MW01600319

Angus Neil was born and raised in Wellington, New Zealand in 1942.
He has always had a love of the sea, from sailing 'P' class to then becoming
2nd Engineer for the Union Company.
It was fitting that he retired at Te Horo Beach, where his love of the written
word came to the fore and he began his writing career.

Dedication

I dedicate this book to my beloved family, to my wife Gloria and to my children, Adam, Sara, Michelle, Katrina & Angela.

Angus Neil Campbell

AHAB'S LEGACY

AUSTIN MACAULEY PUBLISHERS™

LONDON • CAMBRIDGE • NEW YORK • SHARJAH

A CIP catalogue record for this title is available from the British Library.

ISBN 9781786129604 (Paperback)
ISBN 9781786129611 (Hardback)
ISBN 9781786129628 (E-Book)

www.austinmacauley.com

First Published (2018)
Austin Macauley Publishers Ltd.
25 Canada Square
Canary Wharf
London
E14 5LQ

Contents

Chapter 1

Holland

The world in August 1939 was a world that held its breath. The Spanish civil war had ended and the conflict in China had stagnated but few people believed that war would be avoided. The question was where and when.

Adolf Hitler enjoyed tremendous popularity at home in Germany and there were even pro Nazi factions active in the USA, England and France. His recent occupation of Czechoslovakia had raised alarms in capitals across Europe even though many people, ignorant of the violence and terror of the German political machine, still looked to Hitler as a role model for their own governments.

Then the unthinkable happened. von Ribbentrop, Hitler's Foreign Minister, went to Moscow to sign a Soviet-Nazi non-aggression pact. This was signed on August 1939 by Molotov and von Ribbentrop. When the signing was announced to the world, one of the key terms, the dismemberment of Poland was omitted.

As a former province of Czarist Russia, Poland had been guaranteed access to the sea, 'the free corridor of Danzig,' by the League of Nations. This corridor separated Prussia from Greater Germany by cutting a path through to the seaport of Danzig. This did not sit well with Hitler and the German nation who regarded this land as the birthright of all Germans.

Poland was not an Aryan land and the Poles were considered by Germans to be an inferior people. Hitler ordered his general staff to draw up plans for the invasion of Poland. The Germans would enter from the west and the Russians from the east and divide the country as agreed in their treaty.

The SS took 12 prisoners from Buchenwald and forced them to take poison, they then shot them and dressed them in Polish uniforms. Then an SS officer announced over the radio that the executed prisoners were Polish invaders and they had come to invade Germany.

Following this calumny, Hitler, on September 1, 1939, told the Reichstag that Poland had tried to invade Germany and that the German army was returning fire. In fact, the German forces were moving into Poland in a carefully planned mobile invasion, code named 'Fall Weis'.

The Polish army were unprepared for this new fast mobile type of warfare. Poland's army were mainly cavalry forces that were still popular in most armies at that time. The majority of Polish aircraft were caught on the ground and destroyed by the rapidly advancing German forces.

England and France knew that they could not sacrifice Poland as they had Czechoslovakia and so, on September 3, the allies declared war on Nazi Germany. This declaration, however, did not save Poland. Lodz was about to fall, Krakow fell on September 6 and the Fort at Danzig fell on September 7, after a sustained week of shelling from German naval forces. German forces entered Warsaw on October 1.

A nervous Europe became even more spooked as the plight of the conquered Jewish populations in Czechoslovakia and Poland and even the German homeland began to emerge. Telegraph wires were abuzz with the atrocities and Jewish populations in other European countries began to fear for their future in Europe, especially if the Nazi war machine began to flex its muscles in further conquests. What was to become of them?

In Rotterdam, Rudi Levin, a prominent art dealer, art restorer and patron of the arts had called a meeting of all interested Jewish clients at his art gallery. Since arriving in Holland as a teenager with his parents, as refugees from Russia, Rudi had, through sheer diligence and hard work, amassed an enviable art collection.

His gallery was frequented by Jew and gentile alike but his main clientele were the Jewish community and it was this very factor that represented the majority of his audience on that evening as they felt more threatened by the Nazi presence than their contemporaries who seemed to be of the opinion that Holland would remain neutral, as it had in the previous conflict during the 1914–1918 war.

Herr Levin was not a big man, but had an imposing image, with his mane of greying hair, a large moustache and bushy eyebrows that rose and fell like speech inflections or grammatical symbols, as if emphasizing a particular passage of speech.

His eyes roved the seated audience and his gaze met and momentarily fixed on each and every one of the assembled congregation no one was left out, to a man everyone felt personally touched by his sincere concern for their precious belongings.

"And so," he said, "we must consider the serious threat to our valuable works of art, should the Nazis invade Holland. We can expect to receive the same treatment as our fellow Jews in Germany and Poland. Our houses will be plundered and our valuables stolen, maybe to vanish forever, who can tell, I only know that we do have the ability to do something about the situation while we are still free Dutch citizens. Therefore I will outline to you my intentions, as follows.

10

"I have been in contact with our lawyers' London office and together we have devised the following plan.

"Van Oldenbarnevelt & Co have looked after my affairs for some time, through the Rotterdam office, of course. Indeed they are a valued client and will be doing the same as I am about to propose to you tonight.

"Geradus Van Oldenbarnevelt has a farm in Essex and commutes from there to the city every weekday, to attend to the matters of his law firms London office.

"On his farm there is a large unused building that I am told was previously used as stables, it is airy and dry and also secure.

"I propose that we package our valuables, paintings, sculptures, jewellery and the like, in suitable containers, able to endure a sea journey across the Channel from Hook of Holland to the Port of London and thence by truck to Essex.

"Each of us will be responsible for our own packaging and we must ensure that the contents will be able to withstand storage for some time, maybe years, until this conflict is resolved and it will be safe to have our valuables returned home, once peace has again been restored across Europe.

"The law firm will take care of ownership issues should any one of us die in the interim and we 'will' the possessions to our heirs and successors.

"I have contacted the shipping firm of B.V. Boenstens & Sons who operate a small freighter, making regular trips across the channel from European ports. Their home port is Hook of Holland and we can assemble the cargo in their warehouse located near the docks.

"All crates will be clearly marked and the contents detailed in a separate manuscript, duplicates of these plus the respective bills of lading will be held by each shipper with a copy to Van Oldenbarnevelts' London office, to be held in perpetuity.

"My son, Linus, will accompany the shipment and supervise the delivery and storage in Essex. As you are aware, he holds British citizenship, being born there when my wife, who is also British, and I, resided there for several years. He intends to join the British Royal Navy to do whatever he can to help Europe overcome the Nazi threat. He feels he can do more there than from a proposed neutral Holland.

"In the event that none of us survive this conflict, the works will pass onto our heirs and successors, and eventually to the last man standing, as detailed in the documentation that is available from my secretary at the conclusion of the meeting. If, for some reason, that none of us could possibly contemplate or imagine as we sit here now, there are no heirs or successors, it is proposed that a trust be established to manage and control the artworks in the best interests of our wishes in particular and the art world in general.

"The trustees, of course, will be nominated by us but may I suggest that it be comprised of say three people, one of whom will be my son Linus, another our lawyer and a third to be nominated by this or a subsequent meeting convened for that purpose. Perhaps a prominent British art lover.

"It is imperative that we move quickly and with unanimity, because quite frankly, we just do not have the luxury of debating these issues, the whats, ifs, and buts. There are no other options.

"The worst possible scenario is that Britain is invaded by the Nazis, in which case, provided that it will be physically possible to do so, we would consign the entire shipment to North America.

"I therefore propose that we try and get the shipment away from Holland by December end. It is now November 10, so we do not have a lot of time. Are there any questions?"

The meeting sat still and quiet, everyone seemed to be looking inward, contemplating the future. Maybe a full minute went by and then Herman Bortha stood up and spoke.

"For hundreds of years we have pursued the ideals of peace throughout Europe, yet we have been persecuted for following those principals. Our race has contributed to the wealth and culture of every country that we have inhabited and still we are persecuted. We have shuffled our way from border to border until there has been nowhere else for us to go and still we are persecuted. We now face an uncertain future and it seems that there is no place left for us to flee within continental Europe. If I must confront my enemies then I will do so, but it will be me and them and not me and my possessions and my culture, those things they cannot have. If I have to part with them now in order that my heirs can inherit them, then I am more than happy to do so. I think that this is a good and sound plan that Herr Levin has proposed tonight and I am happy to be a part of it and exhort you all to follow."

He sat down as the meeting applauded his contribution.

Rudi Levin rose and put the motion to the meeting which was passed unanimously. They agreed on a date for a further meeting and to engage the services of Heimi Rudzsji, the undertaker, to teach them the secrets of the finer points on packaging valuable items in wooden packaging for an extended confinement. He then declared the meeting over and the attendees departed into the Rotterdam night.

Rudi Levin bolted the door after the last person had departed, turned off the lights and climbed the stairs to the living room where his wife Ester was seated in an easy chair.

"That went well," she said as Rudi entered the room.

"Yes," he replied. "Better than I had imagined, I had thought that there might have been further debate but in retrospect, I feel that we are all reading the situation with the same concern and so we are in accord; which is good."

"You could go to England too," Rudi said.

"Yes I suppose I could," Ester replied, "but I do not want to leave you here alone and in any case, if we saw the situation worsening, we could both go at some future date. I feel certain that we would have no problem crossing the channel on a freighter; after all there are lots of them making regular journeys every day."

"I am sure you are right," Rudi replied. He looked fondly at his wife who had been his lover, friend and companion these past 28 years. "We have had a good life here in Holland my dear, I would hate to see it changed in any way, we have so many good and loyal friends."

Rudi stood up and walked over to his wife, he held out his hand and said, "Come my dear, let us retire now, it has been a long day."

They held hands as they climbed the stairs to their bedroom on the top floor.

Boensten's warehouse, down by the docks, was filling fast with crated works of art and by the middle of December the inward goods had slowed to a trickle. A further meeting revealed that all those who had attended the first meeting had now completed their packaging and apart from a few stragglers who had subsequently heard about the proposed consignment and had elected to join in, the precious cargo was ready for shipment to England.

The *Wipple* was an attractive little steamer, a typical product of Dutch shipbuilding at the time. A vessel of some 400 tons and 43 meters in length she was powered by a triple expansion steam engine. Their modest crews and efficient size made them an economical ship for a small family operation.

Wilz Boensten, the skipper, supervised the loading of his ship and his brother Olaf was the engineer. A fireman completed the engine room staff and on deck there were 3 deckhands and Wilz's wife Edith was the mate. There was ample accommodation for more people to take passage and often their children would live on board when not attending school.

During November, the Germans had begun laying magnetic mines from the air around the UK coast. The allies controlled the English Channel and Germany, now including Austria and Czechoslovakia, were restricted to a short North Sea and Baltic coastline and could exit into the Atlantic either through the Channel or the North Sea.

The Germans were also starting to make air attacks on allied shipping but the casualties were mainly fishing trawlers, which were unprotected and an easy target.

Any transit of the Channel was not now to be taken lightly and Wilz Boensten was aware of the dangers that were lurking in the open waters. Being relatively shallow, the Channel did not afford much protection for German U-Boats and so they preferred to avoid this stretch of water in favour of the deeper water in the Western approaches, which they would access via the North Sea.

Under darkness of night on December 28, the *Wipple* nosed out of her haven at the Hook of Holland and steered a course directly for Harwich. The night was still and the moon and stars were hidden by a blanket of cloud. Conditions could not have been better. The ship was in darkness and all deck hands were on a constant watch. The radio crackled in the wheelhouse and was a sentinel listener. Not that there was much to hear, as most traffic maintained radio silence. There was a slight sea and a small confused chop on the surface and the ship moved easily through the water, almost evenly but then a slight

13

lean to one side and the occasional dip, just to let you know that you were in open water.

The faintest of glows from the compass binnacle cast an eerie light on the face of the helmsman and the lookouts peered intently into the night's dark folds when a shrill whistle from the voice pipe broke their solitude.

Wilz crossed to the tube and removed the plug and put his ear to the device and heard his brother shout into the tube from the engine room, the number of revolutions turned by the propeller shaft, since he rang full ahead, on leaving The Hook.

Navigating as he was by dead reckoning, this information would tell the skipper how far the ship had travelled by the turn of the screw as every time the propeller turned through one revolution the ship advanced a specified distance. Wilz went to the chart room, closed the door behind him and turned on the red lamp above the flat desk and with some simple arithmetic and the help of a slide rule he worked out the distance the ship had moved and made some pencil marks on his chart. He looked at the clock, turned off the lamp and returned to the wheelhouse, looking in the binnacle to check the course.

The lookout came in from the starboard wing of the bridge. "Skipper, there is something out there, I can't make out what it is yet but definitely there is disturbed water." Wilz grabbed his glasses and followed the seaman out onto the wing where he pointed in the direction of the disturbance.

Wilz's glasses traversed the darkness and after some time he was able to make out some flecks of white water and eventually the silhouette of a small boat. "Got it," he said, not taking his eyes away from the object. "Problem is, is it friend or foe? It's too small to be of any danger to us, for sure." He lowered his glasses and told the watch to keep an eye on it and walked back into the wheelhouse and rang slow ahead on the engine room telegraph.

Wilz was concerned about stopping his ship in case this was a decoy from a U-Boat wanting a sitting duck to fire a torpedo into. He told the helmsman to put the wheel hard to starboard which would put them onto a collision course with the small boat, at least that way he could run it down if it was not a friendly encounter.

The boat was now a lot closer and they could make out that it was an open boat, perhaps a ship's life boat and that it contained some people.

At about 200 meters off, Wilz shouted "Who are you?" in Dutch and a voice floated back.

"Do you speak English?"

Linus came on deck, hearing the commotion and shouted up to Wilz, "I can speak fluent English, do you want me to talk to them?"

"Please do," Wilz replied.

"Hello," Linus shouted into the night, "we are a Dutch freighter, do you need assistance?"

"Bloody Oath we do," was the response. "We are trawler men from Hull and the bloody Jerry planes bombed and strafed our boat this morning, we have an injured crewman here as well."

Linus relayed this information to Wilz who immediately rang stop engines on the telegraph and ordered the two seamen to go down to the foredeck and prepare to bring the fishermen aboard.

The *Wipple* nudged toward the small craft and was almost stationary when the lifeboat came alongside. There were four men in the boat and three stood up when the hulls touched and a line was thrown from the *Wipple* to secure their boat alongside.

"Tom here's copped some shrapnel in his legs, you'll have to winch him aboard, perhaps if you have a hammock or just a sheet of canvas we can get him roped into it?"

Linus interpreted again to Wilz who barked out his instructions from the bridge to the foredeck and Edith appeared with a small cargo net and a hammock. The men in the boat wrapped their wounded shipmate in the net and attached the ropes to it thrown to them from the deck of the freighter and the injured man was hauled aboard, followed closely by the three who scrambled up the cargo net.

"What about the dinghy?" Linus relayed the skipper's reply.

"Leave the dinghy, the skipper says it will take too long to retrieve and he would rather be underway than remain a stationery target!"

They carried the injured man into a spare cabin and placed him on the bunk. It is the mate's job to do the doctoring and so Edith gave him a shot of morphine, snipped away the bloody and sodden trousers and set to work cleaning the wounds, of which there were many.

The fishermen were shown the mess and told to help themselves to coffee and any food they wanted while the freighter's crew got back to their watches and the preservation of their ship and its precious cargo.

Linus joined the men in the mess and was glad of the company and spoke English. His English accent had them confused. Here was a Dutchman who spoke like a public school boy. How could that be? They inquired.

Linus explained that he was born in England of an English mother and a Dutch father and his formative years were spent in England where he returned as a boarder at a public school to complete his education. As an English subject he said that he would join the Royal Navy and do his bit to fight the Nazis.

The freighter steamed into the night and when Wilz picked up the Harwich Light, he hove to and waited until dawn. When the morning light came they worked their way down the English coast and toward the River Thames. Boensten's berth was up the Thames River at Tower Hill, where they tied up at 11 o'clock that morning, causing considerable interest with their cargo of human war casualties.

Linus completed his custom formalities and proceeded to the Van Oldenbarnevelts' law offices, where he met with Geradus to arrange the transfer of the artworks from the docks at Tower Hill to the farm in Essex. Linus outlined his plans to join the Royal Navy as the lawyer nodded his head in agreement.

15

He said, "You know, in the last war Holland was neutral, I'm not sure what the Nazis have in mind this time but I do not see any sense in invading countries just for the hell of it."

Linus replied with a little surprise, "I think that this Hitler fellow is an extremist and it seems that he does not like Jews. It seems that he intends to rid Europe of all Jewish people, if that is true then he either has to have the consent of all European countries or be in charge of them, which makes me believe he must invade them. I know Holland would never agree to such outrageous demands and I would imagine that most other nations within Europe would feel the same."

Mr Van Oldenbarnevelt stood up and put out his hand to say goodbye.

"I have to meet a client in half an hour on the other side of the city so best be saying goodbye and good luck. Your treasures are now safely tucked away for the duration and no doubt we will be in touch as the situation dictates."

Linus took his hand and they shook warmly, smiling and nodding, "Thank you for everything, I'll let you know what the Royal Navy does with me. Goodbye."

He turned and was gone.

Formalities completed, Linus returned to the ship where Wilz was overseeing the discharge of the cargo onto the wharf and into the warehouse alongside.

It took several trips by lorries until the cargo had been cleared from the dockside warehouse into storage in Essex. Linus cabled his father to say that the mission had been successfully accomplished and went back to the *Wipple* to say goodbye and thanks to Wilz and Edith who were already loading cargo for their return voyage to Holland. He collected his personal effects and took a taxi to his London hotel.

On May 10 1940, Hitler's armies struck westward across Europe. Within 3 weeks, Holland and Belgium had surrendered and the German Panzer Divisions had split the British and French armies.

The BEF and some French troops were trapped on a diminutive pocket of land centred on the port of Dunkirk. On May 25 Bologne was captured and on the following day Calais fell. That evening, the Admiralty signalled the start of operation Dynamo: "The evacuation of the troops stranded on the beaches of Dunkirk."

The entire mission took from May 26 until June 4 1940 when 338,226 troops were evacuated and taken to the UK.

16

Chapter 2

USS Co's SS Monowai

In August 1946 the Union Steamship Company's liner *Monowai* steamed into Sydney Harbor, released from her contract with the British Government.

Linus was third mate and was paid off on arrival along with the rest of the crew. He had joined the ship in June 1944 when it was in the Solent awaiting the D-Day invasion of Normandy, as part of the Allied D-Day Support Forces.

After joining the Royal Navy and doing his basic training, Linus volunteered for the Submarine Service and served in that division with distinction, being invalided out with the rank of Lieutenant, early in 1944.

He subsequently joined the Merchant Navy and was appointed to *Monowai* as she lay in the Solent, following a refit that saw her transformed from an armed Merchant Cruiser into a troop Transport, capable of carrying and launching up to 1000 troops, from twenty large landing barges, which hung outboard on her port and starboard sides.

On D-Day, June 5, *Monowai* left Cowes Roads for the overnight run to Normandy, anchoring off 'Gold Beach', at dawn and the disembarkation of her troops began with her landing craft splashing down into the sea at 0615 hours as the first wave of assault troops landed on European soil, but not without heavy casualties.

At the end of the day only six of *Monowai*'s landing barges survived. The ship itself was unscathed. Back in Southampton these were replaced and she headed off on her second run, this time to 'Utah Beach'.

As Linus came down the gangway of *Monowai* for the last time he looked up at the black painted hull with the wide oblique stripes and the landing barges hanging over her sides and the memories of those many runs made from England to France came flooding back. In the ensuing 12 months they had made 45 crossings and carried over 100,000 troops and their equipment. Steam had been on her main engines for over a year and not one of her crew had ever complained about the constant workload and vigilance required for such a supreme mission.

He had never experienced such nostalgia, after all this was only a mass of floating iron but it had nurtured within him such a bond that he felt like he was cutting a cord that had attached him to this large womb of a home these past two and a half years.

The fires in the ship's large boilers were now extinguished and with them went the life blood of the vessel. The smell of the engine room that permeates the very soul of a ship had departed. The fires in the galleys and the hot presses in the mess rooms were cold and the smells and aromas of food being prepared and eaten were now only a pleasant memory.

With the other ship's deck and engineering officers, Linus would be repatriated to New Zealand and go on leave before being reappointed to other company vessels.

The Union Steamship Company's head office was in Wellington and it was here that the USS Co. liner *Aorangi* landed them a few days later.

The trip came as a welcome break, traveling as a passenger across the Tasman Sea from Sydney to Wellington. The biggest luxury was enjoying unbroken sleep. A watch keeper's life at sea, which is four hours on and eight hours off, sounds restful enough until you have to endure the routine. Day after endless day until your body cries out for sleep but duty calls you from your precious slumber and your welcoming bunk seduces your tired body like a siren calling to ships.

The land locked harbour that was Port Nicholson, stood clear and crisp in the early morning sunlight as the big liner nosed her way in through the heads and past Point Jerningham, towards Lambton Harbor. Linus stood at the rail on the promenade deck surveying the scenery, his hair ruffled by the breeze of the moving ship. The dark green hills stood high in the sunlight, disappearing altogether at one end of the harbour as they fell away to form a valley.

At the opposite end stood Wellington City, a fine looking city in a fine looking harbour. The wharves appeared to be the front step to the city buildings that soared from the water with a backdrop of hills framing the landscape, hanging beneath a blue firmament.

The consensus of opinion among his shipmates, when Linus enquired about accommodation, was that he should stay at Maximes Hotel, at the bottom of Cuba Street. At one stage or another in their sea going careers it seemed that they all had stopped there. It was known as a 'good feeder', and a man could find all that he wanted there, for his contentment. They all agreed that Flora MacLeod, the owner, would make him feel at home.

He had many offers to come and stay with them and their families but after a couple of years as a shipmate, he felt the need to be on his own, in any event he had unfinished business to attend to in regard to the artworks in England. Linus wrote down their addresses in his book and said that he would keep in touch.

With customs formalities completed, Linus collected his suitcase from the luggage pile and made his way out of the wharf office and into a waiting taxi. He gave the driver the hotel address and settled back in his seat to study what was to become his future home. The streets were full of trucks, cars, people and tramcars, there was movement and bustle and urgency about the place. He saw happy faces and sunlit streets and veranda lined footpaths for shoppers to stroll beneath, sheltered from the weather be it sunshine or rain. Linus thought, *This is a fine city.*

The taxi stopped outside the hotel and Linus paid the driver who carried his case from the cabs trunk to the footpath. He entered the hotel through a revolving door and went over to the reception office. The office was empty but he heard voices through an open door inside the office so rang the bell beneath the sign that read, 'Please ring for attention.' The talking in the adjacent room stopped, he heard a chair scrape on the floor and soon a young lady appeared.

"Good morning," she said, "how can I help you?" Linus returned the warm smile and said that he had booked a room which had been confirmed by telegraphic cable from the liner *Aorangi*.

"You must be Mr Levin," she replied. "Welcome to Maximes Hotel."

Forms appeared in front of him on the top of the counter. "I'll get you to fill these in and then we can get you up to your room. Have you any idea how long you intend to stay with us?" she enquired.

"No idea at this stage," he replied, "I am a ship's officer and am on leave for a few weeks, I may even consider some sort of permanent arrangement if you cater for that sort of thing," he said.

"I can arrange for you to discuss that with the manager, we do have two room suites available for longer term stays, you would probably want to look at them to see if they would be suitable for your requirements, I can arrange that for you Mr Levin."

Linus completed the forms and pushed them back across the counter.

"I'll get you to sign the guest book, here," she indicated with her index finger where Linus was to sign, "and write in you room number which is 303, room three, floor number 3. Elevator's just over there," she pointed in the direction of the elevator. "I will have your bag sent up to your room."

"The dining room is just over there," again she indicated the general direction of the dining room with her out flung arm.

"Breakfast is seven until nine, lunch is midday until two and dinner six until eight. We can cater for any special dietary requirements, just let me know and I can tell the cook."

"My name is Kaetrin," she said, pointing to the name tag pinned on her blouse and handing him the key to his room. "Have a pleasant stay with us, Mr Levin."

"Thank you, Kaetrin, I'm sure I will."

"Oops, I nearly forgot, this mail was delivered here from the Union Company Office," she handed him a packet of letters held together by a rubber band.

Linus sat down at the desk in his room. He had expressed his desire to have a desk in the room when he cabled from the ship and was pleasantly surprised to find that his request had been complied with.

There were several letters from his old submarine shipmates, one from Van Oldenbarnevelts' London office and one from their office in Rotterdam. He opened the Rotterdam letter first.

Dear Mr Levin, it began.

We have made extensive enquires through the Dutch Office of the "Wartime Jewish Displaced Persons," in an endeavour to establish the whereabouts of those Jewish persons removed by the German Occupying Forces during the recent conflict and although we can establish that they were taken to various concentration camps in German Occupied Europe we are unable to find any traces of their movements thereafter and can only conclude that they have been victims of the Nazis' Jewish Extermination programme. For all future legal matters we must therefore declare that they are deceased and we hereby offer our humblest condolences in your sad loss.

In regard to your late parents' property, we can advise that the building is still in a habitable condition despite fierce fighting between the allies and the German army that occurred in and around this vicinity.

We await your instructions as to what, if any, action you require us to undertake on your behalf to either sell the property or lease it out.

It is still a fine building and would command a ready sale or suitable lessee.

We look forward to being of further service to you and remain with kind regards,

Yours sincerely,

Signed by Marinus Johannes Ten Braak. Partner.

Linus folded the letter and carefully placed it back in the envelope, he then picked up the one from the London office and read aloud and to himself.

My Dear Linus,

I am indeed delighted that you have survived a very turbulent time in the history of the world. I sincerely hope that we never witness such atrocities again, ever. My sincere condolences in regards to the tragic loss of your parents [Rotterdam office has done some extensive research and will have conveyed their findings to you by now].

I am at this time reminded of Coleridge who wrote in *The Rime of the Ancient Mariner*:

"A sadder and a wiser man, he rose the morrow morn."

It seems your father was a man of some vision. All across Europe the Nazis confiscated artworks from prominent Jewish collectors and from dealers whose galleries were 'Aryanised' or taken over. Ordinary people too, lost their art treasures, left behind in their homes when they fled to freedom or were sent to death camps. During the war and in the following confusion, many of these artworks, we are starting to realize, and these include works from such well

20

known masters as Manet to Courbet to Picasso, are being snapped up, no questions asked, by prominent museums and galleries. Other works have fallen into the hands of unscrupulous dealers and exported for sale around the world.

It is therefore, most satisfying to know that valuable artworks have been saved through the visionary acumen of your father and I can confirm that they are still very much safe and sound in Essex.

What you do with them now will probably be your call as to date there has not been any other surviving consignee come to light.

As a trustee of this legacy I await your further instructions.

Yours sincerely,

Geradus Van Oldenbarnevelt

Partner

Linus laid the letter on the desk in front of him and scratched a line in pencil across the bottom.

'Sell my parents' collection.'

He did not even know the extent of the collection other than it contained works from some of the old masters. He could recall his father mentioning Jan Steen and Jacob Duck and names of apprentices who had studied under 'the Greats', such as Rembrandt. Barrend Fabritius and Jan Victors rolled out from the memory bank of his mind in the same manner as one might remember how to walk. When you have been immersed in the subject from the very beginning, something sticks. Art stuck with Linus but that did not mean that he had embraced it in the same manner as his parents or as art lovers might do. To Linus it was art – just art, a painting was a painting, nothing to get too emotional over. Brushstrokes were brushstrokes although he had learned enough to tell that some brushstrokes were different than others. Linus remembered when his father had taken him to see a Van Gough exhibition and he marvelled at the sparkle and life in the oils used by the great painter. Tears ran down his father's cheeks as he explained the paintings to his son. Linus liked *First Steps* the best of all. He could still see the peasant in the field, kneeling with outstretched arms, encouraging his off spring who was being supported by the mother, to take the first steps and walk toward the father. A lovely image that he could view again, simply by revisiting the gallery. He did not have to own the painting to enjoy it. Others too, could visit the gallery and enjoy the same image.

Perhaps that is where his parents' collection would be best enjoyed. He would of course keep the icon that his father had given to him when he left for England in 1939. It was one of a set of three from the trinity. Both his father and mother had one each of the other two pieces of the painting. They were to be their guardian angels and be reunited after the war.

The paintings were copied from *Massacio's Trinity* that was painted as a fresco inside the Santa Maria Novello in Florence, circa 1427. The reproduction was an oil on canvas in three parts. The first or top part contained the trilogy which was the Father, the son and the holy ghost, here depicted as a

21

dove. This part his father kept. The middle section contained the lower part of Christ's body on the cross and in particular his legs and feet. To the left was the Virgin Mary and on the right Saint John, each flanked by the figures of the two patrons who serve as models of religious devotion. His mother had this section of the painting. The bottom section was referred to as the 'Cadaver in the Tomb' which depicted a sarcophagus with a skeleton on top. At the simplest level the imagery would suggest mortality. There was an inscription in Latin, which, when translated, read: "I once was what you are and what I am you will also be." And this was the part that his father had given to Linus. The cynics among us may ask what would a Jew or Jews do with the Holy Trinity, but the fact was that Rudi's love of art transcended any religious motivation and at the end of the day it was the painting that mattered.

While Rudi was a Jew, his wife was an English Christian woman when he had married her and Linus was anything he wanted to be. They were Jewish as a race rather than Jewish as a religion.

Linus allowed himself to return to his correspondence.

"I will write a letter to Van Oldenbarnevelts' London Office tomorrow," he said to himself.

It was then that an emotional elevator of feelings ramped up through his body and erupted in a black flood of despair within his head. Linus realized that, in this life anyway, he would never be able to see his parents again. The very idea of this came as a shock to his soul and the loss brought on within him a hollow sinking feeling and he felt faint and had to sit on the side of his bed.

He had never felt this way before. Linus had carried within him a mental picture of his parents as they said goodbye when he left for England in 1939. He had always assumed that they would meet again one day. The war years were filled with danger and despair but nothing could compare with how he felt now.

His letter from the Rotterdam law firm was having an effect on him. Perhaps it was the whole war thing catching up. Maybe both. Four years on submarines. Lost shipmates, blowing up enemy ships with torpedoes. Sending sailors to their death. They would have had parents too! The carnage off the Normandy Coast on D-Day. Confirmation that his parents had perished in the holocaust. It suddenly overwhelmed him. Linus rolled over onto the bed a sobbed until he fell asleep.

Chapter 3

The MacLeods

Flora MacLeod was from the Island of Skye, off the west coast of Scotland. Her parents ran a hotel in Uig, a fishing port and also a ferry terminal for MacBraynes Shipping, which ran numerous ferries from the Western Isles to the mainland. In fact, MacBraynes ferries held a defacto monopoly on the Western Isles and Scottish mainland, that so caused a poetic wag to coin the following rhyme:

The earth belongs unto the lord
and all that it contains.
Except the Kyle's and the Western Isles
and they are all MacBraynes.

Murdo MacLeod came from the Island of Lewis, in the outer Hebrides and was a steward on a ferry that ran from Tarbert in Harris to Uig in Skye.

It was inevitable that a man who enjoyed his ale and a dram of whiskey, in moderation of course, would offer himself to the hospitality of one of Uig's licensed establishments, as occasion allowed.

It was also inevitable that the two should meet, as indeed they did, in Flora's parents' Ferry Inn Hotel.

The relationship flourished into romance and romance into betrothal and following a customary cooling off period they ratified their espousement in a wedding ceremony that the town of Uig had never witnessed before and is likely would ever experience again; such was the energy generated by both a solemn occasion and a bibulous event.

Highland weddings were, by nature of the participants, lively affairs. Given that Flora was, as well, the only daughter of a publican, it was incumbent on the patriarchal Sandy Macleod that his daughter would be given away with all the pomp and ceremony becoming such a local identity.

It was not uncommon in these parts that two clansfolk with the same surname would wed. The convenience factor for the bride, of course was that she got to keep her maiden name and in the reading of the banns preceding the main event, it would be proven beyond any doubt that there was no family connections.

Several pipers were engaged for the occasion, on the basis that the festivities would be of such a duration that one piper could not last the distance, unless they were strictly forbidden from imbibing in the streams of liquid amber that would flow from the cellars.

A teetotal piper was an oxymoron, at least to Mr MacLeod, the father of the bride. He therefore sought assurance in numbers, so that at all times there would be at least one piper capable of carrying a tune.

The musicians were to also include a fiddler and an accordionist and he had employed the skills of a Mrs Mackinnon, who held some renown on the island for her ability to apply secret recipes to revive inebriated persons in general and pipers in particular.

A Presbyterian ceremony of holy matrimony would of course, precede the festivities, of which little public recognition would ever be conceded. The Islanders were a devout congregation of whom many a minister would be proud to lead. On Sundays the pews were full and the minister had their undivided attention for his fire and brimstone Gaelic discourse.

The homily would be stoically received by the attending fellowship and faithfully applied by the matriarchs during the ensuing week, when they again attended at the Kirk for the ongoing installation of the faith.

The MacLeods honeymooned in Glasgow, courtesy of the ferry service to the mainland and returned a week later to resume normal island life on Skye, Murdo having taken up residence with his bride at the hotel where accommodation was plentiful.

Life was easy if not a bit dull at times and so the young MacLeods started to look beyond their horizons for opportunities in the great world beyond. Through their shipping circle contacts they learned that the Union Steam Ship Company of NZ Ltd were having a new passenger liner, *Rangatira*, built for their inter island trade.

Subsequent enquiries revealed that the ship would be sailed to its New Zealand destination by a crew recruited in the United Kingdom and in addition, a full complement of passengers would be embarked for the maiden voyage to the south seas.

Sandy signed on as a steward and his wife Flora as a laundry maid and in August of 1931 they sailed from England by way of the Panama Canal to Wellington, NZ.

They both worked on the ship for a further two years after the ship arrived in New Zealand, saving their money to put into a hotel venture or some other similar activity in the service industry, that had been a part of their working life.

They learned through their inquiries that in order to raise a mortgage they would need to borrow money from an insurance company and their chances would improve greatly if they were to take out life insurance policies, which they did.

The first opportunity arose when a boarding house in Newtown came on the market. Their savings would be enough to purchase the freehold of the land and building with the insurance company advancing the balance on a first mortgage.

Sandy continued working on the *Rangatira* which was making nightly crossings between the north and south islands. He was in Wellington on alternate days and would take a quick tram ride from the railway station which was adjacent to the inter–island wharf, where the *Rangatira* berthed. The ride on a Newtown Zoo tram, which conveniently stopped outside Sanford House, took 15 minutes each way. And so he could spend some time with Flora and even tackle the odd job or two around the place. And there was no end of odd jobs that required a man's attention.

A boarding house is a bit like a box of chocolates or for that matter a collection of shipmates. You are not quite sure what the eclectic mix will turn up. There were regulars, of course, who had been lodgers for some time and who would continue their patronage under the stewardship of the MacLeods. The hotel stood on the main street that ran through Newtown and on up to the zoological gardens.

As buildings go it was rather unremarkable, being wholly constructed from wood, timber framed and planked on the exterior with painted weatherboards. It stood three stories high with the ground floor containing the owner's accommodation, dining room, lounge and kitchen and two floors of single room accommodation above. There were eight single rooms on each floor and communal toilet and bathroom facilities.

The rooms were basic but clean and a person could stay there and feel comfortable and well fed, which was a lot to ask in those days as the depression hit hard into all facets of everyday life. The majority of the guests came from smaller provincial towns, being drawn to the larger city where work was more plentiful, for some.

The occupancy rate was good and the MacLeods were mindful of the economical hard times but grateful that they could make ends meet and pay the mortgage. From time to time a lodger was not able to make a weekly rental payment for their board so they were given seven days' grace to come up with the money or leave. It was a fair and equitable arrangement and on more than one occasion a former lodger would return with the money to 'square away the debt', and take up residence once more. They were welcomed back and Flora would have Cook bake a special 'welcome home cake' that would be shared amongst the diners, in the lounge, following the evening meal.

Mary-Jane Skeffington had been a lodger at Sanford House, which was the name of the MacLeods' boarding house, for seven months, when she lost her job with the wool export company that she had worked for, since moving down from her parents' farm in Horowhenua County. Each week she had been sending money home to help out with the financial crisis that the farm was

25

facing. There was a downturn in wool and meat prices and so the farm income was reduced while mortgage payments still had to be paid to the bank.

Unemployment figures were starting to peak, work was not easy to find and while she had some savings to fall back on, Mary-Jane was able to stay on at Sanford House while she looked for work. Mary-Jane found work but it was not what she had in mind when she answered the advertisement in the evening paper.

The agency said that escort work paid good money, she was not obliged to do anything that she did not want to do, the agency got a cut of the fee and any extra money earned was strictly between Mary-Jane and the client.

Mary-Jane explained her predicament to Flora MacLeod who listened attentively. Flora, who could be as hard as a blacksmith's anvil, was also as soft as a duck's downy breast. She put her arm around Mary-Jane's shoulder and said, "It's a wonderful thing that you are doing for your parents' farm, Mary-Jane, all work is honourable, I am sure that they would be proud of you, I know I am, I do so admire perseverance."

As the depression bit harder into the economy, perseverance became a survivor metaphor. Perseverance put food on the table. Perseverance paid the rent. Perseverance kept the debt collector away. With perseverance one could buy new clothes. With perseverance one could always look one's best. If one could persevere one could get by.

And so it came to pass that Sanford House became home for a few young ladies who appeared to display that admirable quality for survival when economic hardship extracts life's blood from the very soul. Perseverance!

Sanford House prospered while others faced ruin. The MacLeods prospered, they had jobs and an income while others were not so lucky. They seemed to make the right choices while others made bad ones.

Sailing along on a mill pond however is no sinecure as when the pond empties you go down with it. The upside is that you can always walk ashore.

And that is exactly what Flora did when Murdo was tragically killed by a railway wagon in the port of Lyttelton. Murdo had been across at the hotel having a few drinks with his shipmates when he had to return to his ship and go on duty. As most of the sailors did, he took the shortcut across the railway tracks and was run over by a rake of railway wagons being shunted in the yards. Death came quickly, they had said. There would have been no pain or suffering, it was life and then death. Instantly.

Flora the dutiful widow gave her husband a Highland send off. Eulogies were offered in Gaelic and English. And there were plenty of those as Murdo was a social man who liked a dram and a yarn with his shipmates, on and off duty. The piper played a lament as the casket was lowered into the ground. The Seamans' Union paid for the funeral and for his body to be brought from Lyttelton to Wellington and the union president gave a long and emotional eulogy about the faithful: them and us and the struggle which he pronounced as stroogle. What it was to be a member of the union and the great benefits that resulted in membership and brotherhood and comradeship. A wake followed at Sanford House and the residents did not get much sleep that night.

Flora found that she was the recipient of a substantial sum of money when the insurance company paid out on the life policy she and Murdo had taken out. At the time, a life insurance policy seemed an unnecessary expense, but it was the only way that they could qualify for a mortgage as banks serviced commercial institutions only. It seemed that this was the colonial way of doing things and so they signed on the dotted line. And Flora was now grateful that she had. The money would not replace her husband but it did compensate for the income that he earned from his job on the inter-island ferry. They were coming toward the end of the depression, or so they were informed by the daily newspapers, and money was still a very desirable but hard to earn commodity. It always was, of course, but it had been scarcer and those who had some held on to it. It was the mid stream sector, the growers and producers, the buyers and the sellers, traders and merchants, that were generating the ebb and flow of currency. Farm produce was being exported and prices were picking up. This brought an increase in shipping. The ports were hiring labour. The abattoirs were hiring labour. Shipping companies were hiring labour. All this activity created paper war and paper war needed clerks. Business was brisk for the girls at Sanford House and they could spend money on new clothes, a welcome change from stitch and sew and scrimp and save.

Flora had plans too. There was a small hotel in the city for sale and had been for some time. The previous owners went bust during the depression and the bank holding the mortgage had foreclosed and had not been able to sell the building. Well not quite true, they could have sold it but not for what it owed them. At first they put in a manager but it was the depression and the hotel did not have a liquor license so the only source of income was through accommodation. No amount of management could compensate for empty rooms and so they simply shut the doors and waited for a suitable buyer. Flora had made an appointment with the real estate company who were handling the sale to inspect the interior of the building and see if it was suitable for her expansion plans.

The hotel had four floors, ground and three above. It was a reinforced steel and concrete structure. The ground floor consisted of a lobby, dining room, kitchen and food storage facilities, reception desk, office space and a couple of staff bedrooms as well as toilet facilities. There was also a large car park at the back of the building, a necessity when country people came to town in their cars. A hotel with parking facilities was an asset. Especially if a visiting patron required anonymity. The decor was a little jaded but that could be rectified. The dining room tables were neatly set with starched white tablecloths and good silver cutlery. There were napkins and salt and pepper shakers. It was as if dinner would be served at any moment but had been put on hold for a couple of years. It was very 'Marie Celestial' which is how Flora described it to her girls over dinner that evening. Flora inspected the crockery and found it to be acceptable, for now anyway. The elevator had a concertina expanding style

27

wrought iron door and a semi-rotary lever action control device which was the standard of the day. Move the lever one way and the elevator went up. Move it the other way and the car came down. This would need to be upgraded to a push button system that corresponded to the traveller's floor destination requirements. An elevator was considered a luxury, especially when conveying luggage to the upstairs accommodation. On the first floor, one walked from the elevator cage into a large room filled with comfortable leather chairs, low coffee tables with newspapers and magazines strewn about. It was as if the occupants had temporarily vacated the room, gone for a pee and would return any tick of the clock. And ash trays, sans ash. Flora, a non-smoker had noted this and wondered what the smell would have been like with two year old dirty ash trays. Framed landscape paintings hung on the walls and the curtains were velvet and plush. A hallway led off from the back of the room toward the rear of the building and on each side of the hallway there were doors to the accommodation suites, four on each side. On this level the accommodation was of a high standard. The bedrooms had an en-suite, almost unheard of in these earlier colonial times and there was also a sitting room or lounge as they were called in later years. The second and third floors contained twelve single rooms apiece with communal toilet facilities. Not unlike Sanford House. The standard was basic and the chattels in good condition. The bank had paid caretakers who regularly aired the building, dusted and generally kept things looking neat and tidy for any prospective buyer. The beds had covers and looked made up but the linen was stored in the hotel's linen cupboards, in mothballs.

Flora made notes of what she thought would need to be done to the building to make it suitable for occupation by her and the girls.

The real estate agent hovered and kept repeating what a fine building it was so Flora asked him for an engineer's structural report. Atherton Tillbury was his name and she wondered why real estate agents always seemed to have absurd names, talk with a speech affectation, almost always had curly hair and wore light tan coloured rain coats, even when it was fine outside. Mind you, in Flora's eyes any name that was not of Scotch heritage was a strange name. She smiled as she recalled her uncle's comments when she had returned to Skye following her first visit to London.

"What do you think of the English?" he had inquired. "Speak funny, don't they?"

Tillbury replied that if Flora wanted an engineer's report then she had to organize it. It was the buyer's responsibility to find out these things. The agent could supply only what they were given by the vendor and in this case it was a legal description only. These were neither confirm nor deny tactics. "Caveat Emptor," he said.

Flora mumbled 'useless bastard' under her breath and said, "Caveat Actor."

"What?" Tilbury looked startled.

I said, "Caveat actor," Flora repeated. "I had assumed that since you used a common law maxim that you are aware of the general range of caveats and other doctrines common to the legal vernacular."

Tillbury replied, "Yes of course," and turned his back, indicating that he had terminated the conversation. In other words, he had no idea what she was saying to him. He made a mental note to check it out when he got back to the office.

Flora made a notation in her pad to have her lawyer get an engineer's report for the building.

Flora was in no hurry to end her inspection of the building and examined every nook and cranny, making copious notes and refraining from any further contact with Tillbury who by now had sat down in a chair on the first floor and was reading an old paper, examining his pocket watch frequently.

It was two hours before she had satisfied her curiosity and generally felt that she had a good idea on the layout of the hotel. Flora came from a hotel background and knew intimately what worked and what didn't work. It would now be up to her lawyers to see if they could come up with a plan that would satisfy her ideas as to how she could operate from the premises and run a legal and respectful house and hotel.

She left Tillbury asleep in his comfortable chair on the first floor and let herself out of the front door and onto Lower Cuba Street. She walked up to the intersection with Manners Street and caught a tram to Newtown and Sandford House.

Chapter 4

Maximes Palace Hotel

Flora had held her meeting in the dining room at Sanford House on the same evening following her inspection of the Cuba Street Hotel. It was a house rule that the girls should be free between five and seven o'clock in the afternoons. They would have an informal hour together before dinner which was served between six and seven o'clock. There was no agenda set. One came and socialized and Flora provided a sherry for the girls and a scotch for herself. One glass each was all that was allowed and only then if one had a free night ahead. "I do not want anyone breathing alcoholic fumes over a guest," Flora said.

The girls' visitors had always been guests. No questions asked. Flora had managed to keep a good honest boarding house for young ladies and throughout the depression years they had never been visited by the constabulary. It was a record that Flora was keen to keep intact and she knew that once the hard times were over and life got back to some sort of normalcy, it was possible that some smart-assed young copper, keen to make a name for himself might start imagining all sorts of things that would not normally occupy a mind filled with ideas other than where the next feed was coming from.

Booze had occupied the police force during the depression years. Illegal booze operations that distilled and sold illicit whiskey and gin. Excise tax was a large percentage of the price structure when purchasing liquor through legal channels and when the hard times struck the first statistic to register on the economists' scales were taxes received versus alcohol consumed. Alcohol consumption, however, never decreased. Only taxes. Money could always be found for alcohol. An amazing phenomenon in itself. The channels of supply simply moved from the licensed victuallers and hoteliers to the sly grog dens. With the loss in revenue from taxes the governments' first reaction was to plug the holes in the system where the taxes were usually collected. There was no

30

loss in revenue from sex because brothels were illegal, so it was easy to pretend that it never happened. Grog was the whipping boy and so the police force had been busy attempting to bolster the governments' coffers from reduced tax incomes due to sly grog shops and illicit liquor distilleries. Which they were duty bound to find and shut down. They were chasing their tails on this one. As soon as one door shut another one opened and they knew this, but with reduced manpower due to the economic times, they were mere mice on a treadmill. Running fast to standstill. Nonetheless, this gave other factions of the community breathing space.

Tobacco was another tax revenue stream that had slowed to a trickle, as tobacco leaves replaced legal tender in many trader to trader activities. It was not illegal to grow tobacco or sell seeds of tobacco plants but it was illegal to sell tobacco leaves that had been grown by a private grower supposedly for their own consumption. A dried tobacco leaf was commercially superior than a fresh leaf as it was the dry leaf that was smoked and it took about a year to hang a fresh tobacco leaf and air-dry it sufficiently for tobacco production. If a fresh leaf was worth a trey a dry leaf could be worth a zac.

Flora had never felt the need to buy cheap booze or tobacco although traders called in the hope that they could make a sale. The thing was, that her alcohol consumption was low and neither she nor any of the girls smoked. Murdo had his own chain of supply for both products, seaman always had an alternative source of supply. She did however buy underground mutton, as rabbit was referred to, from swaggies who would regularly call following a stint in the hills catching and skinning their prey.

Fish was another item that came at a knock-down price as a lot of her Scots countrymen worked in the local trawler fleet. The trawlers would leave port at a minute past midnight on Sunday and be away at sea all week, returning on Friday morning before daybreak, when the catch would be unloaded from the trawlers and onto trucks lined up at Queens Wharf. One of the reasons that the fleet left port after midnight was the fact that so many trawlermen came from the Hebrides where work on Sundays was forbidden and although they may have left the religious and social restrictions behind, the superstitions remained. And a mariner is a superstitious creature by nature. The fish wholesalers were a fussy lot and would take only the popular species of fish that the locals purchased. Cod ends, the part of the large trawl net that disgorged the catch onto the boat's deck, were not selective and although unwanted or unsaleable species that were caught in the trawl were thrown back, there were also a lot of casualties – dead fish, or near dead fish, that would be retained. This left a number of boxes of fish onboard for the crew's consumption. It was free to a good home and although there were few Catholic families among the Scottish community, everybody ate fish on a Friday, which would have pleased the Pope if he wore a kilt. Flora had her choice of fresh fish every Friday at no cost and as much as she wanted. Her supply lasted well into the week and so fish was on the menu regularly at Sanford House. If Murdo's ship was in port on Friday morning, he would visit the trawlers and collect a bag of fish. If not, then Flora would catch an early tram to Queens Wharf and take a large bag with plenty of newspaper to wrap the fish. This was to contain as much of the fishy smell as possible when she travelled back to Newtown, in the cab of the tram with fellow passengers. If she knew the tram driver she would leave it on the driver's platform which was open and airy.

Flora was looking at the overall picture and her scenario was very clear indeed. The economy was improving and it would not be long before the prosperous times would return. And she wanted to be ready and have all of her chess pieces in place and her castle defended. In her eyes she was not a brothel keeper, madam or any other form of pseudonym that labelled a person's occupation. Flora ran a boarding house for young ladies who, if they wanted, were able to entertain gentlemen friends in their rooms. House rules permitting.

Flora had been discussing ownership issues with her lawyers. She had a plan that she had evolved from reading the Crofters Holding Act of 1886 which provided for security of tenure for the occupier or crofter. She had this desire to ensure that her girls were cared for as if they lived in their own homes. She needed to have some idea of where she was headed as she was not interested in paying a lawyer massive fees to research an area that they had no current knowledge of and so Flora was preparing her ground and somehow had to find a way that would entitle her girls to work from the premises and have ownership of their domain, as if they were living and working from home – so to speak. She was acting on the premise that a man's home was his castle and although she may have been barking up the wrong tree with the Crofters Act, she knew that she had to begin her quest for answers and while she may find nothing there, it could lead to other discoveries. She wrote to a cousin who was living in an apartment in Toronto to ask about the ownership laws pertaining to apartment buildings in Canada and got what she thought would be a good lead to take to her lawyer.

Her plan was to buy the vacant hotel on Cuba Street and turn the first floor into privately owned apartments That way each of her girls could buy their apartments and what they did within the walls of their own home was their business. Providing they were doing nothing illegal, and sex certainly was not illegal. If it was, then all of the good married citizens living in their suburban homes were indulging in illicit behaviour.

The lawyer chuckled as came to realize the import of Flora's anima. Her charisma ran as deep as a Presbyterian discourse on liquor. And she had been on the receiving end of many of those on a Sunday morning church service back in Skye.

"Vertical subdivision," Andrew MacKay said, "is the terminology best used to describe what you are requesting." Mr MacKay was a graduate of Edinburgh University. He had also practised in Canada before settling in New Zealand and so was aware of other forms of land tenure other than New Zealand's 'flat earth' style, as he called it. MacKay was an enthusiastic word-smith and could produce a list of euphemisms, without repeating himself.

32

"I will need building plans as we need to have the exact sizes of the areas involved so you will need to employ a valuer as each apartment has to be valued as well as any common areas. I'm sure I can find something on the statute books that will allow us to find a solution and what an admirable idea too, my dear!" He looked Flora in the eye then addressed his blotter as he wrote some words on a piece of note paper intended for a file.

"You do realize that the occupiers of these, or any similarly titled apartments, must agree that they cannot carry out any illegal activity in the apartment that may bring disrepute to the building as a whole. This is a common law maxim, regardless of the legal description on the title."

Flora looked at her lawyer, whom she had known since arriving in Wellington and buying Sanford House. It was Andrew MacKay who had done the conveyancy work for the purchase of the property and any subsequent legal work that she and Murdo had needed.

"As you are aware, Andrew, I was brought up in the hospitality business. My parents owned – and still do – an hotel in Skye. They are licensed to sell fermented and spirituous liquors, as well as victualling and accommodation. This hotel that I am buying does not have a liquor license, just like Sanford House we are offering victualling and accommodation only. There will be no shenanigans from drunken patrons, brawls and other male dominated misdemeanours that could bring disrepute upon my establishment. Mind you, I would like some form of license that would enable me to offer my guests alcohol with their meals. There are some fine wines being produced in this country from European immigrants. I believe that the Dalmations are very good at it. I envisage some fine cuisine coming from my kitchen and it would be a delight to compliment the occasion with tasty wine beverages. Just a thought, perhaps you could look into that aspect for me during the conveyancing process. Maybe the hotel held a liquor license in its formative years. Who knows what you might find."

Andrew smiled, they both knew what he was angling at and yet again Flora had headed him off at the pass. He was too good a lawyer to make assumptions and took instruction from his client as well as giving guidance. Perhaps he was much too subtle in his approach. He leaned back in his chair and hooked his thumbs into his waistcoat. "If you are selling apartments in your building, then the apartment owner can have liquor in the apartment anyway, so long as it is for their own consumption and not for sale!"

Flora saw her opening. "Yes, that makes sense," she said. "I suppose the same would apply to sex!"

Andrew found cause to examine his blotter once more as the raw noun touched a Presbyterian nerve.

Flora, on the other hand, was raised in the earthy environs of a Highland fishing port. From an early age the young girl's eyes were accustomed to the sexual exploitations of randy young fishermen and crofters enjoying the intimate pleasures of lovemaking with their sweethearts during the long evening twilights, of the high northern latitude summers. What may have been described as a sin on Sunday, had by the following Saturday evening, paled from the hell and brimstone fiery firmament painted by the Reverend Dr Fergus Ferguson. After six days and nights of human toils, travails and endeavours and then fuelled by the island's favourite beverage, young love found the paler twilight evening skies more to their liking as two by two they left the inn and sought refuge in the sweet grasses and hay of the surrounding fields. Young Flora and her friends would often stalk the aspiring lovers and hide in ditches or behind peat piles or stone walls and toss pebbles at the lovers from their hideaways and then run like hell with expletives from the disturbed couples, ringing in their ears.

Andrew looked up from his blotter gazing. "It is my duty to advise you on such matters, I feel you should know the rules."

"Thank you, Andrew, I consider myself well advised. We will conduct our affairs with the utmost discretion at all times."

Flora was not a madam, her establishment was a boarding house and not a brothel. The residents were young ladies who had found employment difficult throughout the depression years and just like Mary-Jane Skeffington had undertaken escort work to make ends meet. Flora had relaxed the house rules, however, and allowed guests to be entertained by her lodgers in their rooms. It paid the rent. The rent paid the mortgage and Sanford House remained solvent. That in itself was a blessing and allowed an economic miracle to occur where tragedy was alive and flourishing in the community. Sanford House was an oasis in a desert of despair and the residents were grateful that a woman with Flora's chutzpah had the temerity to endure with her maxim that perseverance would overcome all difficulties.

Flora had a plan for her new venture. For the nineteen thirties it was perhaps futuristic, but then Flora always was the leader; she didn't follow. Flora was out in front and leading the charge. She had reasoned that real estate was the way ahead and that to get ahead one had to produce. If you produced nothing then you had nothing. She wasn't talking fruit and vegetables either.

Following due diligence, the purchase of the hotel was completed and Sandford House was sold. Both transactions were to prove satisfactory and a bumpless transition followed.

Flora applied for and was granted a license to sell liquor to bona fide quests that were resident in the house but only in the dining room and only with meals.

As the world traded out of the recession, business became brisk. More farmers found time to come to town and political lobbyists and members of the country's unions and ginger groups came to the capital to deal with politicians. The farmers drove cars purchased from their new-found wealth and the car park in back of the hotel proved to be so successful that Flora added an upper level with roof over, so Flora's was the only hotel in the city to have two floors of covered parking. It proved both novel and popular. It was especially friendly to gentlemen callers who were keen on keeping their anonymity. This then allowed visitations at all hours and those in the know could access the hotel building at the first floor level from the car park. Other patrons had to access from the front door on Cuba Street. It was common to see the green Buick of the MP for Miramar exiting the side lane from the car park and into Cuba Street at 2am in the early hours of the morning. He had, of course, as far as his wife and family were concerned, been working late at Parliament for his constituency. "Burning the midnight oil for my constituents," he would say. Those less complimentary about his sentiments would say, "The old fox is dipping his wick again!"

Maximes prospered and Flora added another floor of accommodation and a penthouse suite on to the top of her building. The penthouse suite was her private accommodation and was designed by a firm of prominent architects who were acquainted with the requirements of earthquake strengthened designs as applied to the city building codes of practice at that time. Flora wanted four bedrooms and a couple of lounge areas as well as dining and kitchen spaces. The masterpiece was the exterior landscaping that produced a delightful outdoor arboretum containing exotic and native plantings and even a lawn. There was bespoke outdoor furniture that Flora had especially constructed from locally grown Macrocarpa, also known as Montery Cypress. It was a superb timber for out of doors applications and would last forever. Her evening soirees atop the hotel were memorable occasions and invitations were keenly sought after. The Gaelic speaking community from the Hebridean Islands were well represented as well as their culture and on a still summers evening the sound of bagpipes could be heard wafting through the ambient. Politicians would arrive in chauffeur driven limousines. The police department were not overlooked and the clergy were regular attenders as was the fire department. Fishermen and their wives would rub shoulders with lawyers and other professional people. Union leaders from Trades Hall were always in attendance wherever free booze was being dished out. Flora never forgot the support that she had received from the Seamans' Union when Murdo was killed so a virtual free pass was available at every soiree for the attendance of three union delegates. City Hall, which was a close neighbour, always received two invites. And every attendee left with a sample of haggis, made on the premises to Flora's recipe.

The end of the thirties arrived with the news of a war in Europe. Flora wrote to her brother who was in the British Army. In reply he said that his unit was part of a BEF being sent over to France to help the French in case Hitler invaded France. He said, "Check this out with your local embassy but it has been suggested in Parliament that CORB (Children's Overseas Repatriation Board) be established." He said that Flora could perhaps sponsor her niece and nephew who could come to New Zealand to escape the horrors of war should the Nazis decide to invade Britain. A lot of dithering ensued but when the evacuation of Dunkirk was completed and the Battle of Britain followed, CORB decided to kick-start their abandoned plans and Flora got word from the embassy. They said to contact them if she was still interested in sponsoring the children, as the CORB strategy was now fully reimplemented. Flora never hesitated and in due course she was advised that Kaetrin and Robert would arrive on a vessel [unnamed] during October–November 1940. She should be prepared to receive them. Flora was given two CORB numbers, one each for Kaetrin and Robert. Two weeks before the arrival of the ship Flora was given the name of the wharf at which the ship would be docking, and was told to be there at nine o'clock in the morning. The envelope containing this document came as registered mail and she had to sign a receipt as proof that the mail was delivered into her hands. On opening the mail and reading the contents she was surprised to read the inscription printed along the bottom edge of the parchment paper. 'Loose lips sink ships.'

Flora took a taxi from Maximes to Glasgow Wharf, arriving precisely at nine o'clock in the morning. It was a typical wharf reception for the middle of November. A cool southerly breeze was blowing and on the wharf it seemed to get colder than in the city, when among the buildings. A large black hulled ship was roped to the jetty and Flora, who was well wrapped in a warm fur coat was guided by staff to enter the large shed through big open doors. Inside the shed, passengers' luggage was being neatly stacked by porters and there was a roped area separating those waiting from those arriving. Passengers from the vessel were trickling along the designated path, customs stamped their passports and they were then directed to the baggage claim area and porters would place the claimed baggage onto hand carts and wheel them off towards the shed exit, to waiting taxis and private cars.

Then the children started to arrive. Excited relatives and sponsors craned necks to get a better view of a relative whom they most probably had never met and whom they would try and identify in photographs from the family album. Not all of the children were to be collected here as some were heading to other locations in both north and south islands. These children would arrive last and be put onto buses. Flora watched Kaetrin and Robert negotiate the baggage claim, each coming away with a small suitcase. She tried waving to them which was fruitless as most of the waiting throng were waving excitedly at someone. Each CORB passenger then submitted their numbered paper to an official and that number was broadcast over a loudspeaker. From watching others preceding her, Flora learned that the collection procedure required her to give the paper the embassy had given her to an official who would verify the numbers from the children's papers against her paper and it was simply a matter of saying hello. A redhead in a fur coat was not to be denied recognition in a crowd and very soon Kaetrin was shouting to Robert, "I see Aunty Flora," and in a matter of seconds all three were hugging each other. It was all really quite simple and soon they were riding in a taxicab to Lower Cuba Street and home.

The hotel was now looking grand as Flora had reinvested her profits back into the business, knowing the value that a well presented and maintained building would attract in downtown Wellington.

A liveried bellboy assisted with the baggage and whisked it up to the penthouse suite before the new arrivals and Flora had reached the lobby. Robert, as usual, was taciturn but Kaetrin's eyes traversed the room and took in the simplistic elegance that had transformed a duck into a peacock. "It's beautiful, Aunty," she said, "will I be able to sit here?"

"Of course you can," Flora replied. "This is your home now and you treat it the same as our paying guests do." The lobby of an hotel is a magic space. It can be a classroom for beginners and a laboratory for finishers. There is an education to be had here – you just need to learn to read the signs.

They walked over to the elevator as it was returning to the ground floor sans luggage. The bellboy emerged and said to Flora, "Bags are in the apartment Ma'am."

"Thank you Oliver. Come on Kaetrin, Robert, into the car and I will show you your new home."

Flora decided after the unpacking that both new charges required fresh wardrobes and so the afternoon's activities were established. They didn't have far to walk as James Smiths department store was only a hundred yards up the road and they were able to buy most things there. They were in the dining room over dinner when Jimmy the heartmelt showed up.

In port, watchkeeping ceased and the seaman's workday was eight in the morning until five in the afternoon. The ship was busy loading its cargo of frozen and chilled foodstuffs for Britain. The colonies were a lifeline for an island nation and its merchant navy fleet, the largest in the world. The British Merchant Navy was hard pressed to keep the supply lines open and were suffering terrible losses from the ravaging U-boat packs, which were in the ascendency.

Jimmy had been over the side of the ship on a platform painting the hull of the ship. A task that could not be carried out while the ship was at sea. It wasn't a pleasant duty as the ambient and the sea beneath were relatively cool. At five o'clock he had knocked off for the day and had a hot shower then dressed in his best going ashore clothes, and walked up to the hotel. He had asked for Kaetrin at reception and was directed to the dining room which he entered hesitantly. Formal dining facilities aboard ship were off limits to crew and Jimmy was not certain how the social pecking order placed him when ashore. He soon found out.

Kaetrin let out a shriek of delight and came over to give him a hug. She took his hand and led him over to the dining table where Flora and Robert were sitting.

"Aunty, this is Jimmy, he is a deck boy on the *Rangitata* and this is my Aunt Flora and my brother Robert whom you may have seen on the ship but never met."

Jimmy waved a hello with his hand and managed to say, "Pleased to meet you."

"Have you eaten, Jimmy?"

"No, Ma'am."

"Call me, Flora, everybody does."

"Yes Ma'am."

Flora indicated the fourth place setting at the table that was empty.

"Sit down, young man, I've never known a seaman to refuse a feed."

Kaetrin led him round to the seat alongside where she was sitting and they both sat.

"We've placed our orders, roast leg of lamb with all the trimmings, will that suit you, Jimmy?" Flora asked.

Jimmy nodded, "Yes, thank you, that sounds grand."

Flora got up and walked over to the kitchen, opened the door and shouted into the room, "Another lamb for our table please!"

An audible, "Coming up," was heard in reply and Flora returned to the table and sat down.

Flora was no stranger to romances and she could see that the two teenagers were fizzing at the bung like kegs in a beer cellar. She remembered her father saying to her if you ever see a keg fizzing at the bung either run like hell or get it opened before it explodes! "Whatever you do, relieve the pressure, Flora," he said, "or you'll have a mess to clean up."

Flora excused herself after the mains were finished and she left the youngsters to carry on with dessert.

Hell, she thought to herself, *there will be one very sad kid around here when that ship sails.*

The *Rangitata* sat tied to Glasgow Wharf for twenty days, slowly sinking lower and lower as the cargo spaces were filled with frozen meat carcasses and other valuable foodstuffs, for a nation that the Lufwaffe had failed to bring to its knees. And now the Kriegsmarine was administering the coup-de grace as their lethal submarines attacked merchant ships that were carrying vital supplies, essential for survival.

Leslie had called in briefly to say hello to Kaetrin and meet Kaetrin's Aunt Flora. She was about to leave Wellington for Auckland with twenty CORB children and would oversee their relocation to new homes in the north. She explained that Doug was being transferred to another vessel within the New Zealand Shipping Company fleet and would be leaving for Auckland soon to join the RMS *Rangitane*. He was being promoted to a senior position and the RO from the *Rangitane* who held a junior rank to Doug would be transferred to the *Rangitata* in return.

"Bonus for us," she said. "His new ship will be in Auckland for at least three weeks after the *Rangitata* leaves Wellington for the return trip. I will be in Auckland too! So, hey, bonus time together."

Kaetrin was pleased for her but it was obvious to Leslie who had been in on the start of the romance with Jimmy the heart-melt that the days were drawing nigh for the two youngsters and they would soon have to say their farewells. Kaetrin confided in Leslie and said that Jimmy was talking about jumping ship so he didn't have to leave her. He was badly smitten. His stay in Wellington had cemented a bond within him that was proving to be stronger than a mooring line. So when the ship slipped its lines, Jimmy was not ready to slip his.

Following a tearful farewell, the *Rangitata* left Wellington on November the fourth. Jimmy was required to be aboard by midnight when watches were set and Flora allowed Kaetrin to accompany Jimmy to Glasgow Wharf in a taxicab that she had organized and was owned and driven by a fellow clansman John MacLeod who was from Lewis. She spoke to him in Gaelic as Kaetrin and Jimmy boarded the taxi outside the Hotel. John MacLeod had his instructions, which were to drive his cab to the bottom of the gangway: Kaetrin was not to leave the cab and he was to wait while Jimmy climbed the gangway and was logged in at the top by the MA. Flora knew ships and procedures and she was insistent that her instructions were adhered to.

Five days after the *Rangitata* had sailed, Jimmy turned up at the hotel. He looked rough and he was unshaven. Well it wasn't exactly in the hotel but outside in the street. It was early afternoon and Kaetrin was taking the banking up to the BNZ to deposit the takings when Jimmy fell in alongside her. She smelt him before she realized who it was. Her face must have registered shock because he said. "You don't seem too pleased to see me!"

Kaetrin hesitated. "I'm pleased enough," she said, "but I find it hard to believe that you would pull such a stupid stunt. It was hard enough saying goodbye once, now we both have to go through the agony of doing it again. In six months' time you would have been back here. What the hell has come over you – we talked this through – it's a no brainer."

Jimmy looked hurt.

"I just wanted to be with you – I don't want to be away from you, I love you Kaetrin!"

People were starting to look at them as they walked up Cuba Street toward the bank.

Kaetrin pulled him into an empty doorway. "We talked this over – you can't hide, with your accent the locals will know that you are a ship jumper. There is a war on and you will be jailed and deported. It is a serious offence to desert your ship in wartime. If you were in the Royal Navy you would be shot. You've stuffed it up for all of us. We are in trouble if we are seen harbouring a deserter. How the hell did you think you could pull this off? Yes, I'm mad. Especially since we talked this through already." Jimmy looked hurt. Tears welled in Kaetrin's eyes and with her free hand she banged her fist on his chest while clutching the bank deposit bag in the other. "You've ruined everything," she said. "Don't you see that? We had a plan. I would write to you and you would write to me and we would be together in six months and when the war ends – and it will, then you could come and live here or I could move back to England but we would be together. That's how we arranged it. But not this."

"Is this man annoying you, Miss?"

In their animated discussion they both failed to see a constable approach.

Kaetrin heard herself say no and Jimmy looked like someone had fastened a noose around his neck. There was sufficient guilt from both their demeanours to suggest to the policeman that something was amiss, which is what constables are trained to detect.

39

"Where do you live, Miss, is this man trying to rob you?" The constable pointed at the bank deposit bag that Kaetrin was holding.

Kaetrin said, "Maximes Hotel," and in her best London accent dropped the 'H' from hotel. She held the bag up and said, "No," shaking her head to emphasize that the bag was secure and in no danger.

"And what about you, sir, can I have your address, please?"

Jimmy knew that when he opened his mouth, his best cockney would tumble forth and he would give the game away. He did what any good London lad would do in the circumstances. He scarpered and the lawman followed.

Flora and Kaetrin visited Jimmy who was held in the cells at Wellington Central Police Station. Flora had retained her lawyer to take care of the legal proceedings but she also spoke with the police chief who was an avid attendee at her soirees and was no stranger to a young lady who owned an apartment on the hotel's second floor.

"He can't stay here, Flora," Chief Clarence said. "Pre-war we didn't have much to go on, but with the war the rules have changed. We have to hold him until we can get him onto the next ship leaving for the UK. I don't think it is a hanging offence but the authorities in the UK take desertion of their merchant seamen very seriously – he may even have to do time."

"Silly bugger." Kaetrin whispered.

"What did you say?" the chief asked.

"Nothing, sir, just thinking out-quiet."

"Well keep it quieter, I heard that."

"Can I bring him some fresh clothes? The ones that he is wearing are dirty and need a wash – I can wash them too, if that's okay."

"Sure, Flora, you know you can. He'll go to the prison on the peninsular. If he was a serviceman it would be the army unit at Trentham but merchant seamen are treated as civilians – thank goodness."

Four days later and handcuffed to a constable Jimmy the heartmelt took an overnight train ride from Wellington to Auckland. He was held in a remand cell until the RMS *Rangitane* sailed for the UK on November 24. Under police escort Jimmy went aboard and was held in the ship's brig until the vessel had cleared Rangitoto Channel. After which he resumed ships duties.

Doug was walking along the deck from the radio shack to his cabin when he saw a flash of orange light and seconds later a whistling noise followed by an explosion the percussion from which knocked him over. His ears were not receiving sound but the trampling of his feet on the deck made a reverberating echo, sending the thud of feet on deck through his bones and into the ear drum. It was a weird sensation. He ran for the bridge unaware of further shells exploding around him. His watch relief was a junior RO who was telling the skipper that he had received a message from a foreign vessel telling them to stop the ship and cease any further radio transmission. Doug held his nostrils closed with the thumb and forefinger of his right hand and swallowed several times in an effort to equalize the pressure in his ear cavities. It worked. He could hear again. The skipper was calling out over the din, "Send QQQ," which was radio speak for suspicious vessel. Doug beat his junior to the transmitter and started sending. Then the transmitter received jamming signals and the main set was damaged in further shelling which also took out the steering gear on the big liner. Doug yelled out to his junior RO to crank up the emergency transmitter as the captain's voice called out for RRR to be sent by the ROs. 'RRR' was radio code for raider attack. Once the ROs had confirmed that the signals that they had sent had been received by a New Zealand receiving station the skipper ordered the surrender of his ship. He had no option. He knew that with his twin diesel engines and a top speed of nineteen knots he could outrun the enemy, but his steering gear was not working so it would not be possible to steer his ship. The recent shelling had caused fires to break out all over the liner and there were people injured. Maybe even killed, it was too early to take stock of the injuries at this stage.

There were German raiders operating in the Pacific but *Rangitane* had not received any information suggesting that they were in imminent danger from raiders. The raiders were using disguises to appear as Japanese merchant ships. At this stage in the war Japan was an ally and encountering a Japanese vessel on the high seas was a formality. 'A wink and a nod and on your way'. The German raiders were heavily armed merchant vessels with highly trained Kriegsmarine gun crews on board. They could be likened to the pirates of old who roamed the Spanish main, plundering and looting, and killing too! This mayhem was undertaken under the cloak of war, the irony of which would have been lost on the hapless wasted. It was early in the morning and the darkened night sky was not giving much away but there were three blips on the radar screen and searchlights from the raiders had them silhouetted to the Germans. The captain had tried to get the *Rangitane*'s gun into action but the radio cable from the bridge to the gun had been damaged in the attack and so firing data could not be sent to the gun crew. Even though *Rangitane* had signalled its surrender, shells were still being fired at them. Radio transmission had ceased and the ROs were busy destroying code books and other documents that should not be allowed to fall into enemy hands. A shell hit the emergency battery room that was adjacent to the radio shack and the explosion peeled the steel bulkheads open. Great shards of hot steel were ripped off and sent like projectiles in all directions. Doug was thinking about Leslie when his head became separated from his body by a scrap of hot rampant steel. The heat of the projectile cauterized the separation and no blood was spilled. The Junior RO screamed and departed the scene, babbling incoherently. Doug sat headless in the watch seat, one hand on the code book that he was about to destroy. Fire engulfed both rooms and burned intensely, melting all but the steel deck and what remained of the bulkheads. It was a total cremation. Even the rivets melted.

The captain had sent his first mate to organize the crew and contain the fires that were burning all over his ship. His second mate he dispatched to look after the evacuation of the passengers. His third officer was in charge of the life

41

boats and so he was busy getting them ready for an anticipated abandon ship order. The fourth mate stayed on the bridge to assist his captain.

The shelling had now stopped but not before the *Rangitane* had signalled the attackers from their aldis lamps. The captain had rung the chief engineer and told him to order his staff to sabotage the propulsion and other machinery to prevent the ship being taken as a prize. There were thirty three thousand frozen pork and mutton carcasses aboard as well as twenty four thousand cases of cheese, one hundred and twenty five thousand cases of butter and other perishable foodstuffs. If the refrigeration equipment was not able to operate, the cargo would perish and not be of any use to their enemies. The manifests were destroyed so their captors would have to make physical inspections of the ship's holds to ascertain the cargo aboard.

At daybreak they were able to see three ships standing off, all displaying German flags flying from their stern flagstaffs, from where the *Rangitane*'s 'Red Duster' also fluttered. A proud emblem of the British Merchant Navy. Two of the ships appeared to be armed and the third was most probably a supply vessel. A motorboat with armed escort came alongside and the party boarded the *Rangitane* and met with the captain. The Germans explained that no harm would come to his crew or passengers if their instructions were obeyed. The *Rangitane* would be evacuated and passengers and crew taken aboard the *Kulmerland* which was an unarmed German merchantman and supply vessel to the two raiders, one being the *Komet* and the other *Orion*.

The Captain gave the list of personnel aboard as 192 crew and 111 passengers. A head count following the transfer of the survivors found that there were eight crew and eight passengers unaccounted for and probably dead as a result of the shelling and fires.

Jimmy the heartmelt had been assisting the third mate with the lifeboats along with other seamen. The passengers were first to leave the stricken vessel and Jimmy was tireless in his efforts to calm those fearful passengers, and assist them with their life jackets as he had done with Kaetrin and his general all round cheerful demeanour under adverse conditions was noticed by the officer in charge. Jimmy was wearing a sailor's hat with RMS *Rangitane* on the ribbon, dungarees and barefeet, a life jacket and a bare torso. He was the epitome of an Englishman under fire and could just have easily been riding his steed into the valley of death where the Light Brigade charged. He was so absorbed in his duties that he had not thought about Kaetrin for several hours now and his persona was carrying the moment.

Chapter 5

Rangitata

The New Zealand Shipping Company's vessel, RMS *Rangitata*, sailed from Liverpool on August 29 1940 with a cargo of 126 children, destined for a new life in New Zealand, away from war-torn Britain. The ship formed a part of convoy OB-205 which also contained the Holland America Line vessel SS *Volendam* with 320 children destined for Canada. There were 32 ships in the convoy which was bound for Halifax. On the night of August 30th 1940 the convoy was attacked by a German U-boat, U-60, and the Volendam was torpedoed but not sunk. All crew and passengers, with the exception of a purser, were saved and returned to Britain. The remainder of the convoy continued to Halifax and the *Rangitata* set a course for the Panama Canal and across the Pacific to Wellington.

When war broke out in 1939, the idea to send British children out to the colonies was raised in Parliament and rejected as it might appear that the government was creating a premature defeatist attitude. Instead, relocation of city kids to rural parts of the UK was preferred and implemented. Then in 1940 as the fall of France seemed imminent, the question was again raised in Parliament and received approval. The programme was undertaken by the Children's Overseas Reception Board. The selected or sponsored children were to be looked after by teachers and escorts at a ratio of one per fifteen children, in addition to nurses and doctors. No passports were issued but each child was given a CORB label for themselves and their luggage.

Kaetrin who was fifteen, and her younger brother Robert, who was eleven, were sponsored by their Aunt Flora MacLeod, hotelier from Maxims Hotel, Lower Cuba Street, Wellington New Zealand. Flora had been in touch with her brother Alex, who had moved to London and married a London girl before her and Murdo were married. Her brother Alex had joined the British army and was evacuated from Dunkirk. Alex had previously cabled Flora and suggested that she sponsor the children. This was before CORB finally got approval from

43

Parliament. And so they were ticketed and ready to go on the first sailing. The children's mother, her name was Betty, was making the best of her husband's absence. It was a good time to be at a loose end in London, there were lots of servicemen around and war had become a forgotten threat but a good excuse for a knees-up, just in case it suddenly broke out in earnest. And there were plenty of pubs around the East End where the MacLeods lived, where one could practice the social side of war.

Kaetrin and Robert were delivered by their mother to Euston Station where they were assembled into groups and herded aboard the train to Liverpool which was to be their port of departure from the UK. Saying goodbye was not too hard as it was to be a temporary sojourn for the children who would return once peace had been restored in Europe. For Kaetrin it was a big adventure and she couldn't wait to begin, Robert was a bit more apprehensive but London kids are circumspect and it was "No bovver Mum, I'll be orright." And then on the train and off. Mrs MacLeod returned to her London borough and home via the Pig 'N' Whistle. It was a sad occasion after all and a bevy or two was just what the doctor ordered.

At this stage the children were not segregated. As they arrived, their names were ticked off a clipboard and they were escorted to a carriage compartment and ushered into the compartment and told to sit in the compartment and wait. The train would depart in ten minutes. They each had a suitcase containing their clothes and other personal belongings which they were allowed to take into the compartment with them and both the case and each child was ticketed with their CORB number. In time the CORB number would become less important as identities were formed, names remembered and friendships made.

Eventually a young woman, holding a clipboard, entered the compartment from the corridor and announced her presence. "I'm Miss Corbett," she said, smiling at the four children sitting quietly beside their cases. "I am a teacher and will be accompanying you all the way to New Zealand, what an adventure, are you excited?" Four heads nodded.

"I am in charge of four compartments, yours and the next three along the passage." And she pointed in the direction of 'along the passage.' "There is a toilet at the end of this carriage and it may be used only when the train is in motion." W.C. disposal systems were basic in these early days and if one depressed the flush button and watched, the toilet flap would open and the contents would discharge onto the railway tracks that could be seen rushing past the opened orifice of the discharge system which was a novelty to children wanting to observe railway sleepers rushing past beneath them. This could be turned into a game as at speed it could be difficult to count the sleepers as they sped by. It was not uncommon to observe two or more children in the toilet compartment shouting out the numbers of the sleepers being counted as the train gathered momentum until the wooden slabs became blurs and counting them was impossible. Nonetheless, it was an interesting pastime but not so amusing for those who seriously required relief.

44

"Kaetrin," she called, "which of you is Kaetrin?" she repeated, looking at Kaetrin, who raised her hand. "Right, Kaetrin, you are the eldest and you shall be compartment monitor. And you then, must be Demelza," she said, looking at the other girl, "and so we have a Thomas, which is Thomas? Ah, yes, so then you must be Robert." Miss Corbett ticked a box against her clipboard. "The train journey will take about three and a half hours so we will arrive at Lime Street Station at 1pm. We then are bussed from the station to the dock to board our ship and that is as much as I know." Miss Corbett and her fellow adult travellers were familiar with the maxim 'loose lips sink ships' and while the adults were aware of the perils of their pending journey there was no need to alarm their charges. "I'll leave you all to get acquainted," and she departed just as the train lurched and headed out for Liverpool. She returned some ten minutes later. "Sandwiches and cordial will be brought to you at noon, be back in twenty. You may leave the compartment to go to the toilet or stretch your legs in the passageway but you must not leave the carriage."

The transition from train to liner went smoothly and the children were in awe of what was to be their home for six weeks. The labyrinth of passageways and stairwells was particularly impressive as was the accommodation and ablution facilities. Kaetrin and three other girls were allocated a four berth cabin. Each bunk had fresh white linen sheets and pillow cases that had creases in them where they had been ironed in the ship's laundry. And fresh white fluffy towels with the shipping company's name emblazoned in red across the middle lay neatly folded on each bunk. They had a porthole with blackout curtains and a wooden jalousie that was latched back against the bulkhead.

"This is the Ritz." One of her cabin mates exclaimed.

And then– "Blimey, a bleedin' and basin."

They were equally impressed with their toilet and shower facilities further down the passageway, but they were inboard so there was not a porthole. There was a bath but most intriguing were the six shower cubicles. At that time a lot of homes did not have an indoor bath or toilet, let alone a shower, which they called a shower bath. A flushing toilet was novel too and their discoveries were punctuated with shrieks of delight.

"Shit a brick-piss a pebble and fart a stone," a cockney accent exclaimed – "if my mum could see me now." This was Mary from London's Bermondsey district that had been devastated by the bombing. Her home had been flattened but thankfully she was sheltering in the underground with her mother when the raid happened. Mary was thirteen and epitomized everything that was indomitable in the cockney spirit.

Kaetrin's other cabin mates were Marie, aged twelve from Glasgow and Joan, aged eleven from Liverpool. The children had been matched as close as they could to their chronological peers for social bonding and lights-out discipline. After all, the older children were not expected to bunk down at the same hour as the younger kids.

The dining saloon was something else again. It was the second class dining saloon during peacetime and although class distinctions no longer applied it

45

was allocated to the CORB children who numbered one hundred and twenty six and their twelve escorts who were comprised of eight teachers, three nurses and one doctor. The dining tables ran athwartships and sat fourteen persons at each table. There were ten tables and they had starched white tablecloths, silver cutlery and crockery with shipping company insignia. Each place setting had a starched white napkin in a silver napkin ring. Most of the children had never sat at such a fine table and some seemed more at home eating with their fingers rather than the cutlery which sat precisely placed at each setting.

A large glass decanter filled with water sat in the middle of the table surrounded by seven glass tumblers and there were two of these at each table. In rough weather these were not put out and if you wanted a drink you went to a water fountain in the adjoining lounge.

The children were intrigued with the manner by which each chair was fixed to the deck by a small chain that ran from beneath the seat of the chair to a ringbolt on the deck under the chair.

A ship's steward delivered the food to each diner and this act alone stole the show.

"It is the bleedin' Ritz." Mary's voice could be heard throughout the dining saloon at their first sitting. The children laughed. They were becoming accustomed to their new status and most were enjoying the experience fate had delivered them to.

The U-boat attack on the *Volendam* went unnoticed by the children and they certainly were not informed of the danger that they were in. Life boat drill was one of the first activities that they were involved with and it reinforced upon all the value of safety in life at sea. It was important that they knew which lifeboat they had been assigned to and how to don the life jackets, which were stored in the cabins, and the quickest route from cabin to boat deck. In fact it was a lifeboat drill during which Kaetrin became aware that a young sailor was paying her some attention. The rules of engagement generally, are eye contact and a smile and they had certainly made eye contact and he had smiled. Kaetrin felt her cheeks redden and she looked down. That was when he spoke to her.

"Let me help you with that, darlin'," he said. Kaetrin had been struggling with the device and she had put it on backwards. "Here love, put your hands up and off it comes and round it goes and on it goes." He had turned the jacket around 180 degrees. "See now, whistles in the front, that thing at the back fits up under your neck, holds your head up and now you can do the ties at the side. Remember if you have to jump into the briney, place your hands here." And he took hold of her hands and placed them on the front part of the flotation squab, "And hold tight!"

Kaetrin felt relaxed, he had been kind and not patronizing. His touching of her arms and hands were instructive and not intimidating. She felt hypnotized and not traumatized. They were travellers together. And he was passing on his knowledge to a fellow traveller so that if and when required she may be better equipped to handle the situation. Kaetrin liked him and smiled at him. She was not blushing and she heard herself say an audible, "Thank you," in her best modulated young woman's voice.

He winked at her and replied in his best cockney accent "S'orright luv."

Suddenly life boat drill was over and they were shepherded back to class where Kaetrin daydreamed for the remainder of the morning. She had experienced boy feelings before and there were the usual Saturday afternoon liaisons in the local cinemas. The lads would line up outside viewing the talent as the girls purchased their tickets and entered. Just before the lights were dimmed, in came the lads, checking out who was sitting where and under the cover of darkness. Furtive shadowy figures made their respective hits, ready for rejection or acceptance. Kaetrin was considered a bit of a looker and got her fair share of hits but she also gave out a lot of rejections too. One was regarded as a lucky sod if one got to sit next to Kaetrin. Then it was kiss and hand on breast and hand on knee. A girl had to be alert and alive to survive the afternoon picture sessions. But that's how many a romance got started. There was not a lot of places a young teenager could go and make out during their free time before curfew. Older teens allowed out at night had the cover of darkness but the cinema was the only darkness available to the younger set.

Miss Corbett was making the most of her big adventure. Once the children were in bed the adults who were not on night duties had free time to socialize. There was a ship's bar and a band played dance music in the ball room, as it was rather grandly called. There was a library and a card room and on a moonlit night with a calm sea one could sit on a deck chair and breathe in the iodized air sans dust and grime, that only comes from the great oceans of the world. The convoy was in a blackout condition so unless silhouetted against the moonlight and horizon there was nothing to see but dancing moonbeams on wavelets. Miss Corbett sat in a deckchair on the boat deck and lit a cigarette.

"May I sit down?"

Miss Corbett was surprised at the arrow of intrusion into her solitude. In the darkness she had not been aware of any movement and the noise of the soft sea against the steel of the ship was the only attenuation that her ears focused on. She looked up and saw a young man dressed in the uniform of a ship's officer. With her free hand Miss Corbett indicated the empty deck chair and said, "Please do."

"Lovely evening."

"Yes it is."

The young officer lit a cigarette.

"Allow me to introduce myself," he said, "Doug Thornton is the name, I am a radio officer."

"Hello Doug, I'm Leslie Corbett, pleased to meet you."

Unless one is fluent and confident, once the formalities are done the conversation ceases. The young officer was fluent and more than confident.

"You're with the CORB children, aren't you?" he said.

"Yes, a teacher," she replied.

"I'm from Liverpool, what about you?"

47

"Essex," Leslie said, "South end, actually."

"Nice place, went there last trip with some shipmates, we were in the London docks and we did a day trip to Southend: out on the pier, jellied eels, the whole nine yards. Great day out!"

"Yes, it's a nice place to visit."

Doug looked at his watch, "Must dash, Leslie, I'm on watch at midnight and it's ten o'clock now, I like to get a bit of kip before I go on watch. Tell you what, how about having dinner with me one night soon?"

"I eat with the children."

"I'm sure that you can supervise them and then eat later. We eat in our own mess but also we have access to the main dining saloon." It was the first class saloon when the ship had different classes for travellers. "I tell the chief steward that I would like a table for two at the second sitting which is eight o'clock and bingo. How about it?"

Leslie held back her response so as not to seem too eager.

"Yes, I think that would be agreeable."

"Great, how about tomorrow night?"

"Fine with me."

"See you here at seven thirty, we have time for a quick drink at the bar and then onto dinner."

"I'll look forward to tomorrow."

"Goodnight, Leslie."

"Goodnight, Doug."

And he was gone as mysteriously as he had appeared, swallowed up in the gloom of the boat deck as he moved forward along the ship.

Dinner was a great success. Doug was waiting at the agreed rendezvous and in the darkness he took her hand and said, "Follow me."

It was darker than the previous evening and with the blackout curtains in place it was a dark walk along an unfamiliar deck for Leslie and she held onto Doug's hand tightly, in case she lost him. With the ease of familiarity, Doug opened a door and they entered a lounge that Leslie had not seen before. They sat at a table for two and Doug asked what she would like to drink.

"I don't really know," Leslie said, "at my local I just have a lime and lager."

Doug was a sophisticated man of the world and quietly suggested that they both might like a martini before dinner. "It really is a superb aperitif," he said.

Leslie nodded, "Yes, I like the sound of that, a martini it is."

Doug went over to the bar and Leslie had time out to examine her date in more detail. *Not bad,* she thought, *not bad at all.* Sometimes the moonlight can play tricks but under the lighted interior of the lounge bar Doug was an agreeable and handsome man, in her eyes anyway. On the other hand, Doug had had Leslie under surveillance for some time. In his off duty hours, Doug had strolled around the ship checking out the talent and he had spotted Leslie taking her class for morning lessons. Doug liked what he had seen and resolved to invite her to dinner as soon as he could make a seemingly casual contact with her. And last night on the boat deck was perfect timing.

Leslie's first martini was a visual delight. It came in an elegant martini glass. A green olive sat in the vee shaped glass bottom. It was attached to a wooden toothpick with a small triangular shaped shipping company flag that she saved as a souvenir. She needn't have bothered, as there were many more martinis to be shared on the remaining thirty days of their voyage to Wellington. She found the cocktail agreeable to her palate if a little on the strong side and most certainly not to be quaffed like a mild shandy on a warm day, which was the midday favourite for the CORB staff in the tropics, once they had observed 'tropical hours'.

Tropical hours began when the ship crossed the Tropic of Cancer. The latitude of which was south of the Florida keys and north of Cuba. On a clear warm morning, the high green hills of Cuba could be seen from the deck of the ship and the children were taken out onto the broad reaches of the boat deck on the starboard side to observe this land mass slip silently by, like a huge sea mammal quietly basking in the sun on a tranquil sea. The pre zenith sun lit up the crests while the valleys sulked like creases in a velvet drape. Then it was back to the classroom to finish a geography lesson on their recent sighting. This was the first landfall the ship had made since departing Halifax, they had been two weeks at sea and had adopted a routine that saw the days slip pleasantly by. The sailing was so smooth that table tennis tables were erected for the children to play ping-pong.

The convoy had split up on arrival at Halifax, the destination for the majority of the vessels, others sailed down to New York and other East Coast American ports. The *Rangitata* and another vessel, a Dutch flagged freighter continued south; the Dutch freighter bound for Curacao and the *Rangitata* for Panama.

During peacetime, the *Rangitata* usually bunkered at Curacao, a tropical island, near the coast of Venezuela. The Royal Dutch Shell Oil Company had an oil refinery there and the island was administered by the Dutch. That now was considered a risk and they continued directly on their way toward the Panama Canal, bunkering at Panama before transiting the canal and entering the Pacific Ocean. The heat during the Panama Canal transit was oppressive as the land mass tempered the cooler sea breezes that the moving vessel created, which at fourteen knots was a refreshing gentle breeze. They started the transit at night and black-out regulations were relaxed as they were in neutral and inland navigable waterways. It was the first time that passengers were able to gauge the beauty of a large liner and luminous mass moving across water and past vegetation that had a lush tropical ambience. The children were allowed to stay up late to witness the spectacle and Kaetrin saw her sailor with a senior rating called the master at arms doing night rounds of the ship. He was carrying a torch and looked rather important. Kaetrin waved and he acknowledged her with a toss of the flashlight and an engaging smile.

Kaetrin had seen her sailor at every boat drill but outside of those times he was to be found only in her mind. She had confided in her cabin mate Mary, a fellow Londoner, and all she could offer was "'e's got sailor chores to do, I

49

spose! 'e's workin and we's passengerin'. Don't worry – one day when you least expect it!"

"Least expect what?" Kaetrin replied.

"You know, doin' nuffink and bingo 'e appears and you got your worst gear on, 'air's a mess and there he is!"

Tropical hours were designed to get the day's work done before the heat became too intense. The children were roused early amid grumbles and they had two hours of class before breakfast and three before lunch when work finished for the day. The ship's carpenters had erected a swimming pool fashioned from canvas to hold the sea water and shored up by timber sides. The pool could hold thirty kids at one time and so times were allocated for its use. Adult passengers had morning access as the kids were at class. Following lunch the children were to lie quietly in their bunks for an hour before accessing the pool and then it was segregated. Under eights were mixed but over eights were girls only, then boys only. Boys and water don't mix with girls and water. The teachers bathed with the kids to supervise what was a very active part of the day.

"Bloody exhausting," as Leslie would explain to Doug. "Refreshing but exhausting! I deserve a martini."

Then there was the crossing of the line, one of the reasons the pool was erected in the first place. The ceremony of the equatorial crossing was a mandatory shipping company ceremony and passengers were enrolled to become King Neptune's subjects as part of that ceremony. The crew had rigged up a chair that would tip over at the appropriate part of the ceremony thus committing the subject to the allegorical watery depths of King Neptune's domain. The undignified entry into the pool occurred amid much laughter and applause from the onlookers. Their enthusiasm was fuelled by cold alcoholic beverages delivered by a host of stewards, operating from the open air bar at the after end of the promenade deck. Everybody had a wonderful time and when the adults departed, the CORB children were allowed access and they conducted their own informal ceremony with a crew member supervising the chair mechanics. When it became Kaetrin's turn in the chair there was a change of crew and the gallant young sailor who had refitted her life jacket stepped forward and with a huge grin announced, "Happy dip," and pulled the lever and Kaetrin made a most undignified chair exit and water entry.

She was mortified and totally unprepared for this encounter with her heart-melter. This was not how their next rendezvous was meant to happen. Kaetrin climbed from the pool and marched around to the platform where the chair was situated. She had worked up a good head of steam and was going to let him have a hundred PSI of unvented fury. How dare he! She tapped the sailor on the shoulder and when he turned around it was an older man now in charge. Twice humiliated, she said, "Oh, excuse me, what happened to the young sailor – he was here a minute ago?"

"Young Jimmy the deck boy? He got called away – be back in a mo', Miss, any message?"

Kaetrin shook her head, her wet hair sticking across her face like seaweed. She managed a very subdued no and mustering her dignity, or what she imagined was left of her dignity, walked away, collected her towel and went back to her accommodation for a shower.

Miss Corbett came across Kaetrin in the alleyway of their accommodation and asked her if there was anything wrong because she looked so chapfallen. Kaetrin always exuded a happy demeanour and so it came as a shock to Leslie to see one of her star charges in the doldrums. After some serious coaxing, Kaetrin let out her feelings to the ship mother who understood the young woman's feelings and suggested that they formulate a plan of attack so Kaetrin could recapture her dignity and maybe they could teach Jimmy the heart-melt a lesson. Maybe not a lesson so much as to show him where he stood in the overall opera of romance at sea.

"You have a shower," she said, "and come along to my cabin and we shall fix you up to look like a happy princess on a cruise liner. That should knock his socks off!"

"He's in bare feet."

Leslie nearly said, "Well then we'll knock his pants off," but stopped herself from making such an inappropriate remark. But she managed a wry smile at her witticism.

When Kaetrin returned, Leslie had laid some clothes out on her bunk. They were of similar build but Leslie was a bit taller and that was okay as she had gotten out some flowy sun frocks that can be worn long or short with a similar effect. She had a wide brimmed sun hat that added some mystery and intrigue to the outfit. A hint of make-up and…

"Smile," Leslie said, "Come on, a big smile, it complements the outfit." Kaetrin looked a pretty picture indeed. "Now go and promenade and flaunt," Leslie said, "and don't forget to smile!"

Kaetrin headed for the poolside, her new gladrags fluttering in the gentlest of breezes, feeling like a million bucks. She got admiring glances from some of the adult passengers and this charged her emotional batteries so much so that when she reached poolside she was radiating at top luminosity. Jimmy the heart-melt was hard at work operating the chair mechanism. Kaetrin stood at the rail on the deck adjacent to the pool and let her dress flutter in the breeze while she struck a pose with one hand on the rail and the other lightly holding onto the brim of her hat. Eventually the fluttering caught Jimmy's eye and he looked up. Kaetrin radiated a model smile and Jimmy's jaw dropped, mouth agape. He was in awe of this lovely creature smiling at him. There was a youngster sitting in the chair saying, "Tip me, tip me!" Jimmy finally let go of the lever to wave to Kaetrin and the youngster with a squeal of delight descended into the pool. Kaetrin turned and walked haughtily away. She went over to the outside bar and got a glass of lime squash. Ship's lime juice was available on all British ships by order of the board of trade, a leftover legacy from Captain Cook's antiscorbutic diet to eliminate scurvy. Kaetrin was trying to eliminate nerves and she made a concerted effort to walk as elegantly as possible back to her posse at the ship's rail overlooking the pool. She arrived, drink in hand and gave a regal glance at the pool activities. He was gone! Jimmy had disappeared. She looked frantically in the close proximities of poolside and deck but he was nowhere to be seen. She felt a hand on her elbow and a hot whisper of breath said, "You look bloody ravishing!" Kaetrin turned and looked into the blue eyes of Jimmy the heart-melt and went weak at the knees, recovering in time to stop her glass of lime squash from spilling down the sailor's shirt front.

"I have to get back to my post," he said. "Meet me here tonight at 8 o'clock," and he left. They spent the following twenty minutes passing admiring glances at each other and eventually Jimmy finished his duty cycle and Kaetrin returned to Leslie's cabin.

Leslie was delighted that her plan had worked and said that Kaetrin could meet her man but she was to be back in the cabin by nine o'clock when lights-out was supervised by the duty teacher. "Given time," Leslie said, "I could get a late pass approved, after all you are the senior pupil in the cabin and I'm sure that we can organize dispensation for certain occasions. By the way, keep the dress and the hat, I have others and it does so suit you."

Kaetrin was over the moon and spent an extra hour on her hair before meeting Jimmy at their agreed rendezvous at eight o'clock. He was waiting in the dark. Blackout conditions were in place and she saw a soft red glow from a cigarette that he was smoking. She said, "Hello, Jimmy," and liked the sound and familiarity of his name as she had now known it for several hours and had been practising her pronunciation over and over with various voice modulations.

"You know my name," he said and sounded surprised. "How come you know my name?" She told him about her confrontation with the sailor who had temporarily replaced him on the chair and he laughed. "I am at a disadvantage," he said, "I don't know your name!"

"Kaetrin," said Kaetrin.

Jimmy held out his hand. "Pleased to meet you Kaetrin, a pretty name for a pretty girl, I like it!" and he repeated her name.

They shook hands and he said, "How much time have you got?"

"I have to be back for lights-out at nine."

He took her hand, it was dark and he said, "Follow me, I want to show you something." They walked toward the back of the ship. He had a torch and they came to a set of stairs and he shone the torch down the stairs and they walked along a deck by the rail at the side of the ship and arrived at the stern.

"We can't go any further, we are at the back of the boat. I wanted to show you the wake. Look." And he directed her gaze with a sweep of his arm.

Kaetrin looked at the wake and saw white water that was washed by the light of a moon peeping between scattered clouds.

"I see white water," she said.

"Look deeper," Jimmy said.

She did and let out a surprised and very audible, "What on earth is that?"

"Amazing stuff, isn't it?"

"Looks like emerald explosions and it moves and it spirals and it glows, it's iridescent."

"We call it phosphorescence," Jimmy told her. "The older hands say that it is made up of small sea creatures, god knows what they are but they say they're planktons and they glow when stimulated by the water action such as in the ship's wake."

"They are beautiful," Kaetrin said, "Thank you for showing them to me. I think I shall remember them forever."

"Maybe you will remember this forever," Jimmy said, as he neared her face with his and kissed her firmly on the mouth. And it was not a cinema kiss, fast and furious, but a romantic sea kiss, like a long voyage in fair weather, as they clung desperately together for fear of an ending.

Kaetrin, keen to repeat her experience, made sure she was back in time and found Leslie skulking in the alleyway of their accommodation awaiting Kaetrin's return. Leslie was not duty teacher nor did she have a date with her radio officer, but she was keen to find out how things went and invited Kaetrin into her cabin. "I told the duty teacher that I would cover for you so she knows that you are with me and she is relaxed about that, now how about a nightcap of cocoa and you can tell me all about it? I must be as excited as you."

Leslie had a cabin with facilities for making tea and she had been to the galley and asked one of the cooks for some milk and cocoa. She got the water boiled and added cocoa and milk and handed a hot mug to Kaetrin.

The tacit arrangement was that she should divulge her discoveries to Leslie who was waiting for the first instalment.

"He showed me the wake, that green stuff, it's magnificent!"

"Phosphorescence!"

"Yes that what it's called, phosphorescence – plankton or something."

"That's it, little marine creatures, the bioluminescence of organisms," Leslie said. "I had thought of a classroom lesson on that very topic but with the blackout conditions I simply did not fancy trying to keep track of too many excited children traipsing around a blackened ship at night. It really is a one on one situation. I'm glad you have seen them, it is a wondrous sight."

"They are forever in my memory." Kaetrin seemed rather dreamy as she uttered this statement that was also charged with her first Jimmy kiss. She had finished her cocoa but never tasted it. It may as well have been a ghost drink. She certainly could not remember drinking it.

"Lights-out for you," Leslie said recognizing the signals, "it's almost ten o'clock and you've had a big day."

At this juncture in the voyage the cabin doors were left open and latched back against the bulkhead and curtains were drawn across the doorways instead. The heavy brocade of the fabric was hemmed at the bottom and so gravity ensured that they swayed with any motion of the ship. They worked like a pendulum. This in itself created an air movement, any breath of which was welcome. Punkah louvres in the cabins, ingested a forced air draught at deck head level and outside cabins with portholes had tin scoops that fitted through the round open port and diverted the outside air into the cabin. Any air movement in tropical climes was a bonus especially at night time when one was trying to sleep in the cloying closeness of humid air. First trippers were left to their own devices but those who knew and especially crew who had done many such journeys usually carried electric fans in their luggage. The shipping company certainly did not supply such luxuries. Doug's cabin had two electric fans. One traversed the full length of the bunk and the other was at the foot end of the bunk and blew air onto the bare feet of the bunk occupant. The RO's cabins were high up in the superstructure and were assured of a good flow of air at all times. Doug's cabin sported two portholes and both scoops were deployed and the curtain was moving into the alleyway outside the cabin and then back into the cabin as the ship rolled easily in the long windless tropical swell. Leslie lay in a stupor on the bunk enjoying the luxury of air movement while waiting for Doug to come off watch at midnight. The air blowing onto the soles of her feet and the fan traversing the length of her body from head to foot and back again was regenerating limp molecules. For some obscure reason Doug had changed watches when they exited the Panama Canal. Something to do with time zones and traffic, he had told her.

"We have to give the junior guys experience on the overall system. Fact of the matter is that the chief RO does not want to be woken in the middle of the night and so as a senior among the juniors I get the busier watch as I am less likely to require assistance. If that makes sense?" And so Doug was now off watch from midnight until 0800 hours the next morning and that suited them both. It was a matter of catching some sleep now and seeing what developed when Doug came off watch at midnight.

Doug walked into his cabin and saw Leslie comatose on his bunk. He undressed to his shorts and went off to have a cold shower which was a welcome relief following four hours in the confines of the radio shack. Following the refreshing dunk under cold needles of water, he lightly towelled off. Heavy towelling only produced an excessive heat build up from the energy expended in the operation of towelling, a lesson learned from experience. He wrapped the towel around his midriff and went into the mess and removed a cold bottle of beer from the refrigerator, the label of which he had clearly marked with pen and ink; his rank, as a sign of ownership. He went back to his cabin and poured the beer into a glass from the decanter set on the desk top, sat down on his day bed and surveyed the sleeping form of his lover. He knew the value of sleep in the tropics and decided against waking her. Doug allowed his feelings to surface and he found that his fondness for Leslie was being kindled by the closeness of the tropical environment where shedding garments seemed as natural as donning greatcoats in the Arctic. More skin didn't necessarily mean more sin. On the contrary – to Doug anyway – the mere fact that a lightly clad Leslie asleep on his bunk told Doug that she trusted him implicitly and he would look out for her, asleep or awake. And he felt glad that she had bestowed upon him this role. He was both lover and guardian and he felt good about that.

The beer was gone and Doug got another bottle from the mess and returned to his cabin. He sat again on his daybed, sipping the cold ale and looking fondly at sleeping Leslie. Most of the CORB staff, doctors and nurses, anyway, were doing the round trip but the teachers were staying in New Zealand and that meant that he would have to say goodbye to Leslie. Doug was not sure he wanted to do that. His mind relaxed with the alcohol osmosis and he saw that it was possible to see her again as he would not be leaving the shipping company and Leslie would remain in New Zealand, so their paths should cross once or twice a year at least. If she returned to England the situation would be the same as he would be absent from either country for a similar period in time, so what did it matter, he told himself. What did it matter which end of this globe that he should see her? This reasoning, with some help from his beer, was tiring him and he finished the bottle and lay back on his daybed with a cushion beneath his head and a towel wrapped around his torso and fell asleep.

The monkey island is the highest deck on a ship it is situated above the bridge and contains a compass from where cross bearings may be taken. It is open and therefore exposed to the elements and is a popular place for the ship's officers to sunbathe in private.

Doug took Leslie up onto the monkey island after they woke almost simultaneously at 0500 hours, both having enjoyed a deep and restful sleep in the relative comfort of an ambient air conditioned cabin. Leslie had to get back to her accommodation before the ship awoke and her daily duties began. Doug said, "While you are here, it's a short hop up the ladder to the monkey island, why don't we go there and watch a Pacific sunrise?" And they did. From their lofty perch they had a full 360 degree panoramic view of the Pacific Ocean's horizon and in the east the fingers of the new sun clawing at the watery disc like a crab clambering onto a flat plate, stood up. It then spread the light show with pale cream and yellow and slowly turned to a darker bisque colouring as it rose yet higher before flooding red in a blushing orgy of light. It was pretty to watch and the two lovers breathed in beauty and kissed as the vessel crossed the tropic of Capricorn, heading south on the voyage to New Zealand. With the apparent wind speed at zero the vessel made its own sixteen knot breeze as Doug and Leslie let what little clothing they wore, slip to the deck and they embraced in a love knot. The aromas of fresh morning ozone on the wind were invigorating, it was the only time of the day or night that one could recognize this scent. Try as you may, it was gone before breakfast but stayed until the crew members who were washing down the decks with saltwater hoses had completed this early morning task, washing any flying fish, that had landed on the ships deck during the night, into the scuppers and back into the ocean.

The blue Pacific intensified in colour as the sun's rainbow spectrum of light was absorbed by the ocean and the short-wave blues and violets were reflected. Leslie explained this to Doug who was intrigued by the phenomenon.

"You are a font of knowledge, my love," he said to her, "but then you are a school teacher and I guess the kids come up with some curly questions at times?"

"Not only the kids, I'll be in for a grilling if I am not back in my quarters soon. Matron is the worst, she is like the boss of bosses, for us females anyway."

"Right my love, clothes on and off we go."

Leslie's cabin had not gone unoccupied while she was with Doug. Kaetrin had been given permission to use it to sleep in when Leslie was with Doug, which was most nights when she was not on night duty. It was cooler than sleeping in a four berth cabin and she could extend lights-out to 10pm. As a senior Kaetrin was cut a bit more slack and so she had extra freedoms and could arrange to meet Jimmy and have no fear of disturbing others on her return. The adult on night duty checked on her but it was generally at 11pm, just to ensure that she was tucked up in bed for the night. She was up and away by 0630 hours when Leslie returned from her nightly sojourn with Doug.

Most nights she met Jimmy at 7pm and they had a couple of hours together. Where they shared their intimate thoughts and learned a lot about each other. Jimmy had left school at 14 and went to sea as a cabin boy. His family lived near the Royal Albert docks where his father was a docker and the young Jimmy was hooked on a sea going career from whenever he could remember. "Lord Nelson started his career as a cabin boy," Jimmy had told Kaetrin. "It's the bottom rung. I ran messages, cleaned the brass work, and helped out in all manner of things. I even scrubbed pots and pans in the kitchen – galley they call it. I did a year of that and I became a deck boy, then two years of that, and I have already done one, and I get to be an ordinary seaman. Probably start watchkeeping duties at sea, get to steer the ship and act as lookout apart from the other things we do like chipping and painting and making ropes and strops. Lots of skills to learn. What about you?"

Kaetrin looked startled, she hadn't figured that their conversations would get this personal. "I can't really say," she managed. "Finish school was the goal and then see what I felt like doing I suppose."

"Nothing you fancy?" Jimmy asked.

"I had thought about nursing but I have to be seventeen before I could start training and have all of the required entry level certificates. I didn't think that I could last at school for that much longer. There are lots of jobs available in the factories for the war effort but somehow that seems a cop-out. An excuse to leave school for no reason at all other than to smoke fags and go to the pub with your work mates. I wanted more than that, I think me mum would have loved to shove me out the door to work just so she could charge me rent and spend more in her local. With my dad away in the army she is having a lovely war!

"When my aunty in Wellington offered to sponsor us it solved a lot of problems and maybe answered some questions too. Time will tell."

Jimmy lit a cigarette and blew smoke into the slip stream. He had selected different parts of the ship for their meetings and tonight they were sitting on number five hatch under the cover of some moonlight, courtesy of a cloudless sky.

56

He slid his hand beneath his shirt and pulled out a sheet of document paper. "For you," he said and gave it to Kaetrin. "I don't know if you got one of these when we crossed the equator, if you didn't, you have now." And he passed her the sheet. It was too dark to read the inscription but she could see that the message was contained within a tessellated border and there was a red seal on the lower right end of the paper.

"Looks impressive, what is it?" she asked.

"It's a 'crossing of the line' certificate, from when we crossed the equator. Before the war everyone got one but I don't know what the procedure is now, maybe they are saving paper. Anyway I got it from the writer's office, saw it lying there so I grabbed it."

Kaetrin tried reading it but it was simply too dark to make out the inscription.

"Follow me," he said, "I know where we can read it," and they were off, walking toward the back of the ship. Jimmy opened a door and they stepped over the raised stoop and he guided her down a steep ladder at the bottom, where he switched on a light. It seemed to Kaetrin that they were in some sort of storeroom as there were piles of rope and ships chandlery that were totally foreign and un-nameable. "Bosun's locker," Jimmy said. "Aladdin's cave everything from a needle to an anchor is hidden away in this treasure trove." She wrinkled her nose. "Smells like tar and paint."

"Lots of that too," Jimmy said. "Read the certificate."

Kaetrin held the piece of paper up and saw that it had been specially printed with an intricate patterned border and a red seal at the bottom. It looked impressive. *Just like a diploma,* Kaetrin thought.

Across the top in bold red ink were the words,

'Davey Jones' locker'

And under that the address was given as,

'Trident Place.'

She read aloud.

"Ye Lord Commissioners of ye locker have assured me that ye bigge shippe *Rangitata* did appear within and pass through the limits of our Royale Domaine, on the…"

And there was a dotted line on which the date was to be entered when the event took place, then the word:

'and'

Then under that, another dotted line which was for the recipient's name.

The inscription continued.

"Was admitted into ye ancient fellowship and forever be free to pass over, under or through ye great waters of our Domaine without lette or hindrance.

"Given under my hand and seal.

"The days and years aforesaid

Neptunus Rex. Ruler of the seven seas.

"It's lovely, I love it!" And her eyes shone and she kissed Jimmy on his cheek. "What a lovely gift, thank you. Nobody has one of these."

57

"Better keep it quiet then," Jimmy said, "I don't want to be responsible for starting an epidemic."

"I'll tell no one," Kaetrin replied, "but I do want to put the dates and my name on the appropriate dotted lines, to show my grandchildren, you understand."

Jimmy shook his head, "Yes, Kaetrin, your grandchildren," and he shook his head. And he mimicked in a singy voice, "Come and see your grandmother's diploma she got from King Neptune. The only one presented on the voyage. Tell us, Grannie, what was he like?"

"Actually," Kaetrin joined in the mock. "He was masquerading as a deck boy with large turquoise eyes and green seaweed hair. His skin was scaly, just like a fish but he had lovely kissy lips, boy did he have kissy lips."

"Like this," Jimmy said as he took her in his arms and kissed her long and passionately.

The ship was four days from her destination when they lost their first passenger. The ambience had cooled considerably from the tropics and the porthole scoops were withdrawn. Sleeping was bearable and everybody seemed to have more energy. The man had boarded the ship in Panama and was travelling alone. The chief steward reported that the passenger was buying a bottle of gin a day from the ship's duty free bond store. He was rarely seen about the ship, preferring to keep to himself. His French passport described his occupation as a geologist and by the amount of stamps and visas that adorned the pages therein he travelled extensively and would not have visited his homeland for many years. It was not unusual for a ship to arrive at its destination, following a sea voyage, minus a passenger or two and it was generally conceded they committed suicide by jumping from the ship as was the case here, but in this instance the passenger was observed exiting the vessel. Thus his absence was notified immediately to the captain.

The master at arms was doing his rounds at 2300 hours when he observed an obviously intoxicated person weaving their way along the main deck toward the after part of the ship. He was questioned by the MA but said that he did not require any assistance and was simply taking the night air before retiring. Not being totally satisfied that the person was in a fit state to be wandering around a ship in the dead of night the MA placed him under observation where he was seen to descend a set of stairs onto the lower after deck by number five hold. He went to the port rail and stood there motionless for five minutes. When he was approached by his observers he simply upended himself and fell headfirst from the ship's rail into the sea below. He disappeared from sight as the vessel sped through the blackened watery scrim. Shining a light was forbidden under blackout conditions. The MA could shine his torch beam inboard but not outboard. The only thing that he could do was report the matter to the bridge where he went with great haste and urgency. The third mate was in charge of the watch and he rang the captain who arrived on the bridge to be acquainted with the recent turn of events.

"It's obvious that the man was intending to commit suicide," the captain said. "I see no point in endangering the ship by stopping and searching the ocean in the middle of the night. If we stop and lower a boat we become a stationary target for a submarine. We cannot use lights for the same reasons. Also we have information that suggests there are German raiders operating in the Pacific Ocean so exposing ourselves in a night light search for a body is futile and dangerous. I have no choice but to continue on our course, for the good of my vessel and the safety of the passengers.

"Log the proceedings, time, position etc. Better get the passenger's details. Authorities will want to check the whole thing through."

"Carry on, three-oh."

"Yes, sir," the third mate replied. And the captain left the bridge.

By breakfast the following morning the whole ship was talking about the events of the previous night. The version that was circulating among the CORB staff was that a German spy had come aboard in Panama and had purposefully gone overboard fully dressed but with a life jacket under his coat. He had been in touch with a German U-boat by a radio that was secreted among his luggage. The plan was that at a predetermined spot the spy would fall over-board and be picked up by the submarine. When the large liner stopped for a search of the man's body, the sub would torpedo the *Rangitata*. Survivors would be taken aboard a German raider-merchantman and be taken back to a neutral South American port, and then shipped off to Germany where they would undergo a forced labour existence for the duration of the war and before being freed by the allies. It was a fanciful story and engaged the entire ship's company and passengers for hours discussing the merits of the captain's decision to forsake the life of an individual and save the ship. The captain was an instant hero and the Nazi spy a ratbag.

Two days out from landfall the passengers held a farewell dinner and dance. It was to be a grand affair and the passengers could formally thank the captain and his crew for their safe deliverance. A sea journey was a risky business at the best of times but during a major conflict where adversaries were hurting each other at war, it became a serious undertaking. Fair weather had been their companion and lady luck had a hand in the proceedings too. The captain had ordered a reduction in speed to fourteen knots to make their arrival off the Wellington heads at daybreak- forty eight hours hence. An early arrival then waiting for the pilot was out of the question. He wanted his ship moving at all times.

A special events and dinner menu was printed and at the top of the menus. It was headed in red:

RMS Rangitata.
Dinner Menu:
Hours D'oeuvre
Consomme Clair
Cream of Tomato
Fried Fillets of Turbot-Tartare

Braised Celery au Jus
Vol au Vent a La Reine
Chicken Supreme
Leg of Pork-Apple Sauce
Sirloin of Beef-Horseradish Sauce
Roast and Boiled Potatoes
Brussels Sprouts
Cold Buffet
Cushion of Veal-Roast Lamb
Salad Italienne
Peaches in Jelly
Sponge Fingers
Raspberry Sundae
Croute St Ivel
Pulled Bread-Dinner Bread
Dessert-Coffee
Farewell Dinner
Then, beneath that:
The ship's band will play from 1930 hours until 0100 hours.
It looked very grand.
Kaetrin was devastated to learn that the crew were not allowed to attend.
"Officers only. Officers and passengers."
Leslie had repeated to her.
"Lucky you," Kaetrin said; Doug was an officer.
"Yes he is, but he will also be on watch from 2000 hours until 2400 hours so I may get some dances in following that!"

Leslie used the twenty four hour clock system that she had gotten used to since her association with Doug. "So as you can see, dear girl we both miss out. You will probably meet Jimmy at some stage in the night but I have to wait until the clock strikes twelve. Cinderella would be pleased with that arrangement," she added, hoping some levity might elevate Kaetrin from her gloom.

The CORB children ate as normal with the exception of a few seniors that were allowed to attend the adult function. This was the first time Kaetrin had eaten in the main dining saloon and she was in awe of the grandeur. Normal seating arrangements were abandoned as the organizing committee decided that mix and match would be less formal but Leslie made sure that her and Kaetrin were seated at the same table. The cutlery array was formidable and Kaetrin was in awe of the silver mine displayed on the table. Their table seated four persons and she felt very distant from her knife and fork arrangement on the kitchen table back home in Stepney. If you were having pudding you also got a spoon: three implements from Mum's best 'EPNS.' There were eight pieces per setting on the table in front of her, times four settings, equalling thirty two separate pieces of silverware. Leslie saw that Kaetrin was concerned about the display and in her best teacher's voice said. "I treat it like an equation." Kaetrin looked mystified. Leslie continued. "Now on your left you have three forks and on you right you have two knives and a spoon and above and between the two you have a small fork and a spoon." Kaetrin nodded. "Okay, the two small utensils are like an equals sign so that the three utensils on the left are equal to the three on the right, just like a simultaneous equation: the left satisfies the right, right! So if you are having, say, a four course meal as the setting will suggest, then you will start with outside utensils, which will be the soup spoon on your right and the waiter will remove the fork and so both sides are equal. Then for an entree you have the next two items: the knife on the right and the fork on the left and the equation is still satisfied. Then the main course eliminates the final two utensils leaving the equals sign, which you will use with dessert."

They were joined at the table by two passengers: a Major and Mrs Beresford-Amble. Formerly from the Indian Army, the major had served in the First World War and they had settled in India with the British Army where they enjoyed a colonial lifestyle until the outbreak of war in 1939. The foreign office suddenly discovered the existence of Military establishments that were languishing in the farthest reaches of the British Empire and they were being redistributed to provide the best possible usage of questionable manpower to assist in the formation of fighting units from the colonies and the major had won his New Zealand ticket. He had experience in the African deserts and the New Zealand Government was getting an expeditionary force together from civilian volunteers, to go and fight in North Africa. The Major would give advice on training and conditions to be expected by troops fighting in North Africa. In 1915 the Ottomans had tried to seize the Suez Canal but were repelled by British forces and the major was in the thick of it.

"We were armed to the teeth," he explained, but the three ladies sitting at the dinner table with him were stoic in their receipt of this intelligence. They had started up their own conversation and it was centred around the fashions of the day and what to wear on arrival in Wellington. Mrs Beresford-Amble had declared that the weather would be cold and windy so a good sturdy overcoat would be ideal.

"They get southerly winds, I am told, up from the Antarctic, the South Pole, you understand. Not as cold of course but still unpleasant especially having recently come from warmer climates. I always kept a set of clothes in England you know," she went on, "for when we went back on furlough. I upgraded them each time we were there so I have a reasonably late model wardrobe. Should get me through our sojourn in these southern seas.

"Now when we all get settled in our new land I must get you to come round for a visit and a cup of Darjeeling tea. I have my special supply arriving with our belongings together with my tea set things. Did you know I have several teapots from various Nawabs' collections? Priceless you understand and the tea tastes better. You must preheat the pot. Yes I hear you say an old wives tale but true – it is true and I will prove it to you."

Mrs Beresford-Amble was having a lovely dinner and she found the unexpected female company so enjoyable she was having trouble repressing her natural ability to talk endlessly on any subject concerning Memsahib matters. It was like being back in the Shimla summers where the ladies gathered for their afternoon soirees and drank endless cups of invigorating Darjeeling tea in the relatively benign climate of the hill country and away from the oppressive heat of the Dehli summers.

Horace, the major, sat in silence. His voice may as well have been surgically removed. Previously, their dinner table had consisted of four men and two woman and although everybody engaged in table talk it was predominantly the male voices that logged the most hours and the ladies had to endure listening to the male prattle or talk in undertones between themselves. Now outnumbered three to one, Horace discovered that he had nothing to offer to the conversation and was disgruntled. He was more at home in the mess with a gin and tonic and prattling on about the Sudan or Suez or some other sphere of action that involved the battalion. The major attacked his soup with gusto. *It was*, he thought, *as good as the tomato soup the battalion cooks put together.*

Jimmy was waiting at their usual rendezvous, his cigarette tip glowing in the dark. Kaetrin crept up on him from behind and put her arms around him. They were in southern waters now and the noise from the sea slapping the ship and the wind blowing around the superstructure was enough to blanket out other ambient sounds. He was not startled as he had expected she would do that, as she had before. He turned into her welcoming bosom and they kissed. It was an easy movement now, not awkward and hesitant like the first encounters. Theirs was a romance that had established rituals and they fell into it like old familiar territory and wore it like a cloak.

"One more night," he said.

Kaetrin put her fingers across his lips, "Sssh," she said. "Remember that you have three weeks in port while the ship loads frozen meat and then you'll be back in six months. Just imagine the letters you will get from me and the letters you can write to me. We have lots of ways to share our feelings. Our nightly trysts are just the beginning."

"What was that – twist, you said? Nightly twist? What's it mean?"

"It's trysts, with a 'Y'. It means a lovers meeting. Leslie told me it!"

"We can have trysts in Wellington then," Jimmy said.

"Of course we can, we can go to the cinema, we can't do that here."

"That would be a real tryst," Jimmy said, "going to the pictures with my girl, I like that!"

Chapter 6

The War Years

The sinking of the *Rangitane* made headlines in the evening *Post*, the capital's daily evening newspaper. Kaetrin was reluctant to read the article but her aunty said that she should confront reality with reality.

"Denying it changes nothing!" Flora said. "You can wish for the best but you must accept the inevitable!"

The article described how the liner had been attacked by German raiders. How the captain of the *Rangitane* had successfully gotten his radio signals away and for the good of his passengers and crew had surrendered his ship and overseen the transfer of his charges to the German ships. The raiders already had prisoners of war aboard their ships from previous engagements with allied merchant shipping and they were filled to capacity. The Germans decided therefore to release their prisoners onto Emirau Island in New Guinea. The young men amongst them who qualified for military service would be retained as prisoners of war on the German ships and would be taken to prisoner of war camps in Germany. Jimmy the heartmelt became a prisoner of war. He was also a hero and was mentioned in dispatches for a gallantry medal or some form of recognition for his bravery under enemy fire.

Twenty two perished in the encounter and Kaetrin was horrified to read that one of the radio officers, a Doug Thornton, was among the dead. She had never met Doug but felt great remorse for Leslie whom she knew was very fond of him following their shipboard romance on the recent voyage out from England. She knew that Leslie would be contacting her over this terrible loss and Kaetrin was wondering how she should react. Tragedy was an unknown emotion to the young Kaetrin but she knew that she had to confront it and conquer it if she was to move forward. Flora had explained to her that Jimmy would probably have received some form of custodial sentence on his arrival in England and now that he was a prisoner of war he certainly had a custodial sentence for the duration of the war. His chances of survival were better as a POW than as a merchant seaman in wartime. "Furthermore," Flora had said, "you can write to him, I believe that the Red Cross get mail and food and clothing parcels to POWs. If they can receive letters they must be able to send them!"

Marjory Beresford-Amble's invitation to tea arrived shortly thereafter. It was addressed to Miss Kaetrin MacLeod at Maximes Hotel on Lower Cuba Street, Wellington. The contents also included an invitation for Leslie which Mrs B-A asked Kaetrin to pass on, should she happen to know Leslie's whereabouts. Kaetrin had not heard from Leslie and had no idea where she was. Some weeks had now passed since the sinking of the *Rangitane* and Christmas and New Year had come and gone. For both Kaetrin and Robert it was a most unusual experience to have Christmas in the summertime. Flora had gone to extremes to ensure that her charges enjoyed their first antipodean festive season sans snow. While the hotel staff attended to the in house guests Flora entertained in her penthouse suite, cooking a most sumptuous roast lamb lunch with all the trimmings. Her table was a delight festooned with sufficient tinselry to make a Hollywood tycoon feel secure in the knowledge that no one could have done it better.

Of the eight ladies occupying the second storey apartments, four had either gone home to their families or were staying with friends over the festive season which generally ran through until the New Year. Those remaining, Felicity, Mary, Ethel and Roberta, dined with Flora as part of the extended family. Also at the Christmas table were four seamen from home boats in port. They were from various parts of the Western Isles of Scotland and like Flora were native Gaelic speakers and sought the company of fellow expatriates whenever in a foreign port. It was like being a member of an international family when your birthright became an admission ticket.

Boxing Day however was the big day out. On Boxing Day, Flora hosted the annual picnic for family and staff at the hotel. They took the harbour ferry across from Queens Wharf to Days Bay for a day in the sun at the beach and on the grass in front of the pavilion. It was in the eastern suburbs of Eastbourne, across the harbour from Wellington City. It could be easily accessed by road but the ferry across the water was far more fun and everybody could relax and imbibe in the festive beverages. Hampers of food and drinks had been prepared by the kitchen staff and a skeleton crew remained at the hotel to attend the guests' needs. While the heavy hampers were driven to the wharf by taxi the happy revellers walked the fifteen minute stroll from the hotel to the wharf to board the ferry.

Across the harbour, where the ferry was tied up at the Days Bay Pier, it was a short five minute walk across the road and onto a large grassed picnic area in front of the pavilion and beneath the spreading branches of Norfolk Pines. On a hot day the cool waters of Days Bay offered relief for bathers who took the plunge. It was a popular picnic spot and early arrivals claimed the best spots to spread out their picnic rugs on the grass and take sustenance. Robert was changed into his swimming togs and into the water before the entourage had settled. The *Rangitane* and war seemed so very far away. Even if a little unreal. Felicity, Ethel, Mary and Roberta had kicked off their shoes and were throwing a large beach ball around on the grass. They were dressed in the fashion of the day when modesty required the wearer to display the least amount of bare flesh possible. Shorts were making a summer introduction and unlike the thirties they were becoming shorter as the decades became longer. Roberta had quipped in the changing room that if the trend continued they could expect to wear a handkerchief for cover in the sixties.

Male heads were turning and female hands were slapping the backs of the turned heads. The girls were joined by male staff from the hotel and soon there was just Flora and Kaetrin and Alice the head cook sitting on the rug watching the antics of the ball throwers.

"You should join them," Flora said Kaetrin, "and work off some of your Christmas dinner!"

"No Aunty, thank you, I'm happy to sit here and take it all in. It's still very strange sitting here in the sunshine and it's Christmas. I'm thinking of London and snow anyway I think I like warm."

Robert arrived shivering and dripping water from his swim in the sea. "Bloody freezing, the water is bloody freezing!"

"Of course it is," Flora said, "it comes up from the Antarctic where the icebergs melt and the current flows north." She threw Robert a towel; it had Maximes Hotel written across it in red letters. "Dry off and sit in the sun to warm up, you'll be leaping back into the water in thirty minutes, I guarantee it!"

A beach ball landed in the middle of the picnic rug and one of the male members from the ball game came to retrieve it.

"Watch it, Oliver," Flora said, "I would hate to think what the reaction would be if you managed to land it on another picnicker's site, like in the middle of a cream sponge."

"Yes, Ma'am."

"Call me Flora, everybody does."

"Yes, Ma'am."

Oliver collected the ball and threw it back into play. The game continued with frequent breaks for ales and ciders.

Gymnastic leaps and bounds and delicate ballet type movements were displayed by both genders and became more relaxed and enhanced as the game progressed on the lawn in the sun. A particularly vigorous throw saw the ball soar and catch a wind draft that sent it sailing among a large group of picnickers. Amid whoops and shouts they attempted to lob the ball back toward the players but despite their gallant attempts the ball landed in the middle of their picnic hamper where it settled happily without further movement. The ball players looked at each other, reluctant to volunteer to go and retrieve the ball.

"I'll go," Felicity said, "for gosh sakes, it's a holiday atmosphere what are you afraid of – the fun police?"

Felicity walked over to the picnickers to get the ball. "I'm so sorry about that," she said. "The wind seems to have caught our ball and veered it off course, I hope it hasn't caused any harm?"

A tall man with hair greying slightly at the temples stood up with the ball in his hand. It was James Collins, a young barrister and the Wellington Law Society was having its annual Boxing Day picnic outing. He held the ball in his outstretched hand and then he saw it was Felicity, whom he recognized from his visits to Maximes. It may have been the wine he had consumed or the excitement of an unexpected encounter with a clandestine acquaintance, or the festive season with its goodwill gesture that must be extended toward mankind, which for the most bizarre of reasons renders humankind to behave like kind humans, but without giving the situation his normal and reserved consideration about cause and effect he excitedly heard himself say, "Hello Felicity, fancy seeing you here!" Which in the most well intentioned of deliveries suggested that this meeting was a most unlikely encounter as they usually meet in entirely different circumstances. And then inwardly and to himself upon recognizing his blunder, he thought, *Oh shit, why didn't I keep my big mouth shut!*

Followed a deafening silence, Felicity took the proffered ball and said, "Thank you, Jim." Only James Collins' wife would have known when to address her husband as Jim. The name was reserved for intimate occasions. Realizing her mistaken usage of the bedroom appellation, Felicity escaped to her ball game.

For James Collins there was to be no escape. It got ugly as Mrs Collins questioned her philandering spouse about his acquaintance with a beach belle, in shorts no less and with a crowd of picnickers from Maximes Hotel. "Wasn't that the place that housed, as rumours would have it, loose women?"

Mr and Mrs Collins left the party of the Wellington Law Society Inc picnickers to pursue the argument in the privacy of their large Wellington mansion.

The two sets of picnickers carried on each oblivious of the other's existence.

Flora sent Kaetrin over to the pavilion for hot water. Picnickers would take their own teapot but get hot water from a kiosk in the pavilion. Kaetrin approached the pavilion and her attention was drawn to a band rotunda on which a band was seated and had started to play to an audience seated in deck chairs on the lawn around the rotunda. She stopped to listen to the music and take in the splendour of the rotunda that was in the middle of a tranquil garden setting with a green bushy backdrop, framing the scene like a curtained stage. It was an inviting and cool sanctuary away from the relentless sun. Kaetrin had felt the heat of the sun, as it was intense and far stronger than anything she had ever experienced in London. She became aware of someone standing close behind her and breathing hard. The breath had a strong liquor smell on it and she moved forward to get away from the hot fetid fumes. Looking to one side as she moved she saw a youngish man smiling at her in a lopsided sort of a leer and knew that her admirer was intoxicated. He winked at her and moved closer, attempting to place his arm around her waist and as he did so he suggested that they might venture into the cool lushness of the bush for a bit of 'you know what', as he put it.

"I know that you are on a picnic outing but I am happy to make a business proposition and pay the going rate," he said.

Kaetrin had difficulty believing what he had just said to her and in a state of mild shock she said, "Bugger off!" Her admirer was persistent and obviously had enough alcohol in his system to overlook any feelings other than his own immediate carnal urges. He was not taking no for an answer and became louder with his lewd suggestions. Kaetrin would have fled the scene but he had hold of her arm, his hand by now having slipped from around her waist.

It was at this point that a gentleman said to her, "Is this man annoying you, my dear?" Kaetrin recognized Major Beresford-Amble, impeccably dressed in a cream linen suit, straw boater hat and carrying a walking stick with a carved ivory top.

"Oh, Major," Kaetrin managed to blurt out. "Oh, thank you, Major – yes I need help!"

The major had sized up the situation and brandishing his ivory topped stick he said, "Remove your hand, sir, you insult the young lady."

Kaetrin's assailant looked bemused as his alcohol addled brain failed to comprehend reality. The hot sun and the wine had combined to remove any sense of propriety and decency from the fellow and he was a mere bore. Perhaps not dangerous, but certainly obnoxious.

The major was well used to removing junior officers from the mess who found themselves in a similar state. As recent arrivals from England, sent out to the regiment in India, the young men seemed to have trouble adjusting to the heat when taking alcohol. Perhaps they drank it too quickly in an attempt to cool off.

The young fellow looked at the major and assessed him as being about as much of a hurdle to his amorous aspirations as a felon in the dock under his cross examination.

"Be a good man," he said, "piss off and leave us alone." He had barely finished the sentence when he found himself flat on his back on the grass. A look of profound disbelief spread across his countenance as his brain pieced together, in slow motion, his rather rapid demise. Then a grin slowly creased his face and he started to nod his head, like a fighter who has realized how his opponent decked him and that he could now rise and do the same to the opposition.

The major tipped his hat to Kaetrin and said, "Memsahib's over here, come and say hello, I just know that she would be so pleased to see you. By the way, who is the young man?"

Kaetrin replied, "He's from that group," pointing to the Law Society's picnic gathering. "I recall seeing him traipsing around that gathering showing off and generally making a nuisance of himself – maybe they too have asked him to leave."

As they walked away the inebriated young man who had now regained his feet made a charge at the major. With a side step executed as neatly as a rugby half back, the major moved at exactly the moment his assailant had calculated impact, and he sailed harmlessly by.

The major said, "Excuse me this won't take a minute," as he fell in behind the missile and grabbed him by his collar in the one hand and the belt of his pants in the other and frog marched him over to the Law Society's picnic spot and threw him headlong into their picnic spread.

"This man is a public nuisance!" the major addressed the gathering. "You either control the bounder or I shall ask the police to take care of him!"

"Now look here," a member of the gathering started to address the major but an arm restrained him.

The restrainer said, "Certainly, sir, thank you for bringing the matter to our attention."

The major rejoined Kaetrin and they walked over to see Marjorie Beresford-Amble who was seated in a deck chair enjoying the recital. She was delighted to see Kaetrin who had now remembered that she was originally sent to fetch hot water for tea. Kaetrin had to excuse herself but not before inviting them both over to have a cup of tea with them and she pointed to where they were picnicking. Mrs Beresford-Amble said, "Certainly my dear, Horace and I would be delighted, we'll come in fifteen minutes. The band is about to play Pomp and Circumstance and I simply love Pomp and Circumstance."

Kaetrin arrived back just as Flora was about to send someone to look for her. The ball players were lying on the picnic rugs exhausted from their strenuous activities. Cook had laid out a feast from the goodies contained in the hampers and Flora was waiting to pour tea.

"You obviously got lost," Flora said, "I was about to send out a search party."

Kaetrin recounted her meeting with the Beresford-Ambles and told Flora that she had invited the couple to join them for a cup of tea.

"You'll love them, Aunty. They really are a lovely couple."

"Where's Robert?"

"What?"

"Robert, where is he? We haven't seen him in ages, Jack!" Flora looked at the hotel handyman, "Please go over to the beach and call him for lunch. Drag him by the ear if he won't come!"

"Yes, Ma'am."

"Call me Flora, everyone else does"

"Yes Ma'am."

The Beresford-Ambles were well received by the hotel picnickers. Seated on blankets, Flora had made them cups of tea and Cook was making fresh ham sandwiches. The sun beamed down on the landscape and a gentle southerly breeze middled the air. "Just like a Punkah Wallah," the major said, "the breeze is most welcome." Robert was found by Jack and brought back to the picnic lunch under duress. He was having a grand time jumping from the wharf with his new found friends and it was not until he had consumed the first ham sandwich that he realized how hungry he was. The girls were tanning their legs and minding their weight, Flora had to coax them to eat food to restore energy. "Plenty of fruit to choose from," she reminded them. "Apples, plums, bananas, oranges," she said, "I never saw a banana until I was twenty two!"

"Fish and rice," the major said.

"What?"

"Standard rations in the desert. Salty fish encourages the soldiers to drink water, don't you know! Rice, plenty of rice and dates from the palm trees. By Jove this is a feast. A credit to you, m'dear," he said, nodding his head at Flora.

"I agree," Marjory Beresford-Amble chimed in. "the Lady's Swimming Club at Shimla couldn't have done it better!"

"Where's Shimla?" Ethel asked.

"India m'dear, it's a cooler summer climate in the hills, we go there for the summer because Dehli is simply too hot! Unbearable, you understand." Nobody understood but they never questioned it either. Days Bay was hot enough today. The tall pines sheltered the grassy picnic spot from some of the cooling and pleasant southerly breeze.

It was attired but happy bunch of picnickers that took the six o'clock ferry from Days Bay to Queens Wharf. The contents of the hampers had been consumed and they were now lighter and able to be carried by the menfolk on the ten minute walk back to the hotel. Dinner was just about over and the dining room was clear of patrons but for one. A lone diner was seated in the far corner and although she had her back to the door Kaetrin recognized Leslie as soon as she entered the dining room. Kaetrin ran over and cried out, "Miss Corbett," and nothing more came out as her throat swelled with an onset of a severe bout of emotional sympathy and the words got stuck in the constriction. Leslie rose from her seat at the table, recognizing Kaetrin's voice, they embraced and held onto each other in a wordless but emotional display of grief. When both felt that they could converse coherently they pulled apart and still holding hands, examined each other's countenance as if looking for an inscription in memory of a dearly departed lover and friend. Following the hugs and tears, the two sat down at the table like the old friends that they were, holding hands and laughing about their respective voyage romances as if it were a big adventure. And it was. Leslie told Kaetrin about her trip to Auckland with the twenty CORB children on the overnight express from Wellington. Her contract with CORB had ended with the delivery of her charges to Auckland. Leslie took a room in a downtown boarding house and met Doug most days and nights and they had a wonderful time.

"In fact," she confided in Kaetrin, "I was glad when is ship sailed, we were seeing far too much of each other and while it was fun and all very romantic at sea, in port he had far too much spare time and I seemed to occupy most of that. Don't get me wrong, I liked Doug a lot but I was not in love with him. I was in love with the lifestyle on the ocean wave if you get my meaning. The romance of it all. Hot steamy tropical nights and early morning sunrises. A marine aphrodisiac for sure. We parted amicably enough and agreed to correspond and see each other again in six months' time when his ship was due here again." Leslie bit her lower lip and paused her voice had started to quaver, she composed herself and continued. "But that is not to be – poor Doug – he is gone forever and my memories of our time together will remain forever and they will always be pleasant dreams of a beautiful romance." Leslie looked at her friend and smiled a 'we have a common bond smile' which was like a secret handshake among Freemasons. 'We belong to the love on the ocean wave sorority,' it said.

Flora came and welcomed Leslie and said, "You are staying with us." Leslie confirmed that she was and Flora realized that Leslie had taken her comments as a question and not a request.

"No Leslie, I mean that you are to stay with Kaetrin and myself in the penthouse suite – you are to be our guest! I will get the concierge to bring your case directly to our apartment."

Leslie was speechless and most grateful. "Thank you Mrs MacLeod," she said, after a pause. "That would be lovely."

"Call me Flora – everybody does."

"Thank you, Flora."

At this stage in our story it is necessary to chronicle the war years in Wellington and how Maximes Hotel coped with the influx of fighting men from the United States who came to New Zealand's shores to prepare for an invasion into Japanese occupied Pacific Islands.

Over twenty thousand marines were stationed at Camp MacKay, a forty minute train ride north of Wellington, on the Kapiti Coast. The main influx arrived on June 14 1942 when Wellington Harbor was inundated with troop transports and freighters carrying men and supplies, arms and ammunition to support a major offensive to dislodge the occupying Japanese forces from the near lying South Pacifc Islands. Columns of marines were disembarked at Aotea Quay, they were assembled into their respective platoons and regiments and marched through the city to the train station for the train journey to Camp MacKay. Next the freighters came alongside the quay and unloaded their hardware of fighting equipment. There were tons of food stores, medicines, beer and cigarettes and all of the paraphernalia needed to sustain a bunch of young men with appetites as big as Texas. Trucks came to transport the stores to locations around the city environs where large warehouses had been built to hold such quantities.

Then came the 'brass'. These were the generals and their staff. They were responsible for the planning and logistics and the distribution of both men and stores and they wanted to be housed in accommodation appropriate to their station in the military pecking order. Not for them a canvas tent and a rickety cot, no sir. Clean sheets and a bathroom with hot and cold running water. Formulating policy requires a clear head and that means a good night's sleep. It was division policy to house top brass in the best available billets. If that was a chicken coop, then so be it. It would be the best chicken coop on the island.

Colonel James Peroux was the battalion accommodation expert. He could ferret out a mink lined fox hole on a beach assault landing. And he was at Maximes to see what he could find for his boss General Sherman Winslow.

The colonel had arrived unannounced and called at the front desk to enquire about accommodation and Kaetrin responded to the bell ring when the colonel hit the button. It was obvious to Kaetrin that the man was a military officer of some standing as he seemed to have a lot of badges and insignia displayed on his tunic. Apart from the glitter they held no significance to Kaetrin.

"Good morning," she said, "how can I help you?"

"Morning Ma'am," the colonel said, touching his cap brim with the first two fingers of his right hand in an informal salute.

"I'm from General Winslow's staff. I am here to enquire about the availability of accommodation for the general and his staff members."

"And just how many people would that be?" Kaetrin enquired.

"That depends on how many rooms you can offer. You see we have about fifty persons in the general's staff whom we prefer to house in good quality residential type accommodation. All under the same roof is desirable but hey we can be flexible here. Let's see what you have available?"

Colonel Peroux saw her uncertain expression and said, "Say young lady, you want to fetch the manager? We have a lot to discuss."

Kaetrin was relieved by his suggestion. She excused herself and left to phone Flora.

"Show him to my office please, Kaetrin," Flora said, realizing the opportunity for a business proposition.

Kaetrin showed Colonel Peroux to Flora's office and excused herself.

"Flora MacLeod," Flora said, standing up from her desk and extending her hand.

"James Peroux," the colonel replied and they shook hands.

"Have a seat, colonel," Flora said, indicating the visitor's seat at the end of her desk.

"Thank you."

"Accommodation is what we sell," Flora said. "I believe you are looking for accommodation, if you can tell me what it is you require, how much and for how long, I'll do my best to meet your needs."

Peroux looked impressed by this forthright approach from the red-headed lady with a Scots accent. He just knew they would get along.

"We have up to fifty people that we want to house. If we can get them all under the same roof, great! If not well that's okay too. What can you do for me?"

"I can let you have the top floor and the one below. That will take care of thirty people, more if you want to double up. We have rooms with double beds that can be substituted for two singles. It's a logistics thing. I can show you the rooms, you'll see what I mean."

"Sure, let's do that. The boss would want a suite with a separate bedroom and a lounge that could double as a boardroom. If you get my meaning."

"I know what you mean, we can deliver. Follow me."

They took the elevator to the top floor and Flora showed the colonel the suite that the general would occupy.

The colonel nodded. "That's suitable, but we need a table."

"We have a suitable table that you can use."

Flora showed him another room.

"This is a typical example of the standard double bedrooms that we can substitute with two single beds. All rooms on this floor have en-suites attached."

Peroux made notes.

They went down a floor.

"All rooms on this floor are single rooms and share communal bathroom facilities." She showed him a sample room and then the bathrooms.

"Great," the colonel said, "let's talk costs!"

Two hours later, Colonel Peroux left Maximes with a signed contract in his briefcase. Flora got a good room rate and a guarantee for six months of continual rental with a right of renewal for a further six months. The men would eat [optional] at normal restaurant prices and times. After hours room service for food – boss's suite only – the War Room as it would become known. As for booze, well, they would supply their own.

"Men only on these two floors," Flora insisted, "no guests."

"But of course," Peroux said, "of course."

And so Maximes became a hot spot for the who's who, in the brass section of residential and visiting military bigwigs.

Whilst billing would be effective immediately, it took at least three weeks for the personnel allocated rooms at the hotel to check in. Colonel Peroux was one of them and he handed Flora a typed list of the room numbers and the occupants name and rank. The top floor was reserved for colonels and above. The third floor contained all ranks below. They were majors, captains and lieutenants.

Casuals could still book rooms on the second floor. These were the usual locals and off duty military who came to town for a bit of R&R.

The hotel took on a bit of a military buzz with comings and goings night and day. The girls on the first floor had never been so busy and had to leave town to get a break from work.

The dining room was busy and substituted for a meeting room following long working lunches where the military lingered over endless coffee cup discussions.

The lobby was turned into a press gallery with interviews being conducted by American newspaper journalists and war correspondents, with any brass they could collar either entering or exiting the hotel. In due course those avoiding the media scrimmage would exit via the rear car park in a staff car as the general did.

Flora invested in two milkshake machines and hers was the first establishment in Wellington to install an espresso coffee maker. She had to employ a full time operator, it became so popular. Other hotels trying to emulate her success tried to find a local supplier of these new-fangled coffee makers. They never had the expertise of Colonel Peroux who it seemed had an endless order book with supply Master Sergeant Widowski, Chief of Stores at Seaview Depot which was located at the north-eastern end of Wellington's extensive harbour.

Colonel Peroux and Flora MacLeod formed a good working relationship. It was no accident that the colonel kept his business with the hotel management until the late afternoon or early evenings. He knew that at that time Flora would be pouring herself the hotelier's daily reward which, in Flora's case consisted of a generous helping of a single malt whisky from her favourite distillery on the island of Skye. The war years had taken their toll on supply, however, and the beverage was becoming difficult to locate. Flora had standing orders placed with every seaman who visited Wellington from her homeland to ensure that they had a bottle or two in their locker for Flora when their ship docked. This always challenged the rationale of supply versus carrier's need for the same product for sure the voyage will have started with the bottles fully stacked and accounted for and in the care of the gatekeeper. A lot of water had to pass beneath the keel of a ship from London docks to Port Nicholson and sometimes the carrier had to broach the promised merchandise to satisfy their own requirements. It took a strong will and a steady hand to deliver the goods as intended.

Colonel Peroux asked Chief Widowski for a case of the stuff. Widowski promised nothing but took the money from the colonel anyway. A week later a Jeep arrived at Maximes Hotel. The driver, a marine private, jumped down from the driver's seat and removed a case from the tray behind him. He walked through the lobby of the hotel as the assembled press contingent commented on the arrival of Sherman's booze. Walking smartly to the front office, he placed the case on the polished wooden surface and said to Kaetrin, "Delivery for Mrs MacLeod!" He turned smartly and left.

Flora was overcome with surprise at the manner in which the case had materialized. When confronted by Flora, James Peroux owned up but would not accept any payment, which was another matter as Flora always paid her dues.

"Look Flora," James said one afternoon as they both sat down with a glass of the whiskey, "you gave me a good deal and I came in well below budget! I get a bit of leeway and I can assure you that this case of booze is a drop in the ocean compared with the top brass when they throw a shindig. I'll probably book it against the divisions ball next month which they are holding at the Majestic Cabaret. And before I forget dear lady, I would be honoured if you would agree to be my partner and guest on that occasion."

Flora paused her drink in mid sip and lowered the glass onto her desk. Her late husband Murdo had been gone a few years now and even though she had

73

missed him, she had been so totally absorbed in her business affairs that she had not harboured any thoughts about socializing. Especially with a male. The thought did not scare her, but made her afraid. Their evening drinks together had been a business arrangement, attending a ball would put it on another level.

"No strings attached," James said as if reading her thoughts. "These are good events. If you like dancing you will have plenty of partners and I can guarantee you will not get stuck with a bore!"

Flora raised her glass and sipped delicately from the cut crystal tube. Back in the Hebrides, dancing was a passion. *Same passion*, she thought, *different partners, different island – what the hell – what's to lose!*

"In that case I accept."

"You will have a ball – oops excuse the pun. Bad timing."

The Majestic Cabaret was the premier dance facility in the capital city, if not the entire country. It had been purpose built for dance and cabaret functions when the Majestic Theatre was built in 1929.

Entry from Willis Street was by way of an expansive marble foyer, with several steps of landings. It was built wide to cater for the egress of patrons from the movies. One moved through glass doors onto a plushly carpeted interior foyer with the ticket box office for movie seats straight ahead. To the left was a broad carpeted winding stairway with landings that took movie goers up to the ground floor entrance to the auditorium. On the left hand side of the stairway were windows that allowed a view of the cabaret interior below, it would be spectacularly lit up on dance nights. To the left of the ticket box office in the foyer was the entrance to the cabaret. The ground floor featured a large dance arena set slightly below the carpeted entrance-level floor, cloak rooms and seating. The perimeter of the dance floor was edged in translucent lighted glass bricks that cast a soft and magic glow around the perimeter of the polished wooden dance floor. To the rear of the dance floor stood the bandstand, a rather large and imposing affair that could hold sufficient musicians to play 'Big Band Dance and Swing.' They were seated behind covered music stands displaying a large letter 'M' for Majestic, on the front. A curved stairway ran up either side of the bandstand to the mezzanine above which contained the majority of the seating and tables for the resting dancers and their beverages. Lighting and drapes were of the highest quality and the latest fashions. A large cut crystal ball spun above the dancers reflecting the light images projected on to it from coloured spots strategically place around the auditorium. All up it was written, "The Majestic is the best dance emporium in the Dominion – bar none!"

Marjory Beresford-Amble was going to the Marines Ball. The girls on the first floor were all going. The mayoress was to take the first dance with General Sherman Winslow. It seemed that everybody knew someone who was going to one of the largest social events on the city's calender for many years; Ever since war was declared in Europe, anyway. Ball gowns were being air freshened from their sojourn with moth balls and in some cases alterations were made. Dressmakers and seamstresses were working hard to fulfil their anxious clients' demands. Flora was in two minds – resurrect an existing number from her wardrobe or splash out on a new gown. She decided to buy a new ball gown.

Kaetrin was not going. It was not that she had no offers, because she got requests for dates every day from the young sailors and marines that were swarming around the town. Jimmy the heartmelt was still very much in her dreams and so she was not interested in forming new relationships. Jimmy had her heart and her sacred memories were tucked away in that very sentimental repository.

Mrs Thornton nee Corbett also had requests from admirers, but her interests were in parenting and making a good start in life for young Bravo, who was now eighteen months old.

By elimination, Kaetrin and Leslie were the default hoteliers at Maximes during the Saturday night of the ball.

Flora had no problems with that, as both of them had proved to be capable operators of the business. The police chief had promised Flora that he would ensure that his men kept an eye on the place during their regular beats from the watch at Taranaki Street Police station, two blocks away.

Flora had told James Peroux to come to her penthouse at seven o'clock where they would have a quiet pre ball scotch together before catching a taxi to the venue. The cabaret was walking distance but it was winter. Even in a fur stole, a winter's evening could bring a chill into the ambient temperature, making walking unpleasant and it could rain.

Kaetrin and Leslie and baby Bravo were in the ground floor front desk office – by order! Flora did not want an audience for her one on one full dress meeting with her ball date, who arrived – as one might guess – punctually. James Peroux had admired Flora in her everyday working apparel, but the ravishing redhead in the sapphire ball gown blew him away. Flora could see it in his eyes and didn't need oral confirmation, but she got it anyway.

"Thank you," she said following his flattering remarks. "Please come in." James Peroux was dressed in the Marine Corps' black tie evening dress. It was adorned with a lot of brass buttons, some braid but otherwise conservative enough for his lady to assume the role of peacock. In colour, not gender. The lounge was elegant and plush and their awkwardness at being in formal gender roles for the first time melted with the warmth of the single malt scotch she had poured for them both. The phone rang and Kaetrin informed Flora that her cab had arrived. "Tell him we will be there in five minutes!"

Taxi cabs lined up in Willis Street as elegantly dressed occupants alighted and entered the Majestic foyer. There were many beautifully dressed ladies and Flora was glad she had gone to the trouble of buying a new wardrobe especially for the occasion. James checked in his cap and her stole at the cloakroom and they were ushered to their table on the mezzanine overlooking the dance floor. The band struck up the "Marines Hymn" and General Winslow entered with the mayor and mayoress. They were seated at a table on the ground floor in full view of all attendees. An aide went over and talked to the general who got up and walked over to the bandstand. He addressed the audience through the microphone. The general welcomed everybody to the Second Marine Divisions Memorial Ball and thanked his hosts for their friendly reception of his men. He ordered everyone to enjoy the evening, walked back to his table and requested the first dance with the mayoress. They twirled solo to a foxtrot until the bandmaster ordered, "Everybody up on your feet and dancing!" And the dance floor was crowded. Apart from the first and last dance, Flora and James had to endure 'cutting in', which is considered socially acceptable so long as both parties agree. It was, after all, a social occasion and dancing exclusively with one person all evening was considered gauche. Flora and James had a well-earned rest during supper and visited various tables to talk with other couples. Flora introduced James to Horace and Dorothy Beresford-Amble. James was taken with the colourful British Army Major who was resplendent in his red jacketed dress uniform with black trousers which had a wide red stripe down the outside leg seams. Marjory was effervescent. A perennial socializer, she was in her element. They agreed to meet for a dinner date on some future occasion.

Al too soon, or so it seemed, they were dancing the last waltz and James said they had been invited to an after ball function at the St George Hotel. The exhilaration of the evening's activities had charged their batteries and both had agreed that it would be fun to attend. The close proximity of the hotel was a mitigating factor. A short five minute stroll up Willis Street brought them to the foyer of one of Wellington's finest hotels and they rode the elevator to the functions room. It was thick with the smell of cigar smoke when Flora and James entered. They ordered a scotch at the bar and then mingled. It seemed that James knew a lot of people and was well regarded. They danced more intimately on the small crowded dance floor, to phonograph records. Glenn Millar was popular with the phonograph operator. And so they danced to the classic swing of the day. Bing Crosby turned the mood into cheek to cheek and at three o'clock in the morning they said their goodbyes to the remaining revellers and returned to Maximes. They said goodnight in the elevator and both agreed it was a memorable evening.

Kaetrin had never known her aunty to sleep in so long in the morning. It was Sunday morning and a traditional sleep-in on a Sunday was de rigueur, but not for Flora. There were guests checking out of the hotel already who had attended last evening's ball which had finished at 1am. Public functions were required to end at that time. So, Kaetrin reasoned, if these people were checking out, why was her aunty still asleep? For reasons known only to younger persons, they could not imagine their elders engaging in enchantment of any sort. Kaetrin was brought up on her parents' diet of having a bit of a knees up at the local, a skin full of ale and cider then home to bed; that was as far as older folks' socializing went! Dressing up was a novelty that she felt added a touch of class. Perhaps older folk knew a bit more about romancing than she gave them credit for. Aunty Flora and Colonel Peroux certainly made a handsome couple last evening as they swept through the hotel lobby to the waiting taxi. Kaetrin was busy reassessing her sentiments on the romantic instincts of post teenage humans and she had decided that they had a life after all! Her reverie was interrupted by the phone ringing. It was Flora – her throat sounded raspy.

"Kaetrin," she said, "will you go into my office and bring me up some aspirin, it is in the top right hand drawer of my desk. A cup of tea would be nice too."

"Yes, Aunty." Kaetrin couldn't wait to complete her allotted task. Armed with the aspirin and a glass of water she tapped on Flora's door and waited for the usual, "Come in," which was uttered in a raspy voice. Had there been some light in the room Flora would have seen a smile on Kaetrin's face.

She placed the bottle of aspirin and a glass of water on the bedside table and said, "I'll let some daylight into the room. It is a lovely sunny morning." Kaetrin then left the room saying, "I'm boiling some water for your cuppa, it will not be long."

Flora swallowed two aspirin and squinted her eyes, adjusting to the inrush of bright morning light flooding the room.

When Kaetrin returned with the tea, Flora was sitting up in bed and he cheeks had coloured slightly. Kaetrin eased herself into the comfortable slipper chair by the bed and waited for the post mortem to commence.

"Well."

"Well what!"

"I thought that you would like to tell me about the ball."

"Aah, the ball," Flora teased.

"Yes the ball, Aunty, I'm waiting to hear all about it!"

Kaetrin then received the unexpurgated version of the night's events.

"No wonder you slept late," she said, when Flora had concluded her story. "Dancing off and on for seven hours, you must be tired?"

"Yes, I am, but I have not enjoyed myself that much for many, many years. I have to say it was wonderful!" Flora said it with a passion that Kaetrin, had not heard in her voice – ever!

Flora and James were walking home from the movies one pleasant November evening when James told her about their pending departure. He had been working on their embarkation planning for some time. All that was missing was the date of the departure and he did not want to burst their bubble until he had positive timing information.

"Where will you be going?" she asked him. "Will I see you again?"

"It's all top secret but nothing you cannot guess from reading the newspapers. We don't know our destination but if I have to guess, I would say Soloman Islands. First marines are there now. And some regiments from the second marines also. Looks like we will be the reserve regiment, mopping up the mess. We will return," he said. "I will come back!"

"Is that a promise?"

"President Roosevelt made a promise to Winston Churchill that if Churchill were to keep the New Zealand division in the Middle East, and he did want

77

them to stay and continue fighting in that conflict. Roosevelt would send troops to New Zealand and the Pacific war. We have built army bases, hospitals, store depots, and generally have a strategic location here, that is an asset and a good location to fight a war from. I feel certain that we will be around for a while yet. I can't see us pulling out our tent pegs anytime soon!"

Flora tightened her grip on his arm as they made their way down Cuba Street towards Maximes.

"Don't worry about your contract – we will need the accommodation for sure," he said.

"That's not important, but you are."

"We'll be okay."

"I'm sure you will. If you can organize your men as well as you organized the ball last month – the enemy does not stand a chance!"

Colonel James Peroux sailed with the convoy leaving Wellington for Guadanal Canal on the Solomons, in December 1942. Eighty two ships sailed in single file out from the Wellington Heads early one morning, pitching their noses into the blue Pacific swell.

Christmas at Maximes was a quiet affair, following the boisterous and happy bustle of the marines. There were still plenty of service personnel around, just not as many. There were milestones nonetheless. It was young Bravo's second Christmas. The Beresford-Ambles came for Christmas dinner and stayed three days and nights. Kaetrin received a Christmas card in the mail from Jimmy the heartmelt and Flora opened her present from James Peroux, who was away on active service on Guadal Canal. The gift-wrapped box was hand delivered from Stewart Dawsons, the jewellers on the corner of Willis Street and Lambton Quay. A typical Peroux arrangement. They were emerald earrings of the most exquisite style and colour set in eighteen carat gold orb clasps. The gift was enjoyed by the entire Christmas assembly at Maximes and envied by all of the ladies. Never one to publicly display her emotions, Flora left the room and wept for joy in the privacy of her office. She fortified her emotions with a whiskey from her private bin and rejoined the party, resplendent with the new jewellery in place. Only four girls from the first floor apartments attended the dinner. The rest had gone home to their families. It had been a busy year.

Rain cancelled the Boxing Day picnic at Days Bay. Never stuck for an idea, Flora took them all for a cable car ride to the tea kiosk at the top of the cable car terminus in Kelburn. They were entertained by a brass band and the grand views overlooking the city and the harbour. The Beresford-Ambles commented on the uniqueness of the setting. Marjory said, "The views are exquisite my dears, simply exquisite!"

In February of 1943, the second marines returned to Wellington for some rest and recreation, following the fighting on Guadal Canal which resulted in defeat of the Japanese forces, who sustained severe casualties. None of the hotel's military guests were killed or wounded and they soon settled back into a wartime normalcy that seemed to fluctuate between harmony and mayhem.

"As quick as a tick on a metronome," James Peroux quipped. "Thank goodness for our military police."

"How did you control your men between skirmishes?" James asked Horace one evening over pre dinner drinks. A dinner arrangement that had been in the pipeline since the Majestic Ball.

"Walked the legs off 'em!" Horace replied. "Endless marches sap energy, especially in the heat. Give them a few beers and they fall asleep. Not just an hour, you understand, oh no – dear boy – an all day hike with full field kit! Do it several times a week. Come furlough time, all they want to do is cot duty. Zee and pee, we would say. Then feed 'em salty food and make 'em drink plenty of water."

"I'll mention that to our guys," James said, "sounds interesting."

Kaetrin was by now receiving regular mail from Jimmy the heartmelt. He had been moved to the proper camp for merchant seamen at Wintertimke, the one that Harold had told them about nearly a year ago. His letter, received by Kaetrin at Christmas together with his home-made Christmas card, explained their situation, which by all accounts sounded far better than the earlier days of his confinement. They had a school running and young seamen like himself could learn the rudiments of navigation or engineering. The merchant marine officers, both deck and engineering, were teaching them. After the war, he said that he could become a cadet with a shipping company and together with his sea time, on the job training and studying, he could sit his exams and become a ship's officer, "Just like Lord Nelson!" he said. "I told you he started as a cabin boy and rose to the top. Well I am going to do the same. One day I shall be captain of my own ship!"

Flora and James spent a lot of time together. It became obvious to them both that there would be further offensives and the men could be away to another battle and never return Mortality was a word that was never mentioned, but death lurked in the corridors of security and romance coveted security. In spite of that, romance flourished. Love, it seemed, was the only antidote to war that never induced a hangover. One could get intoxicated on a Saturday night and get lost in the mental labyrinths of fun and laughter. But you still woke up with yourself. Romance, on the other hand, took the path that led the participants through the ecstasy of warmth. You went to bed warm and slept warm and woke up warm. It was a good feeling and could be stored away in that most sacred repository of the soul. It was matters of the heart that took Flora and James away on a tour of the volcanic plateau. It was a first for them both. Mary-Jane Skeffington owned a car and she had said that Flora could use it at any time, but the problem was that Flora did not drive. James could and was happy to take the wheel. Kaetrin and Leslie were able managers in Flora's absence.

"I'll phone in from time to time just to see how you are coping," she had said, before climbing into the 1936 Ford Coupe at the hotel carpark. Coupes have a large luggage boot and Flora had a lot of baggage. James wore civvies and looked different. They could have passed for a couple of farmers until they spoke. Flora with her Scottish lilt and James with his North American drawl. On the first night, they stayed at the Chateau Tongariro, a superb hotel built after a French Chateau, castle style and nestled into the foothills of Mount Ruapehu. Snow had blanketed the higher slopes of the mountain. The chateau and surrounding area was free from snow, but it was cold. The interior décor was definitely French Provincial style and the couches were stuffed with soft compressible fibres which returned to their original shape following an extended stay. She felt that her kitchen at Maximes could produce similar food and James confirmed this observation.

"We all feel that your kitchen puts out great food!" James confirmed. Brandy and cigars followed and they spent their first night in bed together. The next morning, following a cooked breakfast, Flora and James checked out and headed for Rotorua. They were at an altitude of five thousand feet and the ambient was cold but it was a clear and sunny day. Running downhill at the end of the desert road with Mount Pihunga on the left, they saw the blue water expanse of Lake Taupo ahead. At the bottom end of the lake was Turangi, a small settlement that catered for trout fishermen, but it boasted a couple petrol pumps and so they pulled into the gas station to refuel their vehicle. Petrol was rationed, but James had vouchers that were stamped with a military insignia that the cashier recognized as being redeemable and so they were accepted without question. James asked the forecourt attendant to check the oil and water in the engine and they were on their way along the lakeside run up to Taupo where they decided to stop for lunch at De Bretts Hotel. They drove into the carpark outside the reception, which was in the veranda-covered facade of the hotel. Guests milling about indicated that a lot of military personnel on R&R were booked into the well-known Taupo establishment which was popular for its hot mineral water pools. Smoking bodies wrapped in hotel towels and bathrobes could be seen walking back to their rooms from the bath area. The cool ambient allowing the heat to dissipate from off hot flesh just as steam rises from boiling water. Flora and James lunched on lamb chops and the iconic Pavlova dessert which was consumed with relish following their cold beer appetizer.

Rotorua greeted them with its distinctive sulphuric odour, which, on a bad day could be described as rotten eggs. But it was not a bad day. After a few hours the smell was not noticed. Their hotel had private hot mineral pools and it was their first port of call after signing in at the reception desk. In the evenings they went to Maori concerts to soak up the intense Maori culture which was a popular tourist attraction in the Rotorua precinct. During the day, they visited the thermal attractions that included geysers and boiling mud and water pools of the thermal wonderland. It seemed that steam bellowed from every fissure in the ground. The locals used the hot water for cooking, Maori ladies would load flaxen baskets with food and lower them into a hot pool to cook. The culture absorbed them both and at night they returned to the hotel and an hour in their private hot pool would send them off to bed like babies. They were hot, soft and cuddly and sleep was no stranger to them. Never one to abdicate her responsibilities, Flora phoned Maximes Hotel one evening from the hotel in Rotorua. Kaetrin informed her that all was in order and the place was ticking over like a good clock.

They both agreed that a night at the chateau on the way back to Wellington would be nice and this time when they arrived it was snowing. Driving toward the Chateau, beside the golf course, which had been laid out like a large lawn at the front of the classic structure, the snow drops and the fir trees around it gave the appearance of an alpine setting. Soft orange lighting from the windows beckoned the visitors toward the luxurious interior of this mountain resort. It was the most romantic setting that Flora could ever recall. It would remain with her forever.

Dropping in without prior notice, for obvious security reasons, the First Lady of the United States, Eleanor Roosevelt, won the hearts of the American servicemen and women alike. She arrived in Auckland in a Liberator bomber converted to carry VIPs and took an overnight train ride to the capital, arriving early in the morning of August 28 1943. She then undertook a hectic tour of US bases and hospitals and the American Red Cross Club at the Hotel Cecil. On the Sunday evening she held a women-only event at the Majestic Theatre before taking a train to Rotorua the following day. Flora, Kaetrin and Leslie, together with Marjory Beresford-Amble, attended the Majestic Theatre presentation that included two films explaining the work of the Women's Red Cross and the invaluable contribution to the war effort by the many female participants. Dressed in the grey uniform of the Women's Red Cross, the First Lady impressed all with her indefatigable determination to highlight and encourage Women's Red Cross work in the war effort, to encourage more participants and to thank those already involved.

Marjory was already involved and had been for some time. She wore her uniform: Women's Auxiliary Indian Red Cross. Eleanor have her a special wave.

On the Monday and before departing for Rotorua, Eleanor Roosevelt visited the Ford Motor Company's assembly plant at Seaview, where women had replaced the male workers who had enlisted in the armed forces and were fighting overseas, mostly in the Western Desert in North Africa. The women were assembling Bren Gun Carriers for their fighting men.

Flora said that she was already doing her bit, hosting the top brass at the hotel. She encouraged Kaetrin and Leslie to participate in the Red Cross Club at the Cecil Hotel. The hotel was adjacent to the Wellington Railway Station and was the first stop for most of the marines coming into the city from Camp MacKay, on the Kapiti Coast. Kaetrin said it was like a dating agency. Although involved in good works, it was often the first point of contact for young servicemen making contact with young ladies when coming to town on leave.

Eleanor Roosevelt arrived back in Auckland and immediately visited the Navy Hospital, where she spoke to every patient and even attended a Red Cross dance at the Auckland Town Hall, where Artie Shaw's band was in full swing.

81

She then boarded the converted Liberator bomber that took off from Whenuapai Airport, travelling east, out over the Hauraki Gulf and the blue Pacific Ocean before heading west across the Tasman Sea to Sydney Australia, which shared this common stretch of water with her New Zealand neighbour.

The balance of the war years came on fast and in November the marines departed for what was to become another bloody battle, this time on the Pacific Atoll of Tarawa. Flora and James said their goodbyes as the mature adults that they both were. Marriage had never been a topic that either of them had discussed. They had a relationship and they had gotten on with it and enjoyed the moment, both having experienced the previous loss of a loved one. That is not to say that they never felt a great sadness at parting. They both endured their private hells but their maturity allowed them to accept the inevitability of a situation that neither of them had any control over and both knew that if and when control was restored, then they could and would, do something about it. That was the way it was in 1943.

Chapter 7

Letter from Jimmy

On a fine summer's day in December 1941, a letter arrived at Maximes for Kaetrin. It was from Jimmy and it was opened in breathless anticipation.

The letter appeared to be written in part in code and read as follows:

July 13 1941
My Dear Kaetrin,
we are allowed to write letters to our family and I hope you receive mine to you my luv.

I have to keep it short and sweet and can't tell you where I am or where I have been but I am in good health and the rainbows have looked after us and we eat well.

It was sad to see the *Rangitane* sink beneath the waves. Did you know our pay stopped the minute that happened as we had no ship to work on. How nice is that from the shipowners. I was at land tickled to bits with terror but firm about the frogs at sunset.

We took the frog from the rocks and was loaded onto a toby rubber.

All the daisies are called Jack and they look after us with their hooters.

If our switch were nearer to the bed I would be able to concentrate on writing to you rather than work out how to turn it on/off

I am only allowed 200 words so bye luv write to me somehow.

Jimmy. xoxo

The uncoded version read as follows:

I have to keep the message simple and am not allowed to divulge where I am or where I have been but I am in good health and the rainbow trouts [krauts] have looked after us and we eat well.

It was sad to see the *Rangitane* sink beneath the waves. Did you know our pay stopped the minute that happened as we had no ship to work on. How nice is that from the shipowners. I was at land tickled [Atlantic] to bits with terror but firm [ashore, terra-firma] about the frogs [French] at sunset. [west coast]

We took the frog and toad [road] from the pile of rocks [docks] and was loaded onto a toby ale [rail] rubber duck [truck].

All the daisy-roots [boots] are called jack [jackboots: German guards] and they look after us with their car-hooters [shooters].

If our switch [Auschwitz] were nearer to the bed I would be able to concentrate [concentration camp] on writing to you rather than work out [work outside the camp] how to turn it on/off.

I am allowed 200 words only so bye luv. Write to me somehow.

Luv Jimmy. xoxo

"So okay, we can figure out from that that they were landed in France and transported by rail to Auschwitz concentration camp and are doing forced labour. Working outside of the camp perimeter. We can further deduce then that he is being treated as a British civilian and as Britain and Germany are both signatories of the Geneva Convention, his letter has managed to get through to us. It goes through Geneva in Switzerland, you know. The Red Cross HQ is in Geneva. They are even allowed access to the camps to check on conditions, like food accommodation etc. So we can get a letter back to him. Perhaps we can code in some outside information that they would not normally be able to receive. So his letter was dated January 1941 and it was received some 2 months later – not bad I guess – it will take say another... 3 months say, for him to get your reply, Kaetrin."

Kaetrin looked at the Major. Horace Beresford-Amble was the first person that Kaetrin had confronted when her letter had arrived. It must have come in a diplomatic bag from England as the British Embassy had phoned the hotel to advise her that they were holding a letter for her from a POW and that she was to collect and sign for it. It was obvious to Kaetrin that the letter had been read by various interests en-route. No doubt the Germans would have checked it and then the Brits would have run it past their code people too.

On first reading, Kaetrin was puzzled by the contents and then she realized that Jimmy was trying to tell more than he was allowed. She vaguely recognized some cockney speak but did not know enough to understand the riddle, so she had visited Marjory and asked her to pass it on to the Major who no doubt had access to some code people in the military who could unscramble the message. And they did.

"Clever young man," Horace said. "At this pace he will be working for MI5 before the war's over, if he retains his marbles!"

"What do you mean, Major?" Kaetrin asked, hesitating. "Are you implying bonkers?"

"Now, Horace, don't you go alarming Kaetrin with your strange theories." Marjory chided her husband.

84

"Not at all m'dear, not at all. We have a saying in the battalion; it's meant to be humorous."

"Well, if it's funny, tell us," Kaetrin said.

The major cleared his throat, and spoke. "War is a machine that we enter as humans and exit as zombies!"

"Mmmm," Marjory intoned. "Probably funny in the mess with a few gin and tonics under the belt. Well, carry on with the letter. You were saying?"

The major bristled his whiskery lip and continued.

"Now when you reply I must ask you to give us your rough copy and our boys can add some titbits of info for the POWs to lighten their spirits. Jerry has not got the show going all his way now, don't you know! One thing does puzzle our boys and that is his place of detention. Merchant seaman are treated as civilians and we do know that Auschwitz concentration camp was set up as far back as 1934 to take care of dissidents such as German communists and other civilians who were a pain in the Nazis' backside. The idea was to rehabilitate them and reintroduce them back into German society as good German citizens. Perhaps his tenure there is temporary but we have had our people bring this to the attention of the Red Cross. Our Intelligence people tell us that there is a special camp for merchant seamen under construction and should be finished during the first quarter of 1942. It's in the north of Germany, they say, at a place called Wintertimke, wherever that is?"

The rattling of the tea cups by Marjory was the signal for Horace to depart the scene and let the ladies get on with the important matter of tasting some finest Darjeeling tea. Her tea things had arrived and had been unpacked. There were no breakages and Marjory's finest Nawabs tea pot was being used. It featured tiger's rampant, hand painted by the finest Chinese craftspeople. Flora had accompanied Kaetrin as they took the electric train unit from Wellington Railway Station to Trentham, a twenty five minute journey. The house was a short walk from the railway station and close to the military base where Horace worked. The interior was furnished in what could only be described as colonial Indian Raj. There were cane style loungers with comfortable cushion swabs upholstered in the finest Sanderson linen. An umbrella and walking stick stand was at the entrance to the house and there was the preserved foot of an Indian elephant. The major's collection of ivory-topped walking canes and sticks sat in the holder like toothpicks. Randomly placed and randomly selected. A set of elephant tusks, with sterling silver mounts, stood majestically against a wall forming an arch. The remaining wall spaces were adorned with pictures of the Beresford-Ambles in typical tropical garb and at play in the sub-continent. Pith helmets, rifles, elephants and dead tigers were the prominent theme and then there were the polo team photos. As an officer in the mounted rifles it was incumbent on the major to be able to display expert horsemanship and at this he did excel. The major was also chosen by the Nawab to play polo in his personal team when the players were mounted on elephants. All very pukah and simply British India at its best. One expected a turbaned bearer to emerge with the tea things but Marjory coped very well indeed sans servants.

Kaetrin had been to tea at an earlier date when she and Leslie had received invitations to the occasion, after Marjory had unpacked her tea things. But the Beresford-Ambles were in temporary accommodation back then and the furniture and other personal knick-knacks were still in storage. And so they were not exposed to the full extent of their colonial life in British India.

Kaetrin remembered the occasion with great clarity because it was during the train journey from Wellington to Trentham that Leslie had informed Kaetrin that she was pregnant with Doug's child. This was quite a revelation to the young Kaetrin, who had been under the tutelage of Leslie during their voyage to New Zealand. Suddenly they were peers and Kaetrin found that her former mentor was now confiding in her, which was a change in circumstances for Kaetrin. No doubt it was for Leslie too, who had no family in the colony and her closest friend was her former pupil and charge. This however was the early forties and even though the world was at war there still remained certain Christian principles that lay in the hands of the pious populace of Anglicans, who called the shots and shamed the sinners. A spousal arrangement whereby one was voluntarily joined for life was the norm. Outside of this stood the brave and so named sinners and the godsayers preyed on sinners like locusts on field crops. To have a baby out of wedlock was to be ostracized by society, or certain factions of society, who imagined that their righteousness allowed them franchise over the creation and fulfilment of the living soul. To be or not to be was the question. Love was not part of their equation unless it had association with Jesus or the trilogy of the father, the son and the holy ghost. Other than that they were a fairly forlorn bunch of godsayers. Kaetrin was barely able to grapple with the complex nature of Leslie's situation, let alone offer congratulations or condolences. Both sentiments she subscribed to in equal quantities.

Back in pre-war London, Kaetrin was aware of young ladies who would disappear for months at a time to 'Further their education in the French language'. Whether they went to France or Yorkshire was irrelevant. They had their babies who were adopted out and returned refreshed and invigorated from their sojourn in foreign climes and life continued. The odium of giving birth out of wedlock was avoided and the family, with reputation intact, remained in the community pure and unsullied as the congregation who attended soul cleansing at the Sunday temple.

"What are you planning to do?" Kaetrin asked Leslie.

"Have the baby of course!" Leslie replied.

"Are you not concerned about the social consequences?"

"I have not really given it much consideration. But I would hate to think, the part of Doug that still lives could be extinguished because of so-called social virtues. The foetus is alive and well and I want it to flourish."

"And the stigma – born out of wedlock? We are in the colonies and the population is very small here compared with, say, London. I suppose you could return there after the birth and no one would be the wiser for your returning with child."

Leslie's eyes fixed on infinity and she said, "Oh I don't know – at the moment I don't really care what anyone says. Doug and I had fun and this is the result. Poor Doug has ended his days and myself and the unborn baby are here. I'm sure that we are not the only casualties of war. The baby can be our medal for service to our country. If it's a boy I can call him George, Victor or Bravo, and a girl, well that's easy too, she shall be Georgina, Victoria or Brava."

Marjory Beresford-Amble had a different outlook on babies and unwed mothers. Over tea, Leslie had recounted her story and Marjory had very insistently suggested that it would be a rocky road for both mother and child.

"My dears," she had confided, "I have seen some disasters over this issue, believe me. We had lots of young ladies travelling to and from England to India, attending the finest finishing schools in England and Europe and then coming home to their parents in India, in a most unsatisfactory state. Chaperones notwithstanding. When love is in the air, caution is nowhere. And there were plenty of young officers, travelling on the British India run, returning to England on furlough and then back to India to rejoin their regiments. It was a minefield and that was just the start. A hot bath and a bottle of gin. Mother's ruin, causes pregnancies to slip. Also lost a few along the way and all because no one could stand the stigma of birth out of wedlock. Had society been a bit more understanding there would have been a lot more happy families today. Now listen to me – I have a plan."

It was obvious that Marjory had a mind like a steel trap. Behind the facade of the genteel subservient wife of an Indian Army Officer, the memsahib was in possession of an intelligent, agile and lucid imagination, able to transform difficult plots into clear and concise conclusions. She asked Leslie some questions and announced shortly thereafter her plan.

"This is how I see it she said – all quite simple, don't you know! You and Doug were married in Auckland aboard the *Rangitane* shortly before the ship was due to sail, probably on sailing day. The CORB chaplain conducted the ceremony and your witness was another CORB employee. Both now deceased following the sinking of that ship by the German raiders. Doug's witness was a person that you had never met before, obviously one of his fellow officers, but name and rank unknown. The marriage certificate was to have been issued to Doug, once the captain had signed it. He may or may not have received it before the ship went down. The event may or may not have been recorded in the ship's log, but whether or not it was has no effect on the outcome, as all valuable documents were destroyed by the ship's officers and crew, so that they would not fall into enemy hands. Your witness was also a victim of the sinking. Several CORB employees were killed in the incident so you have a name to pick from that list. It doesn't really matter. Sounds awful, I know, but that's the fact of the matter. As for the captain, who survived the incident, he did not perform the ceremony and it would have been written up in the ship's log by one of his officers, who also made log entries on a daily basis. The ship was only some fifteen hours into the voyage so there is little doubt that the paperwork, including the captain's signature on the certificate, would have been completed by that time. In the final analysis, it is your word and your word only that matters as there is no contradicting evidence. How's that!" Even Marjory's final exclamation sounded like a bowler's call to the umpire that one had delivered an unplayable ball.

Leslie and Kaetrin sat in stunned silence and Marjory went for some hot water to replenish her best Nawabs tea pot, the one with the tigers rampant.

"Mrs Douglas Thornton," Leslie intoned in an audible whisper. "Yes, this is my daughter, Brava Thornton, her father was deceased before her birth, killed when the liner *Rangitane* was attacked by German raiders in the Pacific Ocean. He was a radio officer you know, and a brave man too. He was killed while carrying out orders to transmit radio signals and destroy code books – mentioned in dispatches, you know."

Kaetrin turned to Leslie and asked her what she thought about the plan.

"I like it," Leslie replied. "Yes, I think it has merit, Marjory makes a lot of sense and she has had the experience, which is obvious, in the manner of her discourse. I was happy to go it alone but she makes the alternative sound so much easier. No snooping do-gooders making insinuations. I will have a piece of paper that declares, at or around the time of conception, I was wedded to the child's father. It's a good solution. I'm happy about that."

When the Japanese attacked Pearl Harbor, Bravo Douglas Thornton was just three months old. Leslie Thornton nee Corbett had seen out the term of her pregnancy at Maximes Hotel under the insistence of Flora, who had sponsored the finest gynaecologist to attend to Leslie out of her own pocket. Leslie worked at the hotel in the office with Kaetrin and they became very good friends. The department of births deaths and marriages had recognized Leslie's claim, but not before checking with the captain of the *Rangitane* who had confirmed that all documentation was destroyed and that, yes, there probably was a ceremony as they had a chaplain aboard and he, the captain, would at some stage, rubber stamp the certificate by signature. But this never happened as the ship was sunk early into the voyage and way ahead of the paperwork that would inevitably have followed once the routine of a sea voyage had been established. The untimely sinking of his ship meant that all paperwork was destroyed so that it would not fall into enemy hands. The captain could not refute the claim and the department of births, deaths and marriages had no choice but to issue the appropriate documentation.

Marjory Beresford-Amble had her day and travelled specially into Wellington and bought them all lunch at the swank restaurant in Kirkcaldie and Stains upmarket department store. Marjory was so pleased that she never complained about the Ceylon tea that was served in silver pots rather than her preferred Darjeeling in china tea pots.

"We have achieved a victory over bureaucracy and the godsayers," she said. "Let us not forget this day."

For use at a later date in her correspondence to Jimmy, Kaetrin received the following paragraphs from Major Beresford-Amble which he asked her to "include in dispatches, dear girl." Marjory passed it to Kaetrin at the luncheon.

"'After a problem with the Billington trees, uncle has installed a septic tank to help in the effort to overcome the pearl attic. It would not be a lie to say that it is now us and we are not alone anymore. Aunty Flora made this lovely pudding, called Nelson's ship dessert. It's a monty and deserves the prize, as it beat the rainbow trouts in the competition.'

"If they can decipher it and I'm sure they can, it will read as follows:

"'After a problem with the Billington trees [Japanese] Uncle has installed a septic tank [yank] to overcome the pearl attic [Pearl Harbor attack]. It would not be a lie [ally] to say that it is now us [United States] and we are not alone anymore. Aunty Flora made this lovely pudding called Nelson's ship [victory] dessert [desert] It's a monty [Montgomery] and deserves the prize [wins] as it beats the rainbow trouts [krauts] in the competition [battle].'"

It made absolutely no sense to Kaetrin who read it again, or to Leslie when they got back to the hotel. The major had previously explained the artifice but it was not a girl thing and they preferred to talk about other more pressing matters concerning their future.

Chapter 8

The Trinity

Werner Kruger was sent to Dachau in 1936. Dachau was built in 1933 and at that time it was designed to rehabilitate Germans who had strayed from the straight and narrow. They could have been common criminals or political prisoners. Werner was a communist and therefore a political prisoner. German communists were among the first people to be sent to concentration camps. The importance of the name simply means 'an area where dangerous elements are concentrated.'

Hitler once said that his idea for concentration camps came from his studies of the Boer War in South Africa. The British had built camps and concentrated woman and children of Dutch ancestry within their confines. They were not permitted to leave them and return to their homesteads. Nor did the British make an effort to feed the inmates and as a result of this neglect, twenty six thousand of them perished from starvation. German concentration camps were to rehabilitate and release Germans back into society as a true Aryans and Germans, having seen the error of their ways.

Then Jews were sent to concentration camps, not to be confused with death camps that were later established.

German communists were privileged in comparison with Jews, because of their racial purity. They had superior food and accommodation.

The Nazis were fascists, the exact opposite of the communists who ruled Russia. Hitler blamed the communists for Germany's defeat in WWI and feared that the communists were trying to take over Germany. He was determined to destroy the communists in a German society that he was building and concentration camps were just the place to reprogramme these radicals for release into a true and pure German Aryan society.

The third Reich had decreed the round-up of social malefactors and their internment in concentration camps for rehabilitation was a socially proper way to deal with homosexuals, psychopaths, drunkards, lunatics and malingerers.

"There is one way to freedom," they were told. The milestones were: obedience, zeal, honesty, cleanliness, temperance, truth, a sense of sacrifice and love for the fatherland.

Concentration camps were a place of compassion where the incarcerated were not able to harm the new regime and where they were protected from public anger. The government was helping those it committed to concentration camps by placing them in an environment from which they could be rehabilitated and become productive members of the German community.

Werner did not want to be rehabilitated, he felt he could best serve the cause where he was, assisting his fellow incarcerated comrades to carry on their crusade against fascism. An incarcerated communist was better than a rehabilitated communist, who would probably be enlisted into the military and sent to Russia to fight the Red Army. Because of his activities, Werner was shipped to Auschwitz in 1942. Werner had spent five years in Russia and was proficient in the language. His services as an interpreter would be of better use to his masters at Auschwitz which would go on to house some 15,000 Russian prisoners of war, before eventually being liberated by the advancing Red Army in January 1945.

Colonel Franz-Josef Kaiser had a distinguished military career. Following a long family tradition, he joined the military in 1932 and graduated from the academy in 1935 with distinction, as was predicted and expected from any member of the Kaiser family. The treaty of Versailles had reduced the German military forces to what was then called the Reichswehr which consisted of a small army and navy. There was no air force. His father, Otto, had made field marshal in WWI so it was expected that the young aristocratic Franz-Josef would join the ground forces. In 1933, the infamous Third Reich was born and two years later, when the treaty of Versailles was renounced, the Reichwehr became the Wehrmacht, which consisted of an army and a navy. The army was called the Heer and the navy, Kriegsmarine. At the same time, a new air force was created and was known as the Luftwaffe. Unofficially, a German Air Force had existed previous to 1935, finding a way around the rigid treaty of Versailles, and had been operating from a secret training base in the Soviet Union. It was here that Franz-Josef received his basic training and learned to fly the new mono-winged fighter aircraft that were starting to roll out of the German factories, replacing the bi-planes from WWI Vintage, which were good training aircraft. By 1939 he was flying the Fock-Wulf Fw 190-A4 single seat fighter and was very good at it.

Franz-Josef was very good at most things. He had a privileged upbringing as a member of a noble family from landed gentry who had invested wisely in iron and coal in the late nineteenth century, when Germany became the largest steel producer in Europe. The family could trace its roots back to the old Saxon noble Kolditz family and had large land holdings near Dresden. Over the years the family had accumulated a valuable collection of artwork that was housed in the various family estates around Saxony. In 1919 the Weimar Republic abolished all legal privileges of the nobility, but hereditary titles were allowed to exist only as part of a surname. A title is far less important among the nobility than the age and standing of a family. The members of the 'Uradel' are considered by themselves to be of the same status whether they be untitled, or Counts or Barons or whatever. There are a number of noble houses that have never used 'von' or any other noble appellation, but are of fully equal standing with those who do. Franz-Josef's family were of the former type, they had no need for titles. Their name implied their nobility more than a mere title could convey. Then there were those who liked to delude themselves and fool others with such pomposity and whose titles were purchased or merely adopted.

Von Ribbentrop, the Nazi foreign minister, was one of these pretenders. He paid his aunty Gertrud von Ribbentrop to adopt him so he could use the von title. Goebbels, in his diary, said about Ribbentrop: "He bought his name, married his money and swindled his way into office."

Lots were to copy von Ribbentrop during the Weimar Republic. Titles were available from hard up castle owners who were financially crippled with inheritance taxes. One of the more well-known social imposters to come along later in the century was Frederick Prinz von Anhalt. Born Robert Lichtenberg, he had paid a royal to adopt him. This did not make him a royal, but it did give him an impressive name. For those who are impressed by a title. Zsa Gabor was impressed as he became her third husband. Nothing like a title, even if it is bogus, in trumpet and tinsel land.

During WWI, Goering commanded the celebrated squadron in which the German air ace Manfred von Richthofen, the Red Baron, served. The baron was a real title and a member of German nobility. In WWII Goering had a title too, he was commander in chief of the Luftwaffe and a very high ranking Nazi.

Franz-Josef was a popular man in his squadron. He had a regular supply of the best wines from his family's estates and would offer his fellow officers superb entertainment in the mess, wherever the squadron was stationed. His family had brewery and food interests, so beer and special sausages were a common mess item when Franz-Josef entertained. When they were entertaining their young lady friends, champagne and caviar would be on the menu. Most pilots were from good German stock, not necessarily noble but generally well connected. There were very few Nazi pilots and if one ever joined the squadron they were excluded from the social antics of the other young airmen.

This was a paradox, as unlike the army and navy, the Nazis had full control over the Luftwaffe and needed to keep it independent from the old guard officers who controlled the other services.

Herman Goering was mindful of the status that an air ace could attain from the deeds and exploits in the skies of conflict. The actions of the Red Baron in WWI, Franz-Jozef was repeating now. In WWI, while Goering was the Red Baron's squadron commander, the accolades were not his to savour; they belonged to the Red Baron. Goering may have been the boss but his underling was the star. And it was happening again. Goering was the boss of the Luftwaffe but he was upstaged by the exploits of the players in the drama. Air aces were decided following rigid rules concerning the destruction of enemy aircraft. The actual destruction of an aircraft in the air or the bail out of the pilot had to be captured on the gun camera film, or by at least, one other witness. The witness could be a wingman, squadron mate or ground observer. There was no possibility that a victory could be credited because the claiming officer was a gentleman and his word was his bond. On the contrary and unlike his RAF and USAAF counterparts, the Nazi rule was no witness-no kill.

The Nazi system was impartial, inflexible and – so they claimed – less prone to error than the British or American method. German pilots could have to wait several months or longer for a kill confirmation from the German high command. Nonetheless, Franz-Josef was a confirmed war ace with seven kills to his credit soon after the Luftwaffe launched its offensive over the skies of England. This earned him the Knight's Cross and elevation from Lieutenant to Hauptman. His exploits were recorded in the German newspapers, who named him the White Knight. German people just loved war aces and Goering, as the Luftwaffe boss, basked in the propaganda. Again for Goering it was reflected glory but as he told Der Furher. 'It's the results that matter.'

Franz-Josef lived a charmed existence and while he survived, a lot of his colleagues were shot out of the skies as the RAF improved its techniques, especially with their new Supermarine Spitfires. At the start of the conflict, the Germans had entered the arena with a supreme confidence that they had earned with their experiences in the Spanish civil war. It was no accident that the German Condor Legion was fighting on the side of Franco's forces and gaining valuable combat experience. The Spanish war enabled the Germans to test their new technology and was a dress rehearsal for the larger event that would start with the invasion of Poland in 1939. The Spanish experience provided a proving ground for tactics, men and equipment.

The Luftwaffe perfected their new system of fighter aircraft formation and attack in Spain. Traditionally, aircraft flew in a vee formation of three planes, close enough for the pilots to observe the leader's hand signals. They subsequently reasoned that in this close flying formation, the pilots spent too much of their time avoiding making physical contact with each other, rather than taking care of the enemy. With the advent of radio, they perfected a system of flying two aircraft only, at a distance of 600 feet apart. The leading plane or leader assumed the primary attack role. The wingman covered his leader's tail and joined in the attack as required. They called this a 'Rotte' then they duplicated it and called it a 'Schwarm' when four planes flew. They would each be at a different altitude, but when viewed from above, each plane flew at the location of a fingertip of a horizontally extended palm, hand down and the fingertips slightly extended. Subsequently, this system proved so successful that all air forces adopted it. The RAF called it 'the finger four formation' and the USAAF 'the double attack system'.

When it became obvious that England was not about to negotiate an armistice or outright surrender and had in fact occupied the strategic high ground the Luftwaffe was stood down from their day and night time sorties across the channel. Franz-Josef went home on leave and, as a war hero, received the type of welcome reserved for champions. He had also amassed enough kills to add Oak Leaves to his Iron Cross.

On June 22, 1941, thirty German bombers hit ten Soviet airfields in an early dawn raid. This signalled the advance of a ground force of 3.8 million men. Then at sun-up the major Luftwaffe attack was launched with a force of 500 bombers, 270 dive bombers and 480 fighter aircraft. Between them they attacked sixty soviet airfields containing at least three quarters of the Russian combat aircraft. The Russian air force was rendered useless against the might of the Luftwaffe. And so began Hitler's offensive on the Eastern front.

Franz-Josef was in the thick of it from the beginning but, compared with the battle of Britain, this was like shooting fish in a barrel. For the fighter pilots it was no contest as most soviet planes were caught on the ground lined up on the airfields as if they were on display. The German fighters simply flew up and down the line of soviet aircraft and sprayed them with cannon fire. Most of the new recruits thought this was what war was all about and were ecstatic with their easy beat victories. They celebrated with mess parties that went well into the night. The old guard – Franz-Josef was one of them – tried to temper the exuberance of their younger colleagues. This was not aerial combat, it was a turkey shoot. After all, these greenhorns would fly as wingmen in an aerial combat situation and the last thing that the flight leaders needed were over-confident and untried pilots protecting their leaders' unsighted airspace. One young Nazi pilot boasted that he was taking schnapp-shots.

"It is like taking a photograph with the high of a shot of schnapps but without the debilitating alcoholic effects," he claimed. "I get the highs but I land sober!"

As squadron leader, Franz-Josef had them practising their Rotte and Schwarm formations, but in comparison to the live turkey shoots, the new pilots were only interested in shooting up undefended airfields.

The Soviet Mig-3 and Yak-1 were inferior to the German fighters and their pilots were poorly trained but enthusiastic. Franz-Josef's wing were on a sortie to beat up another Russian airfield when they were set upon by a squadron of Mig-3 fighters. The young German fliers were upbeat about another easy day at the office and the wingmen in Franz-Josef's Schwarm failed to see the Russians come out of the sun and fly at them. The Russians used a decoy to attract the leader and while the Schwarm was distracted by that, other Mig fighters pounced. Ordinarily the Russians would have been detected by the old school pilots who flew over Britain and France but the new pilots were far too upbeat to imagine that there would be a Russian plane in the sky, let alone dare to trifle with them. They had placed their flight into a false sense of security and Franz-Josef had more than once told them to stop yapping over their radios and keep a sharp eye out for interlopers. They were caught with their pants down. The Russian decoy drew leader one and a wingman and two Migs flew into the remaining two German BF109s in the Schwarm, creating massive balls of exploding metal and aviation fuel. The wing leader, Franz-Josef, dealt with the Russian decoy easily enough and logged another kill as it hurtled groundward in a smoky spiral, exploding on impact. The wingman was too busy watching his boss at work to notice that there were two further Migs above and behind them. The wingman was raked with cannon fire before the Mig flew into him, which created another aerial fireball. Franz-Josef did what any pilot of his experience would do when his senses perceived fireworks exploding in close proximity: he rolled and dived and the Mig that had him in his sights missed his intended target. Franz-Josef realised from the radio silence that he had lost his entire Schwarm, with the exception of himself. The Mig was trying to pull up but lacked the dexterity of the Be109, which in the hands of the White Knight, levelled out then began a full throttle climb, heading for a piece of cloud and a spot to chill out while he assessed the situation. He was alone and there were still a couple of Migs from the Russian flight stooging about, no doubt waiting for him to come out of hiding and make a run for home. But Franz-Josef was not about to give them that pleasure. He had a good idea of his whereabouts and in his solitude examined the map on his kneepad. The terrain was flat and he was over Russian territory and had about 250km to fly to reach the German lines again. By dead reckoning, he reset his course and headed for home while maintaining radio silence. Franz-Josef maintained his speed and altitude for thirty minutes, by which time he reckoned that he should be over or near the German lines. He then began his descent and broke through the cloud cover at two thousand feet over flat country. Over and beyond the port wing he saw what he thought was a railroad track. Confirming his original discovery in the affirmative, he followed the track on the compass setting that would take him to the German line if he was not already over it. It was simply a matter of finding a landmark and establishing his location. From there he could set a course for the airfield, which was not far from the railroad track near the town of Kursak. Franz-Josef turned on his radio and sent out his call sign which was acknowledged and he followed up with the news about their skirmish with the Russian Migs and that there would be no survivors other than himself. Following a long silence, the tower asked what condition he was in and where he was.

"I'm okay," was his reply. "Aircraft is flying okay, so assume we are good to land, I just need to find some familiar ground and I can set a course for home."

"What do you see?"

"Following a railway line heading SSE; visual are tracks and trees. Nothing I can recognise."

"Okay, we will send up a rocket, at the count of ten start looking."

"Roger."

Franz-Josef scanned his horizon which at altitude was considerable. He turned the aircraft in a horizontal three hundred and sixty degree turn so as not to miss an arc of the circle. He had counted up to twenty when he sighted a trajectory and took a cross bearing.

"Shit, I was out by twenty degrees," he said.

The controller chuckled. "Air ace lost in space."

Franz-Josef grinned – he knew the controller.

"I'll buy you a schnapps in the mess tonight."

"We will drink to our fallen brothers!"

"We will drink their share my friend – talk me down, I'm coming home."

Familiar ground appeared beneath his wings as Franz-Josef flew toward the airfield. The radio crackled and the controller came over the air.

"The boss wants a flyover; he wants a visual of your underbelly before you land – make sure you are all there – you never know what may have hit you with all of the fireworks happening. Put your landing gear down."

"Roger base, I see you now I have a visual, landing gear down, lights on."

Franz-Josef flew low over the airfield and he could see several observers on the ground looking at the plane through binoculars.

"Base to ace."

"Come in base."

"Your landing gear doesn't look too flash, it seems that you have taken a hit beneath the fuselage and the wings. There is damaged and twisted metal and the landing gear bays are messy. The landing gear is down but we cannot tell what state the tyres are in – they may have sustained enough damage to compromise tyre pressure and could blow out on impact. Go round again, we want another look."

Franz-Josef swore and he was a man who rarely cussed. Well-bred Germans didn't cuss. They spoke precise German. He flew over the airfield again, but nothing conclusive could be determined.

"Base to ace, the boss says do a soft landing. Use the grassed runway, stay airborne until we give you clearance to land."

Franz-Josef flew another circuit and the ground observers raised their binoculars, but found nothing conclusive.

"Base to ace, how's your fuel?"

"I have enough for a few circuits, it's all but gone!"

"Good, do a practice run and then come on in."

"Roger that."

Franz-Josef flew low over the grass emergency runway, banked, turned, then came in for the final approach. A post mortem on the remains of the crashed plane found the landing gear hydraulics had been pierced by shrapnel. There was enough juice to lower them and then the fluid was depleted and on impact with the ground they folded. The plane landed heavily and the nose dug unto the soft turf and the aircraft went nose first into a flip, landed upside down then caught fire. Emergency crew were at the scene on standby. They were able to spray the burning aircraft with foam to extinguish the flames and then extract the limp body of the pilot. He was initially treated on the airfield at their hospital, but his injuries were severe and he was transferred to a major field hospital facility for advanced medical care.

The doctors wanted to amputate his left hand as it was severely burnt, but at the last minute movement was apparent in the thumb and forefinger and they decided to repair it as best they could, as limited movement in a disfigured claw was better than no hand. His face had made heavy contact with the dash of the control panel and splintered glass from the instrument gauges had entered the left eye and penetrated deep enough to sever the optical nerve and so they removed his left eye and prepared the empty socket so it could take a glass eye at some later stage in his recuperation. Both femurs were fractured, as were several ribs, a couple of which had punctured his right lung. Other than that, the doctors said he was a fit young man and would make a recovery of sorts. What 'the sorts' were, they couldn't say. He would not fly again, but he could undertake a desk job and maybe even become an instructor in the tactical methods of modern combat flying. He was, after all, 'rather good at it!'

At the appropriate moment in the rehabilitation process, Franz-Josef went home to the family estates in Dresden for further rest and recreation. There he found, to his surprise, his father busy cataloguing new art acquisitions. Registering his surprise that such treasures be available in the middle of a war, his father spoke.

"Many families are selling up before the enemy comes, as they must, as they must! And before they lose it all. We will be pillaged," he continued. "Hitler has really done it for the German people now, taking on the Soviets. We are in the direct line of a Soviet army invasion route so you can expect us the bourgeoisie to be ransacked just as they did to the bourgeoisie in Russia following their revolution. We have to get rid of our valuable treasures, some of which have been in the Kaiser family for centuries and the safest way is to get them out of Germany. And the family too!

"Our iron and steel works in Dresden are making armoured cars for the Africa Corps and a shipment is due to leave for Tunisia in eight weeks. We will have a consignment of artworks in that shipment, in marked cases among the spare parts and they will be destined for our North African friends who will care for them in the dry climes of the desert. The irony is that they will eventually end up in Cairo, having gotten there via a desert camel train. We have had business associations with Abdul Nasser & Sons for years and we still have close ties with the family who are able to move freely, transporting their wares as they have done for centuries throughout their tribal lands and ancient desert routes. So, let us get on with cataloguing and packaging these works of art for shipment to Tunisia. The train leaves Dresden in eight weeks. The consignment, so I am told, will go to Italy and be shipped from Sicily to Tunisia, a secure sea route that is well protected by Italian submarines and German U-boats. We have a lot to do to prepare the shipment."

The Kaiser family threw a welcome home party for their air ace son and heir. Franz-Josef protested saying that he felt uncomfortable in the presence of former friends and admirers. His physical appearance had altered and he felt embarrassed, although he did cut a rather swashbuckling figure in his dress uniform with an eye patch and leather glove on his as of yet unhealed left hand. The Knight's Cross with Oak Leaves and campaign ribbons added a further touch of intrigue and he was a popular figure for photographs taken by the official photographer to the Kaiser family, as all invited attendees wished to have a memento of themselves with a real war hero. There were other service personnel present too, representing all of the German services, but there was only one White Knight.

Brigette von Hapsberg a flame from old family associations and their school days came to him and told him how much she admired his deeds and exploits.

"We do read some interesting articles in the local papers," she said. "There is lots of propaganda, I know, but there are stories that one reads and just know are true accounts. Others you read you realise are fabricated. We have learned to distinguish between fact and fiction." The band struck up a bracket of Viennese waltzes and Franz-Josef asked Brigette if she would care to dance with him.

"You may find me a bit pedestrian," he said. "The schnapps has numbed the pain but I can still feel my legs. We may not finish the bracket but I will give it a damn good try!"

"I would be honoured," she said. And so they danced. They were not the prettiest dancers on the floor, but they were the most admired couple. Eventually the other dancers stopped and formed a circle around the dance floor perimeter and clapped in waltz time as the White Knight and his partner performed on the dance arena. Franz-Jozef could feel his legs weakening as he willed them to continue, but eventually he whispered to Bridgette that he had to stop and take a seat. The crowd parted like the red sea as the couple made their way to a seat away from the dance floor and the band stopped the waltz bracket and broke into the old German national anthem, 'Das Deutschlandlied.' All verses were sung to the wonderful melody penned by Haydn so many years ago. The Nazis would sing the first verse only and then they would switch to the 'Horst Wessel Lied' which was their anthem. Otto Kaiser had instructed the band to play all verses of the German anthem, adopted in 1922 by the Weimar Republic.

"It is a very nationalistic song; not warlike or ferocious as a lot of national anthems are but most pleasing on the ear. A song of much joy to the German heart!" Otto declared.

At the conclusion of the anthem a young lieutenant with U-boat insignia was seen talking with the band leader who was shaking his head and pointing at Otto Kaiser. The fellow than walked over to Otto and was seen in conversation with the great man. He seemed agitated and following the exchange clicked his heels and raised his hand in the Nazi fashion and said, "Heil Hitler," which caused everyone to cease their individual discussions and watch the young fellow make a fool of himself. Otto was puzzled how the young man came to be at the party and had asked him by whose invitation he was present, in his, Otto's, house. His bona fides proving proper and correct Otto wished him a good evening and turned to walk away. The young hothead took Otto's arm and said.

"You didn't return my salute, you insult der Führer!"

His hand was removed from Otto's sleeve by the White Knight who was watching the developments from his seat alongside Brigette.

"That will be enough from you, Lieutenant, I suggest you leave now. The drink has the better of you and you may say something you regret in the morning."

The young mariner looked arrogant and aloof his bravado fuelled by schnapps. "My Führer is insulted," he said, "I demand an apology, a retraction and an affirmation that der Führer is supreme. You must salute der Führer as I did!" He looked around for support and got none. All the Kaiser guests were family friends. They were good Germans but not Nazis.

He looked at Franz-Jozef, noting the Knight's Cross with Oak Leaves. "And what about you, sir?" he said. "Will you salute der Führer?"

"We do so regularly in our mess," he replied. "Here is neither the time or place. You are out of order and I have asked you to withdraw and retire before you regret your actions."

"In the Kreigsmarine we honour our leader," the lieutenant replied in a mocking tone.

"In the house of Kaiser we honour the Fatherland," Franz-Josef responded.

The lieutenant spun around and marched over to the band leader. "You will play the Horst Wessel Lied," he said to the band leader.

The band leader looked very uncomfortable but he had worked for the house of Kaiser for years, as did his father before him. "He who pays the piper calls the tune," he said.

The young fellow had worked himself into a frenzy and was losing any ounce of common sense that may have remained had he stayed sober. He strode over to Franz-Josef and demanded that he tell the band leader to play the Horst Wessel Lied.

"My dear fellow," Franz-Josef intoned in a low threatening voice, "I give you your last chance to leave voluntarily, or you shall be forcibly ejected by our personal guards."

The lieutenant was livid in colour and temperament and before he could control his action, he had slapped Franz-Josef with his open palm across the face.

There was a low murmur among the guests. The last time this was done to a Kaiser, a duel had ensued, and as usual, the antagonist was shot dead.

The lieutenant realised that he had allowed the situation to get out of hand. Not only had he hit a superior officer, he had insulted the host family and a war hero.

Franz-Josef never wavered. His voice was calm and measured. "You have until dawn to find a second and then you and I will meet in a duel. I have a perfectly good set of duelling pistols. Let's hope your man knows how to load yours properly because mine will be loaded by my second who has had a lot of experience in this field. You can leave your contact details with my escritoire on the way out and you will receive full instructions about the time and place for the event later on this evening. These two gentlemen will see you off the premises."

With a uniformed Kaiser house guard on either arm, the hapless and now very quiet lieutenant was led from the ballroom.

Franz-Josef apologised to Brigitte. The dancing continued as if nothing out of the ordinary had happened; after all, this was Saxony and the challenge of a duel, whilst rarer these days, had been a way of life among the high society where points of honour were settled the gentleman's way.

Later in the evening a letter was delivered to the billet of the offending Kriegsmarine lieutenant. It was written on parchment paper and had no letterhead address.

'To the challengee.

The contest weapons will be powder and shot duelling pistols. The points apart will be marked by sabres at a distance of fifty meters.

We shall meet at dawn in the grand garden of Dresden by the palace pond and from there the principal's seconds will conduct the two parties to a secluded dale where the contest can take place.

The rules are:

1. The principals are to act in a respectful manner when meeting and neither by look or expression irritate each other.

2. When once posted they are not to leave their allotted positions under any circumstances without leave or direction from their seconds.

3. When the principals have been posted, the person who is to give the direction to fire, must tell them to stand still until he gives the word to fire. The parties are then at liberty to fire.

4. Following the firing, if either party is touched by ball, the duel is to end. No second who knows his duty will permit a wounded friend to fight and no second who knows his duty will allow his friend to fight a man already hit.

5. If after an exchange of shots neither party is hit, it is the duty of the second of the challengee to approach the second of the challenger to ask "Our friends have exchanged shots, are you satisfied? Or is there any reason why the contest should be continued?" If the meeting is of no serious cause and the point of honour is settled, the second to the challenger will respond as follows: "I propose that our principals meet on middle ground, shake hands and be friends." If this is agreed, then the seconde of the party challenging shall say. "We have agreed that the present duel shall cease. The honour of each of you has been preserved and you will meet on middle grounds, shake hands and be reconciled."

6. If the insult be considered of a serious nature the second of the challenger will respond to the second of the challenge: "We have been deeply wronged and if you are not disposed to repair that injury, the contest will continue." If the challengee offers nothing by way of reparation the contest continues until one or the other of the principals is hit.

Yours Sincerely,

Second of the challenger.'

There were no identifying marks to denote the point of origin, in case the document fell into the wrong hands.

Franz-Josef was driven to the palace pond by the estate chauffeur in the Mercedes estate limousine used for grand occasions as it had extra seating in the back compartment that could accommodate his father, Otto, his second, Albert, and the family surgeon, who may be required to affect repairs, should a ball make contact with either party.

In contrast, the lieutenant and his second arrived in a taxicab.

Both vehicles then drove through a wooded glade, emerging by a large oval that formed a ring for exercising horses for dressage competitions.

The seconds alighted and conferred and returned to their respective vehicles and then all passengers alighted and the two principals were directed by their seconds to enter the arena. Albert strode out to the middle and stuck a sabre into the ground, then strode fifty paces and stuck the other sabre into the ground, marking the two points apart at which the principals must stand. He came back to the cars and removed a portable table that he set up at about the halfway mark and a few meters away from the direct line of fire. He went back to the car and he and Otto returned with the case containing the duelling pistols plus ball and shot and placed them on the table. He opened the case and he and Otto primed and loaded both pistols under the watchful eye of the challangee's second. With the loading completed, the challengee's second was asked to make a choice of pistol. Then, both seconds proceeded into the arena and they handed the loaded weapons to their respective principals. The seconds explained that firing could commence once Otto had dropped a handkerchief, which he would hold up at outstretched arm's length. Silence was deathly and the sound of a bird chirping was amplified in the early morning amphitheatre, ringed by trees. Otto very dramatically raised the handkerchief and a dark stain of pee appeared on the front of the lieutenant's trousers. He was literally pissing himself. Both principals had extended their pistol laden arms to full outstretch, although to the learned eye, one would determine that Franz-Josef had a slight crank at the elbow and was maybe not fully sighted as yet, but his arm never wavered, whereas the pistol held by the lieutenant was trembling at the muzzle. A gentle breeze fluttered the handkerchief as both parties waited for the piece of cloth to be released and butterfly to the ground. When it did, Franz-Josef and his one eyed pilot's vision saw it move first. His eyes, after all, were honed to detect movement and his wide angle of detection of movement was still available, but limited because of the loss of an eye. He had, however, stood in such a manner that the angle of detection was favoured by his sighted eye and he straightened his arm for the fatal shot that would take the outspoken Nazi lieutenant out. The lieutenant picked up the falling handkerchief a second later and realised that he had lost valuable time and loosed off his shot lest he be hit first. The lieutenant waited for the smoke to clear from his fired pistol and for the acrid smell of gunpowder in his nostrils to fade and for his ears to

101

stop ringing from the percussion. He realised that he was unscathed and peered through the clearing smoke to see the standing figure of the challenger, still in pre firing mode, at which point his bowels collapsed internally and he felt a warmness within his pants. Franz-Josef lined up his shot. He aimed for the middle of the forehead and then raised the sight to bring the ball from his pistol just over the challengee's scalp.

"He will feel his hair being parted," Franz-Josef said to himself, "but there will be no indication of injury." He fired and the lieutenant instinctively ducked his head following the sound of the ball nearly creasing his skull. He was now a trembling wreck. Still on his feet, but shaking badly. His second told him to stay his ground.

"Do not move," he called out. The second then approached the challenger's second and said. "Our friends have exchanged shots, are you now satisfied or is there any reason why this contest should be continued?"

Franz-Josef's second relayed this message to the challenger and received further instruction which was then relayed to the challengee's second as follows.

"We believe that we have been grievously wronged and if you are not disposed to repair the injury by reparation or some such manner, the contest must continue."

The challengee's second conveyed this message to his friend and it could be seen that some animated discussion ensued, after which the second returned with pistol in hand and addressed the challenger's second.

"It seems that I have come onto this ground with a coward and I tender my apology for my ignorance of his character. You are at liberty to expose him."

"Thank you for your honesty, you stand excused as his second and may leave the ground."

The challengee's second departed in the cab that he and the lieutenant had arrived in. He did not grant his former friend a departing look or recognition of any kind.

The disgraced lieutenant now lay upon the cindered ground vomiting. He had lost control of all bodily functions and the sight of his image sickened the challenger and his friends. They gathered their chattels and departed the scene in their estate Mercedes vehicle.

"Home please, Sigmund," called the second to the chauffeur. "A breakfast of hot coffee, sausage and eggs await us. You may send a car to attend to the other party, may I suggest that it be able to tow a cart as we do not want the inside of one of our vehicles fouled by the wretched internals of a Nazi coward. Perhaps some buckets of water to douse him with before he climbs onto the cart. Our finest livestock that we carry in the cart may find the smell offensive."

During the contest Otto Kaiser had arranged for one of his security guards to check out the lieutenant's billet to see what evidence he could find concerning the man's background and he had returned with some rather alarming intelligence.

102

"It seems that our coward is not a submariner in the Kriegsmarine, but a Gestapo agent on a mission. He masquerades under the pseudonym of Arnold Fuchs. Obviously not true to label. Arnold means 'the strength of an eagle' and Fuchs is 'fox'. A mismatch if I ever saw one. We must take this slippery eel of a man very seriously, especially if he seeks revenge for the humiliation that he has undergone at our hands. I had my doubts about his ability as a submariner; he simply did not display the demeanour of a member of such a worthy institution. In fact, I was about to phone my old friend Admiral Voss about this very man as I wanted to ask him about their current selection policies. Have we sent a cart to collect the wretch?"

Franz-Josef replied in the affirmative. "The chauffeur has organised suitable transport as discussed. He has taken two gardeners with a barrel of water and a foot operated pressure water pump to decontaminate his befouled personage."

"Good. At least we can deliver the wretch back to his billet. He is in charge of himself from there. When he gains his senses, I sincerely hope his fright will discourage any further actions from the vile person that he is," Otto concluded.

Two weeks later, the Kaiser house received a visit by two people from the Dresden Gestapo Office. It seemed that they were looking for a Kreigsmarine U-Boat lieutenant who had gone missing. Otto Kaiser told them that there was such a person fitting that description who had attended a recent soiree held by the Kaisers. Apart from the fact that he was intoxicated and escorted from the premises, Otto was unable to help them any further with their enquiries and they left. Otto then phoned Albert von Hapsberg and arranged a meeting with his old family friend.

They met at a secluded forest park on the Hapsberg estate where often times they would go hunting for deer that roamed freely over the large wooded grounds. Both men were Knights of the Brotherhood of Saxony, an ancient order that traced its origins back to the death of King Wenceslas in 1402. His successor, Rudolph III, was the son of Wenceslas and was determined he would not succumb to assassins as was the case of his father who had died under mysterious circumstances from suspected poisoning. He formed an elite band of loyal patrons from the respected families throughout the kingdom who swore an oath of fealty to protect the electors and their families from acts of insurgence and intrigue that may cause their unexpected and unexplainable demise. The recruitment and the operations of the brotherhood was highly secretive, so they could circulate throughout the kingdom freely without their identity being jeopardised. Therefore, they were not compromised in any situation as nobody, apart from the select few close to the king and court, knew who they were. Their clandestine meetings were limited to twelve attendees at any one time but these could be arranged at various conclaves throughout Saxony with each conclave sending a delegate to attend the Grand Assembly, again limited to twelve attendees, plus the king. They were identifiable to each other by the use of passwords and signs. These were oral examinations, nothing was written. They were administered under a serious oath of loyalty punishable

103

by death should any knight disclose the secrets to non-members. And they were randomly tested from time to time as they pursued their normal daily lives. Any miscreant was summarily despatched by decapitation. No mercies. No pardons. No mistakes. Despite this rather demanding code they were guided by a peculiar system of morality and their unwritten motto:

'Gentle in manner, resolute in deed'

Prudence and fortitude were the cardinal virtues that should govern society and the knights were there to instil these values and to honour and protect the weaker members of society and maintain peace. Because their role was of a clandestine nature they would use their valets to act as eyes and ears. To collect intelligence as required. It was a good solution and had stood the test of time. Serving twenty seven electors and kings of Saxony before the Weimar Republic was formed in 1919. This transition of power followed the German revolution in 1918 when the Imperial Government was replaced by a Parliamentary Republic and all titles renounced.

The knights had evolved into a sort of club that had stuck to its principles and although there were no longer any kings to protect they were still active in ensuring that law and order prevailed and could wield considerable clout. They were high in the pecking order themselves and had friends in high places. Best of all they were anti-Nazi, as that political leaning was against everything that they had represented for centuries. The best thing was that the Nazis, or anyone else for that matter, knew nothing of their existence. They held trumps.

Otto and Albert decided that they should form a conclave of twelve knights to discuss the matter of the missing Gestapo agent alias submariner. If he were alive, it was their intention to reach him before the Gestapo did.

At first it appeared to be an untimely death to one of Otto Kaiser's hunting dogs. During an autopsy the veterinarian announced that the dog had consumed a poisonous substance. Someone had laid bait, he said, and the dog took it. The next occurrence was a fire in the stables that housed the eventing horses. Fortunately, the horses were released unharmed by a wrangler who lived on the premises. The animals were shaken and frightened but none sustained injuries.

Otto Kaiser had discussed these events with his close friend and fellow knight, Albert von Hapsberg. Were these events coincidences, they mused or was this the work of the fugitive they were seeking? If so, what madness was he capable of reaching? Their valets had taken the word to the populace that there was a madman afoot capable of inflicting serious damage on society. There was a bounty on his head and apart from a loose description there was not a lot of information to go on. These things took time. They had to wait for the fugitive to expose himself in some way so that he stood out from the usual crowd. The locals could spot a stranger a mile away. At some time, he must become vulnerable.

"Let us hope that we can get to him before he does any more damage to us!" Otto remarked to Albert, who quietly acquiesced with a nod while puffing on his favourite Meerschaum pipe.

It was customary for Franz-Josef Kaiser and Brigette von Hapsberg to go horse riding together in the forests on the family estates. Being summer, it was preferable to ride in the early morning when the air was fresh and cool from the night vapours that invigorated the leafy greenness of the forest canopy. Both families kept horses for eventing and breeding so there was never a shortage of good animals to exercise. Generally, the ride would be a leisurely canter with the odd stretch of clear forest in which they would race each other over a distance and fall back into a walk or canter depending on the terrain. The horses would enjoy a drink from a sweet cool spring while the riders dismounted and took sustenance from flasks, especially carried for the occasion. Franz-Josef diluted peach schnapps with fruit juice it had a low alcohol content but satisfied both body and soul following a fast gallop along the forest clearing. The horses knew the path well and could smell the fresh water. They became excited at the thought of a long draught of cold sweet liquid and ran surely and swiftly, the hope of reward redolent in their nostrils. The horses smelled the water and required little coaxing to reach a fast gallop.

Lighter in the saddle, Brigette's horse soon gained the lead and she rode it like a champion jockey, skilfully letting the gelding reach full stride. Brigette looked neither to the right nor the left but kept her eyes on the track ahead, watching the bluff at the back of the water hole loom fuller into her vision as she neared the artesian spring. Brigette could hear the pursuing horse gaining on her as the hoof beats became louder and she coaxed a bit more speed from her mount, finally arriving and dismounting as she reined the excited horse to a halt. She dismounted as Franz-Josef's horse galloped up and Brigette gasped as she saw that the mount was riderless. She looked back down the trail that she had ridden along but could not see Franz-Josef. She was alone. Horse riding was a hazardous business and they had both previously sustained injuries, but it was still an event that was treated with great trepidation lest some serious injury be inflicted upon the rider. Brigette remounted and led Franz-Josef's horse by the reins, walking side by side along the trail that she had just traversed in a gallop.

Hoofmarks were fresh on the soft ground, leaving a trail that would remain until it rained and the ground was re-sculpted by water and soil movement. After five minutes she saw something on the track ahead. A bundle lying prone and a person leaning over the bundle. *There were two people,* she thought. *Someone must have observed the fall. Help would be at hand.* As she approached, the person leaning over the inert figure of Franz Josef stood up and she saw he was in a military uniform and as she neared she realised that it was the Nazi submariner that was ejected from the Kaiser house and whom had had a duel with Franz-Josef the following morning. It was the man they called Arnold Fuchs. Brigette remembered this, as his name was the antithesis of the poltroon that he had since proved to be. Eagle and Fox he was not. Brigette grasped her riding crop firmly in her hand and let the reins go on the trailing horse. Fuchs had retreated from the prone figure of Franz-Josef and was fumbling with a cover on the sheathed pistol attached to his tunic belt when

Brigette struck him violently across his face with her riding crop, the leather causing a large welt to form and then open, exposing flesh under the skin. Fuchs instinctively put his hand on the wound to protect it and Brigette let fly again with another hefty blow that brought a howl of surprise and pain from his snarling lips. Before he could recover, Brigette reared her mount and the front flailing hooves caught the wretch about his head and chest and he fell to the ground where the horse trampled him into unconsciousness. She had no qualms about the punishment that the horse had inflicted on Fuchs as she saw the device that had caused Franz-Josef to fall. It was a rope that had been stretched across the trail. It was raised after she had galloped past. Obviously it was Fuch's plan to harm Franz-Josef and perhaps kidnap Brigette. The thought caused her to shiver with revulsion. Brigette got her horse to stand over the inert form of Fuchs as she dismounted and removed the Luger from his holster. She then went to Franz-Josef and felt for a pulse, which was good and his breathing was steady and full. She rolled him onto his side and considered how she could move him. She needed to get him onto a horse. She would lay him across the saddle if she could, but he was a dead weight and far too heavy for her to lift on her own. Brigette was a resourceful young woman and had the advantage of a liberal upbringing on a large country estate. Her rope work around horses was superb.

Brigette removed the hunting knife from the sheath on Franz-Josef's belt and cut the rope that Fuchs had placed across the path to unseat rider from mount. She then managed to tie one end of the rope around the upper torso and under the armpits of the limp body and then tied the other end to a ring on Fanz Josef's saddle. Her idea was to use the spare horse as a tractor to raise the deadweight. And with some assistance from herself and muscle from the horse she was able to lay Franz-Josef across the saddle of her mount with his head hanging down one side and legs on the other. Brigette then tied his hands to his feet by passing the rope under the belly of the horse. She then moved the horse off from standing over Fuchs who was still out cold and with the spare rope trussed him like a pig ready for the spit. He would need the powers of Houdini to escape the rope bonds that she had skilfully entwined around him. Brigette then thanked both horses for their cooperation and rewarded each with a lump of sugar. She was not surprised at their actions but thankful that they had responded and their training had proved to be a valuable asset in a serious predicament when it all could have gone so terribly wrong. Brigette mounted Franz-Josef's horse and with the reins of her own mount in her spare hand, now carrying the unconscious form of Franz-Josef, she rode slowly down the trail, beneath the canopy of tall beech trees and arrived at the von Hapsbergs' estate stables thirty minutes later.

The stable hands were used to accidents and they carefully removed Franz-Josef from the saddle and laid him on a cot in the stable. He was starting to come round from the concussion and they kept him warm with a blanket.

When a party went back to fetch Fuchs he was conscious but subdued. He was taken to the von Hapsbergs' castle and put into a cell in the basement, built for purpose years ago and still useful.

The only time members of a conclave wore regalia was when sentencing a villain for their crimes against fellow citizens. This was to preserve the anonymity of the conclave members and to add mystique to the occasion and awe to the eye of the person under sentence. The regalia consisted of a long, white, ankle-length smock, tied at the waist with a red braided rope style belt and a white hood with eye holes. The hood had a pointed top and the outfit looked sinister. A sign of mortality in the form of a human skull was displayed on a pedestal to serve as a reminder of all mankind's ultimate destination.

For his crimes against humanity, Arnold Fuchs was to be released as a fugitive deep in a beech forest on the von Hapsberg estate. He would be given a fire arm and ammunition to defend himself, a four-hour head-start and then the pursuers were to start their quest to hunt him down and kill him. If he managed to evade his pursuers and escape from the forest, he was a free man if he left Saxony. But if he was ever found in Saxony again there was a bounty on his head and he could be shot on sight. His pursuers were to be selected from six members of the enclave, each armed with the same firearm as the fugitive. Their job was to find and destroy Fuchs.

The disposal of the body had already been decided in what seemed to be some form of poetic justice. The dead coward would serve his country as part of an armoured car order being constructed at the Kaiser Iron & Steel Works whereby the body would be dropped into a vat of molten metal where it would dissolve on contact with the red hot molten metal used as castings and plate for the vehicles under construction. They were destined for the Afrika Corps and would be shipped to Tunisia on completion.

"He may serve his country yet in some useful form," Otto Kaiser had quipped.

Fuchs was stoic throughout the procedure. On the completion of the ritual the members of the conclave recited the paternoster, perhaps a leftover from the Holy Roman Empire days. Fuchs was taken by the head gamekeeper on horseback deep into what seemed an impenetrable beech forest in rough terrain. He was given rations for a day and if he survived longer he was to hunt for his supper or starve. There would be no shortage of water from the land which contained many springs and streams. Four hours later, the hunting party of six knights rode into the same spot and dismounted. It was all footwork from hereon in as the terrain was too steep for a horse. The hunting party observed the same rights and conditions as Fuchs. They, however, did not need to be selective about making a fire to cook their kill, unlike Fuchs, who could give his position away by lighting a fire. It was, however, hard to spot a cooking fire in the forest as the trees provided good cover and one would have to be above them to observe rising smoke from a cooking fire.

Both Otto and Albert were in the party and knew the land rather well as they had hunted on it for years. It was decided that they would hunt in pairs and signal by rifle fire. Two shots a sighting and three shots a kill. At close quarters, signalling would be by whistling. Two sharps a sighting and three: assistance required. A single shot was generally a food kill and none of them needed more than one shot to fell a deer. There were chosen rendezvous places each night where they could share the spoils and discuss tactics.

Otto was paired with Klaus, Albert with George and that left Bruno and Olaf to form the third party. All had hunted the terrain before but Otto and Albert were most familiar with it and so they took the flanks and left Bruno and Olaf to stay in the middle. At first the walking was easy and as they walked on, the difficulty of the terrain slowed their pace. As the light faded and the party met at the red hunting lodge for the night. Bruno shot a red deer which was not needed that night but it was an easy shot in the twilight as the herd came for a drink at the nearby river. They butchered the animal and hung it in a tree for the night. The kill meant that they could concentrate on their fugitive the next day and not have to worry about food that night. This could be advantageous if they were near their quarry and did not need to give their position away by firing a shot.

The party were away by six in the morning and traversed the rough terrain as fast as they could. Otto knew that Fuchs would have to cross a fast flowing river which was difficult alone and without rope. Otto knew the ford location and unless Fuchs got lucky, he had two choices: attempt a river crossing or double back. It was a difficult choice as both were life threatening. Otto planned their approach so that he and Klaus took the centre and headed for the ford while the other two pairs took the flank at a kilometre apart from the centre. The pairs each distanced themselves by five hundred metres so they were better able to cover ground should Fuchs decide to double back. They stopped at noon for water and trail food then continued on. Otto had estimated that they should all reach the river around three o'clock in the afternoon. They would signal each other on arrival at the river if a visual observation was not made possible. The whistle signal was four shrill blasts similar to the tree creeper birds that inhabit the area.

Otto reached the ford and emitted his bird call imitation but got no replies. He noticed the low level of the water in the channel. It was late summer and the river was not the raging torrent that it would became in the rainy season. It was, however, a formidable crossing if one chose unwisely. Local knowledge was advantageous. Within a space of ten minutes he heard three bird calls and added his own to make a four count. The plan was for the flanks to walk along the riverbank toward the ford where they would meet to discuss the next move.

As each knight arrived at the ford. Otto discussed their findings which in the main were negative. All, however, agreed that unless Fuchs knew about and used the ford, crossing the river would be foolhardy for a person alone. It was agreed that they would spend that night at the blue lodge, an hour's walk from the ford.

They arrived at the blue lodge at six in the evening. Sunshine was casting long shadows through the leafy high beeches and spots of sunlight danced on the ground as the wind soughed through the tree tops. The woodshed door was ajar which was unusual because the gamekeepers always shut doors. It was the gamekeepers that kept the lodges stocked with a good supply of firewood as this was the only fuel available for heating and cooking. The party stopped.

"Maybe Fuchs is inside," Otto commented. He held up his hand and they all stopped.

"We have made enough noise approaching," Olaf added. "If Fuchs were inside he could have shot us as we approached. Maybe he was here and he has gone."

George said, "You guys cover me, I'll take a detour and end up under the window. If he appears at the window or comes out the door – well, you know what to do. I'll have a peek in the window and see what I can see." And he was off on a circuitous route that would take him around the side and back of the lodge and then up to the window. The five knights lined up their rifles. Three on the door and two on the window. George came around the side of the cottage and crept up under the window. He took off his hat and placed it on the muzzle of his rifle and dangled it at the window pane to get a reaction, but nothing happened. Slowly George rose up until he could peek through the glass from one side without exposing his face and this drew no reaction so he cautiously moved his face and looked squarely in the window. The watchers held their breath as he seemed to be looking all around the inside of the building and taking his time. He then stood up. "It's okay to enter," he said to them. "Fuchs is dead."

Sure enough, they were greeted by the sight of Fuchs at the end of a rope. He had hanged himself.

The knights quickly reasoned that Fuchs chose death by hanging over drowning or being shot.

"Looks like he left us a suicide note," Olaf exclaimed as he picked up a folded piece of white paper on the table.

"We know why he killed himself," Otto said, "what the hell more can he say?"

Olaf unfolded the paper and held it up for all to read.

In large print, Fuchs had written: 'Heil Hitler'.

"That explains the man's mentality," George said. "An ideological nutter. One dead Nazi is a good Nazi!"

"Hear, hear," all round. "We can open the medicinal brandy and toast that." And they did.

The knights cut Fuchs' body from the rope, wrapped it in a blanket and tied a rope around the blanket and they stored him in the woodshed.

"I'll get the gamekeeper to bring his men and the mule to collect the body." Otto said. "Now let's get a fire going and cook our venison. I have Onions, potatoes and carrots. We can make a great stew!"

The brandy bottle was passed around while they sat in the lodge and enjoyed their companionship, spoke about a post war Germany without Hitler and relished the aromas of a rich venison stew cooking over an open wood fire.

Fuchs was committed to the molten vat a couple of days later. The mill worked day and night and so they had to choose their moment wisely away from any prying eyes. That vat made steel plate and castings for the last ten vehicles in a total order of 200 units. The last one off the assembly line they christened 'Eagle-Fox' an allusion to Arnold Fuchs, where Arnold meant 'the strength of an eagle' and Fuchs, 'a fox'. It obviously was not his real name and that was good. They would make a special ceremony of presenting car number 200 to the Desert Fox, Rommel. It may bring him luck in his campaign against the allies in the western desert.

"God knows we need luck," Otto lamented.

Franz-Josef received his orders soon after the news of the Japanese attack on Pearl Harbor.

"Japan has joined the axis. But then the United States will have joined the allies. That makes it forty-all or deuce," Brigette quipped as she beat Franz-Josef in a friendly game of indoor tennis. He had beaten her in their previous game.

"Yes," Franz-Josef replied, "and war is the continuation of policy by other means."

"Did not General von Clausewitz also say, war is a trinity of people, army and government?" Bridgette remarked.

"You are the scholar Brigette, I am a mere soldier!" Franz-Josef replied with a grin, "I play tennis and you play war. With you the game is a serious competition."

"And so it is with Hitler and Tojo." Brigette fixed him in a steely glare.

"Then so is this," replied Franz-Josef as he pulled Brigette to him and kissed her passionately on the mouth. After what seemed like a minute their lips parted and Franz-Josef with great sincerity and love looked into Brigette's eyes and said. "My trinity to you is peace, love and harmony."

Colonel Kaiser was to report to Auschwitz. He had received a promotion. Major to colonel. Auschwitz had accumulated a lot of Russian prisoners and Franz-Josef spoke passable Russian following his years of flying training in Russia. His flying days were over but Germany still needed him.

"You know, Auschwitz is not far from here," Franz-Josef said to Brigette. "I can come home for visits. It's about a five hour drive either way."

"I'll look forward to that, I have missed you, you know. I missed the regular outings we used to enjoy before this mad war. I loved our trip to Paris and London. I find it difficult that we have gone to war with such lovely people. I tend to think that von Clausewitz never said that war is a trilogy, people would never have agreed about the war only the leaders and that's policy, or politics. I would say the trilogy is despots or tyrants, armies and governments.

"It may also be violence, hatred and enmity," Franz-Josef offered. "The fog of war is another factor," he continued. "Intelligence is stacked against the odds. The odds are stacked against the receiver. You know I still remember an example that one of our signal guys used to tell us about at the academy. It was taken from a British army manual but it proved a point about messages.

"The sender transmitted: 'Going to advance send reinforcements.' When the message got to HQ they were most puzzled to read, 'Going to a dance, send three and four pence.'"

Brigette laughed. "Well, you can't mistake my message," she said as she gave her lover a long lingering kiss.

"You do know Papa is talking about Mother and I going to North Africa?"

"No, I haven't heard that one." Franz-Josef sounded surprised.

"Yes, apparently your father is going to deliver the shipment of armoured cars to the Africa Corps. It is considered good karma if the head of Kaiser Iron & Steel is in the official handing over party. He's taking your mother too. Dad says that the Nazis are infiltrating the works and Otto is basically redundant. Even though he owns the show. But it will eventually be run by Nazis. Too important to the war effort to remain solely Otto's domain. Anyway, whatever the Nazis do, the Russians will nationalise it when they arrive. Private enterprise is not part of their philosophy. So maybe your father is ahead of his time. Getting out now while he can still call the shots, is probably a very good idea. He didn't make field marshall in the last stoush without being able to interpret the road ahead. I remember him telling me that milestones are markers to pedestrians but signposts to entrepreneurs!"

Franz-Josef recalled his conversation with his father about the artworks and other valuables that were being despatched among the spare parts consignment for the armoured cars and he wondered how permanent his family's sojourn in Africa would be. Maybe the cars were the thin end of the wedge for the Kaisers and von Hapsbergs and their ilk. Otto had mentioned the arrival of the Russians and rape, pillage and general mayhem that would ensue before the top brass had caught up with the troops and managed to settle them with some good old fashioned military discipline, but a hell of a lot could happen to a civilian population who would be cannon fodder for an out of control fighting man fuelled up on vodka. The woman folk would fare the worst – he shuddered and hoped that Brigette would be far away in North Africa when the inevitable happened.

Auschwitz was another matter, as Franz-Josef soon discovered. He arrived on a cold December evening in 1941 having travelled by train from Dresden. The officers' quarters and food was passable, even good, and when compared to the prisoners', sumptuous. A tour of the camp revealed a collection of buildings that had been assembled as the requirements of the camp grew like a cancer. Ten thousand Soviet prisoners had arrived in October, but by March 1942 their numbers had dwindled to about a thousand. Many had been moved on and many died from disease and starvation. The camp was run by Allgemaine SS, (political) and not to be confused with Waffen SS (combat) but there were also other military personnel from the armed forces, like himself perhaps unfit for combat but too valuable to put out to pasture. Franz-Josef felt his presence was a humanitarian offer to observers who would report to the Red

111

Cross in Switzerland. Atrocities were rife but it was foolhardy to intervene. This was indeed as General Carl von Clausewitz had written years earlier. "War is the continuation of policy by other means." The Nazis seemed hell-bent on wiping out communists and now they were turning the blowtorch on Jews. Franz-Josef could not help but notice the train-loads of Jews that were arriving, being disgorged and disappearing. It was while he was watching a train discharge its hapless occupants that his eye caught a couple in the line of Jewish prisoners each carrying a suitcase and heading for the prison gates. He watched them. Something seemed familiar. It was winter and the incoming Jews were swathed in their winter garb. A lot were people of some wealth and influence, they wore good bespoke garments, especially overcoats. Hats and scarves were also popular devices to ward out cold and of course they were dishevelled from days of travel in harrowing conditions. Franz-Josef observed the couple for some time before he realised that he was looking at his family's most revered art dealer in Europe. It was Rudi Levin and his wife Ester from Amsterdam. He could hardly contain himself and started forward only to be given a friendly reminder from a guard that he was to stay clear of the column. Franz-Josef doubted that the Levins would have noticed him. Like the rest of the column, they kept their heads down and shuffled along to the shouts from the guards to get a move on.

Franz-Josef hurried off to find the person in charge from whom he might be able to get permission to see his old friends. He may as well have pushed shit uphill with a fork. The political SS were not impressed with war heroes. It was, of course, a jealousy borne out by the fact that the SS were scumbags, there was a criminal fringe in the corps that would some years later be uncovered during the war crimes trials at Nuremberg. In his travels through the bureaucracy he came upon a German inmate who seemed to have some sort of a trustee status. His name was Werner Kruger who said that he was sent to Auschwitz from Dachau where he was first imprisoned in 1936, for being a communist, no less.

"Hitler hates us," he said, smiling. He realised that his journey would become easier if he renounced communism. He was still inwardly a communist but now as a trustee prisoner he was a far healthier communist and with a bit of cunning, reckoned he could survive the war. Werner explained that he was sent to Auschwitz because he spoke Russian but he had run out of Russian prisoners to converse with. As a German citizen he was a civilian prisoner but had considerable freedom compared with military and Jewish prisoners. He even appeared well fed. Werner told Franz-Josef that the SS considered Auschwitz to be a soft job as there was plenty of slave labour to carry out their dirty work and do menial tasks and the facilities for them were splendid. It was like having servants. Werner explained the complexity of the departments within the system and one just had to know the inner workings to be able to get to the nub quickly and without red tape.

"Tell me who you think the Jewish prisoners are that you know and I will arrange a meeting."

"You can do this?" Franz-Josef sounded incredulous.

"Sure I can – here," he wrote a barrack number on a scrap of paper and handed it to the bewildered Luftwaffe colonel.

"You be here today at 3pm and I will have them meet with you."

Franz-Josef was at the agreed rendezvous at the allotted time. It turned out that the barrack was the living and sleeping quarters for Jewish prisoners – slave labourers and he was aghast at what he considered to be their atrocious conditions. Franz-Josef estimated that the building's floor space would, under humane conditions, have enough area to place twenty five beds along either wall. And there would be an aisle down the middle to take table and chairs for eating and socialising. The gap in the middle was minimal and either side there was a labyrinth of floor to ceiling shelves with just enough space between them to contain a person in a semi prone position and at least three deep back to the wall. They must have packed four hundred people into this space, he estimated. They were like bees in a hive and like bees they relied on the aggregate body temperatures to keep the warmth within the room to a liveable ambient, once you got used to the stench. The building was empty as the occupants were at work. He heard the door open and footsteps and Werner brought in Rudi and Ester. At first there was no recognition from them and they wore quizzical expressions, wondering what was about to happen to them in this newly introduced house of horrors. Franz-Josef removed his hat and smiled at them.

He said, "I am Otto Kaiser's son, do you not remember me?"

Ester was the first to show a flicker as she said, "Franz-Josef! Why yes, of course!" And the mystery evaporated from the encounter as she realised this was a meeting of old friends, she then embraced him. Her voice trembling with emotion and shock she said, "How nice to see you."

Rudi was a little reserved. The sight of a German uniform was not something that he associated with pleasure. Franz-Josef recognised his discomfort and said. "I am not a Nazi. Just a German. Like you, if I do not do as I am told, I get shot!"

Rudi shook his hand, "Is it so obvious? We have been through a lot of changes and are still making adjustments."

Franz-Josef explained that he had been severely wounded and was not able to be a combatant but nonetheless he was able-bodied enough to serve some purpose in the Nazi war machine. "I don't know how I can help you," he said, "but there are ways, I am told by my communist friend here," he said, referring to Werner. "One thing I do recall from the past," he said, addressing Ester. "You are an English national, if you have your British passport I would suggest that you insist that you are transferred to that section of the camp. The living conditions are better, for a start. You would be able to get extra food to Rudi that way at least."

"But we will be separated."

"You will be segregated anyway. This way you will have a better chance of survival. That is what this is all about. Hitler's reign will not be forever – I will predict another three years at the most."

113

They nodded in tacit agreement. They were practical people. Survival was not a sentiment, it was an instinct.

"Okay," Werner said. "Time's up, we can do this again. Any messages in the interim, I can deliver them, either way."

They left the building following Werner's instruction, Franz-Josef first and two minutes later the Levins with Werner in the lead.

Now that Franz-Josef had made contact with Werner Kruger, it did not take long for him to learn about the camp hierarchy. The camp HQ, as with most bureaucracies, had operating branches. "Like octopus tentacles," Werner had said, "all containing suckers."

"Take, for example, the 'Economic Administration' can you imagine what they are responsible for?"

Franz-Josef shook his head. "No idea."

"They," Werner said, waiting for a drum roll, "are responsible for the property of dead prisoners."

Franz-Josef shook his head. "Hard to imagine, apart from some nice civilian clothes, what on earth would they have of any value?"

"They bring suitcases with their valuables, these people are Jews, some wealthy. They have fine jewellery, and paintings, works of art. The canvases are also sewed into their garments. There is a king's ransom in artworks going begging for the want of a German emperor. I have been waiting for the right man to come along. Rudi Levin says you can save these works of art. You have the necessary training to catalogue the loot. To try and save it in some way. Better than it going up in smoke when they burn unwanted garments. The jewellery is spoken for, but no one has realised the extent of the artworks that can be uncovered. Rudi, of course, needs to be involved. If we put a strong enough case forward I'm sure that the bosses, even the dummkopf SS assholes will recognise the significance of these treasures.

"Here's two Rudi has given me for starters. He wants to keep them but they are examples of the sort of paintings that we will find." Werner laid the two canvases of the trinity, painted in three sections, that Rudi had distributed among his family before the war, when Holland was invaded by the Nazis.

"I have no idea what it is," Werner said, "but Rudi thought that you would probably guess."

Franz-Josef looked at the two canvases. "This is a copy of *Massacio's Trinity*, he painted it as a fresco inside the Santa Maria Novella in Florence. Quite old as I recall, maybe fifteenth century. It looks to me as though this painting has been done in three parts." He pointed at the top part. "This part contains the trilogy: the father, the son and the holy ghost, here depicted as a dove. This canvas," he continued, "will be the middle section and depicts the lower part of Christ's body on the cross. To the right is Saint John and on the left the Virgin Mary. Each are flanked by the figures of the two patrons, who serve as models of religious devotion, as I recall. The missing or bottom section is referred to as 'the Cadaver in the Tomb.' It contains a Latin inscription, when

114

translated says. 'I once was what you are and what I am you will also be.' Rather macabre."

"Yes it is," Werner shivered. "Apparently Rudi's son Linus has the bottom part. Rudi hopes that all three parts will be reunited after the war. Hopefully by Linus if neither Rudi nor Ester survive."

Franz-Josef said, "We will need to acquire a large room to work in. I'll put it to the boss and see what the response will be."

"Try Rupert Hessner," Werner said, "I think he will be amenable. Hess is in charge of HQ. Admin, whatever that means, but he is a Wehrmacht officer, and like you, Colonel, he has been sidelined by war wounds. He is not a Nazi sympathiser. You just know some things." Which was an understatement; Werner knew everything!

Chapter 9

North Africa

The Kaisers and von Hapsbergs travelled by train from Dresden to Genoa which was a two day train journey. It could be done quicker in peacetime, but they spent time on rail sidings as military traffic took precedence.

The armoured cars had left the Dresden works of Kaiser Iron and Steel over a four week period as rolling stock became available for their transportation along the same route. Factory engineers had travelled with the consignment in the box cars that also included the crates of spares as well as valuables the two families were shipping out of Germany for safe keeping.

A convoy had amassed in Genoa and they sailed for Palermo in Sicily to connect with a larger convoy that would cross the Mediterranean Sea to Tunis, a journey of about eighteen hours in open water. The route was well protected by German U-boats and Italian submarines as well as fast Italian escort destroyers. This was the supplies that Rommel's Africa Corps were sorely in need of and arrived in February 1943 in time for his offensive against the allies in the battle for Egypt and to push the British and her allies out of North Africa. Apart from the Kaiser armoured cars, there were tanks, ammunitions, guns and fuel supplies as well as food. Also, there were two divisions of Italian reinforcements; everything an army needed to fight and survive. Rommel wanted German troops but Hitler was keeping them for the Russian offensive.

Otto Kaiser presented Rommel with 'Eagle Fox', which was number 200 from off the Kaiser Iron and Steel Works assembly line of armoured cars. The car wore the same livery as the others, but it was emblazoned with the numeral 200 and the name 'Eagle Fox', which Rommel said he rather enjoyed as he was already known as the Desert Fox for his exploits in the North African campaign thus far. In return, Rommel presented Otto with a silver plated Luger pistol with ivory handle grips.

"African ivory," he explained. "It is softer than Indian ivory and much easier to carve. One gets more intricate designs on African ivory than Indian ivory." Otto admired the delicately worked handle grips and thanked Rommel very much.

The parts consignment was housed in a large warehouse fortuitously owned by Abdul Nassar & Sons. The appropriate crates were relieved of their non-military contents and resealed. In what would have normally been regarded as a miracle of warehouse receipt and despatch procedures, the family's valuables were on a caravan, disappearing fast into the hinterlands of the great North African desert. The Kaisers and von Hapsbergs participated in the preliminary rounds of social networking before announcing that they had been invited to stay with a Bedouin Shiek and his family in his dessert oasis. And they then disappeared. Otto had explained to the authorities that they could be gone for a month.

"Do not worry about us," he had said, "we are among old business associates and perfectly safe."

Abdul Nassar sent a large Mercedes limo to collect the families. In Cairo he would have sent a Rolls Royce, but as a Bedouin and mindful of the nuances of European feeling, and in deference to the German occupiers of Tunisia, the Mercedes was a logical choice.

Mahmoud, Abdul Nassar's third son, drove the limo. He had been schooled in England and spoke excellent English but no German. Otto was proficient enough in English to translate to his travelling compatriots. The limo took them as far as the road was sealed and when sand met concrete they were met by a camel train which was to become their transport for some time to come.

The Kaiser party consisted of four Europeans. There was Otto and his valet Konrad, Otto's wife Anna and her maid Kirsten. Both valet and maid had been loyal family servants for years and it was their wish to continue to serve the Kaisers. They were not only servants, but companions and good friends.

The von Hapsberg's party of five were Alfred and his valet Marco, Alfred's wife Claudia and her maid Gerda and their daughter Brigitte who, of the current generation, considered personal servants as degenerate. But she never did get the hang of the personal affections that infiltrate such associations.

Their first camel ride lasted six hours and as dusk came across the desert landscape they approached a bunch of scruffy looking tents that were erected beneath a stony bluff. Smoke rose from cooking fires and the whole scene looked like an unreal attempt at a camping holiday by amateurs. The camels obediently squatted on the ground following strange noises from their drivers and the occupants alighted and were led to what looked like a black open weave tent with a lot of holes in it. Mahmoud observed their expressions and offered an explanation. He explained that the tents were woven from goats' hair, which shrinks when wet to form a very close weave so the tent was weather proof in winter. As the goats' hair dries, the weave loosens and what would appear to be holes, form in the weave. "This allows a breeze to cool the tents," he explained in very good English and Otto translated to their servants, who spoke only German.

117

The interior looked comfortable enough with walled off partitions and beds sufficient for both parties. The entrance contained piles of soft cushions and low tables and this was the general reception and eating and relaxing part of their accommodation. Their travelling bags and valises were brought to the tent by the camel attendants and then they were left to their own devices.

Otto opened a bag and tipped the contents onto a table. They were travelling documents, some old and some new. He picked up the new ones and distributed them around. Saying, "These are your new passports." Each, in turn, examined the front, then opened the book and looked at their photographs. Some winced and some smiled.

"As you know," he said, "I have negotiated Swiss passports for us all. This was part of the deal that Kaiser Iron & SteelWorks did with the Swiss Government. This was arranged in 1936. They got all of our banking business as well as acting as an international buying selling and confirming house for all of our international transactions, in return for these documents and the guarantee that goes with them. As Swiss citizens we are neutral; we can go anywhere, without let or hindrance as the English say. I will burn the old documents tonight and that will be the end of the old era as we enter the new. As you know we can now travel to Cairo and access our financial resources through the Swiss banking system that is operating there. However, we do not proceed with undue haste. It has been discussed with our North African agents, Abdul Nassar & Sons, that we refrain from entering Cairo until the Allies have booted the Africa Corps into the sea. So we will be taking a rather long circuitous route that will see us enter Egypt in the lower Nile region and travel leisurely up and along that magnificent waterway. I have plenty of US dollars available for our immediate needs. Our caravan is prepaid through until we reach the Nile and thereafter we have other arrangements. A lot of our journey upon reaching that large waterway will be by boat, with plenty of stop-offs along the way. As far as the authorities in Tunisia are concerned, we will have perished in the desert, having failed to make it back to Tunis in time for the return convoy. It's not an unlikely story, especially for Europeans without a safe journey guarantee, that goes with our association with Nassars." Otto paused. "Any questions?" There were none and he continued.

"Alcohol is not a part of the Bedouin lifestyle, but I am informed that they are gracious in the benevolence to the comfort of their guests and providing we partake discreetly, there are no objections about our relationship with western refinements. Cuisine is basic in the tented version of our desert sojourn but there will be plenty of opportunities to eat more traditional foods, like meat such as goat and lamb, and even fish when we reach the Nile. Pork, as you will understand, is off the menu. Toilet facilities are as yet to be discovered but no doubt our resourceful host will have appropriate methods of hygiene acceptable to the westerner." At that point, Mahmoud entered the tent with Bedouin ladies in tow. They were carrying ewers with handles, and large wash basins.

"Allow me to introduce Fatima and her team who will take the ladies into their quarters and offer refreshing water for light bathing. Please, thank you."

All of the ladies disappeared behind a curtained off part of the tent which Mahmoud explained was the ladies' quarters, "exclusively."

"I would have thought that water was a precious commodity here?" Alfred enquired.

"Water is always precious, but in some locations we have more than others. Here at Wadi Gin, we have underground springs with plenty of water for the camels and also for bathing. Come, I will show you."

Mahmoud led them to the foot of the large bluff that towered above the camp site like a rock monolith. The four men watched in amazement as he rolled a circular rock aside with ease opening up a passage into the hill. *It was like something out of Ali Baba,* Otto thought, *but then the stories must have come from actual truths in the beginning.* This wasn't science fiction but life in the desert. There were always explanations and Otto was prepared to wait and see what was about to unfold. They walked into a cavern and Mahmoud rolled the rock back in place.

"Keeps out the desert heat," he explained. Lighted torches on the walls illuminated the interior and they walked on a solid rocky floor worn smooth by centuries of people doing exactly as they were doing now. Their journey took them downward through a beautiful limestone cave and soon dripping water could be heard. Turning a corner brought them into a chamber in which a large underground water system in the form a small lake lay before them.

They were all amazed to find an abundance of water in the desert and Mahmoud read their astonishment. He had obviously brought foreigners here before so was prepared for their reactions.

"If you consider," he said, "that for centuries, this rocky monolith has stood and in that time thousands of inches of rain will have fallen on it. We do get rain but not much and in the desert when it falls on the sand it is hardly enough to sustain life at all. But when it falls on rock, the droplets collect and form little rivulets and those little rivulets find crevices and gravity does the rest. The water is away from the pull of the sun and so it does not evaporate but continues down through rock apertures, travelling deeper and deeper underground until it finds a common collection pond to contain it indefinitely. Lovely cool, clear, rock filtered fresh water, as old as civilisation, maybe older. Taste it, gentlemen. It will improve the best scotch. Guaranteed!"

They knelt beside the pool and with cupped hands scooped up the clear, clean, cool fresh water and raised it to their mouths and sipped.

Otto said, "Veritas is in the well, the truth is in the water." and he repeated it in German for his friends.

Mahmoud seemed surprised at this rhetoric and said. "You know I always considered scotch whiskey to be the truth serum without parallel."

"You said it, Mahmoud," Otto replied. "Add this water to Scotch whisky and you may have invented the world's best lie detector!"

They contemplated their genius in amused silence.

"Follow me," Mahmoud said and he led them down another level arriving in a chamber that had wooden sluice gates at head height along one end. He pulled a rope and a wooden gate was raised allowing a deluge of cold water to cascade down onto the bather.

"This is where we have our shower baths," he said. "Men one day and women the next. This is why the ladies are having a sponge bath today. Tomorrow they will be here. Today is men's day. The water is not wasted it is collected and we can pump it up to the desert floor level by semi-rotary hand pumps. It is used for watering the camels and other camp requirements. We cannot afford to waste a drop. Did you realise that a fully grown male camel can drink 200 litres of water in three minutes? Let me know if you want a sluice and I can get towels and soap brought to us."

They all agreed that a cold shower and a good soaping would be the ideal way to end their dusty caravan journey. Atop a camel across the sands of the desert was not the nicest way to travel.

Dinner would be a casual affair and brought to their tent on platters that would be placed on low tables with the diners sitting on cushions that were on the floor around the tables. Mahmoud explained that at Wadi Gin and other major staging posts their meals were a bit more substantial than when travelling in the desert. Both parties, the Kaisers and von Hapsburgs and attendants were having pre-dinner drinks when Mahmoud came to their tent to say that dinner would be an hour away. They hastily tried to hide the alcohol, much to Mahmoud's delight and he said, "You must remember I was in England for a number of years and I made the drinking team at Oxford one year. So if you are offering me a tipple I will gladly accept your offer. Alcohol is a western habit I have come to respect and enjoy."

Otto offered Mahmoud a choice of schnapps, scotch, wine or sherry and he chose sherry. "Bottoms up," he said and they all toasted bottoms up. By the time dinner arrived the tent occupants were in a jovial mood and Otto insisted that Mahmoud join them over dinner and his invitation was endorsed by the others. The meats were goat and sheep which they ate with rice and a mixture of vegetables and all washed down with coffee. "We roast the beans on a shovel over the fire and when sufficiently cooled we grind them." Mahmoud offered. And his audience nodded in silence as Otto translated this piece of intelligence. They all agreed the meal was superb as was the coffee. In an instant, night fell on the encampment and the lighted tents made soft illuminations on the otherwise barren landscape. The sky was big and the stars close. It was all so clear.

When the dinner dishes were cleared away by the Bedouin girls, Mahmoud laid a map of North Africa on the table and explained their journey, pointing out the stopping places and approximate times and distance between each location. "We plan to hook up with the Nile here," he said, a finger resting on a point on the map. "This is the Northern Sudan and the location is Wadi Halfa. It will take us about a month to reach this point. We can boat up the Nile from here, it would be a journey of nearly two thousand miles to Cairo. Some parts are a bit tricky in which case we go overland but generally we have our company dhows traversing the river continuously carrying goods from place to place. For a change we can take a train or go by automobile but hey! It's your call. Also there are some places in the Sahara that we can use four-wheel drive trucks, we cover a lot more ground in one of those. Anyway we are here for another three days while we wait for other camel trains to arrive. This is a bit like a railway shunting yard. We receive, sort and despatch. The next section we traverse is a rather gruelling six day journey until we reach an oasis with water for bathing." When Otto translated this there was a lot of discussion among the ladies in German. Otto conveyed their concerns to Mahmoud, who replied, "There is water for sponge baths such as was administered tonight, but total sluicing or immersion is out of the question during that journey. It's the same for everybody. We have been doing this for centuries and hygiene is not compromised, I can assure you!"

Otto relayed the information which was received with much diffidence and Mahmoud could see the effect it was causing. "Look," he said to Otto, "if I can wangle a spare camel I will carry sufficient water on it to ensure that each female receives a sluice every second day which is same as now. The amount of water per sluice will be less than they get from the caves, but it is better than nothing. We have a device that will do this, not unlike a lavatory cistern effect, you stand beneath the contraption, pull the chain and water is let down over you. We contain the spillage and it can be camel water. No problems, yes?"

Otto relayed the information and the ladies clapped and nodded as they conversed in German among themselves in what was a self-evident agreeable conclusion.

It was a mystery to the Europeans how their tent was left behind but when the evening destination was reached it was erected and fully furnished and ready for the arrival of the occupants. The Kaisers and von Hapsbergs were mounted and away at seven o'clock in the morning. It seemed that there were camels coming and going in all directions. Chaos was a good description of the scene they left behind as they rode off into the vast expanse of desert.

On the last day of their trek across the Benghazi desert, they sighted what at first appeared to be a sand storm approaching. Mahmoud halted the column and suggested that they hunker down beside the prone camels until it blew past. This part of Libya was famous for the 'ghibli', a wind they called the Sirrocco in Europe. One never took chances, especially when vehicles and other machinery was involved. When the dust cloud was about a mile off, Mahmoud trained his binoculars on the storm and announced that they were vehicles.

"Looks like armed army patrol vehicles, without identifying markings," he relayed. He kept his commentary up. "They do not look like German, Italian or English vehicles," he said. "Can't say I have seen anything like them before."

Otto said, "Mind if I have a look?" He held out his hand for the glasses that Mahmoud handed to him. Otto by association with the vehicle manufacturing programme that his company undertook had a good knowledge of all terrain equipment and he studied the approaching convoy. He handed the glasses back to Mahmoud.

"Chevrolets," he said.

"What?"

"Chevrolets; they have Chevrolet grills, but the rest of them look as if they have been modified to suit a particular job. They must be some sort of desert patrol. English or allies is my guess. Looks like the leader is in a Willys Jeep. Never thought I would see either vehicle in the flesh – so to speak. We have the tech specs on them, but that's all."

As the column drew nearer, Mahmoud told his caravan to stay put while he walked out to meet the leading vehicle, his right hand held upright in a peace greeting. The roar of engines subsided as the column came to a halt when the main man in the Jeep held up his hand as a signal to do so. Two Chevrolets came out and flanked the Jeep and Otto could see that they were heavily armed. He was sure that he could recognise an Italian Breda machine gun on one of the vehicles which made recognition equally confusing as there were no identifying insignia painted on the vehicles and they were not flying any flags or pennants, although he did notice strange motifs on the right front bonnet. It appeared to be some sort of green effigy with a red tongue sticking out from the mouth. He thought it very strange.

The officer in the Jeep introduced himself to Mahmoud without alighting from the Jeep but standing up to do so. "Captain Walker," he announced, "we are the Long Range Desert Group, Eighth Army, Allied Command."

"Mahmoud Nasser, third son Abdul Nasser & Sons Cairo." Mahmoud replied. "We are peaceful Bedouin on a trade journey."

"Yes I can see that!" the captain responded, with a wave of his arm toward the column of resting camels and people.

"You are a long way from home?" he replied, turning his remark into a question and raising his eyebrows.

"Normally we would take the coastal route," Mahmoud said, "but that is full of war between Germany and Britain so we play our ancient tribal routes from Timbuktu to Khartoum and all in between where it is safe to go." And as if he forgot to say it he added. "There are no Germans here for you to fight."

"Nothing obvious," the captain said, "but we don't do obvious." He didn't say anymore, not wanting to rouse any suspicions as it was hard to know which way the Arab allegiances lay. Both Axis and Allies had Arab sympathisers and they were not a stable source of support. Loyalties could change at the flip of a coin.

"Your English is very good, Mahmoud," the captain said.

"I was schooled in England, BA Oxon, class of 36. Your English is of a different dialect or accent than I have heard before."

"Yes it is, we are New Zealanders. British subjects of course."

Mahmoud nodded. "New Zealand lamb very nice, I have eaten it in England."

Captain Walker smiled. He was a sheep farmer prior to the war and like the Bedouin he was talking to, enjoyed the great outdoors and wandering around his grassed hills, tending the flock. They probably had a lot in common apart from the landscape, which was in total contrast.

"And what cargo are you carrying?" the captain asked.

"We carry mainly salt and textiles. We have also the normal supplies, feed and water for the animals and I have European friends, business associates of my fathers, who have come to visit him in Cairo."

Captain Walker looked interested in the last declaration. "And who would be travelling from Europe? International travel in wartime would be a risky business I would imagine!"

Otto, who had walked slowly up the file of parked camels and stood behind Mahmoud came alongside and said, "I would sir, Otto Kaiser, a Swiss national. Myself and my entourage are travelling to Wadi Halfa and then up the Nile to Cairo."

The captain touched his cap peak in a casual salute and nodded. "We must check your credentials, sir, you understand. Part of our patrol business is to find German spies. It is my duty, sir, we have to check your credentials."

Otto smiled. "That will not be a problem, I will get my people to present their passports." He turned and walked back down the line to where the Europeans were waiting.

The captain gave a signal to his column and six Chevrolets drove in a line alongside the camel train at a distance of twenty meters away. They spaced themselves equidistant along the length of the camel train. Apart from the driver there was a soldier manning a machine gun in each of the vehicles. They looked competent and efficient. Their dress was less than neat and tidy but to Otto's trained eye it was perfectly practical for the role they were in. Some wore the New Zealand Army shoulder flash on the battle dress tunic and some didn't. Some wore tin hats and others berets.

Otto returned to his entourage and explained their position and they dispersed to find passports. "Do not speak," he said. "I will do the talking. You don't speak English anyway but if they speak to you in German, I will answer."

Captain Walker had alighted from his Jeep at the head of the column and had walked down to meet with Otto who handed him nine passports. Captain Walker was thorough and examined each passport photograph and looked at the owner, each in turn had to remove any headwear so he could get a good head and shoulders likeness.

The captain flicked the passport visa pages and stopped at one. "You arrived in Tunis?" he asked Otto who nodded.

"How did you get to Tunis?"

"By ferry from Palermo," Otto replied.

"A dangerous stretch of water, Herr Kaiser?"

"We were in a convoy and I guess it is no secret that the stretch of water between Tunisia and Sicily is well patrolled by the axis powers."

"What other ships were in the convoy?"

Otto smiled, recognising the question as an intelligence probe.

"I'm no mariner, captain but there were a couple of large liners, a lot of freighters and fast naval craft for protection."

"How many ships would you say?"

"Maybe fifty? Sixty? I never counted. We started at night and ended at night so we had a few hours of daylight in the middle of the trip when the ships were at sea and seemed quite scattered."

"And your ferry? Who was on it apart from yourselves?"

"Civilians like us, just civilians. Mostly Italian, some Spanish, some Tunisians. There were also a few Jewish people hoping to make it to Palestine."

"And you, what is your business here in Africa?"

"Textiles, I am in textiles, we have cotton mills in Egypt and also India. My business associate for Egypt, Abdul Nassar and Sons has organised this trip for us. Before this war we visited on an annual basis but this is our first trip since 1938."

Captain Walker again flicked through Otto's passport and found an arrival stamp for Cairo airport in 1938.

"That all seems to add up," he said, "I have to hang on to these for now as I need verification from our people."

Otto protested. "But that could take days – weeks even, we may never see them again. They are our travel documents, you understand. We need them to travel without let or hindrance, I cannot allow it, Captain."

Captain Walker was a young, but patient and civil man and he realised the importance of the passports, in difficult times.

"This may not take long at all. We have a good radio system with us so we can contact base and let them get back to us, I would say within twenty four hours and we can all be on our way again. Without let or hindrance. If the documents are kosher you will have no problems from us, sir!"

Again, Captain Walker touched the peak of his cap with his right forefinger in a gesture of an informal salute. It was as if he somehow realised that Otto had a military background and he acknowledged that. Otto held his arms firmly at his side, fingers lightly clenched but thumbs pointing down his trouser seams and faintly clicked his heels and nodded his head, which was a natural reaction for a military man in civilian clothes. Otto was certain that he saw Captain Walker smile but it may also have been a reflection of a sun beam glinting off the glass watch face, as his hand arced downward.

Mahmoud spoke to one of his men and then went looking for Otto Kaiser and found him conversing generally among his entourage. They were discussing spending a night in the open which they knew would be cold. He found them Bedouin style, seated in a circle on the ground and he smiled. *Amazing how quick one adapts to the lifestyle,* he thought.

"This is a long way from a comfortable European drawing room," he quipped as he sat on the ground alongside Anna. "We booked the reality guided tour Otto responded with equanimity," he said, echoing Mahmoud's flippant remark.

"For obvious security reasons, Captain Walker has refused us permission to send out a party to let the main camp know what our hold up here is about. I think he suspects that we may be German friendly and give away their position. Anyway we have done what Bedouin tribes have done for centuries and secretly released a carrier pigeon who will take a message of our plight to the forward camp who are expecting us tonight. They will bring suitable cover for your party and extra food and fuel for us all to have a hot meal and coffee and a good night's rest. I can't wait to see the good captain's face when the cavalry appears over the hill – so to speak – in say, three hours' time."

"I see fires going already," Otto said, "obviously there is fuel being carried by the caravan."

Mahmoud gave a low laugh. "Yes, on board and inboard. You see the camel is so efficient in the use and conservation of water that the dung, when it hits the ground is suitable for burning immediately. It is already dry and no further processing is necessary."

"An interesting piece of intelligence," Otto remarked, before relaying it to the others who traded comments amongst themselves in German discussing the merits of a walking log fire fuel dispenser. The great provider had taken care of every contingency, all they had to do was to unlock the secrets to survive.

"That's how Mother Nature works," Mahmoud said. "All we have to figure out is how to work Mother Nature."

Captain Walker talked with his radio operator and they decided to contact Cairo directly for a quick response. This required the erection of a special aerial system, but the results would be worth the extra time in setting up the Windom Dipole system as it was called. He wanted to be away from the restrictions of guarding a large camel train and back to their mission of destroying enemy munitions and fuel dumps that the axis had planted around the desert, for emergency use when the need arose. Mobility was everything and he didn't want to be caught with his pants down should a hostile band of Bedouin tribesmen decide they were easy pickings. Although the patrol was heavily armed and they had plenty of fuel and ammunition, his war was not with the locals – he was fighting the Germans and Italians. One fight at a time was one fight too many. Walker had figured that there was not a problem with the Nassar clan, who were known British sympathisers. But Bedouin tribesmen were exactly that – tribesmen – and arguments between clan factions could flare up in an instant over the most trivial events. He wanted to be away as soon as possible and was keen for a quick reply from Cairo. His next stop was to talk with his second in command, Sergeant Kelvin Ross. Before joining the Second Expeditionary Force, Kelvin was a ranger in the Tongariro National Park. He was a rugged individual and preferred the cold that came with the mountainous topography of the Tongariro. Like most of the Long Range Desert Group, he was chosen along with the other New Zealanders because of their ability to survive on the land. They were rugged individuals who could kill a beast, catch a fish, make a fire, build a shelter, fix anything from a puncture to a blown radiator, ride a cow, a bull, a horse or a camel. There was no on the job training with these boys, they had been training all of their lives.

Insignia of rank was not evident and first names were used. Discipline was what you got when you introduced a snake to a Mongoose. They both respected the other's ability to win the fight. And so peace and common sense prevailed.

125

And each member of the group respected the others' ability to care for themselves and look after their backs in a difficult situation. Kelvin had been in difficult situations in the mountains. He was expected to be named in a future team assault attempt on Mount Everest but war got in the way. Enlisting in the army was as natural as a walk in the mountains for Kelvin and he was quick to join up for his next big adventure. So far he had not been disappointed. The standard issue, long arm Lee Enfield rifle looked like a side arm in his big paws and he had been seen in a skirmish with the enemy firing the rifle in one hand and a revolver in the other. The Italian prisoners later said that they thought he was firing some new form of light machine gun; such was the rapidity of his fire.

"I want you to post two lookouts at all times Kelvin. One hour relieving intervals. The bright light tricks the eyes. Better to change the guard regularly. Also, erect shade over each truck, make them look like a Bedouin camp site. It does anyway with the parked up camels but the trucks stand out."

"Sure thing, boss, how long do you reckon we will be here?"

"Hard to say. I guess we rely on the reply from Cairo. If we get an all clear, we're off like a drover's dog on a rabbit hunt. If not, we have prisoners to take back to base. Either way, I would say we will spend the night here so we may as well make ourselves comfortable."

The captain moved on and his sergeant set about organising the lookouts and the shade camouflage.

Mahmoud singled out Otto and took him aside for a confidential talk. "I expect us to be here until tomorrow. I was not allowed to despatch a messenger to ask for help from our base which we had hoped we would reach tonight. We do need some shelter for the night and our tents have been sent ahead with a fast convoy so I have released a carrier pigeon who will deliver the message to the base, which is his home base. We still use this system. It's foolproof. I expect a camel train to be here in about ninety minutes' time. There may be a problem, however. I have noticed that we are being watched." And he indicated to Otto with his head the direction from which the watching was being done. Otto looked into the distance but all he could see was desert, sand and dunes.

"You sure about this?" Otto asked.

"I'm sure." Mahmoud replied. "Now and again I get a glint, sun on steel which would be a rifle barrel or sun on glass, no doubt a telescope or binoculars. It's not unusual to be under surveillance. Generally, it means that we have something that they want. If the odds look good, then they will attack. If not, they generally disappear into the great wide beyond and seek mischief elsewhere."

Otto looked at the allied convoy. "They would be stupid to try anything with that mobile ammunition dump in our midst."

"Maybe they don't know what they are," Mahmoud said. "We are all a bit far south on this trip and these people may not be aware of the fire power available from those vehicles. I would say they are from the Sudan and we must seem like a ragtag bunch of traders. Foreigners to them, taking our wares to be sold at a market somewhere. We most probably seem easy pickings, but to me it still does not seem a big enough motive to have an all-out battle over. Anyway, just thought that I would let you know. Keep your team together and don't let them wander. Also keep your heads covered and try and look like an Arab. Taking foreigners for a ransom is also a happy payday for some wandering tribes. Fair headed maidens are a specialty. They command good prices in Khartoum. I will send another pigeon to warn the base. I have requested that they despatch an armed relief to ride with horses and catch up with the tent party that is on the way to us."

Otto mulled over Mahmoud's comments about foreigners and fair headed maidens; a description that captured the exact image of Brigette von Hapsberg. It didn't bear thinking about that she would ever fall into the hands of polygamous Muslims and their harems. Sold to the highest bidder at a Khartoum auction. Otto shuddered in revulsion and went in search of his ivory handled silver Luger pistol that Rommel had presented to him in Tunisia.

He instructed his team to cover up and look as Arab as possible. He found his pistol and filled the magazine then tucked it into the waistband of his pants. *If all else fails,* he thought to himself, *I have enough bullets to take us all out, if necessary.*

Sergeant Kelvin Ross found the captain talking with Mahmoud and motioned to him that he wanted to talk. "I reckon we got company, boss," Kelvin said when the captain had withdrawn from his conversation with Mahmoud and was out of earshot.

"Yes, Mahmoud was telling me the same."

"I reckon, boss, I could take my jeep on a bit of a recce and have a look-see"

"How's that, Sarg?"

"Well, I reckon they are laying over them hills, now if I went that way," and he indicated which way, "I can double back with the sun behind me, hard to see me coming out of the sun. I could get close enough for a bit of a look. See who it is, usual stuff, you know the drill."

"How long would it take you?"

"No more than an hour."

"Do it then, take a Bren gun use Barry, he's our best gunner, plenty of ammo and a grenade launcher. Should keep you out of trouble. Wireless me from the Jeep mobile as soon as you have something. I'll turn my transceiver on and wait. I'll have a standby there at all times."

"Roger, boss, be away in five, elapsed time sixty at most."

Captain Walker smiled. His sergeant was on cue as always. He walked back along the line of Chevrolets talking with the crew on the watch vehicles and telling them to keep their eyes alert for any signs of movement from their observers. The number four Chevrolet was firing up their 'Benghazi Burner' to boil water for a cup of tea and Captain Walker was given a cup of the hot brew and stayed and talked with the off duty men. All those not on watch were assembled for the ritual. Tea was a satisfying beverage and more so in a hot

127

climate. It promoted perspiration which was the body's way of lowering blood temperature. Apart from that it was a bloody refreshing tonic and a chance for a chinwag. It built team camaraderie, a word that none of them could spell but it surpassed any other synonym for the condition and so the word was used.

"I want a watch at my Jeep," he said, "waiting for Sergeant Ross to report in on the wireless. Two volunteers, thirty minutes each."

A show of hands indicated four eager privates. The captain pointed at two. "Okay, Frank first and then Tom. Thanks guys, let me know when he's on air. I guess we all want to know what he sees out there in the great sand pit!"

Mahmoud had sent off his second carrier pigeon. Nassar and Sons convoys had access to superior arms than most nomadic Bedouin tribes who were still using the old Martini-Henry rifles, which were a single shot breech loaded carbine. They were effective at 400 yards or less. Over that range the bullets went subsonic and tended to waver and tumble. Still lethal but not accurate. Nassar had the latest Lee-Enfields with the ten shot magazine, current British Army issue. They even ran to light sub-machine guns but Mahmoud was reluctant to use those especially in the presence of the New Zealand patrol who may ask some awkward questions. He mentioned this in his carrier pigeon despatch. Bring the Lee-Enfields and use as required but hold the light machine guns in reserve and use only if necessary. Keep them hidden and silent. Use only if absolutely necessary.

At the agreed time, Captain Walker returned to his Jeep to find Tom manning the wireless set headphones on and tweaking the frequency knob. There was a lot of static, probably from the atmospherics and Tom kept altering the band to allow for distortion. Then a voice was heard and Tom zeroed in.

"Sand Rover One to base, do you hear me? Over."

Tom pressed the transmission button.

"Base to Sand Rover One. I hear you loud and clear. Over."

"Roger base, I can see a large caravan parked up, I've counted eighty five camels and twenty horses. All the men are armed. Looks like the old Martini-Henry rifles. Nothing much happening. There seems to be some sort of forward observation post looking your way. Bit of horse traffic between there and the main body otherwise all quiet. Over."

"Kelvin this is Neil, are our mortars able to reach the position? Over."

"Yes, you could straddle them, fire short and fall in front and then long and go behind. Ideal for mortar fire they are about 300 feet higher in elevation, just behind a hill and about 1500 yards away. No good for Howizter fire. Over."

"Roger. Standby and I'll fire the first round behind them. Let me know where it lands. Over."

Kelvin heard the familiar mortar whoosh and then thump and saw a mound of sand explode about 100 yards behind the parked up camels.

"Sand Rover to base. 100 yards behind. Good shooting, now come forward by 300 yards and that should let them know you have their position. Over."

Whoosh-thump!

128

"Sand Rover to base. Perfect. They seem to have the picture, let's see what happens next. Over."

Kelvin watched the call to arms as the warriors from the camel train ran about brandishing their rifles. It was obvious that they considered themselves under attack as they advanced toward the knoll of the sand dune to observe Mahmoud's convoy going about their business in a normal manner. He could hear them calling in Arabic to each other and was not able to understand what it was they were saying but the tone sounded questioning and anxious. When they realised that an attack was not imminent, the voice traffic decreased and they settled into watching mode. A standard was raised and Kelvin noted the saffron, green and red tricolour. Mahmoud may understand the significance of the colours.

"Base to Sand Rover One. I'm coming up with a billy of tea and to have a look-see. I'll follow your tracks. Okay. Over."

"Roger base, stay on my tracks, you are well out of sight, you will be on higher ground but below ridge line. Over."

Captain Walker's Jeep arrived ten minutes later and dropped off the billy of hot tea. The captain surveyed the situation and left with a wave and a "Keep in touch."

As was normal in these conditions, Kelvin and Barry had rigged up a sun shade over the jeep. It was as much a sun shade as a camouflage tent. Knowing how to deal with the harsh desert environment was the key to creature comforts and they had lots of practice. Their tea was drunk in silence. Both mugs were heavily seasoned with sugar and condensed milk.

"Love a large glass of fresh farm milk right now," Barry said. "Lovely, creamy, white, frothy cow's milk." It was common practice among the patrol to relieve the tedium in the quiet moments by tormenting each other with the smells and tastes of home.

"Yeah well I can smell a venison stew cooking in a large pot over the fire in a mountain hut," Kelvin responded. "It's snowing outside, cold as an Antarctic summer and twice as blustery. Fire's roaring away and I'm just adding onions to the brew. Boy it sure smells delicious." Their reverie was interrupted by a single rifle shot.

Kelvin focused his binoculars on the Bedouins and saw one man on a horse with his rifle pointing toward the sky. He barked out some instructions and the entire caravan came alive as riders mounted both horse and camel and rode off across the desert in a southerly direction which was antipodal to the desert patrol and Mahmoud's position. Kelvin signalled the boss and got his orders to return.

They mentioned the coloured standard to Mahmoud who said, "That sounds like Suileman's men."

"Who's Suileman?" the captain asked.

"He's from the Sudan. A nomadic roque. Not adverse to a bit of mischief. Enjoys a skirmish but obviously has been warned away by those mortar rounds. The odds were not in his favour this time."

Mahmoud thought that it was a good time to let the captain know that he had a caravan arriving from base soon with tents and overnight supplies.

"And how were you able to let them know that these items were required?" Captain Walker asked Mahmoud. He had no sooner finished the question than the answer flashed through his head and he nodded in acknowledgement of his self-probing discovery.

"Carrier pigeon," he said, answering his own question.

Mahmoud nodded. "Yes, my friend, the old Sahara telegraph. Fly-by-wireless! As old as the sands of time. Maybe even older."

The camel train carrying tents and supplies arrived on schedule and thirty minutes later the armed patrol, mounted on horses rode in. There were just twenty warriors in the armed patrol but Captain Walker was impressed with their weaponry which would allow them to repel an attack from most desert rascals such as Suileman's men, with whom they had recently shared territorial sand at close proximity. Having established the security of Mahmoud's convoy, the warriors departed back to their base, but not before returning the two pigeons that Mahmoud had earlier despatched.

With the tents erected, the settlement took on a more relaxed atmosphere and the smell of the cooking fires and food permeated the ambient. Mahmoud explained to Captain Walker that true to Bedouin custom, and as welcome guests, the Long Range Desert Patrol would be fed by food from his fires.

Otto invited Captain Walker and Mahmoud to his tent for pre-dinner drinks. The ladies had refreshed with their daily sluice and they all sat around on comfortable cushions delicately sipping on their beverages. Captain Walker was a scotch drinker and Mahmoud stayed with the sherry that he had enjoyed back at Wadi Gin.

Captain Walker had obviously made some effort to appear presentable and wore his regulation officer's cap. He had on a clean shirt with captain's pips on the epaulettes and New Zealand shoulder flashes. He wore a pair of khaki shorts which bore evidence of creases that had been pressed into them following an historical laundering in the not too distant past and regulation boots and puttees. A Sam Browne belt with a pistol holster were appropriately attached. He cut a passable military figure but then he was a fighting man and not a parade ground pussy. And the desert was no place for spit and polish.

Otto made the introductions again, which were a lot less formal this time. Otto had previously done all of the talking, but now Brigette felt confident enough to chance her English.

"Tell me, Captain," she asked, "what is New Zealand like? I recall eating New Zealand lamb in London when I visited in 1936 and we found it agreeable."

"It's a staple food with us," he replied. "Our biggest export. With sheep the farmers get two clips of the ticket, they get the wool clip, literally, and then the meat. I am a sheep farmer and where I farm we have hot summers and cool winters. No snow, but it gets cold enough, for us anyway."

"And you have mountains, too, and glaciers, such a contrast?" Brigette offered.

"Yes, but not my scene."

"You don't see this scene – I do not understand!"

Captain Walker could see that his indigenous vernacular was not translating at all well for Brigette.

"I'm sorry," he said, "what I mean is that while we have those things, mountains and glaciers, they are not part of my lifestyle. I live in a part of the country that is more like rolling green pastures and gentle streams, whereas the sergeant is a mountain man. He is truly a mountain, snow and glacier person. Mountain climbing is his passion. I understand that he was due to attempt a climb on Mount Everest before the war intervened."

"I understand, a turn of phrase, we might say." Brigette responded. She then translated for the others.

For Captain Walker, this was the nearest he had been to European women for many months and he found the experience pleasant. It is easy to forget one's inhibitions, messing about with war and men and machines continuously. And so a gentle reminder that pleasantries together with the finer points of life, play an important part in the human psyche. To adorn the mind with fine thoughts is a good thing and for sure, the scotch tasted better. As a sheep farmer, Neil Walker had always enjoyed a good lifestyle. And while he ran the farm before he was conscripted into the army, his folks owned it and so they were wealthy people by the standards of the day.

The Kaisers and the von Hapsbergs were land owners and old German aristocrats and while the Weimar Republic had removed their titled ranks and privileges and declared them all equal under the law, it could not remove birthright. But it did remove wealth from a lot of the old aristocracy. Both the von Hapsbergs and Kaisers had transferred their monetary wealth to Switzerland, but their lands were not transferrable and as Otto had so vehemently declared, they would be confiscated by the Soviets who would defeat Hitler and his Nazi regime and Germany, or parts of it, would become Russian occupied.

What Neil Walker was most cognisant of from his hosts was their demeanour. *It was the breeding,* he thought, and he knew a thing or two about breeding from his sheep breeding programmes. His family had been breeding sheep for a long time and it was easy to pick up, with a practised eye the traits of progeny. Starting from an anatomic icon, the basic structure, and adding the ingredients. Protein with a genetic code, he called it. A chromosome arrangement – no genetic drift here. There would be no transporting of pollen to the species on the other side of the river. No seeds from weeds, on the wind. No polymorphic mongrel of a breed. All good aristocratic stock.

He had singled out the two valets and ladies' maids as being your everyday bog standard polymorphics, but with a streak of polish. They had not been introduced as anything other than members of the travelling party. At the end of

131

Neil's professional scrutiny under the powerful lens of his microscope, he had arrived at his conclusion. Nothing escaped the breeder's discerning eye.

Following an hour of social discourse and two generous servings of whisky, Neil excused himself to attend to dinner with his men.

Mahmoud also had other duties to perform and he too excused himself, adding that, "Dinner will be thirty minutes away," and exited the tent.

At around two o'clock in the morning, the radio truck's receiver burst into life as a stream of Morse code was being sent to them. The watch woke their specialist telegraphist who started making notes from the Morse code traffic that lasted five minutes. By the time Mike the telegraphist had transmitted his message received and understood signal, Captain Walker was at the radio truck and Mike was busy with his code book, translating the message into logic for the captain to read.

It made interesting reading indeed.

The message confirmed that the Swiss passports were kosher and the entire party were Swiss nationals who were originally and also quite lately resident in Germany. Otto Kaiser was head of the Kaiser Iron & SteelWorks in Dresden. British Intelligence had had them under surveillance for some years, especially when Kaiser bought interests in cotton mills and production facilities in Egypt and India; both British territories. It turned out that Otto was a field marshal in the German Army during the 1914–18 stoush. Following the armistice, the Weimar Republic that was formed to run Germany according to the Allies' rules, disassembled the aristocracy, annulled titles and subsequent privileges from those titles, thus creating a totally level social ground for all Germans. A good military strategist, (definition could be quite narrow) Otto had foreseen the demise of the Weimar Republic and the rise of fascism and started transferring his wealth to Switzerland. This included all of the Kaiser Empire's commercial trading, which was on an international level, as well as domestic. In so doing he also persuaded his good friends the von Hapsbergs to take similar precautions. The Kaiser Company undertook some large military contracts which included the casting and assembly of large field guns and also armoured cars. There were other top secret projects underway at the Kaiser works and so the German Intelligence Service were keen to locate Otto and his party before they became fully integrated into Cairo society, part of the British Empire. They were aware that the party had been reported missing from Tunisia but did not subscribe to the theory that they were kidnapped by some Bedouin tribe. Instead, they believed that the Germans were headed for Egypt which at that time was a British possession and unless Rommel won the desert conflict would remain so. Therefore, the Third Reich had placed a bounty on Otto's head of US$25,000 for the return of him dead or alive into German hands. The Long Range Desert Patrol was therefore ordered to stay with the Kaiser and von Hapsberg party and ensure their safe passage to Cairo, where they would be relieved of the mission. They were to report back to HQ on fuel, ammunition and food supplies required to complete the mission. If needed, an airdrop of supplies could be arranged.

The captain said, "Thanks Mike, we'll talk about it in the morning."

Captain Walker had a meeting with Mahmoud in the morning where he outlined his plans for a change in direction. Instead of heading for Wadi Haifa which was on the Sudan Egyptian border, he proposed to head for Kufra oasis in Southern Libya and then take a direct eastern route through Egypt, across the Gelf Kebir Plateau to Baris oasis and then Luxor on the Nile, whereas the previous Nassar commercial route would find them in Selima oasis in the Northern Sudan. It was Walker's intention to stay away from the Sudan, where he expected Suileman to have another attempt at the bounty offered by the axis for Otto Kaiser, dead or alive, having now realised what their recent light skirmish with Suileman the previous day was about. It still did not rule out the possibility of Suileman crossing from Sudan and into Egypt. The bounty money was a significant influence. It would enhance the status of his tribe considerably. Money was as valuable as water in a desert. The two men agreed that the camel train would make the rendezvous in the evening as scheduled, at Wadi Sheri. There, they would have to recruit a fresh camel train for the new route. Not being a mercantile venture changed the requirements according to Mahmoud.

Captain Walker consulted his maps. "Do you know that I cannot find any reference to Wadi Gin or Wadi Sheri on my maps."

Mahmoud smiled his all-knowing Bedouin, sand storm smile. That was when he gritted his teeth to stop the windblown sand from entering his mouth, but parted his lips. "That is most possible my dear captain. You see I have code named my depots after forbidden alcoholic drinks. Gin and sherry are the two we have on our current trade route. There are others, of course, but we will not use them on your new proposed course. Only my most trusted accomplices understand where I will be when I say that I will see them at Wadi Gin or some other of my coded way points. That is the upside of a good Oxford education. Imagination to an educated man is puzzlement to a simpleton. We have to keep ahead of the Suilemans in this world. They still live by the old code from which there is no antidote other than death."

Captain Walker regarded Mahmoud with renewed interest and knew that he was glad they were allies in this conflict.

The Long Range Desert Patrol were excited when Neil told them that they would be headed for Al Jawf oasis, Kufra. They were last there in March of 1941 when together with the free French forces they had relieved the Italians of their garrison and sent them packing back toward Tunisia. It had been a significant victory for the LRDP following fierce combat lasting over several days. They had lost one trooper killed in action.

"As for today, we are to break camp and escort Mahmoud's caravan to Wadi Sheri. Our ultimate destination is Luxor by the Nile, where we can all have a swim!" he said, knowing the value of the old carrot and donkey trick. A journey's hardships are endured because of the rewards offered at the final destination. A much admired proposition.

133

Wadi Sheri turned out to be one of Mahmoud Nassar's little gems in the desert of despair. The LRDG were experts in desert navigation but it was not on any of their maps. They were traversing unchartered sands known only to the desert dweller and then only a select few. The wells were plentiful and deep, supporting a modest permanent population, transient camel trains and the irrigation of surrounding fields of crops for the Nassar caravans and the locals. For the first time in two weeks Otto's party were able to be housed in permanent accommodation. Cool airy buildings constructed to hold the desert heat at bay and encourage a breeze should one be available. They had a bath with running water. Cold, of course, as one would prefer in a thirty plus degree Celsius ambient. This was to be home for the next four days at least and so it was to be enjoyed before they tackled the final 1800 mile push to Luxor which, depending on the conditions, could take a month.

Captain Walker and his troops were billeted in a large common barrack. There was an adjoining workshop where they could work on the vehicles and equipment which had to be in top condition for the rigours ahead. His men were fed by Nassar's people and they never went without. Uniforms were washed and dried and then pressed by folding the items neatly and placing beneath the mattress and the wooden bed slats. There was a common table where all ranks ate together and it was at this table that Captain Walker and his sergeant made up the list of supplies that they would need to get the party through to Luxor. All vehicles were put through the workshop and anything suspect was repaired. All arms were cleaned checked and oiled. All stores unpacked, counted and repacked aboard each vehicle. All ammunition was counted. Fuel storage tanks were counted. The water storage tanks were replenished. Food and medical stores were checked and at the end of day two a list of the contents from this stock take was given to the sergeant.

Neil was invited to Mahmoud's quarters one night to discuss the proposed route the caravan would take to Luxor. Neil had maps and Mahmoud marked waypoints on them, writing in neat print the names of the waypoints that he thought would make good stopovers during the journey. Neil was amused with a couple of the names that Mahmoud had pencilled in. Wadi-Ka was one and Wadi-Ker.

"I know that you have named these after alcoholic drinks but they are a bit too cryptic for me!" Neil offered.

Mahmoud chuckled. "Wadi-Ka is vodka, some Europeans pronounce the letter 'V' as a soft 'W' so you hear 'wodka' being pronounced. As for the other, the 'Ker' is the last syllable in Walker from Johnny Walker, so it has to be scotch. Talking of which, how about one, we've got the business end of the evening out of the way – so, fancy a nightcap?"

"Thanks Mahmoud, a scotch would be nice."

Mahmoud poured from a decanter already on the low table adjacent to the cushions they were sitting on.

134

"Single malt, Neil, I think you will like this one. We happen to be the importers of this brand for Egypt. Hard to get supplies because of the war but I have got my secret stashes around the place."

Neil thought to himself, *I wonder why I am not surprised by this statement?*

"Any thoughts about a departure date?" Neil asked.

"Any day suites me, I guess after they air in your supplies. Any idea when that might be?"

Neil sipped his scotch. "We have sent in the shopping list and expect a reply any time now. We'll need a day to stow them and then we are ready to go. Do you think that this Suileman fellow will give any further bother?"

"Hard to say. The bounty is an attractive offer and Suileman has had a taste of what he is up against. To have any modicum of success he would need to launch an offensive that would take us by surprise and have a superior terrain advantage. Other than that, he is wasting his time."

Neil looked at the map. "We are going considerably north of the Sudan Egypt border. He is out of his territory, so how can he find terrain to give his men an advantage, if he is on unfamiliar ground?"

"He could buy a scout who is familiar with the area." Mahmoud put his finger on the map. "This is the spot that I would pick!"

"Why?" Neil sounded a bit anxious.

"Well, it's like a pass, the trail winds through a canyon if you like, with high rock walls. If you hold the high ground and surprise the enemy passing through beneath you, they become sitting ducks providing you can hit them with sufficient firepower and they don't have that with the single shot Martini-Henry rifles, unless they have an overwhelming manpower situation and that is a bit of a longshot too. The more men that Suileman has means the more money he has to outlay. These are guns for hire. Mercenaries. If he still misses the bounty then he is, as you say, up the Swanee!"

Neil smiled at Mahmoud's colourful turn of phrase.

"What about an alternative route; bypass the canyon?" Neil asked the question.

"Yes, can do, but it means that we have to cover some terrible ground. Sandy deserts all around. Once again, if we get caught with the vehicles bogged down in the sand and come under attack from a mobile force we could be on the receiving end of a hiding. It is probably better if we are mobile and they are static. How about those mortars?"

Neil said, "Yes, we have those but if we can't see where the target is and we are moving and they are static it's hard to zero in. I assume that the pass is used by other caravans and if so well how does Suileman know which caravan to attack?"

"I assume that he would attack the caravan that has the trucks," Mahmoud replied.

"So how about we split up and let the camels go through a day earlier on their own? They could be any caravan passing along the trade route and then a day later the vehicles tackle it alone. Maybe we even try a night run, but that

135

can be dodgy if we don't know the road. Hate to hit a rock and puncture a tire with a hundred rifles firing at us. We can take care of ourselves, in fact what we can do is have a couple of our men go through with the camel run and see what they can spot. When they get to the other side they can radio us with their observations."

"What about the Swiss nationals?" Mahmoud asked.

"They can go through with the camels dressed as Bedouins, same as my men, be hard to spot a disguise from their hiding places. Once through, you just keep going and we can keep in touch by radio until we catch up with you. I have to assume that Suileman will expect that the prize, i.e Otto & Co will be protected by the mobile desert patrol so we are his target."

"Sounds like a plausible scheme," Mahmoud said. "The only thing Suileman has to guess is when and if we are going to make the transit."

"Another scotch?"

"Yes, thanks, Mahmoud, that is a nice drop."

"How far away is the pass?"

"Four days by camel."

"Okay, I'll run it past my team tomorrow," Neil said, "see if they can find any deadfalls. They are a canny bunch of fighters. Been in a few scraps now so we have a good collective planning committee."

Mahmoud agreed. "I'm glad we are on the same side!" he said.

"May I enquire what prompts that sentiment?" Neil asked.

"Certainly," Mahmoud grinned and raised his glass. "I much prefer scotch to schnapps!"

The airdrop was made two days later and the contents were counted and stowed away for the journey ahead. The surprise was a small artillery piece that could be towed behind one of the jeeps. It was noticed immediately by Otto who went over and lovingly ran his hand over the weapon. "Something I am familiar with," he said, "it fires at a very high trajectory, we used them a lot in WWI as they were good for trench warfare. Bit like a large mortar, if you like. Longer range, of course. I would imagine it would be handy here in the desert for lobbing projectiles over sand hills, beyond a mortar's range. Happy to give you my knowledge of the weapon. My factory used to produce a similar piece. We call them a Aufinez, but I believe the English word is Howitzer."

The soldiers cleaning the weapon said that they would tell the captain. While they expressed a concern about its usage, they agreed that some instruction on its finer points would be helpful. It came with a hundred rounds and they were wondering where they could stow them. Their vehicles were fully loaded with fresh stores and fuel. "We may have to get the boss to borrow a couple of camels for a few days," one of the men remarked to his mate.

"Yeah, especially the Jerry cans of fuel," came the reply.

A day out from the pass the caravan split up. Two soldiers dressed as Bedouins joined the camelcade. They carried a side arm and a light machine gun each and also a radio to keep in touch with base.

136

Otto's wife Anna and her maid Kirsten, Alfred's wife Claudia and her maid Gerda and the von Hapsbergs' daughter Brigitte went with the camelcade.

Otto and his valet Conrad and Alfred and his valet Marco, joined the mobile convoy. All the men were handy with firearms and Otto, of course, was to be the gunner should their new field piece be needed.

Mahmoud led his team away in the early morning and it was agreed that radio contact be made every four hours and then open during the transit of the pass that would take five hours. They would revert to four hour contact after the pass and until the convoy re-joined the caravan.

The following morning, Captain Walker in his jeep with Otto, led the motorised cavalcade into the desert and toward the pass. The four civilians had been issued with arms of their choice from the considerable arsenal that the desert group carried. Otto wore his ivory handled Luger that Rommel had presented him with and carried a Lee-Enfield rifle. It felt strange in his eyes, a former high ranking German officer carrying the British Army's standard issue rifle. But he had sighted it in and he liked it. Alfred, Marco and Conrad also favoured the Lee-Enfield. They were assigned vehicles and melded into the general background without standing out.

The suspense of transiting the pass seemed to make the time go quickly as they were focused on the task ahead. Every time they stopped they all checked their gear and went over the routine of coming under a sudden attack. The Swiss nationals were treated the same as the rest of the platoon and they fitted in to the procedures like professionals. The radio contacts were kept brief to conserve battery power and on the day of the transit of the pass by the camelcade, the radio truck ran directly behind Walker's jeep and so he was kept up with the news as it came through.

The transit of the pass by the camelcade was a bit of an anticlimax as they went through the area without any sign of being observed or sighting anything untoward that would cause them any alarm. Once through, they continued on their way for a couple of hours and made camp for the night.

At the same time, the motorised convoy was making camp at the other end of the pass and preparing for their transit the next day. The sergeant had made a recce in his Jeep into the pass for a couple of miles and returned with nothing untoward to report. Captain Walker ordered a dawn departure for the following morning and they all turned in with normal reports posted.

It was a dawn boil up of hot mugs of tea and they were into their transit with Neil and Otto taking the vanguard then three Chevrolets, the sergeant's Jeep with Alfred riding shotgun, then three more Chevrolets. Tailend Charlie, the last Chevie, was fitted with an aircraft cannon and could wreak havoc to an unsuspecting aggressor attempting to sneak up from behind.

In the canyon they travelled in the shade, the sun would penetrate the abyss for about an hour when at its zenith but for the majority of the day they travelled in relative comfort from the pervading desert heat. Neil thought that the sides of the canyon were too steep to launch an attack, as their assailants would have trouble accessing the floor from their lofty perches. In places, the walls were so steep that the convoy could shelter in the lee of the attack by driving along the foot of the bluff from which the assailants were shooting. They would literally have to fire vertically downwards, which is impossible to do with any degree of accuracy, if at all. Conversely, it would not be effective to return fire.

They ate rations on the move and the day wore on and the scenery changed from time to time. The lookouts were relieved regularly. The walls of the canyon widened and eventually the way ahead appeared to open up as they neared the end of the pass and would soon arrive in open desert. The canyon sides became less severe and Neil thought they were quite scalable by a man on foot but certainly not with horse or camel. The canyon walls were lessening in height and ahead they disappeared into the desert sands. This was when Otto said to Neil, "We have company ahead," and he handed his binoculars to the captain. Neil held up his hand and bought the convoy to a stop. He stood up on the floorpan of the jeep and surveyed the horizon and sure enough, he saw massed camels.

Otto said, "Allow me to speak, Captain. Our assailant obviously recognises his inability to win a fight within the confines of the canyon. Riding line abreast in the narrow valley would seriously reduce their already limited fire power and we could mow them down at will with our machine guns, like shooting fish in a barrel. They want to goad us into the open where, with a superior number of men, they will surround our little convoy and attack from all sides. I'll bet you that if you could see over that sand dune, behind the visible enemy, there will be a host more Bedouin warriors in hiding. His plan would be to lure us into the open, thinking that what we see is what we fight and when they have us in a vulnerable position, the hidden troops appear. I would also lay odds that he may have some of his hired thugs lurking in the canyon behind us eager to give us a gee-up if we are reluctant to move forward. My suggestion, Captain, if I may offer another, is to have your mountain man scale yonder rock-face and set up a forward observation post. It seems that Suileman has learned one lesson from our previous skirmish and so he stays beyond the reach of our mortars. But what he doesn't know is that we have a field gun that fires high projectile rockets that will fall very nicely behind the dune and give them all a hell of a fright. You could also set up a small mortar battery at the forward observation post. They will be able to see the exposed body of troops and being closer and higher could lob the bombs into their midst. As for our rear, Captain, may I propose that we lay some booby traps in the form of trip-wires to detonate dynamite that we conceal on the valley floor and in rock crevices. That should create a modicum of surprise and panic when combined with some sustained firing down the canyon walls, from the aeroplane cannon mounted on Tailend Charlie. Imagine the effects of those projectiles ricocheting, from side to side off the steep rock walls. If that doesn't get them running, nothing will. One must also surmise that Suileman has brought a bunch of mercenaries along to bolster his manpower. They will have been told that it is money for old rope – no danger. As soon as they recognise that there may be an imbalance of fire power between the two parties, they will value their skins and payment above the call of a desert grave, and – I would be happy to predict – fuck off at a fast camel trot. The pull of a cosy Bedouin tent with happy wives and good coffee outweighs, by far, paradise with a thousand virgins."

Captain Walker looked impressed with the suggestions from his travelling companion and told him so. He walked back to the sergeant's Jeep for a conference and the two of them set Otto's plan in motion.

They had four hours of daylight available to execute the plan. Kelvin the sergeant and a private whom everyone referred to as Cobber, with mortars strapped to their backs, scaled the rock face and then lowered a long rope to be used to haul up mortar rounds. Communications were to be made from the forward post to base by writing on a piece of paper and tying it to a rock dropped to the convoy below. The reciprocal arrangement was to tie notes onto the rope that could be retrieved from above. "Shouting is to be discouraged," Neil said, "as the canyon acts like a sound shell." It seemed that Kelvin and Cobber barely had time to reach their eyrie when a rock dropped to the canyon floor, wrapped in paper.

This was delivered to Captain Walker who read it out loud for Otto to hear.

"Assumption correct – large body of camels and men entrenched behind dune – we estimate eighty camels – compass heading use ninety five degrees and five hundred yards – we will fire mortar barrage when you send in the first round from the field gun – we estimate forward body to comprise of thirty camels – easier to count camels than heads – range two hundred yards ready when you are."

Neil scribbled "Roger. Good hunting," and asked the note to be returned to sender.

Otto had prepared the field piece and was given the co-ordinates from Kelvin's notes. He was allocated two privates who were familiar with gun drills and they waited for the command from Neil to start firing.

From their lofty perch, Kelvin and Cobber watched the opening round fall in the middle of the group hiding beyond the dune and then they set their two mortars to work on the forward band of Bedouin tribesmen.

Suileman was to be seen rallying the troops who were caught unawares. Camels were being mounted and on command were standing and then moving at a slow gait before increasing speed, urged on by concerned riders. Pylons of sand were churned up with each mortar round hitting the ground and exploding. The scene was chaotic and Suileman was desperately riding in circles, mounted on his horse and going around his fleeing army urging them to stay and fight. But at the moment they had other plans. The backup squad from over the dune was in similar disarray. Nobody had mentioned field artillery, they were told it would be rifle to rifle, man on man with Suileman's troops outnumbering their target by about eight to one, which were pretty good odds for the money that Suileman had offered them.

Suileman's troops in the canyon whose job it was to attack from the rear, upon hearing the sound of explosions, assumed attack was underway and so they came at full bore through the narrow gorge. They were well into the trap when the first trip wire set off a dynamite explosion. The aircraft cannon opened up with a terrifying hail of fire, ripping through the narrow gorge at a ferocious velocity. The charging tribesmen mounted on their camels realised that they were no match for the intended target and amid much shouting and confusion, reversed the animals and rode as fast as the camels could take them away from the murderous line of fire. The astonishing thing was that there were no casualties.

Mahmoud chuckled when Neil told him about the conflict two nights later. "About time that old fox was given a spanking," he said, "he was becoming too big for his boots. That should be the last we hear of him. He rarely ventures north of the border. This fright should keep him in the Sudan."

"I have no idea what casualties they sustained," Neil said, "we saw a few dead camels where our mortar rounds landed, but that was it. If I had refrigeration I could have brought some fresh meat for you."

Otto and Alfred could hardly contain themselves when reunited with the rest of the European party. Otto opened his best bottle of scotch and invited Neil, Kelvin and Mahmoud over to his tent for drinks followed by dinner. Mahmoud announced that they would be at Mut el-Kharab oasis in about three days and then Luxor on the Nile was a further 350 kilometres away. "So very close now, our little adventure seems to be coming to an end."

Anna Kaiser said, "Next time I cross a desert, it will be in an aeroplane."

Mahmoud was able to provide some good news. "The ride gets better from the oasis, we have a desert road to Luxor so we will all be in a vehicle. We say goodbye to the camels and hello automobile. That should be more to your liking?"

Cairo seemed a bit of an anti-climax following the desert run.

Chapter 10

Judge Collins

Judge Collins looked at his watch. It told him that the time was eleven o'clock in the morning. Court was due to resume at two o'clock in the afternoon and so he had three hours until his official duties resumed. He buzzed his secretary who came promptly with a notepad and pen ready to take shorthand notes.

"No Josephine," he said, "there is no dictation, what I would like to know is, do I have any appointments in my diary between now and when court resumes at two o'clock this afternoon?"

"Nothing in the diary," she replied, "I checked when you buzzed, just in case."

"Well that's good, please take messages and tell callers that I will phone them back tomorrow if it is a problem that you are unable to deal with."

"You will be back for the resumption of court at two?"

"Yes I will be here."

Josephine left the office and the judge opened a drawer on the side of his desk and took out a sampler box that contained four tablets. It was a new drug that he was trialling for erectile dysfunction and his good friend Doc Gordon had given them to him one evening over drinks at the club.

"James," he said, "ever seen these things?"

The judge picked up the box that his doctor friend had offered to him and he read from the label. "'Eredys.' What the hell do I want with these things anyway, what the hell do they do?" He didn't know if he should act hurt or surprised but inside he felt pleased. The word around the traps was that some of the local GPs were trialling a drug which they had collectively developed from generic drugs available on the open market. The new drug was a godsend, they said it could straighten out a crop of bananas with impunity. The judge decided he should look a little miffed even though he was about to ask his own GP if he could try a dosage.

"What on earth do you think I would need this stuff for?" he heard himself ask.

The doctor chuckled and said, "I have no doubt that you are functioning just fine in that department, but a few of my colleagues got together to talk about it one night over a few beers at the club and it seems that we all have patients on our books with the same problem. Erectile dysfunction is what we call it, that's the clinical reference. We know that the drug companies are experimenting with this problem now. It's in our medical journals. Well, some of us decided to carry out our own trials. We know what's in the pills; it is fairly innocuous over-the-counter stuff anyway, so we just went ahead and pulled in a pharmacy colleague, they have pill making gear, we mixed up a batch and made the pills and now we are trialling it. I've tried it and it works, no side effects. No different than taking aspirin except you have to swallow it quickly in case you get a stiff neck."

The judge looked at his friend strangely.

"It's a joke – 'stiff neck' – get it?"

"Of course," James grinned, "yes, a joke. Very funny indeed!"

"Right then, I take it you'll want to give it a go, all in the name of medical science you understand."

"Sure, I understand," the judge replied, "be happy to help medical science."

That was two weeks ago and the judge couldn't wait to try them out. He had phoned Maximes Palace and booked an appointment with one of his favourite girls there. "Eleven thirty," he had said, "I'll be there at eleven thirty on the dot. Don't keep me waiting; I'm on a tight schedule."

The judge swallowed a pill at ten minutes after eleven and left his office. He walked out into the street and hailed a cab. He preferred to hail a cab rather than book one from the office, to preserve anonymity. He instructed the driver to drive down the side of the hotel and into the carpark at the rear of the building. The judge paid the cabbie and climbed the stairs to the palace entrance where he rang the bell and waited.

The security camera announced his arrival on the monitor in Kaetrin's office, she pressed a button and the entrance door opened and the judge walked into a warm reception from Felicity who was always friendly and pleased to see one of her regulars.

Although he knew the way, Felicity put her arm under his and gently steered him along the plush carpeted hallway to her room. When he got this far, the judge was usually a trembling, excited man, but today he felt anxious and wondered if he should take another tablet. He asked Felicity for a glass of water and swallowed a second pill, some forty minutes after taking the first one.

Felicity looked puzzled; generally the judge came on fairly strongly. "Are you feeling alright, Jim?" She asked him. He liked her calling him by his first name. It felt intimate. On formal occasions it was James, but for intimate contact Jim was the preferred pseudonym.

142

The judge was seated in a comfortable chair and paused slightly before replying. "Well I am due back in court at two o'clock, but I am trying not to let this time restriction play on me. I thought that we would have plenty of time to –"his voice trailed off, "– you know – do the business."

"Just relax and let me get to work on you," Felicity purred as she loosened his tie and took off his shoes. "We will have you on the job in no time."

At twelve thirty, the judge swallowed yet another tablet and left the palace at twenty minutes past one a very disappointed man. Because there was some time left, the judge walked back to his office at the district court building, determined to enjoy at least some of his break.

He was robed up and getting ready to enter the courtroom when there was a knock on his door. "Come in." He called and the door opened. A court secretarial intern walked in with a file in her arm.

"The registrar sent me up with this file, said that you should take it into court with you."

The judge was seated at his desk and the intern came and stood at the edge of his desk facing him. She must have been one from the recent intake of interns as he had not seen her before. She was a tall girl and had very long legs accentuated by a short straight grey skirt and matching body contoured jacket.

"Thank you," he nodded as she placed the file on the edge of the desk, turned and walked from the room. The judge could not take his eyes from off of her very shapely posterior and very long legs with slim ankles riding on patent leather, black shiny high heel shoes. He felt a rousing spasm in his groin and as he rose up from his chair, he realised that he was getting an erection. The cloth of his tailor-made trousers was restricting the growth from within and he was uncomfortable and found walking difficult and painful. He tried some adjustments and his breath was coming in short gasps.

The clerk of the court announced that the court would rise as the judge entered and as they rose, so did the judge's penis. There seemed no end to his out-of-control member's behaviour. The pain was excruciating and the judge was committed to his entry. He found it almost impossible to walk without somehow relieving the pressure from the expanding monster within his pants and even though the folds of his robe hid the disfigurement from the court, he was not able to put his hand down his pants to try and make some adjustments that just might ease the situation. All he could do to lessen the pressure on his distended organ and the cloth restricting its movement was to extend his backside and sort of sidle along, resembling the walking gait of a crab.

In this manner and with the court looking on incredulously, Judge Collins made the bench and attempted to sit down. Muscle and sinew grappled with the natural wool fibres of his tailored pants and true to the tailor's prophesy that the stitching would restrain a bull run at a red flag, it didn't budge. The workmanship was superb, an irony not lost on the Judge.

It became obvious that further adjustments would be necessary to maintain some relief to his extreme discomfort and also to prevent injury. It was not possible for these to be undertaken in the courtroom and so a distressed judge declared a short recess while he attended to an unexpected personal matter. The court rose and the judge sidled, crablike, back to his chambers.

Chapter 11

James Peroux

Flora was settling in nicely after Kaetrin and Linus had departed for the UK. Leslie had stayed on at the hotel was a good manager and their staff were loyal and capable. Bravo was now ten years old and he lived with his mother in an apartment that Flora had made available to her when her child was born. Marjory Beresford-Amble had been instrumental in ensuring that Leslie and her baby would enter society on the right side of the sheets. It was well documented in the best of tea circles that Leslie and her late husband, Radio Officer Doug Thornton, were married by the ship's captain prior to the *Rangitane* sailing for London and disaster. Flora had never relinquished the reins at Maximes but she did rely a lot on Kaetrin and Leslie to manage the day to day business that a busy hotel generates. Above all else, Flora's morning task was as it had always been; to open the mail. Mail was the barometer of any business enterprise. An owner would avoid mail at their peril. Incoming accounts were especially revealing. Flora knew from a glance what the butcher's or grocer's bills for a month's supplies should be. Spikes would be noted and examined and verified. Similarly, a downward trend in purchases would indicate that there had been a fall-off in business. Again, Flora would make a note to check it out with her staff. Same with the liquor suppliers. It was all very simple. One just had to keep one's finger on the pulse. The accountants handled the final percentages but Flora did the mind graphs, the peaks and troughs and could pick a profit or loss with her mental arithmetic. Correspondence was a favourite. There were a lot of begging letters from charities; organisations who railed against the consumption of alcohol but were more than pleased to accept donations from the proceeds of its sale. Red Cross were a regular and Flora obliged them with her donations. She was reminded of the visit to Wellington in 1943 by Elenor Roosevelt who was promoting the organisation and urging all women to champion the cause 'For our boys at war'. That was another life-time away, but the causes were omnipresent. It was the Red Cross that got Kaetrin's letters to Jimmy the heartmelt in the prisoner of war camp in Germany and he was able to reciprocate using the same organisation's channels. Today there were other causes and their bona-fides, Flora reasoned, that were championed by top pedigrees.

She picked up an airmail letter. Airmail letters always came from overseas. They were comprised of lightweight flimsy writing paper and envelopes almost like a cigarette paper, but a bit more robust. They invariably arrived wrinkled, like a well sat in linen suit on a long train journey. Flora saw that it had a USA stamp and wondered who would write to her from there. She was aware of relatives from Scotland who had settled in North America. Flipping the envelope over she read that the sender was a Mrs Reynolds. The post mark was New Hampshire.

"Dear Mrs MacLeod," she read on opening the letter.

"My name is Mary Reynolds and I am the sister of James Peroux. I am aware that James had not replied to your letters and I feel that you deserve an answer. James was wounded at the battle of Saipan. He was invalided home as a double amputee having had both of his legs destroyed by a land mine. The trauma was simply too much for him and he was institutionalised for some time. When he was able to cope we gave him your letters but he refused to answer them. Initially he never wanted to read them and when he did read them he was unable to reply. His psychiatrist believes that he wants to reply but he feels that he is not willing to seek pity which he feels is what people do when they see his disability. He feels that regardless of how you feel that you will, out of compassion, want to look after him and he is not wanting to throw himself at anyone's mercy for such a pitiable outcome. He is not a cripple and can walk perfectly well on his prosthetic limbs. Stubbornness and pride are probably the two biggest obstacles that he has to overcome. I thought that you deserved an answer to your dilemma, as I know from my conversations with James that you both had deep feelings for one another. If you feel that I am interfering, then please disregard this letter. Otherwise let me know your situation as I would dearly love to help you and James see each other again.

Yours Sincerely,
Mary Reynolds"

Flora read the letter a couple of times and waited for her feelings to kick in. It was a long time since they had said their goodbyes back in 1943. It was now 1950 and the world had moved on. Flora had certainly moved on. Her life was good. She had a nice family in Kaetrin and Robert and lovely friends. The hotel was going well. She wanted for nothing. Her memories of the romantic times with James were still active and cherished but she had suppressed them, not having received responses to her letters. It was left to her imagination to try and decide what had happed to James Peroux when he had departed Wellington with the Second Marines for Tarawa and beyond. Her sentiments were scrambled. It was too early for her favourite dram, the very one she would share with James every day when he was at Maximes with the general staff of the Marine Corps. Marjory Beresford-Amble, the nearest thing she had to an

146

agony aunt, was away overseas. Flora put the letter down and finished opening the mail.

Just for no reason she put on a hat and coat. It was bit chilly outside and she went for a walk up Cuba Street then turned right into Manners Street. And again, for just no reason, she stopped at the window of the travel agent that Kaetrin and Linus had used to book their trip to the UK and looked at the visual displays. Travel agents always had spectacular visual displays. If you were not planning a holiday when you stopped to look in the window, you were persuaded that it would be a wonderful experience after taking in the seduction of dramatic scenery in bright colours displaying old castles in Europe or tropical beaches in Fiji. Kaetrin was seduced and enquired how one got to New Hampshire in the United States. She didn't think that sea travel would be an option as it would take too long.

It was all very straight forward.

"You travel by flying boat from Auckland to Fiji then transfer to a land based aircraft and fly to San Francisco. Then over to the East Coast. Be there in five days," the travel agent said. "If you want me to work up an itinerary and pricing for you I would be happy do so, Mrs…?"

"MacLeod," Flora said, "I live just around the corner. You can deliver it to Maximes Hotel. Leave it at the front office. If I go it will be soon. Like this month!"

"Sure thing, Mrs MacLeod, we will have a letter dropped off tomorrow."

Flora left the travel agents and kept walking along Manners Street. She walked aimlessly and before she realised it had arrived at the Majestic Theatre and the Majestic Cabaret where her and James had such a memorable evening at the Second Marines Ball back in 1942. It was a long time ago but could have been last night, the images were so clear. She looked up Willis Street and saw the St George Hotel where they had held the after-ball function. Flora then retraced their steps back home to Maximes. Her and James had traversed this very pavement eight years ago. The same flagstones and kerbing. Their footsteps echoing in the empty streets in the early morning hours. Happy and gay as they made their way back to Maximes and bed. Flora arrived at the hotel without realising it. The revolving door entranceway woke her from her reverie and she entered the foyer, treading firmly on the tiled floor.

The next day in her office, she surveyed the itinerary the travel agent had dropped off. Flying was expensive was her first reaction, but then it was quick; she could be there and back and spend ten days at least in New Hampshire before she could ever reach the same destination on a sea voyage. She had to do it. For both their sakes!

Flora wired Mary Reynolds telling her of her intentions giving an estimated time of arrival and requesting that Mary book her accommodation close to the sanatorium that James was at. Post and telegraph delivered her a reply the following morning.

"All arranged STOP Meet you at the airport-Manchester/Boston STOP You can stay with me STOP letter with more detail following STOP Mary"

147

Flora booked her air fares and then told Leslie of her intentions. Leslie was delighted. "You go!" she said. "I can hold the fort. I have ten years' experience under my belt now at Maximes. This is something you must do because if you don't you will bring a hell of a lot of recriminations against yourself for the rest of your life."

Flora looked at Leslie.

"Does that make sense?" Leslie asked.

"I know what you mean," Flora said. "I will beat myself up!"

"Exactly," Leslie confirmed, "I would probably have to find another job – life would be so miserable around here!"

Flora laughed. "Thank you Leslie, I needed to hear that!"

Flora flew to Fiji in a flying boat. They took off from Mechanics Bay in Auckland and landed several hours later in a lagoon in Suva Fiji. To connect with the flight to San Francisco, she had to transfer from Laucala Bay in Suva to Nandi Airport to catch the land-based planes that would fly directly to San Francisco. Flora had never been in a plane before so the total experience was at the same time terrifying and exhilarating. Then it was east across North America to Chicago and then New York before boarding a much smaller shuttle service to Manchester/Boston airport that serviced New Hampshire. Mary Reynolds met her at the airport. Mary had no trouble identifying the red headed Mrs MacLeod from photographs that her brother had shown her. Mary lived alone in a large brick Georgian styled house of ample proportions. Her children, she explained, were away at college. Her husband was another war victim. He was killed during the D-Day landings in Normandy. It seemed, just as in the commonwealth countries, war deaths had touched most communities.

Following on from her first letter, Mary had sent a further detailed letter to Flora explaining the situation as best she could. James had made considerable progress in the past three years and they were wanting to discharge him from institutional care as they felt that he was fully operational and he had only to decide when and where he wanted to live. They had discussed this and Mary said, "He does not want to live in a climate where he has to contend with snowfall at winter time. He was thinking of California where they trained before shipping out to New Zealand. The Marines have a good support group for their veterans all over so that doesn't matter too much. When I told him you were coming he said good! So it's all positive. The psychiatrists are hopeful that he has accepted his fate and will rehabilitate just fine. As I mentioned in my first letter to you, he was a very bitter person for a long time. No one can say what has prompted the change. Maybe it was time. Healing takes time. Some people can take longer than others but time is an important factor and I am a graduate of that condition."

Flora listened politely but was tired from her extensive travels having gone through several time zones to arrive here in New England. Mary saw her predicament and apologised for keeping her away from some well-earned sleep.

"We'll go visit tomorrow morning, I will drop you off in the morning and you can have the day together. I'm sure there is a lot to talk about." Flora was asleep within two minutes of her head touching the pillow.

Flora had a twelve hour sleep and woke refreshed. Walking downstairs she could smell coffee. Mary was obviously up and about. She enjoyed the luxury of being late to rise. At home the first stirrer was Flora, so she savoured the moment. It was a late summer, sunny morning and the oaks were clad in their generous green livery. Flora could see the scene out of the windows. It was a leafy and an attractive suburb.

Mary enquired, "Coffee?" and Flora confirmed. They both sat at the breakfast table.

"Sleep well?" Mary asked.

"Like a log, thanks."

"You've been travelling for what, five days?"

"Yes, about that, I seem to have lost all sense of time, but I feel that I may have caught up with the sleep-awake pattern thing. Maybe I'll fall asleep at lunch, who knows. For now, I feel fine. When do we leave for the sanatorium?"

"About an hour. Is that okay?"

"Time for a shower-hair-make-up!" Flora was doing some sums. She thought, *I'm not arriving looking like a wreck. Both James and I presented ourselves decently – what's changed?*

"I'm going to need two hours," Flora said.

"I understand," Mary replied, "you take as long as you want."

The drive from Mary's house took just ten minutes and they were walking from the carpark to the main building when the figure of a man appeared. He used a walking stick and had a slight limp but other than that his gait was normal. He waved and Flora waved back at James Peroux. They both increased their pace and soon they were embracing. There was laughter and then there were tears and then laughter again and then excited talk. Mary held back. This was the most animated James had appeared in years and she wondered why she had not written to Flora earlier. Maybe this was the right moment. Earlier may not have been good. Now was good. Mary concluded that she had gotten her timing spot on.

Eventually, they pulled apart, still holding hands and James acknowledged his sister and said, "Thanks, sis! Let's go inside and sit in the lounge, I could do with a drink!"

They kept up the incessant chatter, walking hand in hand and James made them all a coffee in the lounge. Mary had a few goodies that she placed on the table for James. "I'll leave you two love birds alone," she said. "Be back later – much later." She left.

They ate lunch in the cafeteria and then spent the afternoon in the garden beneath spreading oak trees that provided shelter from the sun and were home to copious squirrels who entertained them with their acrobatics. Flora commented on the sanatorium, saying what a nice place it was and James agreed.

149

"Not just a laughing academy," he said.

Flora looked puzzled. "What," she replied, "is a laughing academy?"

James looked a little bemused. "It's a mental hospital – asylum – looney bin!" He rattled off a few pseudonyms.

Flora didn't flinch. "Oh I see," she said, "I had no idea what you meant when you said laughing academy."

"But you do know looney bin?"

"Yes we use the same derogatory description. It's sort of not normal!"

"Normal!" James said. "What's normal? War makes evil look normal," then he laughed. "We talk about it here because it's what those on the outside refer to it as, so we have to be able to cope with that sort of thing. I'm okay with that now as I am with a lot of things that had been bothering me!"

Flora nodded. "I can talk about it with you too," she said. "I am happy to enter into any discussion with you that you want to have with me. I would like to have been there for you when you were first hurt. We could have saved a lot of anguish!"

"I can see that now, it would have been good but there was a war on and we were miles apart and there was no way that you could have crossed those miles and I had no right to ask you to do that either. Had they shipped me back to New Zealand, that would have happened; we would have been together, but they didn't do that. They sent me back to Hawaii and then stateside. Silverstream Hospital in Upper Hutt was by far preferable to me. My favourite supply sergeant who got me that case of scotch had his main depot there too. Can you imagine? You and I could have had sundowners on the veranda at Silverstream Hospital every night. Now that would have been something!"

"Yes and the major and Marjory, you remember the Beresford-Ambles, could have joined us. They lived nearby the Trentham Army Barracks, which is where Horace worked. It's very close to Silverstream."

"Yes I remember them; a lovely couple. Are they still in circulation?"

"Very much so. They have decided to retire in New Zealand. Gone back to England to tie up some loose ends and then they will be back."

James looked at Flora. It was a look that Flora last saw on his face when he left New Zealand for the fighting at Tarawa Atoll. It was a what now look. What do we do now?

Flora took the initiative, which she could now, but not back then. The war was bigger than both of them, but now they were in charge. The war had finished but they were not finished.

"Remember the chateau?" she asked James.

He looked at her and smiled. "Never forgotten it," he said softly and reached for her hand. "That was such a romantic night. I can still smell the pine logs burning on the open fire in the lounge. It permeated the whole of the downstairs area, wafting into the dining room even."

"Would you like to go back there?"

"Oh hell yes, more than anywhere!"

"Well you shall!"

"And just how will I do that?" James looked at Flora.

"Well I suggest that you come back with me and you can have your old room in the hotel back and we take it from where we left off!"

"Hell yes, that is what I always wanted."

"Then let's do it!" Flora sounded adamant.

"Yes, let's do it!" James agreed. "This is what I would call a mink lined foxhole and I haven't been in one of them for many a long day."

They spent the next day sorting out the paperwork with the institution. James had been ready to leave for some time, but he didn't want to stay with his sister Mary and he had not sorted out any alternative solutions. He was working on it. This was not the colonel who solved the regiments' problems during WWII. James was a different man; he needed to regain his confidence and Flora was just the person who knew how these things worked. He would be in transit with Flora for the next two weeks and thereafter his address was Maximes Hotel.

"Where's that, Colonel?"

"Ask General Winslow," James said, "he was a resident there in 1942–43 when I was his chief of staff. If you can't find the general, it's Wellington, New Zealand of course!"

"Sure, Colonel, and good luck!"

They stayed at Mary's for two nights while Flora made travel plans.

It was an interesting time for Flora, as the reticent James was forced to concede some childhood secrets following good natured sibling banter between James and Mary.

Flora learned that their father was a French Canadian. "Montreal's just across the river," Mary said, "we are close to Quebec." Their mother was a Scots immigrant from Nova Scotia, again, "Not too far away, in nearby Canada." Border travel was less restrictive back in the day and their two Canadian parents met in New York where both James and Mary were born. Their father owned a construction company and by all accounts they were never wanting for money. Their mother taught piano and had briefly been a concert pianist and played in various orchestras. Both had a good education and James was a West Point graduate and became a professional soldier, which in peacetime was barely tolerable, but he survived on a diet of minor skirmishes and sea duty on battle wagons and postings to foreign climes. Mary still lectured in botany at the local university and neither appeared to want for money. It was never mentioned, but Flora suspected that they both received an inheritance from their parents' estate when they died several years ago. It was tacitly concluded that James had never been married, other than to the Marine Corps.

All of James' possessions were able to be contained within two medium sized suitcases. "I was a professional soldier," he said. "All I needed were uniforms. I had some civvy clothes too, but not many. All victualling and accommodation was supplied. The corps looked after their professional soldiers!"

James did not use a wheelchair. He was proficient on the use of his 'wooden legs' as he preferred to call the prosthetics. He had crutches and a walking stick. His legs were removed for bed and night time toilet excursions were noisy affairs, using the aid of crutches only and balancing on one stump. For convenience, James slept downstairs next to an adjacent toilet while Mary and Flora used upstairs bedrooms.

The travel agents assured Flora that all Mr Peroux needed for entry into New Zealand was a current passport. Mary drove them to the airport and they were on their way. The only variance to the return journey was that Flora had booked them into a resort in Fiji for five nights. They had their own private pool which they enjoyed and James was able to swim sans prosthetics. Flora could see that the amputations were both below the knee which was probably why James could walk unaided. In time she knew they would talk intimately about that, but she never pushed the issue and they got along the same as back in the war years.

The flying boat in particular impressed James, who said that they used similar planes in the Pacific war. "Smaller," he said, "they were a lot smaller, but boy were they great and could those pilots fly them! Catalinas," he said, "that was what they were called; Catalinas."

They took the overnight train from Auckland to Wellington. "Acclimatisation," Flora explained. She woke James at Waiouru so they could look out of the window and into the alpine darkness and see snow falling on the volcanic plateau. "The chateau is close-by," Flora whispered.

James said, "I know." It was warm and cosy in their sleeper unit.

At Wellington Railway Station, they forwarded their luggage onto the hotel in a taxicab and walked along Lambton Quay, then right into Willis Street where they passed the Majestic Cabaret, and up to the St George Hotel then along Manners Street with James identifying the landmarks and welcoming them like long lost companions. They stopped for a soda at the Kiwi Milkbar and played the juke box then walked onto Cuba Street where they turned left to arrive at Maximes Hotel.

"You've done alterations," James commented.

"A little facelift," Flora replied. "The Second Marines wore out the carpet beating a path to our espresso coffee maker!"

James smiled, "Aagh yes, the famous espresso, courtesy of supply Sergeant Widowski. Bless his soul."

"And how is the Sergeant – do you know what happened to him, after the war?" Flora enquired.

"I do, he's the richest man in Florida!"

"He is?"

"Sure he is – owns a resort, frequented by the rich and famous."

"We should holiday there some time." Flora said with a smile.

"Yeah, yeah… we're rich and famous!"

"You really do mean rich and famous don't you, not just a figure of speech?"

"Yes my dear, he charges for the very air that you breathe. The faucets are gold plated and the bed linen was made in Ireland by hand, by Christ!"

"My God!"

"Exactly!"

"Oh well, welcome to Maximes in that case," Flora said and they kissed in the foyer.

Their embrace was greeted by loud applause from assembled staff whom Leslie had mustered to welcome back the boss and, of course, James. They had discreetly placed themselves and emerged into the foyer on Leslie's signal. A 'Welcome home Flora and James', banner had been erected above the elevators in the foyer and the homecoming was super sweet for them both.

It did not take the American Embassy in Wellington long to realise that they had a war hero residing in the capital city. Flora had no inkling of Colonel Peroux's actions during the battle of Tarawa Atoll or on Saipan in the Marianas. She was as surprised as James was to read about his exploits in the *Evening Post*, the city's daily evening newspaper. Who leaked the information, nobody would say, but the story featured a photograph of Colonel James Peroux being presented with the Medal of Honor by President Hoover in 1946, while in hospital on the mainland, in the USA. The article went on to explain that Colonel Peroux had placed his own life in jeopardy while protecting his boss, General Winslow, while they were on a reconnaissance visit to a strategic position during the battle of Saipan, at a place called Purple Heart Ridge, so-called because of the extreme list of casualties inflicted by the Japanese soldiers in their attempt to defend the island which had been in Japanese possession since 1920. The general wanted to review his tactics in the best interests of his men and so was requiring a hands-on approach in order to save lives. Cognisant of Japanese booby traps, the gallant colonel took the vanguard position in the general's party saying, "Follow me, General, if it's safe for me then it will be safe for you," and he stood on not one, but two, landmines that robbed him of both feet. In so doing, he saved his general and staff from possible life threatening injuries but subsequently placed his own life in jeopardy, thus earning him the highest award for gallantry. No stranger to gallantry, Colonel Peroux had also earned the Navy Cross on Tarawa, so the article revealed.

Flora was shown the piece by Leslie and they were both dumbstruck. Nobody, least of all the man himself, had spoken a word about this to them. When confronted, he was a little agitated and said that it was no one's business but his own.

"If any newspaper reporters come sniffing around," he said, "show them the door. It is obvious that some clerk at the embassy has leaked this information." And he stuck his jaw out at a defiant angle to emphasize his opinion.

Flora knew that that was the end of the matter. James was a doer. Having done it, it was over and as far as James was concerned, *End of story!* Leslie, on the other hand, thought that James should be cognisant of his hero status. Her thoughts were probably championed by the fact that Doug Thornton, her late 'husband' was killed in action doing valuable work for his captain in the radio shack aboard his stricken ship. There was no official recognition given for his deeds, but then the Merchant Marine were not military; it was a civilian organisation. Leslie reasoned that heroism was heroism regardless, whether it was of military or civilian status. Indeed, the shell that killed Doug Thornton was fired by Kreigsmarine gunners on the German raider. A military gun on a merchantman!

"But we are so proud of you," Leslie blurted out.

"Well I'm not so proud of me," James said. "Damn foolish thing to do. Man coulda got himself killed and others too!"

Flora could see where this might go and she was beginning to comprehend the hero's dilemma. James was annoyed with himself for recklessly ignoring his own life and at the same time showing a total disregard for the feelings of others. He wasn't married to the Marine Corps and if for once he could have placed other people ahead of his own impulses he might be married to Flora. He had totally disregarded Flora's feelings for him and done something stupid, something that a thinking man would have avoided. The general's staff could have sent a couple of infantrymen with mine clearing and booby trap clearing experience to clear the way ahead and not rely on some colonel bigshot, with a Navy Cross for gallantry, to add to his string of awards. It was clear to Flora now what had been eating away at James these past few years. All he could offer his lover was a cripple. Not a man. The medals were mere decorations and represented stumps, not gallantry. Stupidity even. Such sweet propinquity to insanity. Flora had never seen the medals. They were not amongst his luggage. She suspected he had thrown them away. A symbolic gesture to love and delirium.

Leslie was not going to be robbed of her association with a hero and so exasperated Flora that she earned herself a sharp rebuke. This was totally out of character as the two women were very close friends but Flora was not about to let Leslie upset James. Fortunately, at that point in time, the telephone rang and Flora barked at Leslie. "Get back to the office and answer that phone!"

In a later quiet moment alone, Flora explained to Leslie her theory about her reluctant hero. "He's put it behind him, now we must do the same. The subject is taboo. If you do see any newspaper people snooping about, tell them that they are not welcome. Unless they have a legitimate reason for being here, invite them to leave. If they get a bit stroppy and start to go on about the truth and public interest and any other claptrap that they often wield to justify breathing air in the same space as real people, call me. I have a few moves of my own that will turn the graphite in their pencils to granite. If that fails, I can phone the editor who was a patron of our first floor establishment for many a year until we closed. He knows the distinction between the sword and the pen. He was a superb swordsman in his day; made the Olympic Fencing team in 1936. Wields a very sharp dart as far as his subordinates are concerned."

Leslie apologised for overstepping the line. "I got excited about the hero status. It would have been nice if Doug was recognised in some way. Survivors are on record as saying how the radio officer got his messages away despite the Germans' insistence to cease communications. Maybe one day he will be recognised."

Flora agreed. "You know," she said, "the Merchant Service lost more people than any of the other services during WWII. They are the forgotten service. But we know the score," she said to Leslie, "and that is what matters."

"Yes it does," Leslie replied. "I just wish that I had something to show Bravo and to say to him: your daddy earned this decoration for bravery!"

Flora got her point. "I see what you mean. I have to agree with you."

Flora made a mental note to contact her friends in the Seamans' Union to see what they knew about decorations for Merchant Seamen. It would be nice to do something for Leslie and especially Bravo, who never knew his father.

Apart from the newspaper incident, James settled into life at Maximes as if he had never been away. He noticed changes and the first obvious one was the first floor. It was previously home for a number of accommodating young ladies.

"When the war ended," Flora explained, "most of them had found love with servicemen and some of them were Marines, so they wanted out. I simply bought the apartments back from them as they became available and turned the floor back into hotel apartments. Mind you, I had been visited by 'Fairy Godparent' groups. Organisations that were previously occupied with wartime activities – knitting socks and the likes – for the troops. But prior to that the depression years, they had occupied their altruistic tendencies. As soon as our men returned from overseas they seemed to want to kill off any distractions that could persuade the boys to have a night out or run some shore leave while mum wasn't looking. You can well imagine the soldiers, who having experienced night life in Cairo and then the Italian delights on the march north through Italy, you know, Naples and Rome and such like. And I do not mean visiting the Vatican – being satisfied with a night at home with the missus! Home would be very tame and boring. And so it became the ladies' campaign to deny menfolk the opportunity to enjoy any of life's wartime pleasures, including pubs. Yes, they even mentioned the temperance word."

"Prohibition," James said incredulously.

"The very one," Flora continued. "Mind you, I did get a lot of opposition from our top patrons – politicians and judiciary, some of our best and most regular customers came from those two professions. The police chief was very good; he said to me, 'You know Flora, peace brings a different kind of policing. During the depression years, we were chasing our tails trying to shut down sly grog dens and smuggling, among other illegal activities. War time, well we had our hands full with drunken servicemen who, you cannot deny, deserved every drop that their bodies could hold. But with peace, we have the time to carry on policing in the time old honoured tradition of keeping the peace. That means everybody gets a say-so; we just cannot turn a blind eye anymore. We cannot

155

say youthful exuberance! Last leave before shipping to the front! Those boys had a helluva time on Guadalcanal! So this is where the bleeding-hearts get their say after having to keep their mouths shut for so long. I'm not saying they are right or wrong, I'm simply a policeman upholding the law! Sooner or later they may want the heat turned on you. I know what you do is legal in the eyes of the law, but the morals might be questioned. The frightening part about that is the questioners will invariably be the lawmakers. Yes, parliamentarians, some of whom frequented Maximes. So there's a thought or two to ponder on!'

"Mind you," Flora continued, "I think the time is right for expansion in the hotel trade. We are experiencing an expanding economy. Our occupancy rate is at an all-time high so we need all the rooms that we can muster and more. I'm thinking of putting another floor or two onto the building. The structural engineers say that it is possible to do this."

"I would make a good clerk of works if you need me to liaise with the engineers and architects," James offered.

"Yes I know, that's why I have mentioned this to you. They make an exploratory visit this week, so I'll get you in on the ground floor, so to speak."

James looked pleased about that. He was good at managing projects.

The next day, Flora received a telegram from London.

'Returning on Dominion Monarch STOP ETA Wellington November 12 STOP letter following Love Kaetrin STOP'

An air mail letter arrived three weeks later in which Kaetrin detailed to her aunty the wonderful news about Linus and his father in Russia. She went on to explain that the Beresford-Ambles were with them on the voyage home. They would be coming via Las Palmas, Cape Town, Durban, Freemantle, Melbourne, Sydney and on to Wellington.

"It's a lovely ship", she wrote, "much bigger than the 'Rangi' boats. All first class too and we have booked great cabins. I'll send you an air mail letter from Cape Town, it will be interesting to see who arrives first us or the mail!"

They had been at sea for about a week when Kaetrin got the shock of her life. There, standing on the deck talking with another passenger, she saw Jimmy the heartmelt and her heart skipped a beat. Kaetrin was not prepared for a meeting with Jimmy, her old flame, and her movements became flustered. She wanted to beat a hasty retreat to her cabin and turned, but not before Jimmy had noticed her. Kaetrin was walking as fast as the moving deck would allow her but he caught up. She felt a hand on her arm and froze. The last time he had touched her was to say goodbye when he was delivered to his ship in Wellington. Nothing had prepared her for this. Kaetrin stopped walking and Jimmy came around so he was in front of her and still holding her arm. He let go her arm and smiled. "Hello Kaetrin, this is a surprise."

Kaetrin was tongue tied but she managed to say, "Jimmy what a surprise, what on earth are you doing here?" After she said it, she thought it sounded silly.

Jimmy replied, "I work here," and he pointed to his epaulettes which sported two gold bands. "I'm the second officer, I'm here for the round voyage, how about you?"

"Returning to Wellington with my husband," Kaetrin heard herself say.

"So you stayed in New Zealand after the war?" Jimmy asked.

"Yes," she replied, "I had no cause to return to London."

Jimmy could see that Kaetrin was struggling with this conversation and he did not want to get off on the wrong foot.

"Look," he said, "why don't you and your husband join me for a drink in the officers' bar. It's far more private there and I'm sure that we will both be a bit more relaxed and we can relate our experiences since we last met. I'm sure that we have a lot to tell each other – how about it?"

Kaetrin smiled for the first time. "Yes," she breathed, "I would like that. How and when?"

"Okay," he said, "I take the twelve to four watch, how about we meet at the purser's office in the foyer at five this evening and I will take you there? How's that!"

"That will be nice. Thank you – yes, see you there – I know where the purser's office is."

Jimmy smiled and nodded. "See you then, Kaetrin." The way he said her name made her shiver.

Linus had already heard the story about Jimmy in one of those pre-nuptial tell-alls when betrothed couples feel it is their duty to confess all now and have no regrets later, if and when skeletons appear in their closet archives.

The officers' bar and smoke room, as it was called, was a cosy secluded hideaway when compared to the open public areas of the large liner. They started very formally when introductions were made and Jimmy fetched their drinks from the bar. He asked the steward to duplicate the order when he signalled. Following two drinks and working on the third delivery they relaxed and laugher started to come more easily into the conversation. Jimmy related his experiences from the sinking of the *Rangitane* until his freedom some five years later when the allies liberated the prisoner of war camp.

"Those five years were the making of me," Jimmy said. "We had school every day. The master mariners and chief engineers ran seamanship, navigation and engineering lectures for those of us who were interested in gaining such knowledge. By the time I got out of there I had passed my third and second mates tickets, on paper, that is. I still needed the sea time and of course I had to take the exams in the proper manner but I had been educated and had sufficient knowledge to sit those exams when the time came. And passed with flying colours. Now that never would have happened in peace time. I was far too busy chasing young ladies on cruise liners," he said, winking at Kaetrin who was able to accept the eye flicker in the same humour with which it had been transmitted.

Kaetrin had worked up enough Dutch courage to ask the question.

157

"You stopped writing," she said. "Suddenly nothing – no communication. We were worried about you. What happened?"

Jimmy nodded and frowned. "Yes, it probably seems like that. I don't know what happened. About a year after we arrived at the camp we had a change in commandant. He was a tyrant and we lost a lot of privileges. He could have destroyed our mail – who knows? He must have upset some of his masters too as he was sent off to the Russian front. His replacement tried getting things back to normal, but somehow that never eventuated. I did write, but you obviously never got my letters so after about a further year of that I just stopped! I was disappointed, but look where I was! What could I do? I simply studied twice as hard and tried to forget you. But that was hard."

Kaetrin smiled wistfully. "At least I can tell Aunty Flora that you survived, she was worried about you. We were all worried about you! Why didn't you write when the war was over?"

"I had intended to, but then I thought that I would simply turn up on a ship and say hello. Give everyone a shock! I joined Bank Line which is a famous old tramp company; they go everywhere and I thought that would be the best way to get my sea time in quickly. They never came to New Zealand, went everywhere but there. Then when I qualified with my first mates ticket I joined Shaw Savil & Albion and this is my first trip on one of their ships. So I guess you beat me to it!"

"Linus is a former seafarer," Kaetrin offered.

"Yes I know."

"How do you know?"

"Mannerisms, walk, talk, you can tell these things. You swallowed the anchor, Linus?" Jimmy enquired.

"Yes I did, some time back now. I inherited a lot of art works. All in a trust but they generate sufficient income and require most of my time to attend to the matters arising from the running of the trust. We display a lot of the works in galleries. New York, London, Paris, Madrid and Rome. People pay to see these famous pieces and it generates a sizable revenue for the trust which is a philanthropic organisation. I am a trustee and have certain obligations. Hence our visit to London to attend to trust affairs. Honeymoon too, for Kaetrin and I."

"Congratulations!"

"Thank you."

They continued with their conversation for another hour and Jimmy said that he had to get his head down and get some sleep before he went on watch at midnight. They agreed to meet again and departed the bar in good spirits.

Kaetrin and Linus walked to the dining saloon and met the Beresford-Ambles for dinner, as they did most evenings at eight o'clock. Kaetrin related the meeting with Jimmy and while Marjory and Horace had been on the same voyage back in 1940 they never did get to meet the young deck boy as he was then. But Horace recalled their coded letter writing when Jimmy was in POW camp in Germany.

"As I said back then, he is a smart lad. Look where he is now! Y'know Admiral Lord Nelson started on the bottom rung, cabin boy to admiral. Where will young Jimmy end up?"

Cape Town was a first time port of call for all of them and so they took all the sightseeing tours that they could while the ship was in port.

Wellington turned on a fine sunny spring day when the DM docked at Aotea Quay. Horace and Marjory went with Linus and Kaetrin to Maximes Hotel where they stayed while the liner discharged their quite considerable cargo of personal and household effects, including Horace's red 1931 MG-M sports car which he couldn't bear to part with. Horace had to oversee the project and work in with the customs agent to ensure that it all went smoothly and no one did smoothly as well as Horace. The customs agent called him an interfering old fool, but he did that out of earshot of Horace. And that was wise. Getting between Horace and the job at hand was like getting between a dog and his bone. It just was not a good idea.

Kaetrin had brought with her a huge china tea set that she was obliged to submit to customs. It required an import entry and duty was also payable. This would be the nucleus for her afternoon tea functions at Maximes that she would style after Claridges in London. It would be a grand occasion and just like the espresso coffee machine in 1942, a first for Wellington.

Homecoming was a joyous occasion. Linus and Kaetrin had been away for ten months, three of those spent at sea. James Peroux was to be Flora's surprise. And he was. Linus of course had never met James but the Beresford-Ambles and Kaetrin were able to recall their wartime association and spent quality time recounting events prior to his call to war, on Tarawa Atoll.

As former servicemen, Linus, James and Horace would regale each other with humorous anecdotes about life in uniform. It seemed to Linus that the time between the two world wars was the time that the services enjoyed some of their happier moments and Horace in particular could entertain for hours with his memoirs of 'My life and times in India and other equally exotic climes.'

And then Jimmy the heartmelt walked in on the second night as the party was settling in for a long, dinner with drinks. This was Kaetrin's turn to surprise her aunty as she had not mentioned his presence at all on the ship back to New Zealand. Jimmy was welcomed like a long lost son, especially by Flora. He joined the party and they got going in a most jovial and noisy fashion. Leslie was very keen to quiz Jimmy about the German raiders that attacked and sunk the *Rangitata* and Jimmy said that he would talk to her alone about that unless present company wanted to listen to the saga as well. It was agreed by all, that now was as good a time as any to hear the story first hand from a survivor. Jimmy told his story to a captive audience. Everyone had read about the sinking of the *Rangitata* by the German raiders but this was the only time that the story could be unfolded to them first hand, from a survivor of the horrors of that night. Leslie was keen to learn about Doug and what actually happened and Jimmy was able to tell her that the junior RO who had survived was also made a prisoner of war and so they had spent the next five years together, in the same POW camp. "I know as much as anyone about that night!" he said.

"It seems," Jimmy related, "that Doug and the junior RO, whose name was Derek, were in the radio shack destroying code books and other secret information that the captain had instructed them to destroy. The enemy were trying to block outgoing transmission from the *Rangitata* and Doug took over from his junior and sat at the desk, transmitting 'QQQ' which was radio code for 'suspicious vessel'. He kept this up until the order came from the bridge to change the transmission to 'RRR' again radio code but this time it stood for raider attack. They were ordered to leave their station and the junior RO was exiting when a shell struck the radio shack, destroying it. The junior RO said that Doug was still transmitting." Jimmy never mentioned the decapitation; when Doug's head was severed at the neck by a red hot piece of steel shrapnel from the shell explosion. Jimmy continued, "Doug was determined that his message get through and in so doing the receivers of his transmission signal could locate the position of the stricken vessel. That was his reason for staying at his post, so I was told. And I now know this to be true. The junior RO made it out by the skin of his teeth. We had also lost our steering gear and our gun controls were shot to bits. We couldn't go anywhere and spent the night putting out fires aboard ship. Come morning, the Germans sent boats with men over and I, with the other seamen, helped our passengers into life boats as instructed by the third officer. They were pretty cut up, as you can imagine, and most needed a hand with their lifejackets – just as you did," Jimmy said, looking at Kaetrin.

Kaetrin recalled the event years ago when Jimmy had helped her put on this strange device when as a CORB passenger at the start of her voyage to New Zealand, they had to go through a life boat drill.

Leslie asked Jimmy why they had not given Doug an award for bravery. "It sounded like he did his bit for the ship and I have been told that the location of the ship was pinpointed as a result of those transmissions, but by the time that help arrived, the *Rangitata* had gone to the bottom of the sea and the German raiders, with their prisoners aboard, had vanished."

Jimmy looked surprised. "I thought that they had done all of that and that Doug was up for some sort of decoration. The captain was put ashore on Nauru with all of the prisoners who were not being detained as prisoners of war. There were some from other ships that the raiders had also sunk. They were picked up soon after by friendly vessels and returned to New Zealand. The ROs are supplied by Marconi in England. I'll ask our ROs on the DM, maybe they can shed some light on the situation. I know that the general feeling among the men was that Doug had done a superb job."

Leslie smiled at the accolade. "It would be nice if his son had something to remember his father by," she said.

Jimmy agreed. "I'll look into it," he said. "He did a good job. We are proud of him in the tradition of seafarers."

The diners continued their table banter and the hotel staff who had been instructed by Flora beforehand were efficient and attentive. They had agreed to work late. Hotel guests had long since finished in the dining room as Flora and her family and friends carried on for some hours. Eventually they dispersed for various reasons, the commonest citing tiredness. But not before all agreeing it had been a tremendous evening and one that should be held more frequently.

As a precedent Horace suggested that they should have a reunion every time that the DM was in port.

"How long is that between feeds?" Linus asked Jimmy.

"Roughly just over five months."

"Let's do it!"

"Agreed."

The additions to Maximes Hotel took fourteen months to complete. It was tricky running the hotel while building work was underway but then James Peroux was running the show and he came into his element as an organiser of men and materials. Flora was given a demonstration of the colonel's organisational abilities and she realised why General Winslow had him on his general staff. He got things done on time. Excuses were not a part of the contract. Every contractor had financial penalties built into their contract and they were upheld to the letter of the law. No one fell behind. There were plenty who worked late and maybe put in more hours than they had allowed for, but the schedule was never compromised. Kaetrin got her tea rooms on the first floor that was remodelled at the same time. It was styled after the fashion of Claridge's Reading Room and they followed the menu as close to the original template as was achievable. One could take a glass of champagne with their sandwiches if that was preferred to a cup of tea. It was, after all, the individual's selection and attendees were there for diverse reasons. Maximes was catering for a broad range of tastes as the occasions arose.

Marjory had considerable input. She had been retained as a consultant having assisted Kaetrin with her selection of the finest bone chinaware from Harrods in London. Tigers rampant may not have been the themes painted on the teapots, but Marjory rampant was certainly evident as she enthusiastically threw herself into the task of duplicating the institution that connected Claridge's with everything that was English, about the custom of taking tea in elegant surroundings, in the most genteel way possible and in the highest scale of good taste. Linus had entered into the venture too and had donated six Turner prints of exquisite English countryside landscapes. The originals, of course, were safely locked away in the British Museum and were part of the Art 1 Trust's collection. At the top end of the building, Flora was supervising the fitting of the new drapes for the penthouse suites. They had decided to forego some of the exterior arboretum area in favour of having two penthouse suites instead of one. Linus and Kaetrin would occupy one and Flora and James the other. Leslie and Bravo would occupy a reworked two bedroom apartment on the first floor.

161

The hotel held a soiree to commemorate the opening of the new additions and was attended by the usual eclectic mix of politicians, socialites, former first floor escorts, judges, fishermen and Seamens' Union officials, and city councillors including the mayor.

The local newspaper gave it a splendid write-up in their 'Town and around with Jane' column. Jane was ecstatic about 'Marjorees', the name given to the new tea rooms on the first floor. "The name was applied in honour of Mrs Marjory Beresford-Amble, former patron of the Simla Swimming Club in India, who had considerable input into the concept." Jane wrote in her column.

Marjory mingled enthusiastically with the guests, pouring cups of tea and handing out the slimmest of her delicate club sandwiches. Those who wanted champagne were attended to by waiters distributing slender champagne flutes from silver trays. Ascending beads clinging to the inner glass and rising to the surface, then exploding, were testament to the pedigree of the genuine French product.

Mary-Jane Horsefield nee Skeffington, had come with her husband, the veterinarian from Shannon in Horowhenua County. Mary-Jane was an 'Old Girl' from Sandford House and one of the first floor residents in Maximes. She had saved her parents' farm during the depression years with her work ethic. They were forever grateful and the farm would be left to her when they passed on. Harry, her vet husband, believed that Mary-Jane had worked for a successful wool export company. She could not bring herself to tell him that her work involved flesh only. And it was not exported.

With the grand opening over, it was time to see if Kaetrin's venture would take off and it did. It proved especially a favourite with farming families. Country visitors were a large proportion of Maximes' guests. They came to the city for a myriad of reasons and while in the country they made up the horse trial set or the polo set and tea, or champagne and sandwiches were a part of that lifestyle. Marjorees at Maximes fitted the bill admirably for their town sojourns. What surprised Kaetrin was that the country menfolk were far more amenable to taking tea with their wives than the city menfolk who were probably encumbered with their work. It was a success and on the way to becoming an institution. No small thanks to Marjory Beresford-Amble, whose attention to detail and knowledge of her subject won her accolades from other social page watcher-writers. On Thursdays and Fridays it was advisable to book a table and that included hotel guests too!

Flora and James flourished as a couple and Flora announced their engagement casually at dinner one evening. Kaetrin started on a guest list immediately but was sidelined in an instant.

"We have decided that we are going to get married in the water in a lodge in Fiji where we stayed on our way back to New Zealand last year. We had a private pool and James was able to swim in the water there sans prosthetics and felt good about that. There will be three at the ceremony; myself and James and a celebrant. And we will all be in the water. I have checked it out already!"

Silence greeted this disclosure which seemed to have deflated the excitement from Flora's original declaration.

Bravo who was now thirteen said, "Good call Aunty Flora."

"Thank you Bravo, we think so, this is for us. We can celebrate with you guys on our return. Nothing big, just close family and friends!"

"And that's an order!" James barked in a military kind of voice.

Kaetrin returned to the dining room table with a couple of bottles of wine from the hotel cellar and a waiter bought glasses and they toasted the bride and groom to be.

James and Flora took the flying boat from Mechanics Bay in Auckland to Laucala Bay in Fiji and spent ten wonderful days and nights at their resort, getting the nuptials completed on the afternoon of the second day. There were just three persons present; James, Flora and the marriage celebrant. A witness was required and they got one of the Fijian hotel workers to assume that responsibility and within a few minutes Mr and Mrs Peroux exited the pool and sat on sun loungers to consume fresh papaya with lemon juice drizzled over. One day they hired a launch and spent the time fishing for wahoo but for the rest of their stay on the island, it was lazy days and lazy nights. They toasted their good luck and fortune to have been reunited again following the years of separation each evening with sundowners. James was later reported to have quipped to close friends that he was legless at his own wedding.

True to her word, Kaetrin had organised a post wedding celebration for Flora and James on their return to Maximes. The event was held late on a Sunday afternoon in Marjorees on the first floor. Kaetrin had organised a wedding cake and a piper who played 'Amazing Grace' and Horace Beresford-Amble gave a father of the bride style speech. The American ambassador said that General Winslow had asked him to say a few words on behalf of the Marine Corps and his old Second Marine Division buddies. Two seamen from the Hebrides who were on a visiting British merchant ship in the port arrived with some of Flora's standing order for her favourite scotch whiskey. And before too long, a memorable shindig got underway that was as good as anyone could ever remember a wedding celebration being.

The occasion rated a mention in the social pages of the local newspaper that week. It seemed that Mr and Mrs Peroux were newsworthy and would remain under the social spotlight for the foreseeable future.

163

Chapter 12

Return to England

Linus and Kaetrin booked their passage to London on the New Zealand Shipping Company's liner, *Rangitoto*. It was a sister ship to the two other vessels of the same class, the others were *Rangitane,* that was sunk by German Raiders in 1940, and *Rangitata*, which was the vessel that delivered the CORB children to New Zealand in 1940. They chose the voyage because the ship was scheduled to transit the Suez Canal on her northbound run to the UK and Linus was keen to visit what was reputed to be, since the end of the war anyway, one of the best art galleries in the Middle East.

Linus had completed as much as he could for the ART1 Foundation Trust by proxy and was required to personally attend a trust meeting in London to sanction some momentous decisions that were being made about the artworks that he had inherited. Also there was a matter of the auctioning off of his parents' art collection by Sotheby's and he wanted to attend what was being billed as one of the biggest art auctions to be held since WWII.

The collection that was stored in Essex for the duration of the war had been taken to the British Museum in London and they in turn had pieces loaned out to some of the biggest names in art institutions, namely the Guggenheim and Metropolitan Museum of Art in New York, Musee d'Orsay in Paris, Reina Sofia in Madrid and Van Gough Museum in Amsterdam.

The money was rolling into the foundation and some investments undertaken. Van Oldenbarnevelts were doing a good job but now some hard decisions had to be made and Linus had to be in attendance when the trustees met to make those decisions. In essence, the professional trustees were Van Oldenbarnevelts and Linus was the inheritance trustee. They had subsequently appointed the British Museum as another professional trustee, so voting was a three way split. The Dutch Government had gotten wind of the Levin collection and were making extradition noises, but as the trustees so rightly pointed out, if the paintings had stayed in Holland where would they be now? They could be anywhere between South America and Moscow and lost to the world forever. This way they were saved for the world by a farsighted art dealer from Amsterdam, Mr Rudi Levin. Proceeds from the collection were going to help repatriated Dutch Jewish families. The paintings were made by various European nationals and the deeds of inheritance were kosher according to Dutch law as it was a Dutch law firm who had originally drawn up the documents.

Kaetrin and Linus were married in Wellington, a month prior to the ship's departure for the UK and this was to be their extended honeymoon. Kaetrin was now twenty five and Linus thirty one. Flora MacLeod had always thought that Linus would be a good match for Kaetrin and she had played an aunty's hand in guiding her niece into what she considered to be a 'very good match indeed!'

Flora herself had not been so fortunate in affairs of the heart, with the early demise of her first husband who was accidently killed in a train shunting accident when returning to his ship in Lyttelton Harbour. James Peroux had entered her life in 1942 and they had a whirlwind romance before the Second Marines left for Tarawa and then Saipan. And that was the end of that. Flora had heard no more from her wartime beau. He was, as far as she was able to tell, not killed in action and had survived the war but it was silent pictures ever since. He had not contacted her nor had she received any replies to her letters or enquiries to the corps. Flora did what Flora had always done. She got on with life! And that what the end of that!

The Beresford-Ambles had booked on the same sailing back to the UK. Major Horace had completed his contract with the New Zealand Army and he had also retired from the British Army. They had both enjoyed their sojourn in New Zealand and decided to stay for their retirement, the army pension sustaining them in reasonable comfort in the colony. They had to return to England to sell a property and pack the majority of their belongings in preparedness to having them shipped to Wellington. Horace had discovered golf and they had purchased a lovely home adjacent to the golf course in Herautaunga which was near the army camp where Horace had worked for the NZ Defence Force at Trentham Camp. Marjory had established a well patronised tea drinkers' circle and she hosted and attended similar functions, in the neighbourhood, regularly. They both had become well respected members of the community. They were a couple of loved English eccentrics who wore their Englishness like a badge of honour. If it were religion that they were selling, they would have made successful missionaries.

The Levins and Beresford-Ambles shared a dinner table every evening and met regularly for afternoon card games and then deck activities when the weather improved. The Tasman Sea showed its mean streak between Wellington and Sydney and they got a bit of a hiding across the Australian Bight. Leaving Fremantle, the weather improved and by the time they were clearing the northern reaches of Australia the ship had settled into tropical mode. From experience, the Levins had booked a balcony cabin set high in the

165

superstructure to maximise any available air movement. They had also packed electric fans in their luggage to assist in cabin cooling. The major had insisted on having their cabin on the starboard side of the ship propounding the maxim 'Port Out Starboard Home.' that had apparently given birth to the acronym 'POSH.' The proposition was that the prevailing wind would be on the port side of the vessel sailing from Blighty to India and the reverse when returning as the ship would present its starboard side to the prevailing wind. Horace merely extended the proposition to include the southern hemisphere. The next port of call was to be Colombo in Ceylon and then Aden, the Red Sea transit and Suez where the Levins had planned to get off the ship for some sight-seeing while it transited the Suez Canal, rejoining the ship in Port Said before heading out into the Mediterranean Sea. The Beresford-Ambles would stay aboard. Having been stationed in Egypt at some stage of their army career, both had seen all they wanted of the sights available in that ancient land. Crossing the equator this time was old hat for Kaetrin who thought about her first transit and the romance with Jimmy the heartmelt. All the passengers received a certificate regardless of taking the plunge and everybody was in a gay mood that evening over dinner when extra wine was ordered and consumed. The band played and the passengers danced and the world was a wonderful place to be a part of once more. The hostilities that ceased a mere five years previously may well have been an event which had occurred last century, if at all.

Colombo was, as usual, a crowded busy port. It was hot and steamy and rained every afternoon at four o'clock. Horace said that they all must go ashore and have a swim at Mount Lavinia, a beautiful ocean beach not far from Colombo. It was a short taxi ride and they all enjoyed the cooling ocean breeze and ocean surf. It turned out that Horace had been stationed in Ceylon at some previous stage in his military career and so they ended their afternoon ashore with a few drinks in the officers' mess at the army barracks in Colombo.

Kaetrin was amazed at her attitude toward the romance of a sea voyage this trip versus her experience ten years ago, when she was shipped out as a CORB export to the colonies. There were no surprises, discoveries maybe, but certainly no surprises. At the end of the war the children were meant to be repatriated. Her father was killed in the North African campaign and her mother had vanished. The authorities had no idea where she was. It seemed that she had simply vanished. One thing was certain. She was not interested in her children. Her children were not interested in becoming repatriated and Flora signed the papers to accept them as her wards until they reached the age of their majority and they could do as they liked. Neither Robert nor Kaetrin wanted to return to London, life in New Zealand with Aunty Flora at Maximes Hotel was just fine!

Jimmy the heartmelt had written his last letter to Kaetrin in 1944. She had sent several letters to him since then but she never got a reply and although she felt vulnerable at the time she had enough local admirers to distract her feelings from a fleeting romance that could have foundered at the first obstacle. Kaetrin never dated a marine, although Leslie was constantly out and about with the

166

American fighting men stationed in the capital. It wasn't hard. There were far more males than females and romances were as common as toast for breakfast. And a lot of them were burnt toast by dinner.

Kaetrin had turned twenty one when Linus moved into Maximes and after some fumbling and awkward beginnings a romance started and then flourished. It must be recorded here that Flora MacLeod was a great selector of partners for other people, but not for herself. With some clever conjuring and sleight of hand Kaetrin seemed to appear in full flirting regalia when least expected and Linus was innocently present due to some covert arrangement that had been made between Flora and cupid. Flora could have been a smash playwright if she had taken the time to write it all down.

Linus and Kaetrin said goodbye to the Beresford-Ambles at Port Suez and joined a tour that would take them to the archaeological sights of Egypt then deliver them to Cairo for three days of sight-seeing before they headed into the Mediterranean Sea on the leg to London. Linus had the address of an art gallery at Karam El Dawia Street in Cairo. Rumour had it that a lot of the artworks on display came from Germany during WWII, secreted over with a shipment of arms and supplies for the Africa Corps. It was, or so the rumour said, an attempt to save European artwork from the clutches of the advancing Soviet Army who were consuming the spoils of war like a voracious feeder with an insatiable appetite. It was, Linus thought, a similar scheme to that proposed by his father. It was such a pity that the two art lovers had never met as they had so much in common. Who knows? They may have become good friends!

It was a sultry afternoon when Linus and Kaetrin took a taxi from their Cairo hotel to the street address of the art gallery. The building was a superb edifice finished in white limestone. It was three stories high and featured pylon-like entrances on the ground floor. The interior was cool as one would expect, being sheltered from the ambient temperatures of midsummer Cairo by three-foot-thick limestone walls. The main entrance was the foyer and there was an information desk selling brochures and guided tours as well as taking entrance fees. On each side of the foyer there was a winding staircase of marble risers with an alabaster balustrade and a highly polished copper handrail on the inboard side. The interior architecture inspired by European grandeur was veneered with Egyptian materials. The Levins paid for a personal guided tour and seated on a comfortable sofa they waited for their guide to arrive. The tours were arranged in a three tiered system starting with introductory, then intermediate and then masters. Each tour was of three hour duration and designed to bring a novice up to speed with art appreciation. Looking at a painting was one thing, but understanding it was another and although Linus was a relative expert compared to Kaetrin, he thought that she would value the lessons that would stand her in good stead for the years ahead, as, by marriage, she was now part-owner of a large art collection. It was to be a lesson a day for the next three days. Their guide was a young art student from Cairo University. She was enthusiastic about the subject and her name was Calliope.

167

She took them to a small lecture room, the walls of which were adorned with paintings in various stages of completion. Linus had had the lecture before and knew what was to come, so his eyes wandered and he never heard the words. To his astonishment he saw a framed copy of the trinity. The top and bottom parts were missing but the middle portion was in place. It was exactly as his father had divided his painting between the three family members when Linus left Holland for England before Germany declared war on The Netherlands. The middle piece was his mother's. Rudi held the top portion and Linus had the bottom piece. His heart was racing. Could this be his mother's part of the painting? He looked at his watch. They had more than two hours to go on the tour. He could get a taxi and go back to the hotel, collect his portion of the painting and be back within half an hour. He had to do it.

"Excuse me," he said to Calliope and then he said to Kaetrin, "I must go back to the hotel and collect something important, you carry on here and I will be back in half an hour. Sorry, I must do this!" and before Kaetrin could utter a word, he departed.

He was away for barely thirty five minutes, but to Linus it seemed half a day. With a racing pulse, he found the lecture room which was now empty and went to the picture and held his piece against the framed portion. It was a perfect match and the work of the same artist. He had found his mother's section of the trinity and he heard himself saying to the picture on the wall, "Hello Mother, I have found you."

Then the tears came. He could feel the wetness brimming the lower eye sockets and he kept thinking, funny how the tears come from the bottom of the eyes never from the top. Always the bottom they well-up and overflow and he felt wetness down his cheeks. He didn't sob or make loud wailing noises he simply wept with quiet dignity.

Eventually the door opened and Kaetrin and Calliope entered. "We came to see if you had returned," Kaetrin said and she noticed the tears running down his cheeks. "Is something wrong?"

"No," Linus said, "something is right, not wrong. I have made a wondrous discovery!" He went on to explain what he had found.

Calliope said, "I'll get Franz-Josef," and left the room.

Footsteps announced the return of Calliope with Franz-Josef. They entered the room and saw a composed Linus holding Kaetrin's hand. The bottom portion of the trinity, 'the Cadavar in the Tomb' was lying on a table for all to see.

Franz-Josef went directly to Linus and took his other hand.

"Hello Linus, I'm Franz-Josef Kaiser. I knew your father at Auschwitz. In fact, you may recall that you and I met at your father's art gallery in Holland before the war. We had visited on several occasions. My father, Otto Kaiser was a regular client of the great Rudi Levin."

Linus was allowing the information to sink in. "You knew my father at Auschwitz... you were at Auschwitz?"

Franz-Josef could see that Linus was joining the dots in the puzzle and before any assumptions were made, he wanted to set the record straight.

"Yes, I worked with Rudi and another German prisoner, Werner Kruger, on artwork. I was a colonel in the Luftwaffe but was wounded and grounded. Unable to fly, I was sent to do guard duty in the Russian sector of Auschwitz. It takes a bit of explaining, but the three of us ran an art workshop cataloguing and repairing the paintings that had been brought into the prison by Jewish prisoners.

"I recognised your parents when they arrived and Werner was able to introduce us; he was a German communist and had been a political prisoner since about 1936. He was a smart prisoner and he knew the systems, so could get things done. We managed to get Rudi transferred to our own little section, but we could not do the same for your mother. We managed to get her transferred from the Jewish section as she was a British subject and non-Jewish. Rudi gave me the middle section of the Trinity as she was not allowed personal belongings. It was to be displayed in the hope that one day the owner would discover it. Rudi has the top section."

"You say 'has' the top section, not 'had' the top section, that would imply that he is alive?"

"Yes very much so, when I last saw him. The Russians had liberated the camp and were very interested in our work. Rudi was originally from Russia so he could converse with his liberators freely. I can only imagine that Rudi and Werner were repatriated to Russia along with some very valuable works of art."

"So my mother was not sent to the gas chamber?"

"No, she was doing forced labour. The non-Jewish prisoners got a better deal, better food and accommodation. Small mercies, but enough to sustain them while the Jews perished. Rudi was a Jew but he was doing valuable work. I managed to get the authorities to let him eat and live in a non-Jewish part of the camp and, with help from Werner, he survived."

"So you think my father is in Russia?"

"Yes."

"What about my mother?"

Franz-Josef, a very composed man, looked uncomfortable. "We don't know. We do know that prior to the arrival of the soviets the SS guards force marched about sixty thousand prisoners west to a place called Wodzislaw. Many perished on that journey through extreme cold weather conditions, it was January so we were in the middle of winter. Starvation, and exposure accounted for many. The SS guards shot anyone who fell behind or could not continue. You must accept that she succumbed at some stage during the march."

"And you survived?"

Franz-Josef felt the bitterness in the remark from Linus.

"Yes I survived – thanks to Werner and your father. Without their intervention I was a deadman!"

Linus relaxed his severe accusing glare and felt uncomfortable. "What happened?" he enquired.

169

"As you can imagine, I was in a German uniform when the Soviets arrived. The troops were a wild bunch who shot first and then asked questions. A German uniform was a fair mark for them. Their ranking officers had yet to arrive so the troops meted out their special form of justice. I was strung up by the feet and left to swing for twenty four hours while the drunken Soviet soldiers performed indecencies on me. Peeing on the uniform was considered great sport so I was washed frequently in vodka smelling urine in my nose and mouth and eyes. Then they cut bits of uniform off me, especially the decorations and my urine soaked clothes froze overnight. I thought that I was a gonner and started to lose consciousness. A Soviet officer finally arrived and I heard Rudi and Werner arguing with him in Russian. Sounded like a hell of a ruckus was going on. I must have passed out because when I came to I was in warm dry clothes in a warm bed. They had spent some hours thawing me out and at one stage thought that I may succumb to hypothermia.

"And then the strangest thing, Werner who pretty much had the run of the camp as a German national, albeit a communist, turned up with this beautiful set of clothes. A new tailor-made suit and overcoat, new shoes, underwear and shirts still in the cellophane wrapping, hat, neckties, scarves. A suitcase to carry a set of spare clothes, same quality, new and bespoke. Apparently there was a huge selection of garments available that had been taken from incoming prisoners. Werner seemed to have access to just about everything. He commandeered a car, ex one of the camp commandants and no longer required where the late owner had been despatched to. But the masterstroke were my travel documents. I became a Red Cross worker from Switzerland, overseeing the transition of prisoners' welfare from their German captors to the Soviet liberators. As I said, Werner had the run of the place so I suppose that within the camp confines there would have been a host of skills from craftsmen of various nationalities from all round Europe. Once on my way I had an unimpeded run through to the Swiss border, and in Switzerland – well – it was all laid on. All I had to do was get to the bank and my strongbox where my father, Otto, had left a Swiss passport and enough money to support me in comfort for a year and buy a passage to Egypt. I eventually had to travel to England to get a passage on a ship travelling via the Suez Canal to Australia and New Zealand. I arrived in Cairo in February 1946. Perhaps you and your wife would do me the honour of dining with us tonight. Us will be my wife Brigette, her parents and my parents. You may remember my father, Otto?"

Kaetrin squeezed Linus's hand as a signal of affirmation and he accepted the invitation on their behalf.

The street address given to Linus by Franz-Josef was a different address to the art gallery but it became apparent that the building occupied a complete section of a block in the shape of a triangle, a plan view of a pyramid and so it had three street frontages. One an art gallery, another a museum and the third was the accommodation block. They all featured the large pylon like entrances and white limestone exterior. At night, lights illuminated the exterior stone, giving the structure a striking white appearance.

If the art gallery entrance was superb the accommodation block ingress was magnificent. Kaetrin remarked, "Palatial, bloody palatial," as they were led into the building by a liveried manservant. Franz-Josef descended a staircase similar in construction to the art gallery stairs only gentler in gradient to enable gowned ladies access without tripping on high risers. Kaetrin and Linus both observed a slight dip of the head and a faint tap of heel as Franz-Josef greeted them both.

"How pleasant to see you both," he said and then, "thank you for coming, we go upstairs to dine," and he ushered them with a wave of his hand toward the stairway.

At the top of the stairway they came onto a landing with a tessellated border, edging the main marble tiled floor. Their footsteps were omnipresent and would have heralded their impending arrival into the living quarters accessed through large cedar doors that had been crafted from the famous cedars of Lebanon. The very same timber used by King Solomon to build his temple in Jerusalem. There were several similar styled doors along the landing.

The apartment was elegant and comfortable and in no way ostentatious. It was decorated in good taste. Following introductions, drinks were served and they sat and conversed. Otto said, "I remember you, Linus. We last visited Amsterdam in 1938. Do you recall our visit? There was my wife Anna, Franz-Josef and myself!"

"Yes I do, Mother made her famous English muffins for lunch as I recall."

"Yes," Anna said, "and I still have the recipe. We make them often."

"Please accept our condolences on the loss of your mother in what was tragic circumstances."

"Thank you."

Anna continued. "We met some gallant New Zealanders here in North Africa when we arrived in 1942. In fact, if it wasn't for them we may not be here now. New Zealand has a special place in our hearts!"

"Yes," Otto confirmed. "The Longe Range Dessert Group. A fine bunch of young men. They went on to fight in Italy from here and we managed to maintain contact when hostilities ceased. They were formed in 1940 to operate behind enemy lines carrying out all sorts of subversive activities. New Zealanders were originally chosen as it was then considered that the New Zealand farmer who was an energetic, self-reliant and mentally tough character had the necessary attributes to handle the job. In practice this proved to be correct. Rommel is on record as saying, 'the LRDG caused us more damage than any other allied force of equal strength!'"

"They used these Chevrolet trucks – we've got one in our museum. They had no identifying marks save this strange looking icon painted onto one side of the bonnet in red and green. I now know it to be 'Tiki' whom I understand from Polynesian culture, was considered to be the first man. Strongly associated with the origin of the procreative act!

"The commander of the Group that helped us through the desert is a Captain Neil Walker, he farms in a place called Masterton. Do you know it, by any chance?" They both nodded.

"Yes," Kaetrin said, "It's about a two hour drive from where we live. Nice country – we get a lot of farmers from that area staying at our hotel."

Franz-Josef was taking second orders for drinks. "We do it ourselves," he explained, "Muslims do not like handling alcohol and we don't want to violate tradition. This way is easier."

Linus asked about their association with the homeland and their intentions on living in Egypt.

Alfred von Hapsberg said. "There is nothing to return to while the Soviets are in charge. Our ancestral lands are confiscated. I would hate to see what destruction has been meted out to our houses and estates. We are now refugees. But hey, thanks to Otto and some excellent political foresight, we had planned our exit long before Hitler started that dreadful conflict, so in a way we escaped with some of our dignity intact. And a small part of our inheritance. I believe that your father, Rudi, was also a forward thinker and managed to get some great artworks out of Holland before the Nazis stole them. All that aside, they still managed to pillage some magnificent collections. Whether they ever see the light of day again will be a vexatious question. Mind you, there are some unscrupulous art dealers who will buy, no questions asked from sellers, no identity given. In other words, a black market, and for what? The buyers can never display their collections in case, they attract awkward questions from those who know about these things in the art world. It is like locking the great artworks of the world away from the beholder. No beholder no beholden." He translated in his head from German into English unaware of syntax, but it made sense.

Brigette came into the room and announced that dinner was ready and they went into the dining room that a few years ago would have brought Kaetrin to her knees. But she was an old hand at it now. Cutlery and plate settings were a part of her stock in trade. After ten years at Maximes Hotel there was not a setting variation to a table that she had not experienced. And she could probably teach the aristocracy a thing or two about table etiquette.

The wines selected were from Franz-Josef's cellar and he had a good one. It contained five thousand bottles stored in a natural limestone cellar beneath the building, where meticulous records were kept of his sublime inventory. If the atmosphere above ground ever got too oppressive and it often did, then an hour or two in the cool dungeons below rejuvenated body and soul. And that was without imbibing from the pleasures bottled within. It was enough to dust the bottles and polish the glass. He imagined that a genie might suddenly spring a cork and pop out. He was, after all, living in a land that inspired such wizardry. But the Genie emerged only when he popped a cork in preparedness for consumption. And that was good enough. Tonight he corked and the genies emerged with a pop. The party toasted, 'good luck', 'good health', 'long life', 'so good to know you', 'please come back' and 'to the future'. At the

172

conclusion of dinner the menfolk took brandy and cigars on the terrace while the ladies relaxed in the lounge with an after dinner coffee and cognac.

The following day while Kaetrin was doing the art appreciation course with Calliope, Franz-Josef and Linus discussed the possibility of attempting to discover the location of Rudi and Werner who Franz-Josef had insisted were taken to Russia along with the substantial collection of art works saved from Auschwitz.

"Also," he said. "Also, I have a list of the artworks we collected and catalogued, Rudi even listed the names of former owners, when he thought he could identify them. Maybe," he said, "we can give them back to the owners when the war is over! He knew so much about paintings but nothing about politics. Surely greatness is canvas and oils not ink and paper."

Franz-Josef continued. "I have tried to contact them before, through the Red Cross, but every time we come up against a blank wall. This cold war thing is a huge obstacle, you just have to look at the situation in Berlin between NATO and the Soviets. It is being stonewalled by the Soviets at every turn. The Soviets insist on arguing the toss! Niggardly things but time consuming and pointless and of course we make no headway whatsoever! We have discovered a Russian Jewish agency who are trying to help with the finding of lost Russian Jews but quite frankly I feel that the Soviets are as like-minded as the Nazis when it come to their Jewish nationals. They really do not want to know."

Linus nodded in agreement. "I'll see what Van Oldenbarnevelts can do from London. They are my lawyers, but they have good international contacts. Do you want me to contact you directly or through your lawyers?"

"Communications here are good; I'll say that for the Brits. Everything seems to work so get in touch with me here." And he gave Linus a business card.

Linus and Kaetrin rejoined the *Rangitoto* in Port Said, saying fond farewells to the von Hapsbergs and Kaisers who had promised to visit them in New Zealand when they came to see Neil Walker of LRDG patrol fame.

Their ship loaded oranges in Cyprus before a scheduled stop at Gibraltar for a run ashore and also another at Lisbon and before long they were in the London docks.

Marjory and Horace Beresford-Amble took the train to Wiltshire and agreed to keep in touch using their lawyers' office as both couples were of no fixed abode for the foreseeable future. Linus and Kaetrin had booked into Claridges and would stay there at least until the trust business was completed and the auction over. Linus had questioned his right to ownership now that his father was alive but his lawyers said that was hearsay and they had to proceed on the legal document in their possession from the Dutch Government saying that both parents were deceased. Linus was not convinced anymore that he wanted to sell and would like time to think about it. He then went to the Russian Embassy to see what they could tell him about his father but he may as well have asked them about the Tsar. So he asked for a visa for both himself and Kaetrin to visit Leningrad to view artworks. His thinking was that perhaps some of the confiscated artworks that his father had catalogued in Auschwitz were already on display in Russia. He knew a few of the more valuable pieces that were in European hands before the war and especially Jewish European hands. Maybe he could start to connect the dots. It was a long shot, but he had nothing else to go on and time to spare. They never got a visa.

"These things take some time. Come back next week, Mr Levin!"

There had been works of art transferred to Russia from Berlin after WWII as reparation for the damage caused by the Germans during the siege of Leningrad and the damage done to the Peterhof Palaces. It was documented that paintings from the Buddhist cave temples along the Great Silk Road that were removed by German researchers early in the 20th century, were sent to Russia from the Museum of Hindi Art in Berlin. The spoils were shared between the Pushkin Museum of Fine Arts and the Hermitage. Those who were suspicious of these motives would suggest that the works were sponsored by the Soviet occupiers for favours that would be reciprocated at some later stage. The Hermitage Museum was one of the oldest and largest in the world, opened in 1852. It had been founded in 1764 by Catherine the Great and comprised six historic buildings one of which, the Winter Palace, was a former residence of Russian emperors. They housed a restoration and storage centre and it was here that Linus figured the services of Rudi and his Auschwitz collection could be easily accommodated, no questions asked, in view of what Berlin had openly presented them with. It could be assumed that other art treasures from Germany had been similarly bestowed, including works purchased by the Nazis from Jews at knockdown prices, as far back as 1935, when the Nazis began to put the heat on German Jews. Linus then telexed Franz-Josef, asking for the list of the artworks catalogued at Auschwitz by Rudi and Werner. Linus recalled that there was something like four thousand items; a serious piece of cataloguing.

Otto had included some art contacts in Berlin in the reply telex from Franz-Josef. There were also some addresses that Werner had given to Franz-Josef as safe houses if he ran into problems in his flight from Auschwitz to Switzerland. Like Dresden, Berlin was in East Germany, annexed by the Soviets since the end of WWII. Linus and Kaetrin could access Berlin by train from Amsterdam. Berlin was divided into four parts administered by the allied NATO forces and the Soviets. Movement within the city was relatively easy unless the Soviets suddenly contracted a malady and everybody caught a cold until the reds had recovered from their distemper. Then what constituted normalcy was restored.

The air corridors into Berlin from the west were neutral territory. Travelling by train however was a different experience. Once the train entered East Germany the barbed wire entrenchments around each train station were plainly evident from the railway carriage. Kaetrin could see overhead walkways and the stations isolation from the general public by the wire constraints. Guards were openly visible as were Soviet tanks and other fortifications deemed necessary to restrict access to escape routes. Passengers were told not to get off the train by a large East German female guard walking through each carriage explaining her caveat in a challenging oration. Kaetrin had no intention of leaving her seat and held Linus' arm tightly lest she be prised from her repose by the gargantuan arms of this female oppressor. She felt intimidated and for the first time in her life understood provocation at a personal level.

Linus felt the pressure of Kaetrin's hand and said, "Relax – she's just a bully – we're actually meant to be on the same side. We are allies, aren't we?"

Kaetrin smiled weakly, "If that is friend I do not want to meet foe!"

Linus chuckled. "Yes, she is over the top. Let's hope she is not representative of the regime. The poor East German people, it seems that they may have leapt out of the frying pan and into the fire!"

"Let's not forget our reason for coming to Berlin," Kaetrin said.

"We may be chasing a dead end," Linus replied. "It's been a few years now since the war ended and Franz-Josef was given those names by Werner Kruger as secure and safe contacts should he get into trouble in his escape to Switzerland. It seems he didn't need them but at least, if what Franz-Josef has told us is true, then if anyone should know where Werner is it would be them.

"Time will tell. We can start looking tomorrow morning. A day and a night on this rattler has my bones in need of a soak in a hot tub and a decent sleep."

They had boarded the train at night in Amsterdam and following a night and then all the next day on board they were both ready for an easy bed in a clean hotel.

"Friedrichstrabe Station Hotel," Kaetrin said, reading from her itinerary, "must be near the railway station?"

"It had better be," Linus said. "I did read that it is like a crossroads for the Berliners, East or West. It's like a big junction, we should be able to find our way around from East to West without too much bother unless we get bother from the border guards."

Kaetrin wasn't as optimistic. "If they are as bolshie as the leviathan on this train we have a problem."

"You have a problem," Linus agreed and received an indignant smack on his arm for his comment.

By agreement they had limited their luggage to one manageable suitcase each for this journey and while Linus chose wisely, Kaetrin's case was bigger than Linus had intended when he laid down the rules for travel luggage. Linus carried Kaetrin's large case and Kaetrin managed the smaller lighter suitcase that Linus had chosen. The Hotel Albrechtshof was just a block away from the station and so they walked.

Spartan clean and larger than usual for European hotels was how Kaetrin described their room over breakfast. "Where do we go first?" she enquired. Linus was scanning some names and addresses on a piece of paper.

"Think that we should start with Werner's parents. They would not be on the list if he had written them off. So he must have kept in touch with them. I'm trying to find which part of the city they are in. East or West. It's a bit confusing!"

"I'm sure that we are in the Eastern sector."

"What makes you say that?" Kaetrin asked.

175

Linus nodded his head in the direction of some other diners. "That large lady over there reminds me of the guard on the train – no don't look, she's looking our way, must have spotted you."

Kaetrin squirmed in her seat.

"She's laughing; you must be okay!"

"So we are being followed?" Kaetrin whispered melodramatically.

"It's okay, I said she looked like her, I didn't say it was her!"

Kaetrin sneaked a look and realised that Linus was having a laugh at her expense.

"Will you be able to speak with them?"

"With whom?"

"Werner's parents."

"My German is rusty but passable, I'm sure we will be able to communicate," Linus replied.

Following breakfast Linus and Kaetrin headed for the station which indeed proved to be a transit hub. Trains from the western sector stopped there and trains from the eastern sector also stopped there. Different lines of course. They were already in the eastern sector and decided to visit Werner's parents who were also in the eastern sector. It was simply a matter of finding a taxi and they were there. Karl and Hilda Kruger were surprised to find two westerners knocking on their door.

"Could tell by your clothes," Hilda said. "Since the war, we have been on rations. Never seems to end if it's not one thing it's another. The Soviets promise the world and deliver zilch."

"Zilch?"

"Nothing, oh sorry, we lived in the states for a few years, it's an American word means nil, zero. Came back in 1930 when the great depression was biting. We thought that things might be better in Germany. They probably were for a while but Hitler put an end to that. Did you say that you were looking for Werner? We haven't seen him since 1936 when he was sent to Auschwitz. The Nazis did not like communists and Werner was one of those, for sure. I did receive a letter from him. He wrote to us after the war, you know. Gone to live in Russia, he said. Be home soon, he said. Nothing to worry about. That was a few years ago now."

"Where was the letter posted from?" Linus asked.

"Not sure, a Stalin or a Lenin something or other, they seem to have changed all the old favourite names. Same around here everything is named after a revolution or a hero."

Hilda came back into the room waving an envelope. "Leningrad," she said, "he mailed it in Leningrad! We never keep documents but this I couldn't part with. My only contact with my son in fourteen years!"

Linus looked at Kaetrin. "Saint Petersburg."

"You must have United States citizenship, yes?" Linus asked.

"No, we never stayed long enough. And Werner was born here."

176

They thanked the Krugers and left. Linus left a card with his London contact address at the Van Oldenbarnevelts' office with a request to let them know if Werner made any further contact and exited into the barren streets. But not before Hilda said, "If you are going into the western sector and plan on coming back here for a visit, bring coffee! Can't buy decent coffee here!"

"Indomitable spirit," Kaetrin observed.

"You would certainly need to have some sort of spirit to live among these ruins," Linus replied. "It's depressing!"

That afternoon, the Levins visited the western sector and were immediately reminded of the difference in the cultures between a democracy and communism. They were in a relatively modern metropolis where people had smiles and shops displayed goods and the latest models of automobiles could be seen. They moved to a Western sector hotel immediately.

Linus got out his list of the artworks that Franz-Josef had given him and scanned it for the Berlin addresses. Rudi, with his intimate knowledge of art, had written the name and address of the owner of a painting that he was able to identify. There were also German art dealers listed. It was obvious that the previous owners would have been murdered in the ovens at Auschwitz. Therefore, any art dealer still standing and most were probably gentile, may have some knowledge about family survivors. Linus felt that if a family heirloom had been saved and was in safekeeping in Saint Petersburg, or Leningrad, as it had been renamed, the owners would have leverage, if there were enough of them, to petition the West German government to do something about it. They were after all stolen works of art. If nothing else, it could lead to the discovery that Rudi Levin was alive and living in Russia.

They visited several galleries, but the owners were extremely cautious. A couple recognised the name of Rudi Levin from Amsterdam. But that was about as much recognition as they got. They probably coerced with the Nazis into buying art works from Jews at knock down prices. So it was a shoulder shrug and "Sorry, can't help you." Even Otto Kaiser's name raised no more than an eyebrow. It seemed that they had hit a brick wall. Nobody wanted to know what had transpired between the Nazis and the Jewish art dealers and subsequently the Russians. Eventually they visited a Jewish gallery run by a survivor from the holocaust. He remembered Rudi Levin from Amsterdam.

"We had dealings over the years. You say he's in Russia. He was originally from Russia. A Russian Jew. He left Russia when the Bolsheviks came to power back in 1917. Wow – he's gone full circle!"

The man's name was Wilbur Weiss and he was in Dachau from 1939 until 1945. He survived but his wife and children and most relatives died. They were either starved or exterminated during the holocaust.

"I had an inkling that the Nazis were going to clean me out, so I sent all of my valuable stock and possessions to my brother in Switzerland," Wilbur said. "Kept rats and mice here to make it look good to the dumb Nazi mobs who burned us out during the pogroms resulting in the crystal night. They really stuck it to us. We knew we were in trouble but left it too late to do anything

177

about it. And then what do the dumb asses do now that the Soviets are in charge of about a third of Germany? They send a heap of valuable artworks from Berlin to Leningrad, that's Saint Petersburg to the educated, as compensation for the damage that the Nazi war machine did to that lovely city during the war. Now that has to be orchestrated. Fiddlers on the loose, wouldn't you say!"

It was obvious Herr Weiss had worked himself into a frenzy over this transfer of artworks from Berlin to Leningrad. "And that's only what they tell us about. What about the secret stuff?"

"So, here I am ranting, is that what you came to hear? A ranting Jew who survived the holocaust! Show me the list again – no, better still – leave a copy with me or get a copy done for me I will see what I can do. It is a lot of work to go through the list but maybe we come up with some trumps. Yes? You like trumps? I like trumps!"

Linus had copies made so was able to comply. "Please feel free to make more copies," he said to Wilbur, "we need to circulate the list. They are stolen Jewish works of art. The Nazis took them, but now the Russians have them, the more we can show the world that these are in Leningrad and the greater shame on Russia. Maybe one day they will be returned to their rightful owners. Silence never taught a deaf man how to talk, so let's make some noise!"

Wilbur thanked them for coming and said he would spread the word. Linus and Kaetrin felt that some progress had been made.

They purchased coffee and planned to visit the Krugers the following day. After talking with residents in the western sector they were encouraged to buy coffee for the border guard too. A small bribe so they could take their gift through to the Krugers. They crossed at the Fiedrichstrabe Station at a street level crossing and paid two jars of coffee for the privilege of taking two jars through. Also they had to buy East German marks which were not redeemable when they returned and valueless in the West. There was nothing in the Eastern sector that they could spend the money on so they decided to give it to the Krugers as well as the coffee. Hilda Kruger was pleased to see them and delighted with the coffee. In fact, she was bubbly and they soon found out why.

"We have had a visit from one of Werner's friends. He has come from Leningrad and says that Werner is in good health and he is working with Rudi Levin, the man he met in Auschwitz. He has a message which is cryptic to us but he says when the right person hears it they will understand. I am not allowed to write it down so if my memory is correct I have to say this. Gee I feel silly." She laughed nervously and cleared her throat in the manner of people not used to passing on information in this manner.

"I once was what you are and what I am you will also be!"

Linus was speechless.

"Did I say it right?"

"Yes you said it perfectly!"

"You are crying!"

"I know."

"Have I upset you?"

"No you have made me very happy – you have just proven to me that my father is still alive. This is proof; what you have said is enough to convince me that my father is alive and living in Leningrad and working with Werner. Same as they did in Auschwitz, according to Franz-Josef."

"We are both happy, then."

"Yes we are both happy."

I will write a letter for your friend to take back to Leningrad."

"No, no letters, oral only. It is too dangerous to carry letters!"

"I can meet this man then?"

"No, it is too dangerous; he is watched closely. He moves freely from Germany to Russia, but he is watched – they trust nobody!"

"What about this house?" Linus asked.

Hilda laughed. "All they will find is coffee!"

Throughout the entire discussion, Karl Kruger was stoic but he now spoke. "You have a message for your father?"

"Obviously we have a lot to tell him. Say that we love him and that we will try and visit as soon as we can get a visa to enter Russia."

Linus and Kaetrin said goodbye to them both and thanked them for their information which was the first positive piece of intelligence that they had received since the war. Rudi and Werner were alive. Linus invited them to contact the London address on the card he left yesterday, if there was anything new that developed.

"Burnt the card," Hilda said. "Dangerous having that sort of information lying about. You never know who's going to shop you. Bring coffee if you come back and good luck!"

Linus and Kaetrin returned to their hotel and purchased a bottle of Champagne. They sat in their room and toasted Rudi and the trinity. At last they had a positive identification with a location all they had to do was get there.

He phoned London that night and asked Van Oldenbarnevelts to get a visa application underway for both himself and Kaetrin to visit Leningrad, as representatives of the Art 1 Trust with a view to display specially selected works of art at the Hermitage, similar to the current display at the Guggenheim in New York. They would be flying directly from Berlin to London as soon as they could get a flight out. Flying out was easier, as they had discovered. If they wanted to go by train they had to go back to the Eastern sector and obtain a visa from the DDR Visa travel office. They were told that the queues were intolerably long. Flying out, did not require a visa.

"We fly," Linus said. Kaetrin agreed, the place was getting on her nerves.

"I'm expecting a tap on the shoulder any tick of the clock," she said to Linus. "It's like living in a fish bowl. I feel watched!"

Linus wanted to wire Franz-Josef in Cairo with their good news but felt that it would be best sent from the safety of London. Berlin seemed a bit too much like a pioneer settlement to him. There was a certain rawness to it. He didn't want a third party to know his business.

179

Back in London they settled into Claridges Hotel and had afternoon tea with the Beresford-Ambles on their first day back. Cucumber sandwiches and Darjeeling tea was the perfect Berlin antidote. There was something profoundly reassuring to Kaetrin about Marjory Beresford-Amble and her adherence to tradition and etiquette. Perhaps that was the secret behind the British Empire, she reasoned. If everyone took time out for cucumber sandwiches and Darjeeling tea the world would be a better place. She immediately imagined Hitler in his Berlin bunker calling a halt for afternoon tea English style. "Sugar, my dear Goering, one lump or two?" She moved on to Stalin sharing a cuppa with Churchill and Roosevelt or should that now be Truman and Attlee?

"You're smiling, my dear."

"What?"

Marjory had woken Kaetrin from her reverie.

"Smiling? Yes, I suppose I was just having a daydream. You know it is so nice to be here with you and the major."

"Enjoying the moment?"

"Yes I was. I love this room, I love your company!" Kaetrin made the statement passionately, unashamedly.

They were seated at a round table covered with a crisp white starched linen table cloth, comfortable cushioned seats and the best china tea service that money could buy. The cups, saucers and plates were superb. Long, airy, translucent glass-paned windows decorated the exterior walls and brought the daylight into the room, highlighting the potted palms and other exotics that emitted an extrinsic ambience. Marjory was in her element and could have been at high tea at the Simla Swimming Club. Her enthusiasm was contagious and set the tone for an enjoyable two hours. The Beresford-Ambles were at a different hotel and had come up to London from Wiltshire to attend to some defence matters concerning Horace's pension. They said their goodbyes at five o'clock in the afternoon.

During their tea absence, a message had been slipped under the door of the Levins' room.

"It's from Van Oldenbarnevelts," Linus said, "I have to get in touch with them. Better do it now."

He phoned the lawyers' office, said a few words and hung up.

"Well," Kaetrin enquired, "what was that all about?"

"It seems that we have our visa. We can visit Leningrad."

It was an 8 hour journey from London to Moscow including a three hour stopover in Moscow and then onto Shosseynaya Airport, just out of Leningrad. The hotel reminded Kaetrin of their first hotel stay in East Berlin; clean and Spartan. They were introduced to their interpreter who went everywhere with them, but as their primary business was in the arts field. They really only travelled to various art galleries and, of course, the Hermitage, which was a beautiful museum housing amazing exhibits. And that was only what was on display. They were desperate to see behind the scenes and Linus was playing on the fact that they were as interested in the display facilities as they were in

180

the handling and storage facilities. It was important that they got Elena's trust. It was Elena that they spent all day with. As their official interpreter, Elena became their shadow and it seemed impossible that they would ever be able to give her the slip which would probably not be a good idea, as that would raise suspicions and God knows they were suspicious enough of Westerners without having a couple roaming at large. The last thing that Linus and Kaetrin wanted to do was to make Elena look bad in the eyes of her superiors. She really was a most pleasant and obliging young lady. Gaining her trust was probably their best strategy.

After several days looking at the various venues for their proposed art display from the Art1 Trust collection they felt that the Hermitage would be their best venue. It certainly was the biggest and they were proposing a large display. Kaetrin discreetly asked Elena if they could meet some of the backroom staff.

"We need to meet the people who will be handling our canvasses," she explained. "We have to form a mutual trust." Elena explained that she would need to get permission from her superiors and the earliest that might be arranged would be tomorrow.

"Earliest," she repeated. "Things move slowly in the USSR; we have procedures, you understand!"

They understood and said that she should take her time. "We are in no hurry, we can go sightseeing until the go-ahead is given."

Elena looked at her papers. "No sight-seeing," she said. "That activity is not on your documents. You need to get permission and they will get you another interpreter for sight-seeing. Take another day or two to organise sightseeing."

"Okay, leave sightseeing," Linus said, "let's get the other matter settled first."

Elena met them at breakfast the following morning and said that she had permission to look behind the scenes at the Hermitage. And they were off. The storage facilities were impressive, they visited room after room, but there was no personal contact. Linus said, "We need to talk with the staff. Get to know who will be looking after our valuables, you understand? Can we meet the people?"

Elena seemed to be struggling with the task. Linus said, "Can we say, meet the person who would be in charge of the display, you know, unpacking from the crates, laying it out, cataloguing the incoming works, deciding on display criteria. That person and their staff. Those are the people we need to talk with." Elena seemed outwardly calm.

"Wait here," she said and went through a door. It was the first time that they had been left alone and it signalled that she trusted them.

She returned very quickly with two persons in tow whom she introduced as Mikhail and Petrov. Following introductions, Mikhail, who spoke passable English, invited them into his office. He said to Elena that he didn't require the services of an interpreter so she could wait outside and Elena indicated that would be okay. "Happy to do that." she said.

They all sat around a table in Mikhail's office and Linus explained the reason for their visit. Mikhail explained that they had been informed about the possibility of the pending art loan for display and they were excited. "We have not had much contact with our allies since the war ended," he said, "so this will be a bit of a coup for us. As you know, the art world just loves to be ahead of the pack and this will be us leading the way. We are honoured. Thank you very much for this honour," he said. "We look forward to working together."

Linus thanked him and said, "You know there is something that you may be able to do for us," and as he finished talking, he pulled a package from his jacket pocket, removed the contents and laid them on the table for all to see.

It was the bottom two paintings of the Trinity that Rudi had had painted in three parts. There was the bottom piece showing the cadaver in the tomb that Linus was given by his father and the middle section which Franz-Josef had added, in Cairo. "We are trying to locate the top section which we believe was lost at some stage during about 1940 and 1945. It alone is not a valuable piece but as a complete package it becomes priceless to the owner."

Mikhail and Petrov looked at it. They both knew what it depicted and admitted that neither was aware that such a copy existed.

"The only reason I ask," Linus said, "is that you have so many works here it just maybe possible that one of your staff may have come across something like this in their research. As I say, singularly it is nothing; collectively it is priceless, if you get my meaning. I was hoping that you might be able to help. I can leave these with you and collect them again on our next visit in a few days' time. You know, after you show them around to see if you get a reaction." Linus raised an eyebrow as he finished the sentence.

Mikhail said, "Sure only too happy to help a colleague. You may contact me directly here by phone," and he gave Linus a card. Linus reciprocated with one of his.

"You can always leave a message at my London Office," he said and thought that he sounded rather grand.

It was a timely meeting and all parties agreed that they had made a good initial contact and said that they would meet again in two days' time. Elena was waiting as they exited the office and said that she had permission to take them for a small sightseeing tour that afternoon. "Where shall we go?"

They had an interesting afternoon, returning to their hotel in time for dinner that waited for no one. It was eat when we serve, or starve. Twilight lasted well into the evening and they strolled around after dinner, but the place was dead. Where on earth were the people? Maybe they came out during the hours of darkness when electricity was turned off to non-essential services and buildings. Street lamps were non-essential. Perhaps people emerged and moved freely under the canopy of darkness!

It was eleven o'clock and night had come at last. Kaetrin and Linus were preparing for bed when they heard a knock on the door. Linus said, "I wonder who that is? We have never had night callers before!"

"You won't know if you don't open it, will you?" They seemed frozen by the surprise of it all.

Linus opened the door and Werner Kruger introduced himself. He spoke in German and Linus responded in German. "Please come in, Herr Kruger," Linus said and waved his entrance into the hotel room with a sweeping arm.

Linus introduced Kaetrin to Werner and they sat down in the chairs that the hotel had provided which Linus had earlier described as "Comfortable – just!"

Linus said, "Can we talk in English so my wife can follow the conversation?"

"Of course."

"My father," Linus said, "how is my father?"

"He is good," Werner replied. "He cannot come because there are too many eyes watching. For me it is not too much of a problem. I have more freedom. I am not so valuable. I have no-where to run to. Here for me is as good as Berlin, maybe better – who knows." Werner seemed a very relaxed individual.

"Can we see my father?"

Werner held up the palm of his hand like a policeman halting traffic. "I don't know how much you know? Have you met Franz-Josef?"

"Yes," Linus said, "we met him recently in Cairo and he was able to explain what happened at Auschwitz."

"A remarkable man," Werner said, "without his help neither Rudi or myself would be here today. We owe him everything."

Linus was impatient. "Can I see my father?"

"That is our intention. That is what brings me here tonight. And at considerable risk if I am caught. They don't like us conversing with Westerners. We are in incubation like a disease ward. You understand!"

Kaetrin and Linus nodded.

"Okay, so here's where we are, today you met Mikhail and Petrov. Mikhail is a good man, Petrov an unknown quantity – he is new here. Anyway Mikhail showed me the Trinity and of course I knew what it meant. I told Rudi and he of course is delighted and he asked me to give you this." Werner laid the top section of the Trinity painting on the table. "Now you will have all three parts when Mikhail returns your two sections. Rudi is a treasure and while he is treated very well and wants for nothing other than to be in Holland, he is kept here as he is too valuable to lose. Therefore, he is watched very closely. As you can imagine any contact with Westerners would be treated suspiciously so his movements are closely monitored. However, I think that we can arrange a meeting when you come back to meet Mikhail again. We all work in the Hermitage, we are just in different sections so it is a matter of making sure that the head count is the same; it doesn't really matter who owns the head. The count is important. We will organise a switch so that when you meet Mikhail instead of Petrov we will have Rudi. As I say, it is the count that matters so we have excluded Petrov and replaced him with one of our trusted staff who will stand in for Rudi. Head count you understand! All you have to do is make that meeting with Mikhail again and we will do the rest. How does that sound?"

Linus recalled Franz-Josef's remarks about Werner having the run of the place at Auschwitz and here he was giving a perfect example of his ability to organise a clandestine meeting and making it sound like one of Marjory Beresford-Amble's tea parties.

"Sounds good to me, how about you, Kaetrin?"

"I am looking forward to it!"

"Well that's settled. I believe you met my parents in Berlin recently?"

Linus knew a good operator when he saw one and replied in kind.

"Did Stalin tell you?"

"No," Werner replied, "Joe's a slow communicator, I have to use faster channels."

They all laughed at the riposte.

Werner looked at his watch, "I have to go, I may not see you again so will say good night, good bye and good luck!"

They all rose and Linus opened the door He held out his hand and they shook. "Thank you for all you have done for my father."

"My pleasure. He is one hell of a man."

It was obvious from the timbre in Werner's voice that he held Rudi in the highest of regards.

Elena collected them from the hotel as usual and they went directly to the Hermitage for another meeting with Mikhail. Linus told Elena that they were making progress now that they were talking with staff. "It is important to have these discussions," he said. "Do you realise that the collection which we are prepared to send is worth in excess of ten million pounds? So we need to ensure that we are dealing with people that we know and trust."

Mikhail met them at the door to his office and asked Elena to wait outside while they conducted their business. There were windows and slatted blinds partially closed, but you could make out a head within, obviously seated in a chair at the table that they would all sit around to hold their discussion. Mikhail said to Linus, "No embracing, that would seem strange to anyone watching. It will have to be a simple and perfunctory handshake. Sorry, but those are the rules."

Rudi stood up as they entered the room. He had received similar instructions from Mikhail which had been anticipated anyway but did not allow the emotions that were welling up within his breast to be contained. With an outstretched hand and an audible stifled sob, Rudi took his son's hand as tears rolled down his cheeks. Linus looked at his father. The mane of grey hair that he remembered was now white. His large moustache was a mixture of grey and white but the handgrip that he felt was warm and firm. It had been ten years. Not a lifetime for sure, but long enough. Their eyes made magnetic contact and never wavered. Linus said three words, "I love you, Father."

Mikhail said, "Release," and their handshake terminated and their brief and only physical contact ended. "Please be seated everybody." Mikhail was keen to present to an outside observer, that their conference was strictly business. Linus introduced Kaetrin and they shook hands. It was Kaetrin's turn to shed a tear. She would dearly have loved to hug her father in law and to tell him that she loved his son and that they had both dreamed about this moment for years.

"It will not be the last," she heard herself say. "We hope to come back with the display."

Linus explained that he was living in New Zealand where he had met Kaetrin.

"She was sent to New Zealand from England in 1940." Linus told Rudi. "Britain had sent a lot of their children out to their colonies during the early stages of the war when major British cities were being bombed by the Luftwaffe."

Linus told Rudi about the artworks that Rudi had saved from the clutches of the Nazis, how they were being displayed in major world galleries and generating income for the trust, that was in turn helping resettle surviving Dutch and other Jewish families, disenfranchised at the end of the war. Rudi explained his existence there at the Hermitage. He said that he had his own apartment, small but comfortable and a good supply of food.

"Not Harrods," he quipped, "but gives me sustenance. And I have a small circle of friends. We gather for drinks and discussions regularly. Vigorous repartee, some humour, of course and heaps of good old fashioned philosophy thrown in for good measure. Just like we did in Holland."

Linus nodded, smiling.

Rudi mentioned that he was aware that Ester, his wife, had perished when the SS guards marched them to Wodzislaw some 35 kilometres away from Auschwitz.

"It was January 1945, a very cold winter," he said, "and the Soviet Army were just nine days away from liberating us at Auschwitz. Fifteen thousand prisoners perished in atrocious winter conditions. It would have been a merciful relief for them, but it does not condone the misguided Nazi thinking, that they were saving German prisoners from the clutches of the Red Army!" he concluded.

"Also I must mention my friend Werner Kruger who has been a big part of my life since we were introduced at Auschwitz. And that meeting only happened by chance, when Franz-Josef Kaiser saw us arrive at Auschwitz."

Linus said, "Yes, we met Werner last evening. We have heard all about his deeds and exploits when we stopped over in Cairo on our journey to the UK. Otto Kaiser did the same for his art collection as you did. He shipped them out of the country as part of an arms shipment bound for the Africa Corps campaign in North Africa. Quite a story. Between the two of you the art world is indebted. One day, my dear father, we all may be able to stand together and toast your greatness!"

Mikhail looked at his watch and said, "Our allocated meeting time is up; we have to say goodbye." And in the same manner that they had greeted one another they said their goodbyes. Mikhail and Rudi left the office and Elena collected Kaetrin and Linus as they exited the office door.

And that was the end of the personal contacts. All further discussions about the proposed art display were conducted through the ministry which was housed in a cold cell of a tall concrete building in downtown Leningrad.

Linus and Kaetrin stuck it out for another week before they boarded their flight to Moscow and then onto London.

Kaetrin could not wait to partake of her antidote as she sat in the reading room at Claridges sipping tea and nibbling delicacies from the afternoon tea menu. Going from Hobson's choice in Leningrad to the exquisite pleasures of her Mayfair hotel was one of the most pleasurable experiences that she could imagine. She made a mental note to introduce the elegant recreational pastime to Maximes on her return. She was sure that Flora would approve.

Chapter 13

Escape from Leningrad

It had taken six years of intense discussions and negotiations before the Russians were able to approve the Art 1 Trust's display of famous paintings at the Hermitage in Leningrad. Linus and Kaetrin had instigated the idea when they first visited in 1951. Since then they had left further negotiations with the trust. Werner Kruger had proved invaluable in despatching intelligence between the two parties. It had not been easy. Werner had freedom to travel between Leningrad and Berlin but he was shadowed by KGB who watched his every move. Barbara Lightfoot, was director of displays for the Art 1 Trust in London. She was also an MI5 operative and was appreciative of any information that Werner was able to pass on to the trust. "However trivial it may seem to you, it is highly valuable to us," she had said. Eventually Werner was contacted by an MI5 operative in Europe who acted as a courier and was able to pass on the despatches directly from Rudi in a safer and more secure manner. One such courier package contained an up to date picture of Rudi with information such as his current weight and dimensions, such as height and girth. He had never regained the weight loss from his Auschwitz diet following three years of incarceration.

It became obvious that Rudi was a bit of a treasure at the Hermitage, an institution that collected treasures, in a less animate form. Rudi was one of the great art dealers of Europe in his time. Pre-war, he had clients across continental Europe as well as contact with other art dealers who in the main were also Jewish. Apart from the cache of artworks that Franz-Josef, Werner and himself were able to collect from Auschwitz, the Russians were also accumulating many more treasures from Germany as they cleaned up their occupied territories in post WWII Europe. These art treasures were being smuggled covertly to Leningrad for examination and valuation by Rudi and his team. Werner was treated a bit like a germ in a laboratory. The Russians were aware of his background as a German dissident communist and he was better

187

kept under their microscope than allowed to run freely among the general populace where who knew what pranks he would be able to get up to. Werner knew this too and played on it so both sides were happy with the status quo.

It was agreed that the forthcoming exhibition should be held during the summer months and stay open during the long twilight evenings in Leningrad. Two Bristol freighters would deliver the display to Leningrad, together with the staff and curators from the London Museum who were to oversee the display. They would uncrate the artworks then set up the display and leave when it was operational. The Russian Hermitage staff would run the display for the following two months. The aircraft would later return to dismantle and recrate the display for the return trip to London. Packaging and loading was a very important part of the whole operation and these people were experts in their field

Among the artefacts to be shipped would be a large, life-size bronze sculptor of a warhorse that had been discovered in a dig on an old Roman village in England. The bronze casting had been unearthed in parts and had been assembled with a few minor bits missing. It was a valuable find, however, as the only comparable example of this kind was in a museum in Athens. The horse was in a heraldry rampant pose, on its hind legs with forelegs in the air. Experts say that there was originally a rider on the horse as there was evidence of reins and bridle that were partially intact. The horse was uncovered early twentieth century and archaeologists were hopeful that the rider would one day be uncovered as the dig continued. They had decided, because the hind legs were cast in a much heavier gage bronze, that they were designed to carry the weight of the horse. The bronze sculpture was three meters long and two meters high and therefore a full life scale model. The Russians were keen to have this in the exhibition as they had nothing like it. History suggested that the bronze statue may have been plundered from Corinth by the Roman General Mummius during the Achaean War, about 150BC and taken to Britain by Julius Caeser in 53BC. A lovely piece indeed; it would draw the crowds.

Barbara Lightfoot was in charge of overseas displays for the Art 1 Trust and had sent works to offshore galleries these past four years, so was experienced in her role. This was the first time that the consignment consisted of a heavy and rather large crate that contained the sculpture of the bronze horse and they needed to find a suitable aircraft to handle it. Also to be crated was a selection of life like and full size mannequins from the famous London waxworks, Madame Tussauds. It was always going to be difficult to select effigies that would not offend the Russians, or rather, Russian politicians. They included Hans Christian Anderson, the Danish storyteller and Peter Tchaikovsky, the Russian composer and were given the thumbs up by Barbara's Russian counterpart, Mikhail Chekov. They were crated and stored in the cargo hold of a Bristol freighter aircraft. Two aircraft were needed as there were also personnel to accompany the precious cargo. The spacious interior of the freighters could accommodate a passenger pod which took up cargo space. The pod could take sixteen persons with luggage but reduced the cargo area. Two aircraft solved the problem. With only a 900 mile maximum flight range the journey was undertaken in several stages. They refuelled at Hamburg, then Copenhagen, Stockholm and finally Leningrad. Unloading of the plane's cargo at Leningrad was performed by the local airport staff and then the Art 1 Trust people, led by Barbara Lightfoot, did the uncrating, checking for any transit damage and then returning the crates back to the aircraft. The planes would fly back to England and return in two months' time, when the exhibition would be dismantled and repacked for the return journey.

The paintings chosen would to appeal to Russians who had never been exposed to the Dutch classics from the Golden Age. Following the long war in the seventeenth century, the Netherlands was the most prosperous nation in Europe. Estimates suggested that 1.3 million paintings were done in the Netherlands in the twenty years following 1640, a definite oversupply, and prices fell. Most of these were painted by the masters' apprentices and they were good, not expensive, but plentiful. Those works that have survived to today are classics and very valuable. No other nation had such a legacy so it was a good exhibition and was popular wherever it showed. Russia would be no exception. Barbara Lightfoot and her team stayed long enough to supervise the display in the best possible light, literally, and when they were satisfied that the paintings had been hung to perfection, they left. Because of his knowledge of the works Rudi Levin assisted Barbara who was able to converse freely with the famous art connoisseur. Repartee that would not normally have been possible was exchanged and Rudi learned that he must be ready for an escape plan when they returned to collect the exhibition and return it to London. Barbara could say no more. All she could suggest was, "You may bring the clothes that you are wearing at the time and nothing more. We can only give you a few minutes warning so be prepared. You will want for nothing back in Amsterdam."

She managed to secure pictures of the exhibition for insurance purposes and in those was able to capture good images of the Russian staff and in particular, Rudi. Werner Kruger was conspicuous by his absence and Rudi said that Werner was visiting his parents in Berlin. He had no travel restrictions within the USSR and its satellite countries.

No paperwork was exchanged other than the cargo manifest that detailed the consignment that the Art 1 Trust had delivered and the Russians verified that they had received the items as described on the manifest. Both figures tallied and both parties were satisfied. By agreement, no other paperwork was to be exported from the Hermitage such as personal letters and papers and this was enforced by Barbara who in no way wanted to jeopardise the display and the access that they had worked so long and hard to establish.

The Bristol freighters left Leningrad for the first refuelling stop at Stockholm on their return journey, where Barbara was able to put a safe call back to a base in London. Not the Art 1 Trust, but MI5. She reported that all had gone as planned and they should be able to complete their assignment when they returned to collect the cargo. "Bring the goods home," was the turn of phrase she used. Barbara Lightfoot was a graduate of the London School of Economics where she studied International Relations following on from her three years at Cambridge where she had earned a degree in Art History. The Art 1 Trust was an obvious choice of employer and MI5 just happened to do what they always did and kept track of suitable alumni from the LSE. Barbara's position opened doors to a lot of influential persons, on her offshore forays into the arts. Famous people, a lot of them politicians, were great patrons of the arts and she got to meet her share of them. The Art 1 Trust was displaying a selection from its famous collection of artworks that Rudi had saved from Holland and the world was starting to appreciate the value of these works and they were in demand. Mind you it was not public knowledge how the Art 1 Trust came by the collection. They just happened to own it. Some art critics had assumed that the collection had been amassed when the allies liberated Europe, whereby, in the natural process of events they had come upon stolen Nazi art treasures. Aryanised works of art that had been taken from Jewish people later incinerated in the ovens in the death camps and now ownerless. The main conspectus was too awful to contemplate and so art lovers were simply happy to be able to view the masterpieces rather than ask the hard questions.

The Leningrad exhibition was the result of a lot of hard work and also it was a chance to see if it would be possible to extract Rudi Levin from his enforced sojourn in Russia, which really was their prime objective. If successful, his disappearance would appear coincidental but not necessarily, because of the appearance of a western art display. If their plan did work – and there was no reason to believe that it would not – it would need to be proven beyond all doubt that Rudi was snatched or stolen away, which seemed a bit farcical. People disappeared for all sorts of obscure reasons within the Soviet Union and Rudi, perhaps, would be no exception. The KGB would be blamed as they always were and they would deny this as they always did. Russian politicians could not really go public and blame Rudi's disappearance on the recent Art 1 Trust exhibition, because as far as the world was concerned, Rudi Levin was not in Russia and never had been, apart from his birth and infant nurture. He was taken to the west, when his parents fled the communist regime in 1918. As far as the world was concerned, Rudi Levin perished at Auschwitz in 1945. The free world would be mortified to learn that the renowned art dealer, Rudi Levin, survived the holocaust, only to have been abducted, along with hundreds of artworks that he had helped save from the Jewish prisoners who had perished in the gas chambers at Auschwitz. The Russians had secretly and furtively removed both treasures and held them under lock and key in Leningrad.

Barbara's job was simply intelligence gathering. This was no Cape and Bodkin stuff. She had a phone number and a name and sent in her reports orally and received her instructions in a reciprocal manner. Her contact was known to her as Stanley and he was a polite and well-mannered individual. They had never met. The Leningrad project was code named Paris after the husband of Helen of Troy. Paris was the son of the King of Troy, he abducted Helen, who was married to the King of Sparta and had taken her back to Troy. It was part of that epic Greek tale. Modern day scholars believe that there is a historical core to the story that gave birth to the phrase, 'Beware of Greeks bearing gifts' – a reference to the wooden horse! *Someone in MI5 has a sense of humour*, she mused.

Operation Paris was kept low-key and mentioned infrequently. Those involved went about their daily work in a normal manner Barbara Lightfoot was the only Art 1 Trust employee that knew of it. Werner was informed through the normal MI5 channels via standard despatches. Surprise and the unexpected were the elements of success in these affairs. Intelligence was now by oral communication only and those conversations were limited to countries outside of the Iron Curtain. Everything was in place. It was now a waiting game.

In early September, two Bristol freighters left London for Leningrad to collect the art display on loan from the Art 1 Trust. The display had proved to be a success and the Russians were upbeat about it. The galleries that held the displays were now closed to the public and so the packaging crew had good space to work in and were pretty much left to their own devices, removing the paintings from the walls and repackaging them in their allotted and marked crates with great care and attention. Packing took a great deal more time than unpacking. Again, Barbara photographed each item that they packaged for insurance purposes. The two largest crates held the horse and the waxworks figurines and were left until last. They were to be the last crates to be fitted into the front of the hold on both planes. Smaller items to the back and larger to the front where the interior dimensions of the aircraft were greatest. The bronze horse was packed and the lid was about to be screwed down when two men in customs uniforms came into the room and asked to inspect the horse. Barbara suspected they were KGB and protested.

"You could have asked us earlier!" she said. "We have to partially dismantle the crate. It's a big job. What is there to inspect?"

"Routine," one said, "it is simply routine, we must examine it. It does not leave here until we have passed examination. Please."

Barbara was going to make as much fuss as she thought she could get away with. She looked at her watch. With a bit of luck, she may be able to get this to work for her and not against her.

"You do realise that this will take several hours. These crates are specifically designed to contain valuable cargo so we have to literally pack the contents as if they were crystal-ware!"

Neither Russian seemed moved by this statement and spoke to each other in Russian. Barbara suspected that only one of them spoke English and to pigeonhole them within her own indexing system, she referred to them as Castor and Pollux. In part, because they had code named the operation to free Rudi, 'Paris', but mainly because she considered them to be a couple of eggs in the most derogatory of ways. In the Greek tale from which the operation was named, Castor and Pollux were born from eggs but far from being oafs, they were accomplished in their field. To Barbara the two Russians were simply a couple of 'eggs' and so her epithets were entirely appropriate. Tag naming had been part of her training to categorise and memorise things and on occasions, it worked.

Castor and Pollux sniffed around the room and looked at the two figurines of Hans Christian Anderson and Peter Tchaikovsky waiting to be crated. Obviously taken by their lifelike appearance, they attempted to touch them, but Barbara intervened.

"Under any circumstances, they are not to be touched. Only our staff wearing the correct apparel are allowed to touch them!" she said in her extremely autocratic voice. Russians responded to authority, it was part of the system. 'Dolce voce' didn't cut the mustard. It took a couple of hours to disassemble the crated horse to the stage where the two customs officers were able to see that it was a large bronze horse. They then asked to see inside it.

"We need to remove the head!" Barbara protested, she sounded exasperated.

The one she had named Pollux responded, "Then remove it!"

"It's a big job!"

"Off with its head!"

"If you insist," and she called a couple of her technicians to remove the head which required removing some rivets and screws that were strategically placed so as not to interfere with the smooth bronze finish of the animal's sleek hide. Barbara pointed out a couple of holes in the bronze; the result of the material decaying naturally during its years in the ground.

"If you get a torch you can look in through those small holes and examine the interior, I really am reluctant to remove the head."

"Remove it please!" Pollux insisted.

And off came the head. That took another two hours.

Castor found a small step-ladder and they both took turns to peer into the interior of the bronze horse.

Pollux said, "It is clear, you may crate it again, we have passed the inspection. Thank you please."

When the head was in place, Castor placed a large orange sticker across the join line which said 'Custom Passed' in both English and Russian. The head could not be removed without destroying the sticker. Satisfied with their inspection, Castor and Pollux departed the scene and let the packers get back to their task. It was now well into the night and the planes were scheduled to fly out at daybreak. There was little time left to complete the packing and loading and so they had no choice but to work through the night until it was completed.

The aircraft were loaded by 0400 hours and the Art 1 Trust staff collected their belongings from the hotel and headed for the airport, where take-off had been scheduled for 0600 hours. Castor and Pollux were conspicuous at the airport and their presence brought a shiver to Barbara's spine. She always felt uneasy under surveillance and wondered what was going through their minds.

Maybe nothing sinister, she concluded with herself. "All of the foreboding is in my head." she said.

"What?"

"Nothing – just talking to myself."

"Are you a nervous flyer?" her questioner was trying to be friendly. He was one of the Art 1 Trust staff.

They were called to board the aircraft and Barbara managed a smile and a nod as she passed the two customs officers when she exited the boarding lounge. The planes were at ten thousand feet, two hours into the flight when Barbara asked her two staff members to don jackets and follow her out of the passenger pod and into the cargo hold which was unpressurized and cold. She told them to take off the side off the crate containing the two wax figurines.

Tchaikovsky seemed normal, but Hans Christian Anderson became animated. "I thought you would never come!" he said. "It's cold in here." With Rudi extricated from his bondage they closed the crate and entered the passenger pod where Barbara explained the presence of Rudi Levin on the flight.

The question on everyone's lips was, "How did you do that?"

For those not in on the ruse, Barbara explained to her staff.

"As with any deception, the trick is never obvious. The Russians must at some stage have looked at the bronze horse and recalled the story about the siege of Troy. If we were going to conceal a person it would seem obvious that the horse would be the vehicle to use. That will be why they asked us to unpack it so they could check it out. No point in checking it before we crated up. All the while we had our two wax figurines in full view awaiting packaging. Moving the crating of them into the night further enhanced our plan and it was simply a matter of switching Hans Christian for Rudi at the final minute before the crate was sealed. Hans Christian was taken by Werner to Rudi's office and the heads and clothes were switched to a Rudi wax lookalike head that we had made.

"It appears that Rudi is sitting at his desk working, and a do not disturb sign is on the door. Werner then brought the old head and clothes back to the crate, tossed them in and the bingo crate was sealed. Job done! All we needed was enough time to clear Soviet air space and we have now done that! So all can be revealed. I may add that you cannot mention any of this. It's in the secrecy clause in your contracts.

"You were all selectively chosen for this exhibition and loyalty will ensure that you will have many chances to take part in further offshore displays. Nothing as exciting as this, however. This is a oncer."

Barbara ended her discourse and sat with Rudi to debrief him over coffee. He was offered something stronger but declined. Linus received an aerogram from the Art 1 Trust telling him that his father had been secreted out of Russia.

"You wouldn't read about it in any newspaper because the Russians didn't make a fuss. They dare not. As far as Pravda is concerned, it is silent pictures – silent night!"

Dispatches from British agents operating behind the Iron Curtain suggested that the Russians were not sure what happened. Some say that he went away with Werner, as Werner was also missing. Naturally they were looking for them both but as yet there were no sightings. Werner was in fact in the hands of MI5 and was being taken care of at safe-houses, moving as secretively as possible. They would get him out from behind the Iron Curtain. That was, if Werner wanted to leave! Ultimately, Werner did what suited Werner. End of story. Werner left MI5 when they got to Berlin. The Russians took no further interest in him. If he needed to get to the west from Berlin, he told MI5 he was up to the task. "Goodbye and thanks!" MI5 had a plan to publicise Rudi's arrival in the West some six months on from the actual escape. In the interim they had to keep him undercover and out of the way of wandering KGB operatives in the West, who would have been sent his file. It was not clear what the Russians would do if they got their hands on Rudi, as he was past his use-by date. For years, Rudi was the jewel; not only was he the great painting that art people craved to own he was also the artiste. Eventually, the artificer becomes irrelevant when the owner has amassed sufficient treasures to admire. He had done his work. The world had changed in the past decade. Then there was the ego factor. No one likes having a swift one put over them, but revenge is not the best motive for retribution. Especially in the espionage business.

Linus learned most of this during a telephone discussion with Mr Van Oldenbarnevelt, his London lawyer and a fellow trustee. Linus was not allowed to phone his father for security reasons but he was encouraged to come to London, which he did. He travelled alone, arriving at Mr Van Oldenbarnevelt's office early on a Monday morning where he was introduced to Barbara Lightfoot. Barbara took Linus to a house in Chelsea where he was reunited with his father Rudi. He persuaded his father to come back to New Zealand with him, visiting Cairo along the way so he could be re-acquainted with his wartime accomplice, Franz-Josef. Barbara Lightfoot looked after the detail and Rudi was given a new identity and a British passport under the name of Hans Christian. Barbara said that the name was her contribution and they all laughed at her wit. His occupation was described as a taxidermist, an inventive reference to the escape mechanism employed when Rudi was substituted for a waxworks model. Barbara had them booked on a flight to Cairo via Zurich. A common B.O.A.C. Route. In Cairo, they would have to confirm the remainder of their flight to New Zealand through the British Embassy. No doubt it would all be orchestrated from Whitehall – a metonym for all things governmental and mysterious. Linus had a direct phone-line to Barbara Lightfoot and was requested to contact her weekly. Before leaving London, Linus phoned Kaetrin and acquainted her with proceedings to date. Kaetrin had the Kaisers' contact details in Cairo but Linus said that he would phone her on arrival. The Art 1 Trust had kitted Rudi out with a new set of clothes. He was raring to go and expressed his delight at making contact with Franz-Josef once more. Two days later they were on their way.

Linus was an observer, a mere onlooker when Franz-Josef and Rudi finally met in Cairo. Brigette had come to the airport with FJ but like Linus, once introduced, the two old wartime adversaries, who in fact were the greatest of friends, were inseparable. Brigette and Linus became extras on a film set, while the heroes hogged the limelight. Rudi and FJ were, to a certain degree, scripted in their performance but the extras hovered in the background and made small talk. Linus and Brigette had met previously, of course, when he and Kaetrin were en-route to the UK and they stopped off in Cairo for a few days, while their ship transited the Suez Canal. Brigette was now the mother of Nixie and Franco and life was full-on and interesting. Brigette and FJ's parents were in good health and while the parents hankered for Germany, Brigette and FJ were content with their life in Cairo. The Kaisers' car and driver were waiting outside the terminal. A Mercedes, no less.

"What else would an expatriate German drive?" FJ said as they clambered aboard. They drove to the Kaiser residence where Linus and Rudi were to stay for the duration of their visit to Cairo. Linus sat in on the conversation that Rudi and FJ were having, they were in a large comfortable study seated in stuffed leather chairs and drinking schnapps. It was past dinner time and as they had eaten on the plane, Brigette said that it was a waste of time going through the motions of dinner. She would eat with the kids and FJ – well he could fend for himself. Brigette said that she would see them in the morning which was a blanket invitation for FJ and Rudi to reminisce into the night. Linus was happy to listen as he had not been brought up to date with his father's movements post-war. Cigar smoke wafted heavily in the ambient and the rotating ceiling fans pumped the air through the up-down cycle, distributing the fumes evenly. FJ and Rudi conversed in German in which they were both fluent, unlike Linus who was struggling to keep up with the ebb and flow of conversation. Eventually Linus asked if they could converse in English as he was having trouble keeping up with their rapid conversation and they obliged.

"You were lucky to get away from the Red Army," Rudi said to FJ.

Franz-Josef inspected his drink. "It was a good plan. Werner had crafted the detail superbly. The Russian soldiers that had liberated the camp had moved on and so the fresh intake had never seen me at all. I guess that was a bit of luck but the reality was that the plan made sense. Timing is everything and the timing was as good as it gets. Of course the Red Cross would want to oversee the Red Army liberate a concentration camp and report it to the world so my role was fortuitous. Once the Russians had approved my credentials I was off, lickety-split."

Rudi looked puzzled. "Lickety-split?" he questioned.

"Sorry, Schnell! English jargon is integrated into the language here in Cairo already. Actually, I think it is an Americanism, but whatever, it means fast, quick, at speed!"

Rudi nodded at FJ's explanation.

"Remember Rupert Hessner?" FJ asked Rudi

"Yes, I do. He was a good man."

195

"You say 'was'?"

"I do. The Russians killed him, poor fellow. They were out for blood as you can imagine but the SS thugs had vanished leaving the good guys like Hessner behind to face the music. Hessner wore a German uniform, Wermacht, major in fact. But to the Russians he represented the combined crimes of the SS. He was given a trial in a kangaroo court and summarily sentenced to death. It was the manner of his sentence that is of concern to us who were there, but I guess it seems insignificant when the crimes of the SS guards over the years preceding it were unveiled at Neuremburg."

"So what happened?" Linus was drawn into the discussion.

Rudi looked at his son, reluctant to relate the procedure of sentences imposed by the court. He took a deep breath and a slug of schnapps and started.

"First, they fastened him to the top of a wooden ladder which they placed upright against a wall. Then he was disembowelled and emasculated. His entrails were wrapped around the wooden ladder frames. Still alive, you understand. Next they lit a fire at the base of the ladder and as the fire licked up the wooden sides and rungs, his entrails were slowly cooked as one would sizzle a sausage above a naked flame. He must have died in terrible pain but it took some time before he was quietened by the flames that were enveloping him. Eventually, the fire consumed him and the ladder and there remained a pile of ashes on the ground. The ashes were gathered up into a bucket which was emptied into a latrine used by the soldiers."

"Poor bastard," FJ said.

Linus shook his head in disbelief.

"The Russians endured terrible atrocities by order of the Nazi hierarchy. Retribution is the accelerator for vengeance at the hands of the victors. Nothing new in the annals of warfare!" Rudi sounded almost belligerent. "Read the scriptures, it's well documented; an eye for an eye!"

It was strong stuff and the three men sat reflecting inwardly and sipped schnapps.

"So what happened next?" FJ restarted the discussion with an innocuous enquiry.

"A Russian big wig arrived, Marshall or something big like that, and he got some law and order going. Now, he was interested in our works, the paintings that we had saved and documented. He asked us if we could prepare them for shipment to Leningrad. He was specific about that! Leningrad. I suspect that this was his hobby, war loot, or he was genuinely interested in preserving them lest they fall into less desirable hands. So Werner and I packed them into crates and then he asked us to accompany them on their journey – look after them – be their guardians. Well that was it really, we did that and then after a while in Leningrad I suggested that I would like to return to Amsterdam and they said they would see. And that was all they did for the next ten years. They would see. They would look into it. Werner, on the other hand, was free to travel within the Soviet Union, so he went to Berlin often. I was not allowed to travel

196

so I figured that I was one of those prisoners who were not called prisoners but really were prisoners. I have no word for it."

"Detention, maybe," Linus offered. "You were being kept under restraint. Not free to travel but free within a confined area. A prisoner by any other name!"

"They were good to me."

"You were good to them!"

"I guess so."

"Did you get paid?"

"I got an allowance, they supplied accommodation and I had to buy food and clothes. I was warm in the winter which is saying something for Leningrad. I had people visit me socially, but was never allowed more than five persons in one gathering, which was more than adequate for my socialising. I missed my wife and my son and our friends in Amsterdam. From what I am told, they have all gone. Killed in the holocaust. I think that I would still like to live in our old house in Amsterdam Mr Van Oldenbarnevelt says that it is currently leased and is in good condition. I would need to wait until the lease has expired. Two years, he says. But hey, I can wait two years. I waited ten for freedom."

FJ offered cigars and more schnapps.

Rudi blew a smoke ring and said, "I thought that when you and Kaetrin turned up they might release me, but instead they put me under increased scrutiny. Werner told me that the Russians didn't know who you were. I guess they were just being their usual old suspicious selves. Then when they realised your credentials were kosher, they relaxed. I was actually permitted to attend that meeting, which was a milestone. My first contact with Westerners in five years! I must say, the escape ruse that they pulled following the recent exhibition was brilliant. I sort of felt that they were ready to let me go. I mean what the hell else could I do for them. Perhaps they were pleased to see the last of me?"

"Where do you suppose Werner is?" FJ asked.

"Werner could be anywhere, he's that sort of person. Had he lived in a free Western economy he would have been a millionaire by now. You know he was originally imprisoned in Dachau as a communist. The Nazis were hell-bent on eradicating communism and any dissidents were incarcerated. In hindsight, he made the right choice at the time. Anyhow he is cured of communism now, I know that!" Rudi took a sip of schnapps and a puff on his cigar. "He made the switch in Auschwitz, before we joined forces and then when the Red Army came, he made sure that he had the red communist triangle sewn back onto his prison garb. Not a silly move. But that was Werner; his moves were calculated and correct every time. That man could organise a fire sale in Satan's cave. He looked out for his parents too. Made sure that they had the necessities in life, especially when they were in short supply, as in Berlin just after the war. I get the feeling that he wants to bring them to the West. Get away from East Germany. He says there will be no future in a Soviet satellite country. The spoils in communism work in the reverse ratio to supply and demand. He called

197

them "Plunder and live. Kill and survive." Lots of euphemisms. Werner was never stuck for a word. He would often say "if you are ever stuck for a word I will slit your throat and extract it from you, to save you from choking." He would let that sink in and say, "mind you I doubt that you would ever thank me!" Well, you couldn't with a slit throat could you? I'm sure Franz-Josef could tell you a tale or two about Werner as we all worked together for about three years at Auschwitz."

FJ nodded, "Yes, he had the run of the place alright. If only the commandant knew who was giving the orders!"

The three talked on into the night and Linus was the first to excuse himself. He left Rudi and FJ deep in discussion and retired to his comfortable room. It was a warm Cairo night and the ceiling fans were circulating cooling downdraughts. He slept fitfully with the evening's stories circulating through his head. *They certainly had the worst of it,* he thought as he compared his war to their nightmare.

Morning dawned warm and humid and over breakfast FJ announced that he would show Rudi through the art gallery and in the afternoon they all might enjoy a guided tour by Otto Kaiser through his museum of war relics that he had collected since arriving in North Africa over a decade ago. There were a lot of interesting relics left over from Rommel's Afrika Corps' Campaign against Monty of Alamein, as he was now called. "And some of our own artefacts thrown in for good measure. Some days I get a bigger turnover than the art gallery," he said with pride.

Rudi was impressed with the gallery. A lot of the display were pieces that Otto Kaiser and Albert von Hapsberg had secreted out of Germany with the armoured car shipment from the Kaiser Iron and SteelWorks in 1943. They had been buying works since the war ended, going on buying forays into Europe and the Middle East. They were getting a lot of interest from buyers in North America, India, South Africa and Greece. Hong Kong and South America were to be avoided, they said, as the majority of works on sale were stolen Nazi loot that had been resurfacing.

Lunch was a family affair. Brigette introduced Rudi to Claudia and Alfred von Hapsberg, her parents. Rudi was already a familiar figure to the Kaisers as Anna and Otto, Franz-Josef's parents, were clients of Rudi's before the war, and had been for many years. Brigitte explained that her children, Nixie and Falco were at school so would not be joining them. Beer and wine were served and then the food was brought to the table by bearers.

"The main course is schaufele," Anna announced. "It is popular where we come from and is a roast shoulder of lamb, we do it slowly in a cooler oven to get tender and succulent results. It is accompanied by a side salad and dumplings and a rich dark gravy, we use a dark beer to make the gravy." They ate the delicious meal amid much talk and good natured banter. For afters, Claudia had made pfefferkuchen.

"It's our version of gingerbread," she proudly announced, "and especially from Pulsnitz near Dresden." The two older ladies were responsible for the menu that had been concocted following consultation with Linus who had confirmed that Rudi's dietary regime was to gratefully eat whatever was put in front of him. An enlightened condition, emanating from years of starvation at Auschwitz.

Following the lunch break, Otto took Rudi and Linus on a guided tour through his museum of war relics that he and Alfred had collected following the end of hostilities in 1945. The 'Western Desert' was littered with destroyed or abandoned equipment used by the armed forces during their campaigns and the dry desert air had preserved them very well indeed. Pride of place was taken by the exhibit of Eagle Fox, which had been armoured car number 200 off the assembly line at the Kaiser Iron and Steel Works in Dresden. It was barely marked and needed little restoration work before being put on show. This was the vehicle that Otto had personally presented to Field Marshall Rommel who in return had presented Otto with a silver plated Luger pistol with carved ivory handle grips which was also on display. Linus pointed to a small drip tray on the floor. It contained a small drop of water.

"If you drain the coolant from the engine," he said, "you can eliminate that!"

"The coolant has been drained," Otto replied. He watched Linus puzzle with this enigma.

"Then where on earth can it come from?" Linus asked.

"We think they are tears," Otto said.

It was the tone in Otto's voice that curbed what naturally would have earned some ribald comment from Linus. But Linus was silent.

Otto went on to explain about Arnold Fuchs, the gestapo agent who had tried to infiltrate the Dresden social scene posing as a submarine lieutenant.

"After all," Otto said, "we were very good Germans but not very good Nazis. We think they were looking to pin some anti-Nazi activities on us. Anyway, he ended up having to face a duelling contest with Franz-Josef and lost his nerve. His second posted him as a coward and apologised, then departed the scene. We cleaned him up as he had soiled himself and dropped him off at his lodgings. That was when we discovered he was a gestapo agent. Then strange things happened. He disappeared, vanished. We found some of our prized hounds poisoned and then a fire in one of our horse stables that housed some very valuable eventing horses. And then he tried to kill Franz-Josef. That's when we said enough and we plotted his demise. He really was an evil person. Unfortunately, he beat us to it by hanging himself and so to conceal the body and of course his death, as you can imagine the gestapo were snooping around, we dropped his body into a vat of molten metal at the works. This vat contained the raw material for the steel on the bodies of our last batch of armoured cars. We named car number 200, the last armoured car off the assembly line, Eagle Fox. Part of his, Fuchs name, meaning Eagle and we named the Fox part after The Desert Fox, Rommel. We said at least the dead coward may still have the honour to serve his country. As this was to be Rommel's personal car, we added extras such as a headlamp, leather seats, map

199

light and so on. You will observe that the drip is below the headlamp. The eye, so to speak. So you see we conclude that we have repentant tears. Signs of lamentation and regret perhaps – who knows."

"A fascinating tale," Rudi said and Linus remained silent looking at the water in the drip tray.

Otto took them to an old battered Chevrolet truck. "Now this," he said, "is a vehicle ahead of its time!" and he went on to tell them about the Long Range Desert Group. "I couldn't find one of these in Africa so I went searching and got this one in Italy. That was where they went once the African campaign was over. They did the same thing in Italy operating behind enemy lines. Boy, were they armed to the teeth. They had a weapon for everything. Even an aircraft cannon on one of the vehicles that we travelled in, when they found us in the desert. We were escorted by them to Cairo as Hitler had placed a bounty on my head and a Bedouin mercenary was keen to claim that bounty."

"So you were in the thick of it," Linus said.

"Yes, we had a couple of stoushes with them, the Bedouin that is, but they had no show against mortars and a field gun."

Linus pointed at the bonnet. "That looks like a Tiki," he said.

"What's a Tiki?" Rudi asked.

"It's a Polynesian fertility icon. 'Breeding' is a term that Captain Walker used. Mind you as a sheep farmer, he was always talking about breeding!" Otto continued. Neil Walker had told him about Tiki. "Very common in Maori carvings. Yes, the New Zealanders decorated their vehicles with a Tiki on one side of the bonnet and a Maori place name on the other – this one is called 'Kokiri'. The Kiwis were fiercely independent and capable men. That's why they were especially chosen for their work. Rommel paid them high commendation."

They came to an artillery field piece. "Now this," Otto said enthusiastically, "is another product of the Kaiser Iron and Steel Works. We made them in the 1914–18 conflict and also for the last war. We call them Aufinez, I believe you know them as Howitzers."

Otto was entertaining and he was very proud of the collection that he had put together. "We are adding new items all the time it's amazing what the desert turns up. Like the archaeologists and the pyramids, my team uncovers relics from the past, as the sands blow and waft their grains. I may need to look for larger premises or premises to show larger exhibits. We have some large pieces of ironmongery that we cannot display here and I refer to battle tanks from all sides. I have several examples under restoration now. At another place of course. No room here for that sort of work."

Over dinner that evening, they discussed the possibility of the Kaisers and von Hapsbergs visiting New Zealand. "Captain Walker farms in Masterton and is always asking you to visit. Now may be a good time," Franz-Josef said to his parents. "Brigette and myself can hold the fort. Besides, we don't want the children to miss school so we prefer to stay in Cairo."

"It would be a good time to visit," Linus said. "You would see a farm in full production, with spring lambing underway and also sheep shearing will be underway. The weather will be pleasant and also we usually have plenty of beds available at our hotel as the farmers are too busy with their spring farming activities to come to town. They usually book us out about two weeks before Christmas when they come to Christmas shop in the city." Amid much discussion, the elders slept on the idea and confirmed their decision to make the journey the following day.

They all a came on the same flight and the party was met at the airport by Kaetrin who was pleased to be reunited with Rudi again. They drove to the hotel and were introduced to Flora and James and then the party retired to their rooms to recover from the ordeal of travelling such a long distance in what seemed a short time, although they had been on the go for three days, including stopovers. Kaetrin had volunteered to drive them to Neil Walker's farm, a drive of some two and a half hours. They would do that in three days' time. As Neil had explained to Kaetrin, he was busy with the early summer farm activities and there were chilled and frozen lamb shipments to get to England before Christmas so farmers were busy rounding up their spring lambs and sending them off to the works for processing.

Neil Walker was delighted to be reunited with his North African charges that his unit had escorted across the Sahara Desert to Cairo in 1943. Kaetrin and Linus drove their guests in the large and comfortable Chevrolet which the hotel kept for special occasions. It was a sunny day and the vista of their destination lay before them when they breasted the summit of the divide that separated the Wairarapa farmlands from the more densely populated and urban Wellington region. Linus pulled into the parking area at the summit and all of the passengers got out from the vehicle to stretch their legs, make a comfort stop at the nearby tea rooms and take in the view of the vast farmland plain below. On such a clear day the scene was of well-maintained farming pastures that stretched to the east and the Pacific Ocean beyond. The paddocks and tree lines of shelter belts marked out the well-defined patchwork of a handsomely stitched quilt. The colours were vibrant in the bright sunshine that caused the viewers to place an open palm across their foreheads to protect their eyes from the cloudless glare. Anna Kaiser remarked, "It's pretty countryside. You know during our desert trek, Neil used to talk about the lushness of his farmlands when we were surrounded by sand. At the time we thought that he was exaggerating in inverse proportion to our barren waste of a desert but, you know, he was right!"

Neil descended the steps from the homestead porch as the Chevrolet bearing his old friends and guests arrived, tyres crunching on the gravel drive. The sign above the porch said 'Waikorea Station' and underneath in smaller print: 'Neil and Alison Walker'. The building was a large wooden structure, bounded on all four sides by a four meter wide roofed over porch. Neil was accompanied by his wife and their two children. It was obvious from the enthusiasm of the welcoming that both sides were equally excited about this visit and following introductions, embracing and cheek pressing, Neil ushered the party onto the verandah to a large table that had been arranged with lunch things. Alison, Neil's wife, excused herself and went into the house. Their two boys, whom Neil called Kel and Cob, raced off to do whatever it was that boys do on the farm and the remainder of the adults seated themselves on the seats provided. Otto remarked on the boy's name.

"I recall Kelvin, your sergeant, and Cobber, the soldier who set up the forward observation and mortar battery in the canyon." He looked at Neil with raised eyebrows. Neil nodded, anticipating the question.

"Yes," he said. "We lost both men killed in action during the Italian campaign. Kel is for Kelvin and Cob – well, Alison wouldn't have Cobber – but we do have a family name, Cobham so I guess Cob is for Cobber via Cobham." The Swiss nationals expressed their dismay on learning about the two Kiwi soldiers who had played an important role in protecting them from the clutches of the Bedouin Suilleman in the desert. It was a long time ago, but important memories are etched into the mind and are never forgotten.

A man appeared from around the house leading a small horse pulling a trailer. He unloaded the guests' luggage from the boot of the car and disappeared into the direction from whence he had come. Neil said, "He'll put the luggage in your rooms." And they nodded. Alison appeared with another lady and they placed food and plates on the table. The lady left and Alison sat down. They ate lunch that was prepared from cold cuts of lamb leg roast, salad with eggs and tomatoes, home-made relish and home baked bread with farm butter. There was a jug of cold milk and one of cold ginger beer.

Anticipating the question, Alison said, "Cook will feed the boys in the kitchen, they tend to eat on the run when they have a project underway. At present they are attempting to dam one of the streams to make a swimming hole for summer. They do this every year and come the winter rains, the streams flood and their dams get washed away."

Otto laughed, "Sounds like me as a boy, you and me, Alfred, do you remember our efforts?"

Alfred agreed, "Sure do," he said, "sounds like boys are boys the whole world over, a stream is a potential ocean to swim in, never just a stream. There's something soothing about water on a hot day. Remember Mahmoud's underground cavern with that gorgeous spring of cool clear water?"

They all nodded. Neil said, "Never heard of that one!"

"It's at a place that Mahmoud referred to as Wadi Gin."

"Yes well we know about Mahmoud's place names." Neil offered. "He would name them after alcoholic drinks. It would probably have a proper place name among the Bedouin tribe names – but Wadi Gin," Neil shook his head, "never heard of such a place!"

Albert said, "I have a better understanding now of the Arab language and that 'Wadi', pronounced 'oudi' is an Arabic term traditionally referring to a valley but it may also refer to a dry ephemeral riverbed. A transitory flow of water following a sustained fall of heavy rain."

202

"Whatever," Otto replied "Wadi Gin was pure tonic – 'scuse the pun – following a day's hot ride on camel-back."

"Well what do you say, Anna?" Otto asked his wife.

"Yes I agree, it was a lovely spot, we sluiced under those wooden gates in the coolness of the cavern, a really lovely spot – magic even."

"Do you people ever see Mahmoud?" Neil enquired.

"Yes we do," Otto said. "He is still part of the family business and we maintain our business arrangement with Abdul Nassar and Sons. We don't go, but Franz-Josef says he is a regular at the All Cairo Polo Club where he has been known to enjoy a mild shandy on a warm afternoon. He maintains their export and import contacts and keeps an apartment in London, Mayfair actually, which we hear is a regular bachelor pad where he can engage his Western indulgences away from the restrictions of religious restraints imposed by the family and culture in Cairo. He has never married and must be one of the most eligible bachelors in Egypt. And he is not restricted to taking just one wife either. Old Abdul has several, you know. He keeps adding a new one every so often. Younger, of course! Don't know how they get away with it. You have to be born into the system to understand it I suppose."

"And what about that rascal Suilleman from the Sudan? Is he still causing mayhem?" Neil asked casually.

"We haven't heard about him since the pass when you guys peppered his troops with the field gun and mortar rounds. He obviously got his second fright in as many weeks and headed off for the Sudan, never to cross the border again. Maybe his own troops dealt to him for promising them an easy battle for large rewards. Instead they got their asses kicked and no doubt lost some valuable camels. A camel is an asset and a dead one can be sustenance but a dead camel that has to be abandoned in a hurry is a double wammy, so to speak. I'm using American jargon. My English is contaminated," Otto said.

"Cairo is an international city now, a crossroads," Alfred offered. "Some of the German spoken is simply awful. I'm sure we speak better English these days!"

"Speak for yourself," his wife Claudia said.

"We certainly had some good times there," Neil said. "Great place for a bit of rest and recreation following a stint in the desert eating sand between drinks."

Linus excused himself and Kaetrin. "Sounds like you folk have a lot to catch up on, so Kaetrin and myself will hit the road. Just let us know when you want to come back and we can drive over the hill and collect you and, more importantly, ensure that we have your rooms ready!" They said their goodbyes and departed, the Chevrolet Belair Sedan crunching the gravel on the drive as it negotiated the semi-circle driveway to exit the homestead entrance. It was a ten minute drive through the Walkers' farmland before they would make the main highway.

They all waved goodbye from the shady porch and Alfred started the conversation again by asking about the name of the station.

"Waikorea," he said, "we have a conflict in Korea, can't imagine the tie up!" he said.

Neil smiled. "It's a Maori place name and means 'Water of the Small Canoe' absolutely irrelevant to these parts, but we had one of our trucks named as such. It survived the war unscathed and I thought that it was a lucky name. You will recall our vehicles? They had the Tiki on one side of the bonnet and a place name on the other side, so we renamed our sheep station after it. Originally, my parents called the place after some Scottish village where their parents were born and married: Locheil. When we bought them out and they moved into Masterton I talked to Alison about it one night and we both liked the sound of the name and the relevance to our lives."

The gathering sat in the warmth of a late spring afternoon and then a man turned up on horseback leading a horse that was fully saddled and bridled. Neil excused himself. "Work calls," he said, "I have to help out with some cattle that we are bringing into the yards. Not only sheep here," he said, "we run a few hundred head of cattle too. Fattening them for the works!" he said, and he was off.

Alison suggested that they would like to go inside and freshen up for dinner. "I'll show you your rooms, follow me," and she led them up a wide winding staircase to the second story landing where the bedroom accommodation was. "Take your time," she said, "Neil will not be back for a couple of hours and he likes to have a drink before dinner. Your rooms have en-suites and we have plenty of water, so please take a bath or shower as you wish. Come on down when you are ready, we can have sundowners on the verandah."

Neil and Alison were gracious hosts and had arranged horse riding treks around the station where they were able to observe first-hand the wonderful spectacle of sheep dogs working the cattle and sheep on whistle commands from their handlers. The party could be two or three hours' ride from the homestead, but at lunchtime a chuck wagon in the form of a couple of pack horses would turn up and a veritable feast was laid on for the farm workers and the guests. Neil took Albert and Otto deer hunting and they bagged a hind and a stag. It was as near as they both had been to their own activities that they would engage in, on their ancestral lands near Dresden, from whence they had fled in 1942. The bush was so different but the venison. "It's as good as the German venison," Alfred declared.

The station even boasted a landing strip for aeroplanes that were used as 'dung dusters' which was how Neil referred to them. These were planes equipped for dropping fertiliser onto the land from the air. It was officially called 'aerial top-dressing' and it was a new method of adding fertiliser to the landscape and had been pioneered in New Zealand. As Neil explained to his guests, "The practice originated back in 1906 from a hot air balloon when a chap by the name of Chaytor dropped seed from his balloon, near Wairoa which is in the Hawkes Bay, just to the north of here," Neil said. "The practice had been nurtured by far sighted New Zealand agriculturists and has become especially popular following WWII when an excess of cheap Gypsy Tiger

Moth bi-planes became available. The front seat was used as a hopper to store the fertiliser," Neil said, "sometimes we also launch seed from the air." Neil owned two such aircraft and he could turn one of them back to a two seater, which he did and used it to take his guests, each in turn for an aerial tour of the spread. "We are in our own way," Neil continued, "cultivating and polishing the procedure and we have plans afoot to actually build a dedicated version of such an aircraft. Designed exclusively for the distribution of fertiliser from the air. How about that!" he said proudly.

Otto and Albert were impressed. "Well," Otto said, "if you ever want some venture capital for the project, let me know, we have funds available and I like the idea. I was in manufacturing, as you know, before the Nazis dealt to our plans. I know a good idea when I see one! In fact, I can foresee uses for this type of plane in Africa, flying over some of the large tracts of land, jettisoning seed and fertiliser. My God!" he said, "The saving of time and money, such a plane could create." An aeriform method of broadcasting seeds and fertiliser is the answer, I am convinced." Otto seemed won over by his own rhetoric.

Neil was upbeat. "You know," he said, "I mentioned, there is a group of us talking about it. We have plans on the drawing board already. I should get them to a meeting here at the station, maybe we can get some ideas floated before you leave. Good excuse for you to come back to view the proposed Kaiser-Walker Aero Works!" Neil joked, but it had serious undertones and an amazing punch line.

"Our research," Otto said, "shows that there is a tremendous amount of underground water reserves in North Africa. A lot is from aquifers but the majority is from underground storage cells that have accumulated from rainwater that has fallen on the ground and been preserved by filtering through porous rock and crevices such as has accumulated at Wadi Gin. These deposits are not replaceable. Once the water has been used it is gone. It does not replenish itself. It has to accumulate as it already did, over a very long period of time. Hundreds of years. Aquifers are another matter; they are self-replenishing but not as plentiful as the underground storage reservoirs. Mind you, some of them are oceans big." Otto still translated some phrases from his native tongue literally. "But as I said, once used they are gone. We think that we could fertilise large tracts of land from the aquifers. We have to be careful as over exploitation may lead to us exceeding the practical sustained yield. We also must consider artificial recharge as an option too. We have a lot of data to investigate but maybe we can get it onto the right side of the ledger. In a way it's a bit like banking. If we take out more than we put in, we could bankrupt ourselves. In preparation for this, we have also been land banking for some time. Buying land especially adjacent to limestone hills where they do have a known rainfall each year, sand hills that nobody wants but buying them in the right places where we can access the aquifers. Seeding and fertilising these large tracts from aeroplanes is the ideal way to take the proposed land transformation to the next level. So you see, the planes that you propose are exactly what we have been looking for. The logistics of carrying out those chores on the ground were starting to make the project an unrealistic dream. I'm sure that you have answered our dilemma."

"Perhaps you need a bigger bird," Neil said. "There is a guy who, so I am told, has converted a Douglas DC3 into a dung duster. Big plane with a big payload flying over big land areas. I understand that they can take several tons of fertiliser in one lift. That would cover a large piece of desert!"

It was an excited mix of people that met for sundowners that evening on the veranda at Waikorea Station. Alison had prepared a large jug of cold punch of her own concoction. She filled large glass tumblers with ice cubes and poured punch over the contents and garnished with fresh mint leaves.

Anna said, "I remember Neil telling us about his favourite time of day back home, as he called it, when we were in the desert trekking to Cairo across the Sahara sands. Evening time, at sundown, as he would say, the wind would die, not a discernible breeze, and the land was still, as still as a leaf on a Nikau palm. You must show me a Nikau palm, Neil!" she said and continued. "Nothing moved, even the cattle stopped chewing. And the flying insects paused their endless flickering of tiffany wings. A peace comes across the land as time stands still." Neil puffed on his pipe.

"A reflective moment," he said. "Just like now," and they all stopped and listened to the sound of quietness.

Chapter 14

Bravo

Bravo had never met his father who was killed when the ship that he was a radio officer on was shelled by German raiders in the Pacific in 1940. One of his earliest memories about his father was a ceremony held in the lounge of the person that he had come to call Aunty Flora. A man had called on them and had presented his mother with some medals that he later would know as the Atlantic Star, the Pacific Star and the Marconi Medal for Bravery at Sea by one of its members. His mother had wept openly, which young Bravo thought were tears of sadness for his dead father but in fact she was crying for joy. She was happy that at last his father's actions were being recognised and Bravo would have something to remember his father by. Bravo wore the medals on ANZAC day when they attended the service at the cenotaph to commemorate the brave servicemen and woman who had died in the service of their country, at war. He was three years old when James Peroux left for Tarawa Atoll but the vision of military uniforms was etched in his earliest memories as the hotel where he lived with his mother, was home to the Second Marine Divisions' general staff and young Bravo was a popular figure among the married marines who had left young families behind when they went to fight their war in foreign lands. Between ANZAC days, Bravos late father's medals were displayed in a case alongside a photograph of the man himself, given to his mother when she and Bravo's father, Douglas, parted in 1940, before the *Rangitata* sailed from Auckland for London. It was a lovely image and showed the young merchant navy officer resplendent in peaked cap and double breasted navy jacket with a double row of brass buttons, four in each row. On each cuff he wore the insignia of his rank which was two gold rings. Bravo grew up in the pleasant surroundings of Maximes Hotel where his mother worked. He had a host of people looking out for him. There was Aunty Flora, Aunty Kaetrin and Aunty Marjory and Uncle James, Uncle Linus and Uncle Horace. They were generous in bringing him presents on his birthday and at Christmas and were always ready with words of encouragement as he was growing up and playing sport and studying for exams at school. It came as no surprise to any of them when he announced that he wanted to join the air force and fly aeroplanes. By 1963, Bravo was flying the big air force transport planes to Vietnam and Malaya and by 1970 he had retired from the air force and joined Air New Zealand, where he flew their jet airliners. Then, in 1976 Uncle Linus suggested that he might like to join the Art 1 Trust as a pilot to fly the new class of business jets that they were now using. Following training on the new planes, he would be a captain and not first officer, as he now was. He would receive excellent pay and conditions. Bravo was hooked and he was sent to Wichita, Kansas, to the Lear Jet Works to undertake flight training and receipt of a new plane that he and his co-pilot would fly to Wellington and then fly Linus to London for a meeting. The Art 1 Trust had several such planes in their fleet which they found superior in getting their executives around the world quickly for meetings. Since the early days following the war, the trust had accumulated considerable income from their artwork collection exhibitions and also from trading in artworks. With spare cash available, they had invested in coal and ore mining, iron and steel smelters, shipbuilding and aircraft manufacturing, all of which were in the ascendancy following the war years when millions of tons of shipping were sunk and old battle relics of iron mongery lay rusting around the globe, in their previous theatres of war. The Art 1 Trust got into iron and steel production on the ground floor and never looked back. Linus was now an extremely wealthy man and a philanthropist looking for places around the world where his money could achieve good works in fledgling economies. He desperately wanted to help his brother-in-law, Kaetrin's brother Robert, who lived with his Tongan wife Tia, on Vavai a small island in the Tongan Archipelago. Robert said that he couldn't enter into any deals, as much as he would like to.

"You would have to see the royal family and even if they agreed," he said, "I doubt that we would see any of the money. They get aid now!" he continued, "God knows what they do with it – we never see any! We need to raise our own money somehow, money that we earn from our own enterprises that the government cannot take from us. We don't mind paying taxes if we are to receive government funded improvements but so far we have received none of those things. Also be aware that the royal family own all of the money systems in the kingdom. Nothing gets passed them. The bottom feeders get the scraps. I have put my own money into this island from my engineering business in Nukualofa, but really it's a pittance. We need a large capital injection of funds. One day," he said, "one day we'll find a way. You'll see. What you may be able to do to help us is to give our daughter Maree a good education in New Zealand. Knowledge will be the bank of the future – with knowledge, we can prosper and that knowledge will not be taxable!"

Linus listened to the discourse and agreed that it would be a good idea to have Maree schooled in New Zealand. Kaetrin would love to have her niece stay with them at the Hotel. He couldn't wait to ask her about it. There was a lot to discuss.

Maree came to live with them in 1978, a year that was also a milestone in the Tongan calendar as the year the king, by royal decree, placed a moratorium on whaling in Tonga. The taking of whales was banned. This placed a formidable downward spiral in the Tongans food cycle where the graphs were mercurial in the best of times. Whale meat had been taken now for nearly one hundred years. The smell of whale meat cooking in the umus was as Tongan as eating coconuts or drinking kava. Whales were a valuable source of protein and the Island of Vavai had two of the best whale boats and crews which enabled them to sell or barter the extra meat for goods and services from neighbouring islands. Aboriginal hunters were no threat to the whale population. It was in 1890 that a young Maori harpooner named Albert Cook came to Tonga and established the Tongan Whale Fishery and it became an established part of the Tongan food chain and commerce during the twentieth century. The brave Tongan whalers took on what no other Polynesian society had done. They killed whales. They truly were Polynesia's hunting elite. The whales took no prisoners for sure and many a brave Tongan had fallen foul of the whales' flukes and had his brains bashed out on contact with fifty tons and more of live threshing whale meat. Vavai had a one legged whaler named Homeguard, and his impairment came from an encounter with a particularly lively sperm whale, happily puffing his way along the ocean tops when he became annoyed by the prick of a dart in his flesh. The leviathan sounded suddenly, taking fathoms of line with him. The speed at which the rope was leaving the container in the boat, required water to be poured on to it, to cool it lest it catch fire. The hapless whaler got a leg entangled in the rope and it sliced through his limb as easily as a wire slices through cheese.

It was Bravo who flew Kaetrin and Linus to Tonga to collect Maree. They landed at Nukualofa Airport and then had to take a boat to Vavai as there was no airport on the island. Kaetrin had not seen her brother for a few years and they spent an enjoyable time together getting reacquainted. Maree was a charming ten year old and she had utilised the best features from the gene pool provided by her Tongan mother and European father. She was a very pretty girl and had a smooth, even, light coppery completion and olive eyes. An unusual combination, maybe, but it worked very well, especially with her generous mouth and white-toothed smile. Kaetrin thought, *I will have to keep an eye on her, a future heart stealer for sure.* Kaetrin found the island everything that a tropical island should be. A sea locked atoll with a lagoon and a reef. Sandy white beaches and coconut trees fringing the green sward of land where it merged with the white sand. The sea was an emerald green colour in the shallower water where the sunlight was reflected off the sand and reefs near the surface of the sea. Beyond, in the deep waters, the surface shimmered in an irradiated blue topaz glow. It was a tempting kaleidoscope of enchantment and Kaetrin just had to go swimming. At fifty three years of age, she maintained a svelte sylph like figure and was soon joined in the lagoon shallows on a sandy beach by Maree, Linus, Robert and Tia. Tia's parents, Aba and Ata, joined them, but like most Tongans swam with their clothes on. The afternoon was a family event that was far too infrequent and all agreed that they should put in some effort to get together more often. With Maree staying in Wellington, Linus suggested that Robert and Tia had cause to visit.

"You get yourselves to Nukualofa," he said, "and I'll get the plane to meet you! The plane journey is taken care of by my trust. Your accommodation is the same for you in Wellington as it is for us here. You are our guests and we would love to have you. All you have to spend is the time. How hard is that?" he said.

Bravo and his co-pilot stayed in a hotel at Nukualofa where they were visited by a government official who was being nosy. He wanted to know what their business was in Tonga. Obviously a privately owned jet aeroplane created a bit of interest. It was not a common mode of transport for visitors to the small Pacific kingdom and so curiosity levels rose. Bravo said nothing other than he flew his boss and his wife to visit friends. Bravo was not even aware of the island that they had gone to. He did have an emergency phone number, but apart from that Linus had said, "Wait for my further instructions, we'll be a few days!" The government official left without learning anything from Bravo but they had the registration number of the plane and so were able to trace the owner as the Art 1 Trust, an organisation, it seemed, that operated from a London address. Further intelligence revealed that the trust was involved in art collections and dealing in artworks. It also operated a large aid portfolio loaning and gifting monies to developing and needy nations and worthy causes and offered venture capital where the usual bank loans were too prohibitive for a lot of developing nations to participate in. It proposed a no cure, no pay strategy that saw them lose money occasionally but more frequently, cream excessive profits from successful enterprises that they had shrewdly backed. Anything Jewish was a shoo-in, it seemed. The government official was able to relay this information to the palace from where the enquiry had originated.

Bravo spent his days on the beach and when night fell he moved into party mode and frequented night spots looking for a piece of the action. The action, according to Bravo, could be provided by male or female accomplices. He was, as they say, AC/DC. Bravo was a late developer, as initially he was consumed by his love of all things aeronautical. This absorbed all of his energy and as such he found little need for sustenance from the intimate love of another person. Growing up, he had all the love and nurturing that a developing human being could possibly hope for. His mother had tried to compensate for the lack of a father to the little boy with her constant love and attention and also he had lots of male contact during his formative years as he was the marines' mascot when they stayed at the hotel during WWII. Then there was Uncle Horace and more lately Uncle Linus and Auntie Flora's new husband Uncle James. Bravo enjoyed both sets of relations with equal fervour. He was relaxed in the company of both genders. He had not been able to categorise this feeling between the sexes when puberty started and seemed equally content and excited by contact with a member of either sex. Bravo never questioned this, as his main motivation was his career, which was flying aeroplanes. In commercial aviation he had his share of affairs with female cabin crew members. A bachelor pilot was always a popular man in the crew with the ladies and why not? Bravo was a fine looking specimen of a man. The trouble with Bravo, was that he never took his relationships beyond the first night or two; they were never long liaisons. There was always another tour of duty and another crew. He had one rule, however, and that was to never have a relationship with a male member of his crew. Any homosexual activities were limited to after hours and off duty playtime and whatever was available, when he desired intimate contact with a male, wherever he was staying in the world. He knew where to go to make contact with what he was looking for. They were generally one night stands and very secretive. On his first trip to Cairo while on a tour of flying duty with the Art 1 Trust, Franz-Josef had taken him to the All Cairo Polo Club where he met Mahmoud, who insisted that they make contact on some future visit to London. Answering in the affirmative, Mahmoud had given Bravo his Mayfair address.

"Even if I am not there," Mahmoud said, "my permanent staff will look after you." And they did. Mahmoud had insatiable excesses which he curbed when in Cairo but they ballooned when he visited London. Mahmoud's Mayfair flat turned out to be a rather sumptuous dwelling of six bedrooms and several bathrooms. It contained luxurious lounge and reception areas and was staffed by a permanent butler, who would organise all of the functions that one would expect to receive from staying at a five star plus hotel in the city. What couldn't be found at the apartment, the butler could discreetly arrange. One simply had to enquire. It was all one could desire and more. Once Bravo had stayed a few times and got the lay of the land, so to speak, with a bit of planning his London sojourns could be turned into endearing stopovers of great pleasure. And he was in London a lot. Bravo flew Linus when Linus needed to be somewhere quickly, otherwise he flew a variety of Art 1 Trust executives around the world, but, generally, with London as the star point of his universal pilotage. In 1982 Bravo had flown Linus from Wellington to London for a meeting of the Art 1 Trust and he then flew Linus to Amsterdam to collect Rudi and then the two of them were flown to Cairo for a meeting with Otto Kaiser and Alfred von Hapsberg on matters of art. On the return flight to Amsterdam and London, they carried Mahmoud as a guest. Linus stayed in Amsterdam with Rudi who had since moved back into his old house and art studio and Mahmoud and Bravo carried on to London. They shared a taxi from the airport to Mahmoud's Mayfair apartment. Mahmoud, as usual, was in party mode. He was an older man than Bravo, but still very virile and active. Bravo excused himself and went to bed. Mahmoud went out on the town visiting his usual haunts, including the Playboy Club where he invited some playmates home for a bit of fun. The noise from Mahmoud's frolicsome friends eventually woke Bravo who, clad in a bathrobe, descended a floor and came upon an orgy of bodies, all in an advanced state of intoxication and, he thought, no doubt fuelled by drugs, cavorting around in the nude, some in very uncompromising positions. Bravo was no prude but he had always conducted himself in a conservative manner. The scene that he was observing was downright depravity and indulgence. He was conspicuous by the style of dress. He wore clothes, albeit a bathrobe and all others present were naked and they took no notice. He could have been an elephant in the room and to the spaced out participants that would seem perfectly normal. Bravo looked around for Mahmoud who was nowhere to be seen. As he started to leave the room, the elevator car bell rang, announcing the arrival of the lift car onto the second floor. The door of the lift opened and two naked eunuchs emerged. They were superbly muscled and their smooth skin was oiled to a glisten. Both carried scimitar style swords and wore turbans in the manner of eunuchs from a Hollywood movie. The two eunuchs took station, one each side of the elevator door, and a Sheik emerged. Again, the figure was naked, but he wore the turban of a Sheik and belted around his midriff was the traditional Bedouin dagger. It was Mahmoud.

The eunuchs were indeed true to label. There was no evidence of a scrotum or testicles and Bravo thought that they may have come from one of Mahmoud's family harems, where they were known in their own language as 'chief of the girls'. Eunuchs and concubines, the girls that made up a harem and who were not wives of the Sheik or Sultan, were slaves. The eunuchs would instruct the concubines in the manner of their master's preferences in the bed chamber and would also issue punishment if the master were displeased by his concubine. The punishment was usually in the form of a whipping severe enough to be unpleasant so that one would want to conform with the master's wishes on future occasions. The eunuch would also keep a ledger of the concubines' menses, an important cycle in the life of the harem. It was not unusual for a master to favour a handsome young eunuch to perform fellatio as an alternative sexual deviation. This was especially important in observing prohibited sexual activity, which, according to Islamic literature, is during menstrual cycles. The eunuch indeed had many duties in his life. Fellatio is still a common ritual among the Sambia people. From age seven, their young males undertake the regular ingestion of an older boy's semen, in the belief that it is necessary to achieve sexual maturity and masculinity. And by the time he reaches mid puberty, he in turn participates in passing his semen on to younger males. Thus, as the young men become adolescents, they will have the younger males practice fellatio on them to keep the ritual alive and obviously producing the desired results as the young men take wives and produce families. *Who can argue with that proof and logic,* Bravo thought to himself as he eyed the eunuchs' physical prowess. Mahmoud entered the room and acknowledged Bravo.

"Allow me to introduce you to my two flute players," he said and noticing Bravo's concerned look as he nodded toward the eunuchs, he continued. "They do not speak English, they have no understanding of the term. In Japan," Mahmoud continued, "the persons performing fellatio are commonly referred to as flute players. Take your pick, my boy, I offer you the use of either or both of my excellent musicians." Mahmoud gave his rascally grin.

"Thank you, Mahmoud, but not tonight. I am still jet-lagged. I came down to see what all of the noise was about. I suppose this is standard party routine?"

Mahmoud nodded, "Yes this is about as raunchy as it gets, I cannot do this stuff in Cairo, well some anyway, so I tend to crack the whip a bit when I first hit London. Don't worry, it's not a nightly occurrence. Too old for that now, you know." Mahmoud delivered his statement in such a manner suggesting, that in his younger days, they may well have partied thus every night. As a parting quip, when Bravo excused himself, he said, "Did you know that the fruit bat has been observed to engage in fellatio during mating?"

Bravo walked toward the stairs shaking his head and grinning.

Ten hours later, Bravo awoke, freshened from a long sleep and his body clock more in sync with local time. He ordered breakfast to be brought to his room even though it was two o'clock in the afternoon. Nothing was too much trouble to the resident butler who had the staff to perform the required tasks. A knock on his door signalled the arrival of the food and Bravo opened it. The bearer of the food was one of the eunuchs that Bravo had seen last evening. Passively and with no hint of recognition the breakfast was set down on a table and the waiter, dressed appropriately in a waiter's uniform with a badge on his jacket that read Yousef, wheeled the trolley out from the room. Bravo mumbled a 'thank you' and tackled the food with gusto. Mahmoud may have been a Muslim but obviously bacon was not a prohibited meat in his Mayfair digs. No doubt the butler would have been responsible for provisioning and only the best was bought. The eggs were large and beautifully cooked and presented and the bacon rashers were like the ones that you saw in cooking articles in glossy magazines. His orange juice was freshly squeezed and the coffee was a delight. He savoured a cigarette and checked for messages on the phone. There was one from the Art 1 Trust, he would ring them when he came to. They knew the procedure and were aware that he would be sleeping following his long flight.

It seemed that he was to fly to Amsterdam tomorrow to collect Linus and bring him back to London. He notified his co-pilot, who was staying at a Holiday Inn and asked him to file flight plans. He thought that he might go shopping and buy his mother some duty free perfume. Leslie loved her Chanel and Bravo was a son who liked to please his mother.

On arrival at Amsterdam's Schiphol Airport, Bravo received a message from Linus saying that there was a change of plans and they would be staying on for a few more days. 'If you are free,' the message read, 'come over to Rudi's house and stay here with us.' Bravo got approval from head office that he was not needed in the interim and that he was free to stop in at Holland so long as they had a contact address. They parked the plane up and Bravo and his co-pilot, Ted, shared a taxi to Ted's hotel where they parted company and Bravo continued on in the cab to Rudi's address. Linus answered Bravo's door knock and they shook hands and embraced, as was their custom when greeting each other.

"This is where I grew up," Linus said. "Welcome to our humble home." The ground floor entrance led to a stairway ahead and an art studio to the right.

They walked up the flight of stairs and came into the first floor living accommodation. Bravo was surprised by the compactness of the space. There was room for everything but space for nothing. Bravo had heard stories about some of the older Dutch houses and the economy of scale on a square metre basis. On this floor there was a kitchen, and a dining room and a lounge. In the lounge he was introduced an elderly couple who were watching television. It was a German channel, Bravo could tell by the language.

"They are Werner Kruger's parents, you will have heard Rudi mention Werner; they were in Auschwitz together. When Werner moved to Holland his parents, who are from Berlin, came too. Franz-Josef was at Auschwitz, but you know that. The three of them saved lots of paintings from the clutches of the Nazis only to see them settled in Russia when the Russians liberated Auschwitz. You know the story?"

Bravo nodded. "Yes I do, it's a great story too. One day maybe the paintings will be returned to Germany or somewhere in Europe so that the paintings can be claimed by the rightful owners or their heirs," Bravo concluded.

Linus agreed. "Yes, I think that is what both Rudi and Werner would like to see but it is difficult to imagine the Russians playing ball at this stage, but, who knows. Come on up these stairs and I will show you your bedroom. There are three on the next floor and one on the floor above that. You are on the next floor. Rudi takes the top floor. It was always his and my late mother's bedroom. Even though he is ageing, he insists that he climb the stairs. We want him to move to a modern dwelling – god knows we can afford it, but this is his home. I fear he will die here. Werner does not stay here; he is a bit of a loner and lives in a small flat not far from here. At present he is away in France on a mission for Rudi. The art world is a busy place, Rudi stays at home and leaves Werner to do the travelling. They work well together. I couldn't imagine a more diverse couple but I think their links were forged in Auschwitz and would be extremely hard to break." Linus showed Bravo his bedroom. "Bathroom's just across the hall," he indicated. Bravo unloaded his pilot case which contained his emergency kit for when he was unexpectedly delayed. "Now we can go down to the studio and I'll show you some paintings."

Bravo liked art and had been an early disciple when Linus had shown him some of his paintings that he had shipped to New Zealand from the London collection, which was his inheritance. While Linus had sold most of his parents' collection, he did keep a few favourites and these adorned the walls at Maximes Hotel. If the local villains knew what they were, the paintings would have needed special security, but Linus said nothing and no guests knew any different so they merely were passed off as general background pictures that hotels hang around the place. All hotels have strange pictures and so Maximes had their share too!

The ground floor studio was an interesting and an intimate space. Rudi had a special way of displaying artwork that only time and experience can replicate. While the artist created the masterpiece, the gallery had to display it to the best

214

advantage. A badly hung painting may as well be facing the wall. The effect would be the same, maybe better. Light is important as is the angle of the light beams that shine onto the surface. Oils have peaks and valleys and, like sun rays on a distant hill, the scene can appear to change colour and definition as the sun moves across the sky and the image transforms. Some scenes are better in early morning sun and some are better in the late sunlight that is lower in the sky and the angle more obtuse. So it is the same with light on an artwork. Rudi has the touch of the finest artificer and he displayed the work at its best and the artists knew this and so he got the finest works to display and sell. And that translated to the best prices, too!

At the rear of the gallery was an office. This was where Rudi would spend his time when not hanging paintings or talking with customers. Here he would entertain his friends who may have been artists or buyers. Apart from a desk, there was a low table and comfortable sofas. There was also an endless coffee pot that Werner kept going when he was here. In his absence, Rudi tried to keep the device percolating but he did not have Werner's touch and so it was lifeless. Linus turned it on and suggested that they sit and have a coffee. Bravo asked where Rudi was.

"Rudi went out this morning on one of his forays," Linus replied. "We have no idea where he is going, he simply goes and does his thing and when he is ready he comes home. Time is not of the essence. He may be getting on in years but he seems to have the energy and enthusiasm of a much younger person. If he is in discussion with an artist or a buyer about business, it may continue for hours. They might visit a coffee shop or maybe have a few drinks; Rudi likes a beer as much as the next Dutchman. He thinks of himself as a Dutchman. He always comes home to sleep. Maybe he eats out some times if he is in a deep philosophical discussion about some piece of art. He may visit various artists' studios or galleries. He gets around the traps and keeps his finger on the pulse. He lives and breathes his passion. I cannot imagine him in any other form of occupation. It is his life blood!"

The coffee was percolating and a fine aroma enveloped them. Linus poured two cups of the hot black liquid and gave one to Bravo and then he sat down placing his coffee on the table.

"I have heard about the great escape when Rudi was spirited away from Leningrad. I never was told how Werner escaped or got away from the Soviets. He is here now, so obviously he managed to get out and bring his parents with him."

"Yes he did. Werner has always been a resourceful fellow. You heard how he set Franz-Josef up as a Red Cross worker from Switzerland so that he managed to evade the Soviets at Auschwitz. The Russians would have executed him otherwise."

Bravo nodded. "Yes I heard them talking about it in Cairo, Franz-Josef will be eternally grateful to Werner, they literally fried that poor German guard and he was a good guy – not SS – but a German Army officer. Weremacht, I believe – what a horrible end. I simply cannot imagine such cruelty."

215

"That is war, that is what war does to humans. For some reason we need to punish those that have punished us but we want to do it with compound interest, to borrow a mercantile term. I have become a business man so find that the aphorism is easily forthcoming. Anyway, Werner had always been free to travel within the Soviet Union and their satellite countries. He moved freely between Leningrad and Berlin. I understand that after Rudi left, the Soviets could not implicate Werner. Werner said that they were quite philosophical about the whole affair and apart from having egg on their face, the Hermitage carried on, business as usual. Werner also said that the Soviets did not wish to make a fuss, lest the reasons for Rudi's incarceration became general knowledge and the cache of artworks that they had accumulated from Auschwitz turned into a political hot potato. Werner had no intrinsic value to the Soviets other than being Rudi's assistant. With Rudi gone, Werner was of no use to the Leningrad cadre, so he returned to Berlin where his parents lived and moved in with them for a while. Or rather, for as long as they could endure his lifestyle. Then, one day, he learned the earth shattering news from his contacts within the communist hierarchy that Moscow wanted to erect a wall that would dissect the two political ideologies contained within Berlin. The primary objective for this hideous structure was to prevent the East Germans escaping to the West and freedom. After all, everyday Berliners made the transition with minimum hindrance of movement but it had become obvious to the communists that this relative freedom was bolstering the escape mechanism for the Germans' resident within the communist regime of East Germany. Werner decided that it was time to get out and so he planned the escape with his usual meticulous attention to detail. His parents would come with him. He had contacted Rudi using his underground network and Rudi was ready and waiting on his side of the Iron Curtain. Drawing on his pool of talented artisans, a lot of them from his Auschwitz days, Werner was able to produce three United States passports. These were costly, but Rudi had transmitted the money to an art dealer friend in West Berlin. The Krugers had previously immigrated to America, but never stayed long enough to apply for citizenship so Werner used their old addresses in Baltimore, as, if questioned, they could describe the neighbourhood and environs in great detail. Enough to satisfy the most vigorous oral examination.

"All they had to do was to present these to the passport visa office which happened to be in East Berlin, obtain the necessary DDR transitvisum stamp to travel by train from Berlin to Amsterdam, where Rudi would be waiting for them. Crossing into West Berlin presented little problem at this stage as Berliners travelled freely between the sectors prior to the wall being erected. The transit visa would allow them to travel via the rail corridor from Berlin which was inside East German territory, to and through the border with West Germany. In May of 1961 the Krugers left East Berlin each carrying a light satchel and a small backpack containing the items that they could not bear to part with. The erection of the wall began in August of the same year and was called the 'anti fascist protection rampart' by the East German authorities, thus

216

implying that neighbouring West Berlin had not been fully de-Nazified. However, the main reason for the structure was to prevent mass immigration and defection of the East German people fleeing to the west via East Berlin. So that's it!" Linus concluded, "Now you know all about Werner – quite a story, don't you think?"

Bravo agreed, "What a life, reminds me of the *Scarlet Pimpernel*, I never did read the book but I had the classic comic and enjoyed the story. In fact I had an excellent collection of classic comics, I often wondered why they never used them in schools. I recall in French lessons we were given comics to teach us the finer points of French grammar. It was the quietest moment in class when the French teacher handed out the comics. We were totally absorbed."

Linus smiled at this reflection. "I remember those comics from my schooldays in England."

Bravo looked startled. "I thought that you were from Holland?"

"Oh, yes I am, but my mother was English and she insisted that I was schooled in England. How else do you think I came to talk like this. Mine is not a Dutch accent – maybe you think it is?"

Bravo looked pensive and paused before replying. "Yes you're right, I did wonder about that but never bothered to ask or I guess I didn't want to appear nosy. None of my business. But you're right, very English, yes I agree!"

At that point Rudi walked in.

"Ah Bravo," he said, "welcome to my house. I see Linus has fired the coffee percolator up. Might have a cup myself; been a hard day."

Rudi poured himself a cup and sat down in one of the comfy sofa divans. "Everywhere I go reeks of marijuana," he said, "seems the whole of Amsterdam is one big reefer joint and a lot of today's artists are smoking the stuff in the coffee houses. The smell puts me off!"

Bravo asked why he went to coffee houses.

"It's where my business is, artists, the young and even the older painters all patronise the coffee houses, you can buy marijuana there and smoke it. It sure has changed since my young days. I'm getting the hang of it though. The well-heeled artists, those selling their works, tend to go to coffee houses in the red light district, that's where the more expensive pot is. The more expensive it is the better quality it is. The further away from the city centre, the cheaper the pot. The quality is not so good but still better by international standards, I am told by my artist friends. Anyway I move around, the established artists are in the town centre and the lesser or up and coming talent, further out. Excuse me." Rudi went out from the office and returned with a parcel, unwrapping it as he re-entered the room. "Almost forgot this," he said. "I actually bought it from a young man in one of the coffee shops further out from the city centre. Probably felt a bit sorry for him he is on the bones of his ass but also I liked his work." He stood the painting upright on the desk for all to see. "Bit dark in here but I'll get it in the right light and it will make a nice display. What do you think?"

As is the habit with all connoisseurs, they tend to absentmindedly assume that everybody shares their knowledge. Bravo looked nonplussed. He saw a portrait of a young woman, attractive enough, in gloomy colours with what he imagined was oil paint that had been squeezed on directly form the tube container. Then moved around with a knife or some sort of spatula.

"Well?" Rudi enquired.

"Nice one, Father," Linus said.

"What about you Bravo – what do you think?"

Bravo searched about in his mind to think of something to say. Searching about in Bravo's mind for words was generally productive but this one had him stumped. He didn't know enough about art to make a comment.

"The structure is fine," he heard himself say, "but the application, well what can I say, other than the artist has gone berserk with the toothpaste tubes."

"You just nailed it," Rudi said. "They all think that they are Van Gogh first up and run short on funds, wasting oils, which are costly. Nonetheless it is interesting. I want to experiment with light on this one. Come and see it tomorrow once I have set up the display. I think that it will be an interesting look! I call these first issues. When they become rich and famous, first issues are priceless."

"And if they don't become rich and famous?"

"I've still had an interesting day," Rudi said, "come on let's eat out, I'm buying."

"What about the Krugers?" Bravo enquired.

"They never move from the television set."

It was a mere half a kilometre walk to the town centre where some of the best cafes were. They ate a sumptuous meal and drank beer and wine and enjoyed convivial conversation while embracing the pleasures of living in a prosperous era in relative peace.

"There were times in Auschwitz," Rudi said, "when I doubted that I would ever see the outside world again. Prison wire and death chambers were our bill of fare, nice food was a dream and a nightmare was a good sleep. The waking hours were worse than a bad dream. So come nightfall it was good to relax into the relative comfort of a benign nightmare!"

Bravo almost felt guilty that he had had an easy life thus far. Linus survived the fighting of his war at sea and mentioned very little about that. It was in jovial spirits that the three men left the cafe and walked among the throngs in the red light district which was busy at this time of night. There was jostling and one had to be aware of pickpockets. At one stage Rudi became aware of a potential pickpocket using an umbrella to try and hook his wallet from out of his jacket pocket but they scared him off with some shouting and much gesticulation. "They get cheekier," he said, "usually they jostle and it's over – what next?"

The following morning Rudi was taken ill with a cough and fever and he also complained of stomach pains. "I felt sick in the night but put it down to over-indulgence, I took a sleeping pill and that was me out to it. Now I feel awful. I can't make the doctor's office, you better see if he can come to me!"

The doctor visited around noon by which time Rudi was visibly worse and the doctor suspected poisoning.

"Could be food, you say you ate out last night; what did you have?"

"Rudi had chicken and we had the beef," Linus said, indicating himself and Bravo.

"Chicken can be dodgy if it's not thawed and cooked properly."

"It was a first rate cafe, near the red light district. Good food in all of that area."

"We'll see, I'll get an ambulance and we will get Rudi to hospital and carry out some tests. How old is Rudi?" The doctor asked Linus.

Linus looked a bit sheepish. "You know I'm not sure. He was always coy about age. We do know that he came from Russia about 1917, as a young man. I recall my mother mentioning 1890 as a birthdate but that cannot be confirmed and I doubt we can get any records out of Russia."

"That would make him ninety two," the doctor looked incredulous. "He sure does not look ninety two!"

"Considering the hard times he has endured it's a wonder he is here at all," Linus said.

"All the more reason for haste," the doctor said. He wrote a letter and phoned the hospital and left them to wait for the ambulance.

Rudi was on oxygen by the time the ambulance delivered him to the hospital and Linus and Bravo sat alongside him on the short ride to the hospital's emergency admission suite. They were left in the waiting room as a team of medics swarmed around the inert frame and wheeled him away on a gurney, to begin their medical examination and test procedures, which they all knew could take considerable time.

Two hours later, police arrived to question Linus and Bravo. The examining doctor, Dr Arens, joined them in an interview room and explained that they had determined that Rudi had been poisoned and following the normal hospital procedures when this type of poisoning was detected, the police had to be informed.

"It's not food poisoning?" Linus asked.

"No, it's not food poisoning, although the poisoning may have been ingested by eating but we tend to think differently at the moment."

"Tell me," the policeman asked, it was the plain clothed officer who had introduced himself as Inspector Joos Zervas and his accomplice as Constable Behrens. "Tell us exactly what happened last night, anything out of the ordinary. Did anything out of the ordinary occur?"

Linus started. "Well as you know we went for a meal and had some beers and a few wines with our meal and following that, we walked among the crowds in the red light district, taking in the atmosphere and Rudi said that this pickpocket had used an umbrella to try and take his wallet from his jacket pocket."

The doctor looked at the policeman in a conspiratorial way.

"And what did this person look like?"

"Didn't take much notice, he was in and out, just like that I guess. Rudi shouted at him and that's when we realised that something had happened and he vanished into the milling throng of people. You know what it's like in the area. We were not really watching and it was all over so quickly. Why the interest in the pickpocket?"

The inspector looked very serious. "We believe that Rudi has been the victim of a Bulgarian umbrella attack."

"And just what is a Bulgarian umbrella attack?" Linus enquired with a bemused look.

The inspector maintained his serious demeanour. "It is a usually fatal method of delivering a highly poisonous toxin in the form of a small pellet containing ricin."

His statement was met by blank stares.

He continued. "Ricin is a toxin that is fatal to humans, it comes from the castor bean plant and can be delivered as a powder, mist or in a pill or pellet form. If fatal, the victim will die within five days and there is no known antidote."

Everyone looked very serious.

"If fatal, you say, implying that it may not be fatal?"

"There have been known instances when the victim has recovered, usually due to the dosage not being administered correctly. The Bulgarian umbrella is a device that injects a prepared pellet of a fixed dosage from the tip of an umbrella. The pointy end. The trigger is in the handle of the umbrella and the attacker simply places the umbrella tip next to the victim and pushes a button that releases a charge of compressed air that, in turn, propels the pellet from the umbrella tip-nozzle, not unlike an air pistol. Maybe the victim feels a small sting which he may expect if he had been touched by the supposed pickpocket with the umbrella tip. The pellet is placed within the skin of the assailed, just beneath the surface and it melts as designed, at thirty seven degrees Celsius, when it is absorbed into the body. Absorption takes a few hours, all very innocuous, I assure you. In this instance I regret to say that the full dosage will have been discharged and absorbed by the victim. Do you know of any reason why someone would want to kill Rudi Levin?"

Linus froze at the words implying that his father was on his deathbed. The Dutch people do not pull any punches. They are too honest to be polite.

"My father, a Jew, was taken to Russia from Auschwitz by the liberating red army in WWII. He was kept there involuntarily until we managed to stage his escape back in 1952. At the time the Russians did not seem overly worried about him getting away. He had served his purpose and they didn't want to make a fuss about a matter best left unpublicised. It may have been embarrassing to the Russians to divulge too much information about their collection of great artworks which they had managed to spirit out of Germany and secretly stockpile at the Hermitage in Leningrad! Maybe he was classified as too low a priority at the time. As far as we were aware, he was not declared persona non grata. Following on from that, they must have slowly worked their way through the people on their hit list, then decided they wanted to upgrade Rudi, to a villain. So you think that this was the work of an assassin?" Linus looked questioningly at Inspector Zervas

"Yes, we think most definitely KGB. This is a known KGB assassination device. You say that you spirited him away in 1952, can you elaborate please?"

"Sure; when I say we, I mean that MI5 planned it and it was done in conjunction with an art exhibition that we had staged at the Hermitage in Leningrad, that is to say, my trust, the Art 1 Trust."

Inspector Zervas raised his eyebrows, "The art treasures that were secreted away from Holland prior to WWII. Is that the one?" A penny had dropped. The inspector may not have been old enough to recall the event but he had obviously read about it. He looked anew at Linus. Linus was not sure if it was a look of scorn or awe. They could easily be transposed depending on who was wearing the expression.

"Yes, Inspector, Rudi, my father that is, arranged to save priceless artworks from the hands of the Nazis. The world is indebted to his foresight. Furthermore, when the Nazis imprisoned both him and his wife, my mother, in Auschwitz, he went on to save another four thousand works from the belongings of the Jews who were exterminated in that camp. Now those pieces are the artworks that the Soviets claimed, when the red army liberated Auschwitz and removed both the paintings and Rudi and Werner Kruger to Leningrad. We managed to rescue Rudi some years later, but the art collection is still in Soviet hands. At the time we figured that the Soviets made little fuss over the matter as they were reluctant to divulge their illegal cache of Jewish owned paintings that they had had stolen. It would have been embarrassing for sure. They were keen to avoid bad press. I think that they were getting enough of that over Berlin at the time. Now, some thirty years on, they see fit to exterminate the very man who saved that art collection. Sounds absolutely preposterous, don't you think?"

"Well we have our ways of finding out some of these things, so I intend to get investigations underway. I'm sorry, Mr Levin, please accept my condolences. You father will be made as comfortable as possible until the end."

Linus was in no mood for pleasantries. "Yes, well, rest assured that we have our own intelligence network," he said, thinking of Werner Kruger. "We will probably have some idea who is behind this even before your people, in which case I will let you know."

The inspector and his uniformed officer said a formal goodbye and left the interview room. The doctor invited Linus and Bravo to accompany him to visit Rudi who was resting comfortably in an isolated cubicle.

"The toxin will slowly shut down his organs," Doctor Arens said. "He will get diarrhoea and probably die from circulatory shock. Prior to that, he will fall into a coma and will simply stop breathing as his time arrives. Not a lot of difference from natural causes, but it will be managed and he will be very comfortable and there will be no pain."

Linus turned to Bravo. "I had better get hold of Werner, not sure of his whereabouts but there must be something in Rudi's diary back at the office. We can't do much here at the moment."

Bravo and Linus left the hospital and returned to Rudi's place where they informed the Krugers of Rudi's predicament. The Krugers offered their condolences and returned to watching television.

Bravo and Linus entered Rudi's office to examine his diary and found a phone number for Werner who, it seemed, was in Spain. Werner was mortified to hear the news and said that he would be on the next flight and Linus said, "I can send my plane to you, just sit still and Bravo will collect you." Linus looked at Bravo as he said this and Bravo nodded in agreement.

When Linus had hung up, Bravo asked, "When do you want me to leave?"

"Go now, let me know your ETA when you have filed your flight plans and I will tell Werner to get to the airport and wait for you. Once you have him aboard, come back."

When Bravo had departed for the airport, Linus contacted Werner again and made him aware of the plans afoot. "We'll talk when you get back," he said, "but I want you to have a good think about how the hell and who the hell could have done this?"

It was almost twenty four hours later when Bravo returned with Werner and Linus and Werner went to the hospital to visit Rudi who was conscious – just. It pained Werner to see his friend and companion of these past thirty nine years lying in a hospital bed dying. Rudi had been made aware of his predicament by Dr Arens and he was submissive and had accepted his fate with great dignity.

"Father."

"Yes, my son."

"Dr Arens has asked me your date of birth."

"Can you keep a secret, son?"

"Yes, Father."

Rudi motioned for Linus to come closer as one does when imparting a secret. Linus moved close to hear the words.

"Well, so can I son!" Rudi said and smiled.

Werner looked at Linus and shrugged. "Vintage Rudi," he said. "Keep schtum, it's a hangover from Auschwitz, and comes from the German stumm, meaning 'silent'. We said nothing. Nothing cannot hurt you!"

"Yeah well, he hasn't lost his sense of humour either," Linus said. They could see Rudi's body convulsing beneath the blankets. He wasn't wracked with pain, he was laughing.

Rudi slipped into a coma the following day and died the day after that.

The funeral was a very private affair, family, art patrons, local artists, Art 1 Trust executives ferried in by Bravo from London. Linus asked Kaetrin not to come. It was too far away and Bravo was busy shuttling local dignitaries between London and Amsterdam and couldn't fly to Wellington to collect her. Franz-Josef made it to London and was ferried across to Holland in one of Bravo's many runs. As was requested by the rabbi, the internment was to be made as soon as practicably possible and in a plain wooden box with no metal fittings. There was graveside service only, thus observing some Jewish traditions.

Inspector Zervas was at the graveside and afterward Linus introduced him to Werner.

"Inspector!" Werner started the conversation, "I have some intelligence for you. Maybe you already have the same information?"

"Nothing to report as yet," Inspector Zervas replied. "We have our own intelligence agency, LAMID, as well as Interpol on the case, but we have no leads as yet."

"And you most probably never will, but here's what happened anyway, you can file it in your report and write 'closed' on the file!"

Joos Zervas was an experienced police officer and the candour of Werner's delivery surprised him, but he remained stoic.

"Go on," he said.

"There is a new man in charge of foreign operations at the Kremlin, KGB HQ, Moscow. His name is Putin. A young Turk by all accounts, he has dragged up all of the old files and reissued instructions on dealing with persons who are declared persona non grata. They are to be eliminated and their file closed. Russia will not be humiliated, he says. Russia is to reinforce its superiority in subversive affairs. The Bulgarian umbrella was last used by the Bulgarian secret police back in 1978, but it is a KGB tool and was made in Russia and issued to the Bulgarians to be used on one of their own dissidents in London. No doubt you will recall the case. In this instance, the tool will have been supplied by KGB and was used by a KGB agent. You will find neither."

"Rudi was never persona non grata," Inspector Zervas said.

"Well he is, or was, now," Werner replied. "Putin says so and if he says so, then it is so. He is very powerful. You have a new face to put up in your hall of rogues and throw darts at. This guy plays Cape and Bodkin with real knives and guns and other nasty little devices!"

"Thank you, Mr Kruger. Are you sure about this?"

"I am, Inspector, my contacts are impeccable!"

Joos Zervas nodded in agreement. Somethings you just knew and never questioned. It was not logic but that was how detective work happened, sometimes. You just knew. "Seat of the pants is not always for sitting on!" he reminded himself.

Linus asked Werner to move into Rudi's house. "Keep an eye on the place and your parents, they're getting on a bit. Get a housekeeper. The trust will pay. Okay?"

Werner nodded. "Business as usual?" he asked.

"Yes business as usual," Linus replied. "I'll get London to make some adjustments to their payment schedule but yes, carry on as Rudi would have, you have the skills that Rudi has passed onto you. Use them wisely."

Bravo and Linus returned to London and in a matter of days they were flying off to Cairo to deliver Franz-Josef and Mahmoud back to Egypt and then it was onto Wellington.

It was only two months since they left but so much had happened it may well have been a lifetime. Bravo had Chanel perfume for his mother Leslie and Linus came bearing gifts for Kaetrin and Flora. They landed at Rongotai Airport in Wellington at 0130 hours and the three of them. Linus, Bravo and the co-pilot shared a taxi to Maximes Hotel.

Over breakfast, Linus brought everyone up to date with the events in Holland and Rudi's untimely death. Bravo and the co-pilot were still asleep but Linus had slept during the flight and so had arrived in a relatively fresh condition. It was good to be back and eating the food from the hotel's kitchen. Despite having some memorable repasts in his travels, Linus still maintained that Maximes' kitchen was the best. Cooks come and cooks go, but Kaetrin somehow managed to get the best out of the staff that she hired to maintain the culinary standards of the hotel. Marjorees afternoon teas at Maximes were now an institution in the social activities of the city and during summer it was necessary to book, so as to avoid disappointment.

Flora and James had retired from the everyday running of Maximes, the task being entrusted to the ever reliable and capable Kaetrin who was now into her forty second year of hotel life. The only regret Kaetrin had was that her and Linus had been far too busy in their business lives to even contemplate raising a family. During the past four years they had the responsibility of taking care of Maree, who was about to start university. She wanted to become a marine biologist and was already into her underwater diving activities with one of the local diving clubs. Maree's parents visited infrequently, not that Maree was bothered about that; she was too busy enjoying life in the big city following her childhood on Vavai. Maree had a good circle of friends and all the maternal love that a young girl would require from her Aunty Kaetrin. The two were becoming inseparable and in a way, Kaetrin was reminded of her friendship with Leslie when she came to New Zealand as a CORB child, during WWII on the liner RMS *Rangitata*. Those memories were still as fresh as a sea breeze in the doldrums, and as welcome. Leslie was a part of the family. She resided and worked at Maximes and Bravo worked for the Art 1 Trust. Life was hectic but somehow extremely orderly considering the shock start they both had. Their love interests of the day had been washed away by the tides of war. Both young women had to make the best of a difficult start in life and they did and they had won through. Best of all, Kaetrin and Leslie remained very good friends and spent time together, especially when Linus was away on one of his business trips. Maximes was centrally located and they would take themselves off to a movie of an evening as there was a choice of several picture theatres within walking distance from the hotel. It was on one of these outings that Leslie had confided in Kaetrin her fears about Bravo.

"I mean, he is well into his adult life now and I have never known him to look at a woman. Do you think he might be homosexual?"

224

Kaetrin looked bemused. "He's never here, I guess it would be hard to answer that. All of his adult life he has been away from home. At first he trained in the air force, so we hardly saw him. When he was flying the big jumbo planes he was never here and now that he is with the Art 1 Trust flying their executives around the globe we never see much of him. Quite frankly I cannot imagine when he would ever get the time for romance, unless they were one night stands!"

Leslie was aghast.

"Relax, Leslie," Kaetrin said. "A man's a man. If he needs it, he'll get it! Imagine the talent that would have been available from his commercial airline days. I mean cabin crew, very attractive young ladies for sure. You ever heard of the mile high club?"

Leslie shook her head, confirming a negative response.

"It's the industry's reference to having sex in the aeroplane when flying, you know, way the hell up there." And Kaetrin flung her arm upward to indicate airborne. "Up there – a mile high," she repeated. "High in the sky."

"Sex in the plane," Leslie exclaimed incredulously.

"Sure, there are plenty of private spaces. If your fellow crew members know, they give you a wide berth. It's a badge of honour!"

"I'm sure Bravo wouldn't condone such activity!" Leslie sounded defensive.

"Ask him."

"What!"

"Go on, ask him. I'm sure you and Doug got up to a bit of slap and tickle on the ship. In strange places too!"

Leslie reddened as she remembered an early morning outdoor sexual encounter in the South Pacific Ocean, at sunrise and on the monkey island of the *Rangitata*.

Kaetrin noticed the blushing Leslie and turned the blow torch off.

She could see that Leslie was working through a raft of discoveries.

"You know," Leslie said after a long silence between them, "if Bravo is anything like his father I'm sure that he would have taken his chances as they presented."

"Feel better?"

"Yes, feel a lot better – thanks, Kaetrin."

They walked back to the hotel and went into lobby and made a cup of coffee from the endless coffee cup and sat down in one of the comfortable sofas, of which there were many.

"Thanks, Kaetrin. I needed that. What strange creatures we are. We forget our own indiscretions and yet challenge our successors to be saints without sinning. I fear I have become an old maid. I feel a sea cruise coming on, maybe I will rediscover some libido."

Bravo had five days at home before a telex arrived sending him on his next mission which surprised both Linus and himself. It seemed that the Art 1 Trust had purchased a new aeroplane from Lear in Witchita, Kansas. It was a larger plane, but carried the same number of passengers. The extended fuselage was designed to carry extra fuel tanks for longer flights or it could carry more freight if the tanks were removed. The trust had decided that they needed a plane that could transport artworks to and from their worldwide displays and auctions. They would retain their existing planes and Bravo's co-pilot would oversee the refit and be given the rank of captain. He would train a new co-pilot who would receive initial training at the works on their flight simulator. Bravo was to collect the new plane and his new co-pilot and report to London for further instruction.

Leslie said a teary goodbye to her son and Bravo and Ted the co-pilot took a taxi to Rongotai Airport and they flew to Kansas. At Kansas, Bravo was told that he would need to do simulator time with his new co-pilot and the first stint was scheduled twenty four hours following their arrival. Bravo said goodbye to Ted and wished him all the best with his new command. "Our paths must cross," he said, "so I'll simply say, see you later! We have different schedules and I know mine is full on here until we leave in a week's time."

"So's mine," Ted confirmed. "Pound of flesh – noun and verb!"

The following morning, Bravo arrived at the simulator where he met a stunning young lady whom he imagined managed the flight programmes in the simulator. She introduced herself.

"Hi," she said and held out her hand in greeting. Bravo took it and they shook.

"I'm Bravo," he said.

"Hi, I'm Georgia, I'm your new co-pilot."

Bravo thought about this for at least a second before the penny dropped. Georgia must have noticed the surprised expression on Bravo's face and smiled. She had been used to her male counterparts categorising her as anything but a pilot. Bravo was too professional to let the encounter pass as anything other than workmanlike, even though his thoughts were anything other than workmanlike.

"Welcome aboard, Georgia," he said. "What's your background?"

"I flew sea harriers off carriers: navy," she replied. "Been commercial for the past year, but that was boring and I spotted an advert for this job, applied and here I am!"

Bravo nodded, "Impressive stuff; carriers! Falkland Islands, you involved in that stoush?"

"No, before my time. They probably would not have deployed females. We talked about that, consensus was no but my time was up and I was ready to leave anyway – so I left!"

Their instructor arrived and the small talk ceased. Following the morning session, the instructor excused Bravo saying, "You seem to know the equipment very well. I'll take Georgia only for the next couple of days. You should take your new plane for a spin with one of our pilots and Georgia can join you after that."

A week later they were winging their way to London. Georgia was a competent co-pilot and so she should be, with her background. Bravo was pleased to have her aboard.

"Where do you stay in London?" Georgia asked.

"A friend's flat in Mayfair, usually," Bravo replied.

They had just landed the plane having flown directly from Kansas to Gatwick.

"The Art 1 Trust has a standing order at the Travelodge near the airport, but I stay in Mayfair," Bravo repeated. "It's central and a butler attends to my every need. Best of all, it's free. As is the hotel of course."

"Some friend, flats in Mayfair don't come cheap!"

"They don't, the owner lives in Cairo. Chap by the name of Mahmoud Nassar. Bit of a playboy in his day," Bravo offered. "If he's in town there is usually a bit of action, but most times it's quiet and respectable. I can offer you your own room there if you would like to try it out. I have the run of the place."

"Better than wasting out here at Gatwick – yes, sounds interesting I'll take you up on the offer. Sounds like a girl could go shopping."

"Very central, parks, shops the lot and quiet too. Remember we have to check in with HQ tomorrow. It will be better for both of us."

They took a taxi and Bravo gave the driver an Art 1 Trust taxi chit. The flat was empty and they had the choice of bedrooms. "Nice little pub around the corner if you fancy a drink?" Bravo suggested. "Freshen up, say, see you here in the lobby in an hour – yes?"

"Yes, can do, see you then," and she went to her room.

Before they left for the pub, Bravo introduced Georgia to the butler who had until now remained nameless, but today he wore a badge on his lapel, engraved 'Gregory'.

"We'll grab a bite out tonight," Bravo told Gregory, "but will order breakfast for the morning. We have to be up and away to a meeting so if we could have breakfast at seven thirty that would be great."

"Certainly, Mr Thornton. May I suggest breakfast in the conservatory tomorrow? It will be a sunny morning."

"Yes, of course, thank you. Good evening," and they left. On the flight over each had in turn managed an hour's sleep, mid-Atlantic. The passenger seats on this plane could be laid horizontal and turned into a comfortable bed. There was even a twin berther at the rear of the fuselage. The plane had some modern features. This was their first social outing since meeting and they were both a little reserved initially, but a couple of drinks soon dissipated the awkwardness and soon they were chatting like old friends. Bravo was not sure that he wanted to be old friends or even good friends. Boyfriend was what Bravo had in mind. He was attracted to the lady but it was too early for him to say so. It was getting to know you time and he decided that he did want to know Georgia. He was looking for return signals, but could not detect any. Georgia was business-like. She was flying her single seater jet fighter plane, he felt. Maybe that's how the lady played. Bravo was cool with that. They had a lot of flying to do together.

The following morning, they reported to HQ and learned that they would be flying some paintings and people to South Africa to an art exhibition and then they were to go to Perth, Australia, and collect one of their executives and take him to Hong Kong for a meeting and then it would be back to London. They would be away for two weeks, then it was back to South Africa to collect what they had already delivered and off to another exhibition in Cairo.

"Wait in Cairo for the next leg." The despatcher said.

Bravo added a bar to his mile high club gong, on the leg between Cape Town and Perth. Georgia became a new member of the club and as she said to Bravo, "You can't fuck yourself in a sea harrier, I know it's called a jump jet but it's not that sort of jump!" Over the vast expanse of the Indian Ocean Bravo had put the Lear Jet on auto pilot as they checked out the double berther at the rear of the fuselage. They had both worked themselves into a frenzy for this first encounter and for Bravo, it was as epic as Julius Caesar crossing the Rubicon in 49BC. He had flushed his demons and consecrated his manhood and was advancing on Rome.

Chapter 15

Otto

Otto Kaiser died at the ripe old age of 92, in Cairo. He had wanted to return to his native Germany but the ruling communist regime of Erich Honecker, the head of the Communist Party of East Germany, were in essence communist quislings of Moscow and they instituted a Stalinist style police state. The Kaiser Iron & Steel Works where the field guns and armoured vehicles were made for the German Military were now owned and run by the state. Their estates were communes and the palatial homes were institutionalised. One was a sanatorium and the other an orphanage. The von Hapsbergs and the Kaisers did not want to return under the current regime. Otto was born in 1888 and in the First World War he was a field marshall. One of the youngest, they said, but then the Kaiser family had supplied military greatness to Germany's war efforts over the years and back in the day name and rank went hand in glove. That's how it worked before the formation of the Weimar Republic, following Germany's defeat in WWI. The aristocracy were blended with the hoi-poloi, or so they would have you believe. The reality was, that now everybody was equal, it became as it does with all doctrines. It demonstrated that nature's contribution, by making things different, was for a reason. Meddle with nature and you risk compromising the outcome. Every race has winners and losers. The Jews were the race losers in WWII. But Emile Zatopek was a race winner, with three gold medals to his credit in the 1952 Helsinki Olympics. Not a level playing surface for sure.

While Anna and her maid Kirsten and Claudia and her maid Gerda were happy in Cairo, the men's two valets, Marco and Conrad, were pining for the green coolness of their native land and were keen to return to the verdant hunting wilderness that was the Dresden estates of the von Hapsbergs and the Kaisers. Technically they were homeless, but they knew the hunting lodges and the terrain and felt that they could quietly melt into the forests and enjoy their twilight years in familiar surrounds. They both held Swiss citizenship and their respective employers arranged for an annuity to be paid into Swiss bank accounts set up for the purpose. It was simply a matter of them accessing those funds as required and they could live in relative comfort anywhere in Europe, if the wilds of Saxony got too much for either of them. It was with great sadness that the two faithful valets departed Cairo for Zurich on a B.O.A.C. flight one May afternoon in 1963.

Otto and Albert had persevered with their irrigation schemes and had purchased suitable tracts of land that could become arable cropping farms with the correct application of water, seeds and fertiliser. They purchased their first aerial top dressing plane from Neil Walker's fledgling crop dusting aviation factory in the Wairarapa and the delivering pilot stayed on for three months to instruct local pilots in the nuances of the aerial spraying and dusting business. The plane was a Douglas Dakota DC3, of which there were many specimens left in North Africa and Europe following WWII. Alfred and Otto started a factory to convert the planes according to Neil Walker's designs, which were implemented under a licensing agreement and they became the pioneers in the aerial crop spraying and seeding industry for North Africa.

Neither Otto nor Albert ever lost their flair for innovation and when the elder of the two, which was Otto by six years, died, Albert had lost a friend that had been his intellectual mentor and companion for over sixty years.

It was Otto's wish to be interred within the family crypt in Dresden, but that was not possible at the time of his death and so they put his embalmed body in a specially built, lead lined coffin that was placed in an underground crypt, adjacent to the wine cellar in their Cairo building. The instructions were that as soon as their lands in Germany were restored to their former rightful owners, his remains and any other deceased persons awaiting transportation back to their native land would be repatriated to a permanent home in the family burial sites on their estates in Saxony.

The funeral service was attended by people from many different parts of the world, all of whom had had contact with Otto during his varied and colourful military and civilian life. The military personnel were thin and few on the ground, with a great many of Otto's military acquaintances beneath it – their demise was hastened by participating in WWII. A large contingent came from India where the Kaisers had cotton mill interests. The ladies were resplendent in colourful saris and the men in sober Nehru style jackets and hats. Neil and Alison Walker came, having flown in with Kaetrin and Linus in an Art 1 Trust Lear Jet from Wellington and piloted by Bravo and his co-pilot Georgia. The service was conducted in the military museum, among the relics that Alfred and Otto had so lovingly restored or overseen the restoration of by their team of artisans. Alfred gave the eulogy and Mahmoud talked about their desert experiences when Otto had a bounty on his head and was eagerly sought after by the Bedouin, Suilleman from the Sudan. It was an orthodox Lutheran service conducted by a Lutheran church minister and a relative of the family, who had come from Germany for the ceremony.

Otto's casket was placed on Eagle Fox, the scout car that he had presented to Rommel in 1942 and which was made by the Kaiser Iron and Steel Works in Dresden. It was coupled to a Kaiser Aufinez field piece, also a product from the Kaiser Works at Dresden. A Chevrolet from the LRDG carried the official party of Anna Kaiser, and Kirsten her maid, Claudia von Hapsberg and Gerda, Claudia's maid. Up front was Neil Walker, the driver, and sitting alongside him was his wife Alison. Alfred drove Eagle Fox and the funeral cortege headed out to the desert where they would fire a 21 gun salute from the Kaiser field gun in honour of the old warrior. Linus and Kaetrin were in an air conditioned Mercedes with FJ and Brigette. Their children, now adults, were Nixie, who was 30 and Falco 28. They rode together in Falco's open top green Jaguar sports car. The cavalcade created considerable interest and the traffic in downtown Cairo was brought to a halt as it passed intersections, patrolled by policemen directing and halting traffic, to allow the official cortege right of way. The German and Swiss ambassadors, as well as Egyptian politicians, were in the cavalcade, so traffic control was briefed on the importance of it moving with no unscheduled stops or hold-ups. A police escort on motorcycles completed the spectacle. Mahmoud was there, as were several family members from Abdul Nassar and Sons but Abdul himself was too frail to attend. He was, after all, 101.

The guests assembled back at the museum for the committal, when Otto's casket was taken down into the underground vault where he would lie until he could be repatriated to the family crypt in Saxony.

Traditionally and by Otto's explicit request, alcohol was offered to the guests. Mindful of accusing Muslim eyes, Mahmoud deferred his alcohol consumption until a more private moment, when the guests had departed and close friends and family only remained.

Mahmoud ordered a scotch, it was a favourite of Otto's and one that they both had enjoyed during their sojourn in the desert, all those years ago. Many things had changed, but the scotch remained the same.

"It's been forty years," Neil said as they both raised their glasses said, "Cheers," and sipped the fine amber liquid.

"So you never married, Mahmoud?" Neil asked.

"No, my father wanted me to, many times, but I just could not settle down, I had wanderlust, now there's a German word for you!"

"We have the same word in English," Neil said.

"Yes you do, but it is a loan word, Otto said that it has now been superseded by a later German word 'farweh' which means 'farsickness'."

"Strange word!"

"Yes, I suppose it is if you are not a German, Otto told me it was coined as an antonym for 'heimweh' which is homesickness, a condition that Otto had to contend with since leaving Saxony in 1942. Otto said that I was like the adolescent wanderbird seeking oneness with nature. I suppose I get that from my Bedouin genes, the world is my desert and London an oasis. I call my home in Mayfair Wadi-Shira." Mahmoud placed the emphasis on the last syllable.

Neil smiled, "Now, let me guess, same as for Wadi-Gin and your other boltholes around the desert named for alcoholic drinks, and I would guess that 'Shira' is for 'Shiraz', the wine."

Mahmoud acquiesced with a smile and a nod of his head. "Am I that transparent?" he mused. "I go there when I get dissatisfied with the restrictions of home. Having a liberal education helps, or doesn't help, as the case may be. Mind you, we have our customs that Westerners find difficult to comprehend. My father has many wives, he is a happy man. I have no wives. I'm a happy man. When in London, you and Alison must stay with me, if you ever go to London that is. If I am not there you can still use the place, be my guest. I would be honoured to have you as a guest in my house. Bedouin are benevolent hosts."

"Thank you Mahmoud," Neil replied, "in fact we are heading off to London when we leave Cairo. Linus has invited us to do the return trip Wellington to London. Alison has never been away from New Zealand so she is keen to take in the sights of London town. Buckingham Palace, the Tower of London, the usual touristy things. I know that Linus and Kaetrin will be staying at Claridges but that is a bit beyond a farmer's income, so I will accept your kind offer and stay at your place – if that's okay?"

"Absolutely, dear boy," Mahmoud beamed. "I'll let Gregory, the butler, know you'll be coming. All you have to do is knock on the door and the rest happens, as they say. I may be there a week or so later, I have few things to take care of here with our Indian guests and then I'll come on over too."

Alison was delighted with the arrangements when Neil told her and she mentioned it to Kaetrin, who agreed. "Mayfair is a nice part of town," she told Alison. "Claridges is in Mayfair, so you must join us for afternoon tea at the hotel, it's the best experience ever. I can guarantee that you will simply adore the occasion."

"Similar to your very own Marjorees at Maximes," Alison replied, "we had tea there and found it to be superb!"

Kaetrin smiled at the response from Alison. "Well, you see that was inspired by the Claridges experience. Marjory Beresford-Amble, who is a tea connoisseur, learnt her craft in India. Marjory and myself formulated our plans over tea at Claridges one afternoon – it's been a hit for us for sure, no small thanks to Marjory's input and her expert knowledge of the subject!"

"Neil and myself will look forward to that," Alison replied. "I'll call you when we have settled in and make a date for sure."

Alfred cornered Neil and invited him and Alison to visit the museum that Otto and himself had built up over the years.

"You will be amazed at the material we have managed to salvage from the desert," he said. "The dry atmosphere has helped preserve a lot of what might normally be scrap metal. Our superb staff have resurrected some amazing artefacts. Even got one of your so called Benghazi burners – you remember those things your team used to boil water for a cuppa?"

232

Neil was impressed, "Yes I do, the Benghazi burner, what an invention. When Mahmoud explained the use of camel dung for fuel, the boys would scavenge for that ubiquitous item whenever we came across a watering hole. Sadly, so did the camel owners. Nonetheless our sand and petrol mix usually sufficed once you got the ratio right you could just about set your watch on the time it took to boil up for a brew. Our shepherds use the same device back home on the sheep station. You must show me the one in the museum."

"Tomorrow we'll do the grand tour," Alfred said. "You know we've had Germans through the place who served in the Africa Corps. They said that the Benghazi burner had them fooled for a long time!"

"Can't imagine why," Neil said.

"It was the round burnt circle in the sand, every time that they overran a former Kiwi post they were puzzled by the number of circular blackened discs on the sand. At first they thought it was left by some sort of rocket launcher that they knew nothing about. Eventually they discovered a Benghazi burner in situ having been left in place by a hastily departing enemy. Lifting the thing up revealed the fire box which of course was round and they discovered the mystery behind the burnt round rings of sand. The discovery went to the highest level in army intelligence. It had them worried for some time."

Guests slowly left the reception as the afternoon wore on but not before they had paid their respects to Anna Kaiser who was being morally supported by her granddaughter Nixie who was a great comfort to her. Nixie had inherited her father's ice blue Germanic eyes and her mother's flaxen hair. A fair Germanic beauty who had left many a young man floundering in the wake of would be suitors that had tried and failed to make an impression on her. She had attended a Swiss finishing school and studied art in Paris and was fluent in Arabic, German, French and English. A modern world product, she moved effortlessly through a myriad of social customs displaying charm, grace and the refinement of a princess. Her interest was in the family art business where Franz-Josef had made her CEO. And he was pleased about that. 'Kaiser Art' also worked with the Art 1 Trust and their European counterparts in locating and returning stolen Nazi paintings. They were the art world's equivalent of the Nazi hunters, that Jewish organisation which hunted down Nazi fugitives and brought them to justice. FJ reflected on Nixie's ability, he could retire knowing that the art business was in good hands.

Falco, on the other hand, was a bit of a problem. Franz-Josef often wondered where he came from. He never seemed to display any family traits inherited from the von Hapsbergs or the Kaisers. As a young boy he had spoken German at home with his family as was their custom when together as a family unit to keep the language alive. English was the Lingua Franca of the European community and the business community in Cairo. He attended an English school in Cairo as a boy before being sent off to a boarding school in West Germany, to be taught in the traditional German fashion, in a German curriculum and it seems that is when he probably rebelled. He was separated from his earlier school friends who continued on at the English school in Cairo or were sent to schools in England to receive schooling according to the English tradition. Falco desperately missed his sporting activities that he had become rather proficient in which were cricket and rugby. German schools simply did not do cricket and rugby. Falco missed playing cricket and rugby and when he was home on holidays from his boarding school he would immerse himself with his English friends playing cricket and rugby. He begged his parents to allow him to go to school in England which was unpalatable to FJ, but not so much Brigitte. FJ discussed this with Otto and Anna, his parents and the von Hapsbergs, who all agreed that the boy could be schooled in England, where he could indulge himself in the sports he enjoyed so much.

"God knows," Alfred said and his wife agreed, "at least he is in an era of relative peace. At his age we were so insular we believed the propaganda dished out to us about anything that was not German, or German as the case may be. It was all very nationalistic. Maybe that is where our generation erred. Let us grasp another's culture and understand it. Surely we can only learn by assimilation. Isolation is oppressive. Look at us now, Swiss nationals, German by birth, sons and daughters of Saxony. Where did all of that nationalistic fervour get any of us? Nothing but grief. Now here we are living alongside our vanquishers and getting along famously. Where lies Germany? Defeated and divided! Maybe Falco is the way of the future. Let him go to England and learn their strange customs." And so he did.

Falco became so good at cricket that he played county cricket for Sussex at the age of eighteen. They were allowed to have a certain amount of players in the team who were not English nationals and besides Falco, there was a Pakistani and a South African also in the side. At twenty two, he would have made the English national side but he was not an Englishman, nor did it seem that he could qualify other than applying and waiting through the normal immigration channels. Falco got the genealogists on the job. His grandmother, Claudia von Hapsberg had long ago told him that they were descended from a line of Prussian royalty and that with all of the German connections with the British royal family, if they ever wanted to dig deep enough she said that they would be in the line of succession to the English throne. The genealogists dug and announced that Franco was 189th in line for the throne. This evidence was submitted with his application and the procedure was speeded along somewhat. With his new nationality he made the tour that summer with the team for an Ashes series in Australia and proved to be a very useful middle order batsman and spin bowler. He received favourable write ups in the newspapers back in England which is a no mean achievement, considering the fickleness of the English sports press. 'Prince of Blades' and 'Our Knight in White Flannels' were a couple of the epithets bestowed upon the young sportsman.

Franz-Josef was bemused. In a way, they mirrored his own successes as a young man. His were on the field of combat.

"So what!" Brigette said, "Franco's are also on the field of combat!" FJ couldn't see any similarities between the achievements of father and son.

234

"Don't you see?" Bridgette continued, "In both cases a young person is striving to achieve excellence in their chosen arena!"

"My arena was chosen for me!" FJ retorted, with a hint of frustration. His one eye had widened and his eyebrows were raised in a questioning way. FJ never did get a glass eye fitted but wore a black eyepatch which seemed to accentuate his Germaness.

"As I recall," Brigette replied, "you were training as a pilot in Russia long before a sniff of the future war years were in the o-zone. You had already chosen your game. You followed Otto into a military career as it seemed most of the Kaisers did back in the day. Your son," Bridgette started and then corrected herself, "our son, has chosen his arenas and they are on the green playing fields of England. Yours were in the Russian skies, so again we have similarities. Both of you honing your skills in foreign lands."

Falco had considered what the English might say to him if they ever found out about his father's exploits in the skies above Britain during the Battle of Britain. In their perverse way, Britons had always celebrated defeat as much as victory in the same way as they admired great warriors over the years. It mattered not to them what side they were on but how good they were. They were merely doing what any Englishman would do for their own country and if they were good at it – well so be it. The greatness and fairmindedness was epitomised in the songs he learned, especially from the rugby fraternity. They would sing after a game with a few beers in the belly and roar away shouting.

"Follow up, follow up, follow up, follow up, till the fields ring again and again with the sound of the thirty true men."

It was not about the one team of fifteen men, their team alone but the two sides who played the game. Thirty men. The opposition were given the same accolades as they gave to themselves. It didn't seem to matter too much who won the day, but how good the game was and how much they enjoyed the encounter. Franco thought that it was very English and he liked it. Of course, they were competitive and they went on the field to win but if, at the end of the day, they were beaten by a better team then, hey, next time we'll beat them! They didn't angst about it or beat themselves up as a lot of cultures might do. They sang about it and some of the words to their rugby songs were downright filthy. Falco was no prude but it took him a full season to accept the singing and drinking for what it was: a lot of fun; young men's rituals. His father would have drunk alcohol and sung songs too, young men's rituals in the mess. They would have sung nationalistic songs about the fatherland and the purity of good German bloodlines.

Brigette could not gauge if her husband was weakening in his stance against the anglicising of Falco, but the subject was not raised as fervently or as often since Otto had passed away. Maybe he was accepting the inevitability of a less insular world.

Linus, Kaetrin, Neil and Alison said their goodbyes the day after the funeral and flew off to London. Linus had Art 1 Trust business to attend to and Neil and Alison were on a sight-seeing junket. Kaetrin thought that she might try

235

and flush out her childhood haunts to see if there were any traces of her mother's existence that might give her a lead as to what had happened to her. Was she dead or alive? She had last seen her mother some forty years ago when she had put her and Robert on the train to Liverpool to catch the ship that would take them to New Zealand. And that was the last memory that Kaetrin and Robert had of their mother. Kaetrin thought that it was about time she found out what had happened to her. It did after all seem rather strange; surely, even in wartime, one just simply did not disappear?

Kaetrin took a ten minute walk from her hotel to Oxford Circus and boarded a bus that took her to Bethnal Green Tube Station, a forty nine minute ride. Nothing looked familiar, especially as they neared her old neighbourhood. Mind you she, told herself, this area took a pasting during the blitz so I guess a lot has been rebuilt. Kaetrin had been reading up on her old home town and it was recorded that eighty tons of bombs fell on the Metropolitan Borough of Bethnal Green during WWII. *I wonder if I could find our old street?* she mused, as she remembered Everard Street where they had lived before her and Robert were shipped out to New Zealand. The bus stopped at the Bethnal Green Tube Station and she remembered that this was an air raid shelter when they lived here and had often sought its shelter when the air raid sirens wailed. They must have extended the underground line here since the war. Kaetrin found the Metropolitan Borough Council Offices and entered the doors with some trepidation as she thought to herself, *When I exit this doorway I may know what happened to my mother.* She felt a shiver down her spine. 'Maybe I don't want to know?' she then chided herself for harbouring such a counter-productive idea. Kaetrin found the department she needed and gave them her mother's information that she had gotten from Aunty Flora. It was her mother's maiden name and date of birth and also she had a copy of the marriage certificate that her father had sent to Flora, his sister.

"What are you looking for?" the clerk enquired, having inspected the proffered paper work.

"My mother," Kaetrin said. "I want to find out if my mother is still alive. If she were dead, I would expect that you would have a death certificate!"

"I see, when did she die?"

"That's what I am here to find out!"

"I see, is she a missing person?"

"I suppose you could say she is to me, you see," and Kaetrin was starting to get annoyed with the nosy clerk, "I have not seen my mother since 1940!"

The clerk examined Kaetrin as if she had made a confession for a heinous crime.

Kaetrin returned the compliment with a challenging glare.

"In 1940," she said, "my mother took my brother and myself to Euston Station where we boarded a train for Liverpool to catch a ship that took us to New Zealand. We were CORB children!"

The clerk gave her a blank look.

"Children's Overseas Repatriation Board, do you know what that is –was?" Kaetrin said. "There was a war on, it was 1940, how old are you?"

"I was born in 1956 so no I don't know much about the war years other than what my folks say, after a few beers in the local, that is."

"Maybe an older staff member would be more helpful to me," Kaetrin suggested and received a stony glare for her effort.

"Please wait!" the clerk said, "I'll pull the file," and she left the booth, returning two minutes later with a manila folder, appropriately marked with identification embellishments that never failed to impress Kaetrin. She had never worked in an environment that kept lots of files and so the emblazoned coding was a source of wonderment to her. The clerk read the file flicking pages then retracing and flicking back again making audible noises and nodding to herself and saying, "I see," from time to time. Eventually she put her finger on a spot on a page and said, "This should tell us what we are looking for!" She looked at Kaetrin with a wan smile. It was a look that you just knew did not accompany a happy outcome. It was a sympathetic smile, Kaetrin concluded. The messenger was softening the blow. If you were an assassin, you would have screwed a silencer into the gun. Oral deliveries required wan smiles. It was a wan smile.

"Bethnal Green air raid shelter, third of March, 1943." The clerk looked at Kaetrin and then back at the file. "On the evening of 3rd March 1943, 1500 people were queueing to enter what was then the Bethnal Green Underground air raid shelter when the sound of an explosion caused what they now call a stampede, a lady stumbled on the stairway leading down into the shelter and in the resulting panic three hundred were crushed in the stairwell, resulting in 179 deaths."

Kaetrin felt a twinge of fear in her breast as the messenger continued reading from the file and a strange emotion swept over her. She had an urge to burn the file before more bad news escaped.

"The result of the official investigation was not released until 1946. From the records, it shows that Mrs Betty MacLeod was among the deceased. Next of kin was a Mr Alex MacLeod, also deceased. Killed in action, North Africa, 1942. I can check your birth certificate if you like? It seems that we had no alternative address of next of kin for your mother, unfortunately.

"I'm sorry the news could not have been more favourable," the clerk said. She seemed genuinely remorseful, like a puppy that had behaved badly and desperately wanted to still be friends. The clerk thumbed the file, stopping at another page. "You have siblings," she said, "that's nice."

"I have a brother who came to New Zealand with me," Kaetrin replied, "Robert is his name."

"The file says that Mrs MacLeod had three children."

"No, two!" Kaetrin corrected.

"Just a minute," the clerk said, and left the booth returning with another three files.

She opened the top one and said, "You would be Kaetrin?"

237

Kaetrin agreed.

"You have a brother, Robert?"

Kaetrin agreed.

"You have a sister, Muriel?"

"Not to my knowledge!"

"We have a birth certificate here for your sister, born February 21 1943. She would have been a few months old when your mother died. We have no record of this person's death. Just a record that she was born. Same parents on all three birth certificates."

By now, Kaetrin's head was swimming with all of this new information. She had had enough discoveries for one day and wanted to go away and digest it all. In particular, she wanted to share it with Linus.

"Can I get copies of the birth certificates?" she asked the clerk.

"Yes you can, I can do a photocopies now, or you can order replicas to be collected in a week."

"I'll take the photocopies now," Kaetrin said.

Kaetrin paid for the purchases.

"Thank you," she said faintly, "you have been very kind," and she left, passing through the portal from which she had only recently entered the place of disclosure and shock. She exited carrying both emotions and travelled back to the city on the underground through a labyrinth of tunnels, where she digested the revelations that had been unfolded before her by the borough clerk.

Back at the hotel, Linus listened to Kaetrin's tale unfold. He was as shocked as she was to hear about the third sibling. They both agreed that it was a good thing that they could now close the book on Betty MacLeod's life. Ending as tragically as it did, it was agreed that she would have probably written to Kaetrin and Robert had she lived. Obviously she had been very busy living in war-torn England and being pregnant and running to the air raid shelters every time the sirens wailed their banshees as harbingers of mayhem and destruction. Then, receiving the news about the death of her husband in the African desert. The question they kept asking was, where was the baby Muriel the night of the tragedy, in the air raid shelter at Bethnal Green? Was the baby with her? Did it miraculously survive? If so, who looked after it? The questions were coming faster than answers could be found.

Linus broke a long silence when they were both sitting with these thoughts, struggling to see how they could get some answers to what appeared to be a riddle that would be difficult to find answers to.

"You know," Linus said, "we have had to unravel some fairly intensive mysteries at the Art 1 Trust. There are similarities. We deal with paintings and genealogy. Here we have the genealogy already known, but the subject is a person, and is the unknown. It's the same riddle but in reverse proportion. Normally we start with a tangible article such as the painting and deal with the intangibles like who owns it. Now we start with the intangible part of the riddle, we know the genealogy, but we need to find, the definite article; where is she? If that makes sense. We are looking for the positive – the tangible – the person – where is Muriel, your little sister? I'm sure our team can work with these concepts and find an answer. They always do. We have considerable resources at our disposable, what do you say?" Linus was upbeat.

Kaetrin kissed her husband on the forehead. "Yes, my love," she said, "I'm sure that you are right. We can do no more than that. I must let Aunty Flora know that she has a new niece and Robert another sister."

Mahmoud arrived in London ten days later and promptly sent an invitation to Linus and Kaetrin to attend a soiree that he was hosting to formally welcome Neil and Alison Walker to London. Bravo and Georgia were also invited, as was Falco, who had returned to England on the same flight as Mahmoud. Mahmoud's usual eclectic mix of party animals from the London jungles would also be in attendance in one form or another. Suggested dress was 'comfortable' and the starting time was to be 8pm sharp.

A jazz quartet would play until 10pm and then an illusionist would do something astonishing, no clues given. Queen, the band, would perform until midnight. Mahmoud had somehow managed to obtain archive footage of the LRDP activities shot during WWII that he would screen next. Some footage showed Neil Walker's patrol at work which would be a big surprise to Neil. A rock band would play for an hour following the film and from then until whenever a DJ would entertain. Food was to be available at all times on request and served in the banquet room. Mahmoud's two large African eunuchs would supply drinks and food service to all. Gregory the butler would oversee the total show. It seemed a bit like a last hurrah, but then a lot of Mahmoud's plans were to excess, so he had hosted a lot of last hurrahs over the years.

Mahmoud greeted his guests as they arrived. He was resplendent in flowing Bedouin robes, a plain white Kufiya headdress held in place with a black circlet of rope called an Agal with desert sandals to complete the ensemble. At the clap of his hands, a eunuch would appear and take any garments not required by the guests for their indoor sojourn for the evening and place them in the cloakroom adjacent to the entrance hallway. Throughout this procedure, Mahmoud was seen to be talking with and fondly stroking the posterior of a pretty Indian woman of tender years. Her name, as the guests would learn as the night wore on, was Lalita, a Hindu name meaning 'beautiful woman.' And she was resplendent in a saffron and green sari and garlanded with jewels.

Linus and Kaetrin mingled with Alison and Neil as they compared notes about the Walkers' sight-seeing in London. Bravo and Georgia arrived and their little party expanded as they continued to discuss the London tourist spots. Falco turned up with several members of the cricketing fraternity in tow. They were members of his county team and also two were in the England Eleven. No other party goers were aware of such sporting prowess among them and so they largely went unnoticed. The exception being a couple of outrageously homosexual men who made it obvious that they would be agreeable to approaches from young athletic males with suntans and expansive, white-toothed smiles. Their flaunting was ignored by the young cricketers and eventually the queer men tired of their unreciprocated flirting and took themselves off to pester some of their own friends of similar ilk.

The magicians, or illusionists, were hosting in a special studio that was normally reserved for Mahmoud's art displays. He often would host an Egyptian art exhibition. These were restricted to young Egyptian artists who were breaking into the art world at large and Mahmoud had managed to see a few off to a start on the world stage. Otto Kaiser's gallery in Cairo was not the place for home grown talent as Otto tended to favour European artists who had made their mark and were now out to make some money by selling their works to wealthy Arabs with oil money. The studio was cleaned out and seating for the audience was placed in front of a slightly raised stage and had a drawn curtain which, when opened, revealed a large and alarming piece of equipment. It appeared to be a drop saw, the type seen on building sites for cutting planks of wood. This was the same apparatus but of larger proportions. A long wooden box sat on the table beneath the drop saw and it was obvious to the guests that the illusionist would cut a person in half with the drop saw. A large and terrifying act indeed, but to a lot, still very ho-hum. It had to be the oldest trick in the book. The illusionist and his accomplice explained the history of the illusion and said that they would show them how the trick was done. After all, they said one literally does not saw a person in half. It simply would kill them. The two male illusionists introduced the usual lovely lady accomplice dressed in a shimmery costume type swimsuit top and black stockings with high heels. Blonde hair and a pony tail accentuated the beauty about to be dissected and she dutifully climbed into the box. The lid was shut and you could see her feet protruding from one end and her head at the other, wiggling and smiling, the animations projected life and vitality. The huge circular saw was started and it screamed as the blades tip speed-cut through the air at subsonic speed but still fast enough to make an audibly disturbing noise. The saw made the cut and returned to the pre-cut position, but still running. At this juncture the two illusionists explained the trick to their audience and by sliding part of the table away they exposed the posterior of the person sitting in the box and she was clearly sitting in a lower position than the bottom of the box and so was clearly safe from the sawblade when it had reached the nadir of the descent of its travel. The feet poking out at one end were fakes but the other end, the head, was for real.

The illusionists were upbeat as they revealed this part of their act which is what they had said they would do before they started. They were out to expose the tricks of the trade. It was to be a journey of discovery. Suddenly without warning, the saw descended and failed to stop at the bottom of its controlled trajectory. It continued downward and severed the exposed body of the illusionists' accomplice completely in two. Entrails and blood and guts fell out and the illusionists went into a panic. The audience shrieked and howled and then someone had the good sense to dowse the lights.

In the darkness, sobbing could be heard and in the background the haunting sound of the large circular sawblade lessened as it slowed down and eventually came to a standstill. Then there was absolute silence in the blacked-out auditorium. Suddenly the lights came on and the curtain had been drawn across the stage. The audience were asked to leave the room as quickly as possible.

They exited to the strains of 'Bohemian Rhapsody' from Queen and standing on the stage with the band were the two illusionists and their lovely female accomplice. A mighty roar of approval went up as the previously shocked revellers threw themselves into dance routines to the music from the famous band. The eunuchs were kept doubly busy distributing drinks that were gratefully received and thankfully applied by guests, having witnessed, or so they were led to believe, the horrible spectacle of a live person being sawn in half, before their very eyes. Their dry throats had quickly turned to thirsty emotional conduits as they downed the alcoholic drinks as fast as they could be dispensed. Mahmoud knew how to throw a party.

Linus and Kaetrin were having a break from the festivities, nibbling food in the banquet room when Mahmoud came up to them. Lalita was at his side. Mahmoud introduced his partner to them. "She came to Cairo with the Indian contingent for Otto's funeral," he said. "I promised to show her London. She does not speak any English." They all nodded and smiled at each other.

"So how do you two communicate?" Kaetrin asked.

Mahmoud gave one of his 'desert storm' grins. The one where he grits his teeth to prevent sand from entering his mouth but parts his lips – just.

"We have our ways," he said. "Bedouins do sand storms best in bed. Why do you think we have harems?" He looked at her mischievously.

Before she could comment Neil and Alison Walker entered the room and came over to where they were standing. It was plain to see that there was an easy alliance between the two men.

"Some act Mahmoud," Neil said.

"We do our best," Mahmoud replied. "The problem with hosting these things in London is that you need to excel to succeed. We looked everywhere for that act. Now that it's been done it's become yesterday's news. Imagine what it must be like for the illusionists. They have to be continually looking for new material. A tough business for sure. How's the sight-seeing going?" he asked Alison.

"We have seen a lot and we have a lot to see. I'm not sure how much time we have left. We leave when Linus and Kaetrin leave." Alison replied.

Linus looked at Kaetrin, "We have some extra work to do, something has come up so if you are in no hurry we can stay at least another two weeks. How does that suit you?"

"Great!" Alison replied. "I hope that fits in with Mahmoud's plans, we are after all, guests in his lovely house."

"You stay regardless of if I am here or away, Gregory the butler knows what to do – come and go as you please my dear friends." Mahmoud was effusive but he was genuine.

Falco and friends joined them in the banquet room and like all young men they were ravenous and would feed like locusts on a wheat crop. Mahmoud

241

was generous. "Eat as much as you like," he said, "you will not get the better of Gregory. If there is something that you like to eat but it is not on the table ask Gregory; he has never been stumped yet."

"A cricketing pun!"

"What?"

"Never mind!"

Falco's friends were talking about the illusionists but between food and talk Falco managed to introduce them all round. Neil, it seemed, was the only one who was into cricket and was able to identify the two England players. The three men went into a huddle for a cricket discussion. Mahmoud excused himself. "I must circulate," he said and left with his hand around Lalita's waist.

It was obvious that a couple of the young men who were Falco's cricketing buddies were impressed with Mahmoud's Indian lady.

"She's hijra!" Falco announced.

"Whats hijra?"

"India's third sex!"

"They have three sexes?"

"In a way –yes, hijra is a eunuch, usually castrated at a young age, maybe a shortage of girls in the village to do the women's chores so, bang! Off with the appendages, bollocks, penis the lot. No messing about. A lot make a living singing and dancing at weddings. Prostitution is an obvious occupation as normal employment is often not available to them. Lalita is a slave. Mahmoud bought her from the Indians who came to Otto's funeral. He told me so. Probably a favourite because she is so pretty. I guess beauty makes a difference regardless of sex! Mahmoud said she is an avatar which in Hindi mythology is a deity descended to earth in an incarnate form. It's his way of saying she is an angel." Falco finished talking and spread some caviar on a wafer and devoured it. There was a silence while everybody thought about Falco's disclosure.

"How do you know this?" Kaetrin asked Falco.

"Mahmoud told me, on the way over, I flew here with Mahmoud and Lalita. He talked freely about it. Lalita had no idea what he was talking about, so he talked candidly and freely. It seems par for the course for Mahmoud from what I have learned about his preferences. I guess the same applies to the band Queen; it's all about sexual preferences, part of Mahmoud's London scene. Homosexuality or sexual deviation, it's Mahmoud's choice. It happens in Cairo but is hush hush, extremely discrete. Delicate even – tolerated maybe – but only just. Here he can be himself I guess. Katzenjammer!"

"What the hell does that mean?"

"Katzenjammer?"

"Yes, that word."

"It's an old German word, my grandfather Alfred von Hapsberg used it a lot to describe chaos, mayhem, generally a noisy mess. He would say to my mother when my sister and I would play rowdy and rough as kids do. They make more noise than the 'Katzenjammer Kids.'

Linus looked at Kaetrin, "Ready to leave?" he asked.

242

"I think so, can't handle any more surprises, had enough for one night."

They said their goodnights and exited quietly, leaving the party animals to continue with the revelry.

It was a nice evening and so they walked the short distance from Mahmoud's apartment to their hotel on Bond Street.

"That Mahmoud's a party animal," Kaetrin said, as they strolled hand in hand.

"Yes he is, here in London. I believe, according to FJ, that he is a lot more subdued back in Cairo but then he has to be, the Nassars are a prominent family. I do not think that his father would tolerate too much nonsense. I believe that he cuts him a bit of slack but will haul him in for a dressing down if he gets a whiff of any misbehaviour."

"He is the only son to have a college education and from all reports no other offspring was allowed to follow in his footsteps. Far too radical and old Abdul, the father, is not a prude, but I hear that Mahmoud tries his patience at times. If he ever found out about the London escapades, Abdul would pronounce the equivalent of Islam's ban on worldly activities," Kaetrin concluded.

"Mahmoud would be confined to the desert trade for sure. Perhaps given the Arabs' equivalent of the black spot!" Linus continued, referring to the pirates sign from *Treasure Island*. "From what Neil Walker tells me, even the desert routes are littered with his boltholes. He seems to have the propensity to make whoopee almost anywhere. If you could bottle him he would make a good fun-genie."

They walked on in silence reflecting on the conversation about Mahmoud and Kaetrin said, "He has never done anyone any harm. Everybody that I have talked about Mahmoud with, has only had positive things to say about the man."

"This is true," Linus said, "but I think the problem is the generalities that one associates with his behaviour. I am reminded about that wartime saying we had, you remember it: 'loose lips sink ships'."

"I can't say I get your meaning!" Kaetrin said.

"Maybe not in that way but let's alter it slightly and drop the first 'ess' from ships and we get, 'loose lips sink hips'."

"Sexual promiscuity?"

"Exactly!"

The doorman at Claridges welcomed them back and opened the door for them and they entered into the rich closeness enjoyed by the privileged people who entered the portals of the prestigious address.

"I guess you have not heard from your team of sleuths checking out the riddle of Muriel?" Kaetrin enquired.

"Not yet, they go all quiet as they make enquiries and then suddenly the answers stream in. It may take days, weeks or months. We don't know until it happens. There are usually no questions – just answers."

243

Gregory, Mahmoud's butler, phoned the Levins at their hotel the following morning to explain that Mahmoud had taken ill and was admitted to hospital.

"Saint Marys Hospital," Gregory said and gave them the phone number. "They think that he is suffering from exhaustion."

"Thank you," Kaetrin said and then, "Good bye."

"The party beast is suffering from exhaustion, can you imagine!" Kaetrin said to Linus.

"He doesn't stop," Linus replied. "I suppose one can become exhausted enjoying oneself, especially at his pace!"

"I'll ring the hospital later," Kaetrin said, "we should go and visit him, it's not far from here."

"Leave it for a day or so," Linus said. "Give them a chance to run tests and confirm their results. Didn't you invite Alison and Neil for tea here this afternoon?"

"Yes I have," Kaetrin said, "I have made the bookings, I could never overlook such an important occasion."

Linus grinned knowing how much Kaetrin enjoyed her afternoon teas at Claridges. If Kaetrin had a choice between tea at Claridges or a garden party at Buckingham Palace, Claridges would win. He was sure of that.

Mahmoud looked drawn and haggard when they visited. "I feel like I have the flu," he said. "Generally yuk. No energy, I have a temperature and ache here and there. I thought that I was a bit run down, exhausted, I think is how they say it in press releases. Anyway they are taking bloods from me regularly and doing all manner of tests. They want to know if I need a blood transfusion, is it okay to give me the standard stuff, like do I have to have Muslim blood. I told them I eat bacon and ham and lots of Western food so the standard blood is fine. I had no idea you could have designer blood. Make mine a double!" he said. Mahmoud never stopped when he was chasing a theme or talking about a situation that had comical overtures. "I'll have double bacon on rye with a scotch chaser. That should have my ancestors spinning in their sandy long homes among the camel dung."

Kaetrin had brought a large bunch of flowers to brighten the room up. They exuded a delicate aroma which took the edge off the sharp hospital scent. She went in search of a nurse to find a vase for the flowers and met Neil and Alison Walker in the corridor.

"Human Immunodeficiency Virus is the tag the doctors are giving to his symptoms," Neil said to Kaetrin. "They say that it can be transmitted due to unprotected homosexual relations. It has only recently been identified by doctors in San Francisco where there is a large promiscuous homosexual population. The prognosis is not good. I thought that I would tell you this as I am sure Mahmoud will say nothing."

Kaetrin said she would see them in Mahmoud's room and continued on her quest for a vase. Kaetrin found a utility room that she saw a nurse enter and so she knocked and entered and asked the nurse for a vase. It seemed that Kaetrin was addressing the matron who seemed a bit put out that she should be bothered by this hospital visitor for a vase for some flowers but she managed to find a large glass jar which she offered to Kaetrin.

"Flowers are not allowed in wards," she said, "only in private rooms."

"These are for a private room, Mr Nassar's room," Kaetrin replied.

"Yes, well some people are allergic to pollen and other nasties that come with flowers, but if it's a private room well I suppose that is alright."

Kaetrin thought, *What an officious person, no doubt a bloody good matron, hate to be one of the nurses working under her.* She noted from her name tag that she was Matron Coombes. She had what Aunty Flora called the Scottish skin, a bit like corned beef, red and ruddy but green, green eyes and her hair was hidden by her large veil-style headdress.

Kaetrin thanked the matron and headed back down the corridor to Mahmoud's room where she filled the vase with water and arranged the flowers and placed them on a small table, next to a visitor's chair.

Mahmoud had rallied to his visitors' esprit and was happily talking in his usual lively manner.

"Sometimes I feel normal," he said, "and then I seem to relapse from the effort and have to have a rest. Just now I feel great and I'm sure it is the company so please keep coming and I shall be out of here in no time," he said with one of his rascally grins. No sooner than Mahmoud had said that he fell back on his pillow and closed his eyes. He had exhausted himself and had fallen into an instant sleep. His visitors left the hospital and walked along the street in the sunshine talking about their friend and his strange condition.

"It's new apparently, the disease is a new one, recently identified. The doctor said that at the moment there is no cure or effective vaccine. They have coined a term for it, as it has evolved and that is, Acquired Immune Deficiency Syndrome or AIDS for short. The doctor says that it lets life threatening infections and cancers survive, where a previously healthy immune system would suppress these things. It is passed on in body fluids, apparently kissing is okay, but blood, such as drug addicts using dirty needles from other users, and semen, vaginal fluids and even breast milk are transmitters, so it is a very insidious wee beastie!" Alison said.

"So, what's the prognosis?" Kaetrin asked.

"Not sure, bit of a wait and see, some sufferers in America have developed certain cancers that kill them quickly, others hang in. it's a bit of a lottery at the moment. He must tell his sexual partners for sure, some of whom are probably already infected. He must have caught it from one of them, maybe he has carried the virus for some time. It's frightening when you imagine the significance of the activities around which the virus is spread. I mean if you caught it from playing dominoes the disease could be controlled, but sex and drugs…" Alison trailed off.

They walked on in silence and then Linus said, "Shall we catch a taxi?"

Neil looked at the sky and replied, "Well it is nice day and I haven't walked much in the past few weeks. Farmers do a bit of walking; I feel like a walk."

Alison agreed. "Why not? Let's walk to Hyde Park, I am a tourist and have seen more of the underground than above the ground."

"Kaetrin, what about you?" Alison enquired. "Nice day for a stroll?"

"Yes I'm in!"

"Linus?"

"How far is it?"

"About three miles down the Edgeware Road to Marble Arch."

"No choice," Linus said, "I don't fancy a taxi ride on my own. Perhaps we can stop for refreshments along the way?"

It was after all a very nice afternoon. Late summer, but still warm. And so they set off with Alison and Kaetrin leading the way and the two men following on. Forty minutes into their task, Linus saw a watering hole that looked interesting and they sought refuge within for refreshments. They were sitting and sipping when Kaetrin spoke.

"You know I can't imagine Mahmoud returning to Cairo and receiving treatment for a disease that they see as being socially unacceptable. He would be treated like a leper. Give him a bell to ring and call out 'unclean, unclean' as he made his way around the city. Can you imagine that!"

"I can imagine the unacceptance. Their society accepts the normal. Variations are a bit of a problem. Their rules are virtually unchanged for two thousand years," Neil said. "We discovered that in the war and I doubt that things have changed since my time among them. Mahmoud may have to live in exile, a rather pleasant one. How do you tell your family that you cannot come home?"

The conversation so consumed the walking party that they found themselves having a second drink and then a third and then it was a taxi ride and Kaetrin convinced Neil and Alison to join herself and Linus in the reading room at Claridges for a glass of champagne and some sandwiches; it was late afternoon and there were spare tables.

"I don't have a booking but they do know me and I'm certain we shall be accommodated." She said, and she was correct.

They continued talking about Mahmoud and AIDS and HIV as they had come to know the condition in the short time that they had been told about Mahmoud's illness. The gravity intensified but never reached mortality despite their best efforts in dispensing two bottles of France's finest bubblies. Instead, they were finding cures and congratulating the scientific expertise of today's clinicians. And before long, Mahmoud would be cured and returned to Egypt where he would eventually die a very old and contented man.

A week following on from the disclosure about Kaetrin's lost sister, they had still not had any news from the Art 1 Trust and their research team's efforts to come up with some answers.

Kaetrin was visiting the hospital on her own one afternoon while Linus was busy with Art 1 Trust business. She had just entered the hospital and was making her way along the corridor when she saw the doppelganger of her Aunty Flora walking toward her. It was most uncanny and her mouth fell open in amazed awe, as the redheaded figure of the matron in street clothes neared her. Kaetrin thought that the matron recognised her from the vase incident and she nodded and said hello as they came abreast.

The matron must have been unnerved by Kaetrin's stare and she stopped.

"Is something wrong?" she asked.

Kaetrin was flummoxed and she was speechless for what seemed ages but in reality was mere seconds.

"I'm sorry," Kaetrin managed to get out, "I did not mean to be rude, it's just that you remind me so much of someone I know. The word doppelganger comes to mind."

Instead of being crabby as she was when she found a vase for Kaetrin's flowers she smiled. "That's okay," she said. "My red hair often gets me comparisons. You are not the first person, I can assure you." She paused. "As a matter of interest, who do I remind you of?"

Again Kaetrin was caught unawares. She hadn't expected the conversation to go this far. Most people gave embarrassed laughs and it was all over. The encounter usually passed, as ships do in the night.

"I have an aunty," she said, "my Aunty Flora. She lives in New Zealand now but came from Skye originally. Her brother had children, my brother and I, and we went to New Zealand in 1940 as CORB children. You look like my aunty did when we first arrived in New Zealand. It's uncanny."

For some reason this strange piece of intelligence from a complete stranger did not faze the matron.

"I'm an orphan," she said. "I have no idea who my parents were or what happened to them. The best they can suggest is that they may have been killed in the blitz. The bombing raids. London suffered terribly from German bombs."

Kaetrin heart was now beating fast. "I have just learned that I have a sister. She was born in 1943, probably in or near Bethnal Green. My mother was killed in the Bethnal Green air raid shelter tragedy in 1943 and my father in North Africa in 1943. There is a birth certificate for my younger sister Muriel, but no one knows what happened after that. It's just that you are a dead ringer for my aunty. I have just found out about all of this. Gosh I hope I'm not upsetting you?"

Kaetrin reached out and touched the matron's arm in the manner that one does when apologising for being a nuisance.

"Not at all, it's as much a mystery to me as it is to you. I have been down many blind allies in pursuit of answers. I find your assumptions plausible and am grateful that you had the courage to make them. What shall we do now?"

Kaetrin was nearly in tears when she heard this eager response. It seemed too easy to be real, she thought and then, *Damn it no! It can be this way!*

"If you are keen, I would like to meet you and we can discuss what happened and see if we can find a solution," Kaetrin suggested, her heart racing. And then "Will you be home tonight, could I visit you, or you could visit me at my hotel?"

"I'll be home." The matron passed a card to Kaetrin. "This is my phone number, ring me at seven tonight and I'll give you directions." The matron held out her hand. "I'm Helen," she said.

"Kaetrin," Kaetrin replied, "I'll phone you at seven."

Reluctantly, they parted. It seemed both wanted to solve the riddle on the spot.

Kaetrin hardly remembered what she had said to Mahmoud, he had some of his party crowd visiting and so she never had to go through the torment of being somewhere she wasn't interested in being. Her mind was fizzing with the meeting of the matron in the corridor and emotionally was elsewhere. She left early and walked very quickly from the hospital and caught a taxi back to Bond Street.

Linus was still away and Kaetrin got out the birth certificates that she had paid the clerk for, at the municipal offices and read and reread them. She put them back in the heavy envelope and put them in a small leather attached folder. She looked through her small photo album that she would take with her to show matron. There were pictures of herself and Robert, Aunty Flora and her mother and father. She looked at the large chiming clock on the mantelpiece. It was four thirty and it chimed accordingly as if to confirm the fact. The suspense was killing her. She desperately wanted it to be seven.

'Tempus Fugit' was the inscription on the brass clock face. Kaetrin had remembered asking Linus what it meant. "It's Latin," he had told her, "it means 'time flies'." It was not flying at the moment. Kaetrin phoned Linus at the Art 1 Trust office but he had left for the day. She was becoming frustrated and decided that she was too worked up to eat dinner so she did what Marjory would have done. She went to the reading room and ordered a pot of tea and a plate of club sandwiches. Kaetrin wrote a note for Linus and left it on the bureau in the entrance to their hotel apartment, in case he should come in while she was out.

Linus was late getting back to the hotel as he and Roger Van Oldenbarnevelt met for a drink after work which they often did.

They were talking about the investigation that the Art 1 Trust was conducting for the missing MacLeod sibling known as Muriel. Roger was wearing his lawyer's hat which was not unusual and he said to Linus.

"You know you have to be very careful about this."

"In what way?"

"Well let's say that someone gets wind that Kaetrin has a sister. She is unknown, neither sibling is known to the other, and have been apart forever. Both parents are dead. Now, Kaetrin is a wealthy lady these days, so would be a good catch for a homeless waif to claim as a prize. You can imagine Kaetrin showering her newfound sister with kindness, especially if she were disadvantaged, so to speak. I'm sure that you are understanding my inference. You only have to look at the Russian royalty pretenders to imagine the proliferation of wannabee relatives. Every day, a new Russian count or prince or countess pops up and claims some long lost title. I mean they can, can't they? The Bolsheviks put most of them to the sword. Records of their ancestors have been obliterated. All one needs is to inherit a trait that ran through the Russian court and they are suddenly the descendant of the one that got away. Escaped the Bolshevik swords. Mind you there is no money in it – just the title, you understand. The prince of holey socks, a title but no money."

Linus sipped from his beer and nodded, "Carry on," he said.

"In my legal practice I am currently working on a thing called DNA. It all started with the study of genetics. Genetics is the study of genes. Genes are units inside cells that decide how living organisms inherit features from their ancestors."

Linus continued nodding and sipping. Roger was always interesting. "Carry on," he said again.

Roger whetted his talking voice with a drink from his glass and continued.

"In genetics, a feature of a living thing is called a trait. Some traits are exhibited in a physical appearance, such as height and weight, maybe eye or hair colour and complexion. Like skin, you know olive, ruddy, white, brown, whatever. Other traits not discernible may be blood type, a genetic illness, like cystic fibrosis and so on but you get my drift. Genes are made from a long molecule called DNA which is copied and inherited across generations."

"Sounds plausible," Linus said, "but how does it help us?"

"Well," Roger leaned into it. "My clients tell me that soon we will be able to carry out, what they call, DNA fingerprinting. That means that by cross referencing the DNA of two people it will be possible to state whether they are related or not. A yes or no decision. No guessing, but scientific fact! Simply saying they have similar traits, they look alike, is not conclusive in most cases."

"Another drink on the strength of that disclosure?" Linus enquired and headed for the bar, knowing the response in advance.

"Recently, the practise has been inundated with scientists and their various research institutions who are keen to patent what they call their inventions on DNA sequences which they contend they have discovered."

"A rational commercial reaction, no doubt," Linus said. "I understand that drug companies are making billions from some of these discoveries, hoping to cream it until the patent expires! I can't disagree with that sentiment," he concluded.

"Well therein lies the rub," Roger replied.

"It does?"

"Yes it does!"

"You see; the purpose of a patent is to allow the inventor sufficient time to develop a saleable product from said invention. The patent holder usually gets a twenty year moratorium."

"Makes sense," Linus said.

"Yes it does, no problem thus far, however inventions originally are for artificial things that are not part of a normal or natural phenomena. DNA falls into the latter category. Some scientists argue differently and there are some who say that DNA bears the image of God!"

249

"Now I'm starting to get the picture," Linus said. "It should be a good money spinner for the old firm."

Roger grinned. They knew each other well enough not to get too embarrassed about profits.

"God may have invented it, but failed to patent it!"

"Twenty years is peanuts; God is probably not interested in a paltry twenty years when he is working in perpetuity."

"Suppose not, do we have time for another?" Roger held up his empty glass.

"Why not? Got nothing on tonight, I'm sure Kaetrin would have phoned the office if there were something happening."

Linus arrived at their hotel at six thirty and was greeted by a highly excited Kaetrin, exploding with news and no one to share it with. A lesser person would have been unkind and run off at the mouth but Kaetrin had been under the wing of her Aunt Flora for forty odd years and knew when to hold her tongue and when to let rip.

"You look mighty pleased with yourself," Linus suggested.

Kaetrin told Linus about her encounter with the matron at the hospital when she went to visit Mahmoud.

"Well say something!"

"I'm flabbergasted!" Linus said and wondered where the word came from. He could not remember ever having used it before.

"I have to phone her at seven o'clock to get directions to her place." Kaetrin really did not want Linus to come but said. "I guess we'll get a taxi?" and made it sound like a question.

"Yes, probably the quickest way this time of day. Tube will be full for sure. Anyway, let's find out where she lives. You know – if it's okay? I think that you and her would talk better without me hovering in the background."

"Do you really think so?"

"Yes, you two are the central characters in the drama, I think that you will cover a lot of ground without interruptions."

Kaetrin described Helen to Linus.

"Sounds like she has family traits," he said, "you know, red hair, green eyes, small of stature, corned beef complexion, just like Flora. Traits are an important marker. Not sure-fire, but definitely a genetic marker. You have any photographs of family with you?"

"Yes, I always travel with my miniature photo album," Kaetrin said. "Where did you get this information on traits. Sounds like you have swallowed a book on the subject."

"Roger has brought me up to speed, they are doing work on this very subject. He says that soon we will have DNA fingerprinting. We will be able to tell who our relatives are by DNA samples. Eliminate the guessing and work on scientific facts. It's a year or so away I am told."

Kaetrin made her phone call to Helen at seven o'clock she wrote down the address and said that she would be there in half an hour.

"Where does she live?" Linus asked when Kaetrin had hung up.

"Near the hospital, makes sense, she works at the hospital so yeah, near makes sense. I'll leave an address and phone number here for you in case you need to get hold of me, otherwise I'll be home in a couple of hours, any delays I'll let you know."

The matron lived in a nice flat in Paddington which was a short cab ride from the hotel. She opened the door as soon as Kaetrin knocked and they walked into a comfortable downstairs living room. Helen seemed even shorter without her street shoes which obviously had higher heels than the house slippers that she wore when greeting Kaetrin. A family trait, Kaetrin observed, both herself and Flora wore slippers, they put them on as soon as they got home. Off went the shoes and on went the slippers.

After a few awkward words of greeting they sat down and the conversation flowed.

"I have no record of birth or parents," Helen said. "They say I was born in early 1943. Not sure of the exact date obviously. You see I was left at a minister's home one evening. In a portable cot with a note that said my mother was dead and my father was in the army and the person who was baby-sitting me at the time could not afford to keep me. Obviously they did not want any trail left so no names were mentioned. I was the original mystery child. The thing is, I do not know any difference. My formative years I imagined were the same for all children. We were in an orphanage, we were warm and well fed. Probably fared better than a lot of wartime waifs who were wandering about London looking for food and shelter. No complaints there. How about a drink? Tea, gin and tonic, wine?" she trailed off.

"Tea is fine, I would like a cuppa, hard to beat my standby favourite." Kaetrin replied.

"How do you like it?"

"As it comes, not too strong, milk no sugar."

"Same as me."

"Really?"

"Yes my adoptive parents in Perth always had sugar, I couldn't stand the sweetness."

Neither Flora nor Kaetrin took sugar. *Maybe it was a family trait,* Kaetrin thought.

"Mind you, back in the day, sugar was rationed, we never got anything sweet in the orphanage."

Helen left the room and Kaetrin looked around, she was looking for photographs and saw a framed picture of two older people whom she assumed were the foster parents. *Nothing remarkable, just another picture,* Kaetrin thought. There was another framed photo, looked like a younger Helen in her nurse's uniform, maybe a graduation photo. Further along was another photograph of a group of young people in what seemed to be an informal gathering around a life ring against a ship's rail. Obviously on a cruise ship holiday. Kaetrin smiled, having done similar things herself.

251

Helen returned with the tea and a plate of biscuits and they continued with their banter.

Helen said that she was sent to Perth in Western Australia where she had been allocated a home with a childless couple. She was five years old and it seemed that the British Government were giving away their war orphans to the colonies, as they had done with the CORB children during the war. "Britain exported about 250,000 orphans in this manner. Help keep the colonies British, so they said!" Helen had her figures off pat. "Arthur and Audrey were dear people," she continued. "They had a farm near Albany which is where I grew up. They adopted me and I assumed their surname of Coombes, but retained Helen, the name that the orphanage had given me. I felt like a Helen," she said, "so it sorta stuck. I went nursing and passed my state finals then decided on the big 'OE' which a lot of Aussies do and ended up here in Earls Court with the usual mix of colonials from down under. I have been here, London that is, ever since. I feel I belong here. I was born here so it felt right when I came back. Then Mum and Dad died, that's what I called them, and they left their farm to me, I sold it and with the proceeds from that I was able to buy this place in Paddington which is a nice part of London and best of all is near to Saint Marys Hospital. In a way I suppose I have fallen on my feet, so I am not angry or mad about life. I have been given a leg up following a bad start. It would be nice to be able to trace your roots, so to speak. Like where did I come from? Is there family out there that I don't know about? That's the worst one. I could be talking with a stranger who is a relation and I have no idea!

"What about you, Kaetrin? What's your story?"

Kaetrin took the birth certificates from her attaché satchel as she spoke.

"Robert, my younger brother and me, were sent off to New Zealand in 1940. We were what they referred to as CORB children, sent offshore for safe keeping, I suppose. Repatriation was to occur at the conclusion of hostilities but that never happened. We never heard from our mother and our father was killed in North Africa in 1943. So we stayed in Wellington and lived with Dad's sister, our Aunty Flora – here is a photo of her taken when we arrived," Kaetrin passed the open book across to Helen. "The photo is black and white which is all that was available back in those days but I think that you can see a likeness there. I can anyway."

Helen studied the picture in the album and saw a vibrant Flora smiling with her arms around the shoulders of her newly arrived niece and nephew fresh off the boat. Helen then got the picture of herself in her nurse's uniform from off the sideboard and looked at the two images. She had to admit there were similarities.

"Yes, I think I can say that we do have similar features. We are a similar body mass and height. Nose and mouth, mmmmmmm?"

"It would be great to see the colouring," Kaetrin added, "but, hey that can be done. How about this for the green eye trait. Robert, my brother is married to a Tongan girl Tia, and their daughter Maree has olive eyes. There is a picture of Robert, Tia and Maree on the next page."

Helen flipped the leaf and stared at the image. "I can see a likeness between Robert and Aunty Flora – so how did you find out about your other sister, Muriel?" Helen asked.

"All I wanted to do was find out if Mother was still alive. That's when I went to the municipal offices at Bethnal Green and got the info." Kaetrin opened the birth certificates and handed them over to Helen, who read them in great detail, especially the one concerning Muriel. It could be, after all, the first time in her life that Helen had seen her own birth certificate and it was an extremely traumatic moment. Her hands were shaking when she reluctantly handed them back to Kaetrin.

"We have had an agency – experts on finding missing people and objects, searching for a couple of weeks now but have not heard back from them. It would be hard to know where they would start their search from. There is really nothing to go on."

"It is a riddle for sure," Helen said. "I cannot offer any more to the story but I can say this: as you know, I work in the top hospital for sexually transmitted diseases and we have a lot of contact with laboratories who are working in the field of genetics, it is after all how a lot of things are transmitted – genetically. Our experts are telling us that soon they will be able to examine blood and other body fluid samples and tell us more than we probably want to know for example, they say that they will be able to tell who is related to whom! Now there's a scary thought."

"My husband was only saying that this very afternoon," Kaetrin replied. "But in the interim I hope that we can keep in touch and hope for a positive result when that time comes. How do you feel about that?"

"I feel relaxed about that," Helen said. "Perhaps I can get a nice colour photograph for you to send to Aunty Flora." She said it as if it was her aunty too. It was a new experience for Helen to even imagine having an Aunty and Kaetrin wanted her to hang on to the sentiment with all of her being.

It had been two hours since Kaetrin arrived and the two had gotten along famously. They agreed that they should keep in touch and Kaetrin gave Helen her New Zealand contact details

"I'm not sure when we are leaving London," she told Helen, "but I will phone you every week at least and may even run into you at the hospital."

"Mr Nassar, of course, you are a friend of Mr Nassar's. I do a normal daily shift so please feel free to call on me if you are at the hospital. I can certainly make time to talk with you. I'm mainly admin. This has been a very interesting evening. I'm so pleased you stopped me in the corridor. Thank you so much."

Helen's impassioned cry of thanks was so intense that Kaetrin forgot to phone for a taxi and she was walking along the street blinking away teary eyes when she remembered: taxi!

Chapter 16

The Life and Times and Passing of Horace

Horace died in the most appropriate spot on the golf course. A sand bunker! Since retirement, the major had taken to golf just as he had taken to life and his army career. He grasped the club firmly in both hands and swung vigorously. Horace was born in 1898. He had enlisted in the British Army in 1915 and served in the Middle East and India before peacetime came. His regiment stayed in India and Horace received a line commission. The regiment moved from India to Ceylon, Egypt then Palestine and back to India. As a young subaltern he was a vigorous sportsman participating in swimming and athletics and playing on the regiment's cricket and polo teams. He also made the Nawab's elephant polo team, by invitation. The Nawab had the best elephants and he wanted the best riders too. It was an honour for the regiment and indeed Horace. Horace Beresford-Amble met Marjory, the daughter of one of his senior officers in the regiment. They married in Colombo, honeymooned in Cairo and settled down in Lucknow. Marjory was a much sought after young lady of twenty two years when she married Horace in 1932. She had been born in India and had never been to England.

Marjory was as English as the best of them and referred to England as home, a mysterious and mythological place, where all white people came from to run the rest of the world not fortunate enough to be British. On the world maps in the classrooms, all of the countries coloured red represented the British Empire and the colonial kids were told how fortunate they were to be a part of the Empire. The expats were out there running 'them places', and 'making a damn fine job of it too –don't ya know!' Having the sort of upbringing in India away from the provinces of England, Marjory spoke English with an accent that could place her anywhere between the Cotswolds and South Africa. A lot of the colonials sent their children to England when they were young so as to avoid developing a colonial accent, but Marjory's parents employed an English nanny who spoke well and this proved moderately successful. Horace's in-laws were snobs, but they did concede that their son-in-law would be a good husband and best of all, would remain an army man for life. Marjory, their daughter, therefore, was assured of a stable marriage, to a good man who would remain employed in an honourable profession. Horace, on the other hand, was from Wiltshire and could bend an 'R' as well as any Englishman from them parts.

The army sent Horace to the military college in Sandhurst for a one-year course and study and he and Marjory sailed on the British India ship S.S. *Hooghly* departing the Kidderpore Docks in Calcutta for the Tilbury Docks in London, in 1933.

The Indian bearers carried out the menial domestic chores in the barracks and the homes of the English army personnel and it was the same on the ship on which they took passage to England. It came as a shock, therefore, when Marjory discovered, on her arrival in England, that there were no Indian bearers to carry the bags, serve tea, wait on tables and clean up afterwards. Everyone was English – English to Marjory was a euphemism for white skin or European. It took a while for the penny to drop and Marjory suddenly realised that her life thus far had been anything but normal. In India, Marjory rationalised, servants were a part of the European household. Marjory couldn't remember her mother ever washing and drying a plate. Making the beds and all of the household chores that one took for granted was totally carried out by servants. She mused about this and declared, "I have a lot to learn," and she set about doing so rather than lamenting the drudgery of choredom. Marjory was a doer and so she got on with it, as the saying went.

They found suitable accommodation in nearby Berkshire and Horace purchased a red MG convertible sports car, to travel to and fro each day as he did not need to live at the academy. His was not a cadet training course but a specialty course for experienced officers who were line or field commissioned. In the snobbery ranks, he was never going to achieve high regimental status, but he was a good man and a capable soldier and well-liked by the enlisted men and officers alike. Dependable was the word to describe Horace. Plus, a very good bowler in the regimental cricket team.

Marjory was learning to cook, as previously food was something that had been magically created by the servants. Marjory's contribution to food processing in India was to be present at the table at meal times and consume the wondrous dishes that were presented to her. Now she was consumed with food preparation, cooking and cleaning up afterward. It was a never ending cycle. She had hardly gotten Horace out of the door following breakfast than he was home in the evening enquiring after the fine gastronomical delights that she had prepared for the evening repast. Marjory did manage to get in her tea breaks but they were solo affairs in the beginning. After a while, when she had made friends who would visit during the day, Marjory found that dinner was late when she lingered too long over the tea cups. As was her custom, Marjory served only the best Darjeeling teas, brewed in her china teapots. Her favourite tea pot was the one presented to her by the Nawab of Ranpur. It was hand painted with tigers rampant. It didn't take long to figure that a cook was needed to at least help prepare an evening meal. Their budget ran to that little extra and Marjory was glad of the help.

Horaces' parents lived in Devizes and they visited them one weekend, soon after arriving in England. It was an easy drive completed in about eighty minutes. The elder Beresford-Ambles lived in a comfortable villa in the countryside. They had retired there from London where Horace's father, Wilford, was in the customs service. His mother, Winnie, was a quiet person and Wilford did most of the talking and Winnie did the action bits like fetching. Horace was their only child and he was the pride and joy of both parents. They made it abundantly clear that Horace would inherit their country villa, which Marjory agreed was a nice place to retire to. A place in the country.

"You'll find," Wilfred had said, "when you retire, you'll enjoy peace and quiet. A place in the country is just the thing, don't you know." Marjory was recently married and far from retirement, so a place in the country was not even registering in her sentimental memory bank but nonetheless she decided that perhaps she could store this data in her long term working memory for later retrieval. *Like, forty years later,* she thought. *I should be ready for retirement then?*

Six months after they had arrived in England, Marjory had a miscarriage. A hysterectomy followed and that ended any hopes of raising children of their own. Marjory was crestfallen and Winnie was better than her own mother as she consoled her daughter-in-law.

"India is not a good place to raise kids," Horace had said. "The mortality rate of infants in India is very high. Perhaps it is just as well," he continued. "You've seen what infant deaths do to a family. We'll just have to be happy with ourselves, you and me, my love." Marjory recovered from her operation and they holidayed in Devizes with Horace's parents, who were very understanding. Marjory thought that they were disappointed too, but they managed to conceal their disappointment to the degree that nobody felt compromised in any way. It was what it was and that was the end of the matter. Winnie, Mrs Beresford-Amble, that is, was very nice to Marjory and they did a lot of trips into the markets in the village which were a joy to Marjory after the chaotic market scenes that she was used to in India. Here she was able to peruse the goods at a leisurely pace without being constantly accosted to buy something. It was a pleasure to shop and one that she would remember when she had returned to India and the raucous hectic pace of the local markets they would go to. She would recall Devizes and the local farmers' markets that Winnie had taken her to. A small matter indeed, you might think, but it was the cultural sensitivity of the English that prevailed upon her senses. Marjory thought it rather genteel.

Horace and Wilford went to Wilford's golf club where Horace was introduced to the game for the first time. As with most sports, Horace took to the game like a natural athlete. "A few more rounds, my son," Wilford said, "and you will be playing off a single figure handicap for sure." And he was right. The game, however, was not popular in India and so his skills lapsed until later in life when Horace was reintroduced to the game, following his retirement, in New Zealand.

Time passed quickly and soon they were boarding SS *Hooghly* at Tilbury Docks, London, for the return run to Kiddepore Docks in Calcutta. They had been entrusted with chaperoning duties. In those days, it was customary in the Indian based regiments, for those who could afford it, to send offspring to England for schooling. One had to pay for a suitable chaperone to accompany the children and although the young folk who had finished their education were no longer able to be called children, young ladies required chaperones as a matter of propriety. And the Beresford-Ambles had acquiesced when their services were requested by anxious parents who were also regimental friends and acquaintances. Just as kettle becomes the metonym for water, a ship undergoes a metamorphosis of a similar nature for love, or passion or romance. After all, aboard a ship, afloat on a luminous moonlit sea and moving gently through the warm ambience of the Mediterranean or Indian Ocean, a young person's highly charged chemical circuits are in need of a circuit breaker. Marjory and Horace were to become those safety devices. Theirs was not an enviable task, but Horace had recruited some young married subalterns to act as sheriff deputies, whom he recompensed with generous splashes from his duty free gin supplies. There were nights when Marjory and Horace both slept peacefully for the duration of their sleeping hours. The daytime watch was less demanding but nonetheless, one couldn't shirk the duties of a thankless chore. It was with some relief that they viewed the Hooghly River transit from the Bay of Bengal and into the safety of the Kiddepore Docks at Calcutta, where duties ceased and their young charges were claimed by waiting parents or agents.

The Beresford-Ambles settled into the routine of army life where Marjory proved a popular member of the ladies' auxiliary of anything that required due diligence and fervent application. Marjory was in demand and barely had a spare day on her calendar. And then the regiment was shipped to Egypt for two years. Married men and families were accommodated in comfortable quarters with as many servants as they enjoyed in India.

Horace had received special training in desert warfare during his sojourn at the military academy. It was now obvious that he had been sent there for this purpose. They stayed until 1936 when a young King Farouk inherited the Egyptian throne at the tender age of sixteen years. All British troops subsequently departed Egypt, except for those in the Suez Canal zone.

When war with Germany was declared in 1939, Horace, now a major, was ordered back to England where he became an instructor at the college that he had attended in 1933. In 1940 he was seconded to the New Zealand Army to train their soldiers in desert warfare at Trentham Army Barracks in Upper Hutt, which was a satellite town, just north of the capital city of Wellington.

257

Marjory and Horace boarded the RMS *Rangitane* and sailed for Wellington in November of 1940. During the six week voyage they met people whom they would befriend for life. In fact, their New Zealand sojourn was so enjoyable that when Horace retired from the army, they returned to England and sold the country villa in Wiltshire which Horace had inherited and shipped the remainder of their belongings, including the red MG sports car, to New Zealand. Horace rediscovered golf, playing on the lovely Heretaunga course where he became a member. He found the camaraderie in the clubhouse similar to the officers' mess in India and enjoyed many a gin and tonic after an enjoyable round of golf.

On the day he died, Horace was in a sand trap and had swung his sand wedge stroking the ball onto the green. As he was raking the sand he fell to his knees. His head was swimming and he imagined that he was in a bunker his men had dug for him in the desert. He put the head of the sand wedge golf club to his shoulder and sighted along the handle of the iron, as if sighting a rifle.

"Hold your fire, men," he called out. "When you see the whites of their eyes, give 'em hell!" He gave a lopsided smile and fell prone onto the sand where he expired. He was eighty six years of age. There was a chapel at the Trentham Army Barracks and his service was held there. An old friend, also an army man, gave the eulogy and after the service they bore his casket on a gun carriage to the camp perimeter, where the honour guard transferred it to a hearse for the journey to the crematorium. Marjory had remained stoic throughout the ordeal but when she was finally alone in her house, she sobbed for hours as she relived her fifty one years of life with a wonderful lover, friend and partner. "I could not have wanted for a better man," she told her best Nawabs China tea pot, the one with tigers rampant.

Chapter17

Maree and Ken

If you have ever sat in an hotel lobby you will know how the comings and goings of everyday life can seduce your intellectual powers and observations. It is a vibrant atmosphere. A kaleidoscope of humanity. A fashion parade. Anything goes, and it generally does. Fine feathers make fine birds. But do clothes really maketh the man, or woman? Who can tell what lurks beneath the veneer. At best you can guess or imagine from whence one may have come and where one may be going. Transitory life is a bewildering array of allegory. Signs and symbols abound. But how you interpret them is another thing.

Maree sat in a leather seat in the lobby at Maximes reading a book, or at least trying to concentrate on it, but there were so many distractions. To Maree this was the attraction of being in the lobby, the book a mere catalyst, like a jewel in a tapestry. The vacuum was omnipresent, the portals were the magnets and the flux of humanity moved within these precincts.

People ebbed and flowed like the waters of a tidal pool. Some scurried while others just sat and the swirl went around them and never touched them. Some attracted attention and others were left alone in their own space, untouched by the kinetics of the human flywheel that spun with cyclic energy. It was an open space in which one could be ambushed.

"Excuse me," Maree looked up to see an Asian face confronting her, "excuse me," he said again, "I couldn't help but notice the book that you have there," he said, referring to the book in Maree's hand.

Maree turned the book over to look at the cover as if to confirm to herself that she did have a book. "Yes", she said out loud, "a book on whales, yes, it is about whales."

"I have the same book," said the owner of the voice, "by the way I am Ken, Ken Nakamoto, I do whale research, that is why it caught my eye."

"Gosh," said Maree, "that is what I want to do, I have only just finished my degree in marine biology, my major was in this subject."

"Mind if I sit down?" Ken indicated to the vacant seat alongside.

"Yeah that's fine, please do," said Maree, more than eager to continue the conversation.

Ken sat down and smiled at Maree, "I am on a research ship, we have just returned from the Antarctic and have docked in Wellington for some minor repairs and to replenish stores before we head off to Tonga for some more whale research."

Maree nearly fell out of her seat with excitement. "Tonga," she said, "Tonga," she repeated, "that is my home, that's where I'm from."

Ken nodded, "You will be familiar with the humpback whale," he said, "the singer," he added.

"But of course," she replied, "they have a large presence in Tongan waters, in fact Tongans are the only Polynesian people to have hunted whales."

"Yes I know," Ken said. "I have read extensively on the subject and have learned quite a lot about the Tongan whaling years. Must have come as a shock to the Tongan people when the king banned the killing of whales in 1979, I understand that they were a very important part of the Tongan diet."

Marie was just 5 years old when the king's edict was sanctioned, but she could still recall the cooking smells wafting from the umus around the village as the whale meat was cooked for the evening meal. In the scented warm tropical night air, the aromas took on a distinctive exotic flavour. Sensory perceptions sharpened as the meal hour drew near. There was nothing that would ever replace such redolent ambiance, from a bygone era.

"You get over, it I guess," she said, "Tongans certainly never took enough whales to upset the survival equation, if you will pardon the pun, barely a drop in the ocean. Although they are still on the endangered species list, aren't they?"

Ken nodded in agreement.

"Yes I think at last count there were some twenty thousand of the species estimated to be swimming around the world. They will certainly survive, providing we don't upset their food chain, mind you what we do not know is what the population was prior to being hunted commercially, they could have been much less in number and thus able to maintain their feed stocks, this is where our research is taking us. Conversely, the population may have been considerably larger, in which case we may have to keep the moratorium on commercial whaling for a number of years yet.

"There are a lot of tree huggers out there that will hang their hat on any 'save the whatever,' pegs. They are not helpful. Scientific research will deliver the answers we need, but we do have to collate the data and firstly we have to collect it. And that is what we are doing, collecting and collating data to ensure the survival of these wonderful creatures."

Maree hung on every word, this was so much her world, this what she wanted to be a part of.

The conversation was at a temporary pause and Maree was keen to keep it going.

"And what is it like in the Antarctic?" she said, probing the gap.

"Different than anything I had ever imagined," Ken replied, emphasizing 'ever imagined.' 'We have a quota of Minke whales that we were allowed to take for scientific examination and so, that kept us scientists busy dissecting, measuring, weighing and examining every part of each whale that came aboard the research vessel. As for the seascape, well," he said, pausing after the 'well' for effect, "it's a huge green rolling mass of water, endless horizon that never seems to have a start or an end, like sailing through space. When it blows water, spumes hurtle at you with intense ferocity, we did not have to work outside very often, thank goodness. Apart from measuring the catch as it came aboard, most of our work was done in the comparative luxury of the laboratory. I can tell you, those deck workers earn their money, the conditions are atrocious."

Maree hung on every word, conjuring up a picture of whales, ships and wild seas and winds. "That must have been exciting," she said, "really exciting."

"It certainly is different," Ken replied, "it's not a part of the planet that a lot of people venture into and I can't see the point in going there unless you have a good reason. Not holiday or touristy stuff, really. Be nice to go to some warmer climes, so we are all looking forward to the Tongan leg of our voyage."

At that point, Ken waved to two Japanese men that had entered the lobby. "I have to go," he said standing up suddenly, "just when the conversation was getting interesting, tell you what, are you able to join me for lunch on the ship tomorrow?"

Maree, who was looking forward to a longer conversation looked up at Ken and smiled. "Oh yes, that would be wonderful."

"Great, I will meet you here, I assume that you are staying here?"

"I live here," said Maree.

Ken looked a little surprised, "Okay then, let's say 11.30 tomorrow and we can walk down to Queens Wharf, that's where the ship is berthed, I can give you the grand tour as well, you'll love the facilities we have on board."

Ken waved as he exited the lobby.

Maree sat back and folded the book shut, she was too excited to read, her head racing with the thought of visiting a real live research vessel. She couldn't wait to tell her aunty of her good fortune and went into the front office and called Kaetrin's extension. "You'll never guess what has just happened to me," was Maree's breathless outburst as her aunty answered the phone. Kaetrin could hear Maree's smile down the phone.

"It sounds like something so good I could never guess; what has just happened to you?" Kaetrin replied.

"Well," said Maree, "I have been invited to lunch tomorrow, by a scientist from a whale research vessel. I have been talking with him in the lobby, he saw me reading a book on whales and came over and introduced himself, yeah, so we just talked and then his two friends arrived and he left with them but said that he would pick me up here at 11.30 tomorrow and we will go and have a tour of the ship and have lunch there, isn't that great?"

"Sounds like a lovely experience, good for you, can I talk to you in the morning about it? I am a bit busy here at the moment."

"Wait, wait, Aunty, what will I wear?"

Kaetrin returned the transmitted smile, "I'll talk to you tomorrow. Bye."

Maree went up to her room to examine her wardrobe.

The following morning, Kaetrin and Maree discussed the day's forthcoming events over breakfast in the hotel dining room.

"Let me tell you, young lady," Kaetrin was saying to her niece. "If you are going onto a ship and are going to be taken for a tour, then you wear pants and flat heels. There is no way that you will able to negotiate those steep ladders and other strange obstacles that you will encounter without compromising your modesty. Do I make myself clear? You must dress appropriately."

Maree had presented her aunty with a dress code that was not appropriate for the occasion and she was having some difficulty accepting changes.

"You're right," Maree said at last, "sneakers and jeans it is."

And so at 11.30 am, Maree stood in the lobby waiting for Ken to arrive. And he did, wearing jeans and sneakers too. She felt relieved and made a mental note to thank Kaetrin for her sage advice.

They exited the lobby onto Cuba Street and turned left and crossed Wakefield Street and walked past the town hall and onto Jervois Quay making small talk as they went. At Queens Wharf they crossed the quay amid the traffic and entered through the wharf's large iron gates. The research vessel *Koto Maru No 2*, lay at the outer tee berth and was visible from the wharf gates.

Ken explained that they had strict security because of the nature of their work and so he would sign her in at the top of the gangway and then take her directly up onto the bridge to meet the captain. They would then lunch in the ship's dining room, which he explained was called a mess, and after that he would show her the ship's facilities, such as laboratories and anything else that she wanted to see.

The ship's gangway was a new experience for Maree, if you looked down you could see between the steps onto the wharf and water below. It was not wide enough for two people to climb side by side but was too wide for one person to have a hand on each of the side rails and so she felt a bit vulnerable on this, her first attempt. As if that was not enough to cope with, it also wobbled. Ken called from behind with encouragement. "Keep going," he said, "don't stop and don't look down, just keep climbing." At the top of the gangway, Maree stepped onto the deck and Ken came up beside her, "Go through that door," he said, "and we will sign you in on the visitors' register."

A circuitous passage and stairway route brought them onto the ship's bridge with its 360 degree panoramic view. Ken explained that unlike conventional ships, they had action going on all around, especially on the after deck when deploying or retrieving scientific devices or fish-stock.

"Whales?" Maree asked,

"Yes, whales too." Ken replied.

"Excuse me, I'll see if the captain is in his usual place," Ken disappeared and she heard him talking with another man in Japanese.

Maree heard footsteps on the highly polished wooden deck of the bridge and then Ken appeared with a short fat man. "May I introduce Captain Kyoto," he said. The captain bowed deeply from the waist and then straightened and extended his right hand, he spoke with a rather imperial English accent without ever using the letter 'L'.

"Prease to meet you," he said. Maree shook his hand.

"Thank you, Captain, you have a lovely ship," she said, not really knowing what her response should be.

"Yes," replied Captain Kyoto. "Company poricy is to have ship rooking good orra time, you enjoy runch." He bowed spoke in Japanese to Ken and walked away.

"Okay, let's have a look around here and get some lunch." Ken led her over to a bunch of screens. "This is a multibeam echo sounder which is used to produce the equivalent of an aerial photograph of the sea floor, the operator sits here and monitors all of those screens." It looked like what Maree imagined a space ship control panel should look like.

"There are six dry laboratories on board, this is where the computers take over. The main one is here on the bridge where the chief scientists direct operations and process the main data." Ken opened the door and they stepped into another world. Maree was blown away by the equipment display.

"This is amazing, I never imagined anything like this."

"It is a nice working environment, I suppose if you want to get answers you have to spend the money on equipment," Ken said. "Any new technology is added before each voyage, so we are up to date."

They went down to the mess for lunch, which was buffet service, mainly Japanese food but there were western style dishes available. Maree commented on the lack of diners and Ken explained that in port the scientists would be hosted by scientific institutions ashore, and crew not on duty would take shore leave and some even book into hotels for a bit of R&R. After their lunch they sat in one of the lounges and had coffee and talked about the ship and its mission.

"Are you ready to do some more exploring?" Ken asked.

"I'm ready," Maree replied and they got up and walked out on deck.

"This is a davit for instrument deployment, we have several on each side of the ship and also one at the stern – that's the back end."

They went down some stairs and onto the main working deck but under the covered part where apparatus could be prepared for deployment.

"And this strange looking device is a continuous plankton recorder."

"Yes I know this one," said Maree. "I believe that a lot of merchant vessels tow these on a voluntary basis for research institutions, they provide a valuable insight into environmental and climatic indicators, once the results have been analysed."

"We have six wet laboratories on board. They are used for sorting, processing and storage of fish, plankton and any other type of marine biological material, they all have hot and cold running water and work benches and ample storage for containers and equipment. Here we have our marine samples sorted into jars and preserved in alcohol. As you can see, these wet laboratories are situated adjacent to the main deck where the trawl or larger fish and whale samples are hauled aboard."

"And then there is the dark room for processing photographs." Ken and Maree kept poking their heads into new places around this main working area.

"Here we have a radioisotope laboratory and a temperature controlled laboratory.

"You have seen the mess and a lounge but there are three lounges in all, one is for smokers, a ship's office and a store where you can by confectionary, cigarettes and alcohol."

They went down an internal stairway. "Here we have our doctor's surgery and a two bed infirmary. It can be used as an emergency operating theatre." It looked like a room at A&E.

"And here we have a gymnasium and a Japanese bath and a sauna which is the best place to be in the Antarctic, believe me."

"Amazing," Maree said, "just amazing."

"Yes," said Ken, "to attract the calibre of staff that we require we have to offer reasonably comfortable accommodation. Come and let me show you what a scientist's cabin looks like." They went down a long alleyway with doors on one side only and Ken opened one that had a label that read "Science 6," above it and above that Maree assumed that the Japanese characters said the same. He opened the door and they entered. "As you can tell by the porthole this is an outside cabin, most are." Maree could see a bunk on one side that was neatly made up with crisp clean white linen. Against the opposite bulkhead was a built in wardrobe and a couch and at the end a desk under the porthole with a chair that was fastened to the deck by a chain. To the left as one entered the cabin, there was a door that opened into an en-suite that was shared by the adjoining cabin. "Senior scientists have their own en-suite. All very elitist. The higher up the pecking order the better the perks," Ken said as he watched the wonderment on Maree's face.

"We haven't finished yet," he said, "follow me," and he led her up several flights of stairs ending on a landing which seemed to be a dead end but for a steel door set into a bulkhead. Ken opened the door and they entered a large cavernous empty space. "Helicopter hangar," he announced, "sans chopper. We usually send the chopper ashore for service and maintenance work whenever need or like now when we want it out of the way."

Maree took in the large empty space. "So why would you want it out of the way?" she asked.

"Cocktail party! The Japanese ambassador is holding a cocktail party here tomorrow night. Mainly for the scientific community and a general gesture of goodwill toward our New Zealand friends." He saw Maree raise her eyebrows, questioning the suitability of the venue.

"They dress it up for the occasion," Ken said. "You wouldn't believe the transformation but, hey, you don't have to. You can see it for yourself!"

Maree looked at him, she held one hand, flat-palm up as if carrying a tray. "What am I, a cocktail waitress?" she mocked.

"Oh no, you are my guest."

Maree's upturned hand went over her mouth as she gasped in disbelief.

Ken saw her delight and said. "Your car will collect you from the hotel at seven in the evening. Simply climb aboard, enjoy the ride and I will meet you at the bottom of the gangway where there will be a large reception tent erected."

Maree was speechless and couldn't wait to get home to break the news to Kaetrin. The news caused a flap that saw the entire wardrobes of the first floor apartments as well as Kaetrin's and Maree's, ransacked for suitable apparel. Armistice Day was received with less pandemonium. And that was riotous. Hotel clientele who took rooms to display their wares to clothing store buyers were phoned and consulted. They were able to direct Kaetrin and Maree to stores who had purchased suitable collections. The stores were visited and fittings arranged. And, 'certainly Madam', for a price, they could have alterations done overnight.

Back at the hotel, chaos had replaced sanity. This would be the closest any of them would ever get to prepare their very own Cinderella for the ball. Maree had more mothers than a religious house full of women under vows and every one was an expert in their field. But no one had ever attended an ambassador's cocktail party. They had been invited to political shindigs and Roberta said that she had even sat naked in the speaker's chair in parliament one evening after a particularly intoxicating experience at a politicians' cocktail hour. But ambassadors were not elected politicians, they were career gentlemen. Not for them the rough and tumble of politics. Oh no! They were uncrowned royalty. Men with plenipotentiary commissions. Achievers without vanity. They were gracious, dignified and polite. Princes of polite, even. And so it was important that the dress code be appropriate for the occasion. Despite a committee being appointed to oversee the transformation of Cinderella, they managed to produce a winner.

On the evening of the main event, Maree exited the elevator and walked through the lobby to the waiting embassy car amid admiring glances and ooohs and aahhs from the tidal pool occupants. She wore a black chiffon dress that hung loosely from her shoulders in waves that overlapped a short formed skirt. Kaetrin had loaned Maree her diamond pendant earrings and matching necklace. Her hair was a masterpiece of shapes and coils that bounced like flowing silk, but never lost its form. Felicity had a way with hair and she had excelled herself on this occasion. Maree had a flawless light coppery skin, a legacy from her Tongan mother and European father. She had a pretty face and pretty legs and her walk was usually under control but her camp mothers had insisted on her wearing heels that she was not used to and so they had spent a lot of the evening instructing her in high heel walking practice and performance.

Maree was not impressed with the shoes and said that she would have to remove them to negotiate the gangway. "A most hideous device," she called it. "It is the nearest thing that I can imagine to negotiating a ladder in an earthquake."

But she need not have bothered. When the embassy car delivered her to the side of the ship and into the reception tent there was an elevator that had been erected to carry guests from the wharf and up to the hangar deck level. It was an enclosed affair so that even the most timorous soul could take the ride without compromising their intolerance of temporary mechanical contraptions, and heights. Maree had no such qualms and rode the platform hanging onto Ken's arm. He had told her that she looked lovely and that he was proud to be entering the hangar with her on his arm. A liveried concierge announced the arrival of Mr Ken Nakamoto from Nakamoto Scientific with Miss Maree MacLeod.

It was just as Ken said. The hangar had been transformed. Bunting, flags and flowers commanded the most attention. A wooden floor was laid over the steel deck and there was seating, a bar, a dance floor and a small orchestra playing predominantly stringed instruments to Japanese themed music. The ambassador would make his grand entrance once all guests were received. He was currently being entertained in the captain's cabin with cocktails and finger food supplied and served by the ship's catering staff.

A waiter offered them a glass of champagne each and they took the glass tubes with bubbles rising, clinked the transparent cylinders together and said cheers then sipped delicately in silence.

Guests were starting to fill the hangar and the background noise became the 'rhubarb scene' in a street full of extras for a random movie shot. A large hirsute face came into frame and Maree said, "Hello, Professor."

"Hello, Maree, this is our first meet since your graduation. What are you up to? Joining the whaling fraternity are you?" He presented the question as if he were disapproving of Japanese whaling procedures.

"Professor," she said, "this is Ken Nakamoto, Ken meet Professor Barry Roper. He was my professor at uni." Ken and Barry shook hands and acknowledged that it was good to meet one another.

"You on the ship, Ken?" Barry asked.

"Yes, I am one of the scientists."

"I spent time in the Southern Ocean some years back now," the professor reminisced. "We were counting whales," he said, "not killing them. Back in the day it was called the Blue Whale Unit. The blue whale was the standard reference against which all other whales were compared in terms of bounty. What they produced in oil and meat basically. A strange method but that was what the IWC used and who were we to argue?"

266

Ken nodded, "Yes, well, we are using more exact methods today, Professor. We have to kill stock in order to properly assess them but we believe that we are getting some accurate results."

"Ever eaten whale meat?"

"What?"

"Whale meat!" Barry repeated. "Ever eaten it?"

"Well yes I have, it has been a part of the Japanese diet for centuries."

"And the meat from your whale kill, is that sold in Japan?"

Ken was surprised at the question.

"We do not waste what we catch for scientific examination. After we have finished the science project the remainder is retained for human consumption in Japan. I suppose it is what you might call fish and chips!"

Barry laughed. "Well put, Ken, I have never heard it called that before. Heard all the euphemisms but you cut through all of that bureaucratic nonsense like a flensing knife. Well done, boy!"

Just as Barry was getting into his loquacious stride, the public address system crackled and asked Ken Nakamoto to come to the captain's suite. Ken said good bye to Barry and took Maree by her elbow and steered her through the throngs that had amassed in the hangar.

"Me too?" Maree asked. "They did ask for you, not me!"

"You too," Ken replied. "The ambassador wants to meet us both."

"What about my glass?"

"It's okay to carry your glass, but only when the ship is docked."

They entered an alleyway that was wider than any Maree had seen before on board ship. It was like moving from a lane to a boulevard where you just knew the houses were about to get bigger. The deck was carpeted from bulkhead to bulkhead and framed pictures were hung on the walls. Ken knocked on an impressive oak door and it was opened by a steward who ushered them into a roomy cabin with all the trappings of a stateroom.

The ambassador bowed, the captain bowed, Ken bowed and Maree bowed. Ken introduced Maree to his excellency, Ambassador Fitsui, who came forward, hand extended, and Maree took and shook the proffered hand just as she had been trained to do by Kaetrin, and Flora before her. Maree had met Captain Kyoto at an earlier time and so they shook hands and reminisced about their earlier encounter on the bridge. A steward freshened their glasses and the ambassador thanked Neil for the support of Nakamoto Scientific in Japan's scientific whaling endeavours and then Ken and Maree were ushered out with much bowing and smiling. The entire procedure would not have taken longer than five minutes but to Maree it seemed a lifetime.

Ken said, "Time for some fresh air," and led them onto an open deck, where they could view the twinkling lights of Oriental Bay across the water from Queens Wharf.

"It's a lovely harbour," Ken said.

Maree looked over the water. "Yes, I guess it is, I live here. You never stop to enjoy the view. I guess I just take it for granted, isn't that how natives treat their own back yard?"

"Perhaps," Ken replied, "I think you need to have reference conditions, a set of values to assess against. If you never leave your own backyard, there is no yardstick – excuse the pun!"

Maree laughed. "I see what you mean. I can only relate to my own home which is an island in Tonga. We don't have a lot of lights but we have smells. Tropical flower scents. Warm air aromas that hang suspended. You can smell the sea, and when you are at sea, you can smell the land. I was very young when they stopped taking whales but even now I can smell the cooking of whale meat from the umus, the ovens that Tongans use. And the bright lights from the lanterns burning whale oil. Especially spermaceti from cachelot."

Ken laughed.

Maree said, "What's so funny?"

"You know," he said, "I can smell the whale meat cooking too and I thought that maybe the champagne had got to my senses and was playing tricks on me. Maybe it is the atmosphere; pretty girl, lovely scenery, starry firmament and then I realised we are standing near the extraction vents from the galley and whale meat is on the menu. Finger food for the cocktail party. We actually are smelling whale meat cooking. It's coming straight at us from the galley extraction fans."

Maree burst into laughter, "That's so funny," she managed to gasp out and started to do a little dance on the deck both arms extended. One with the champagne flute in her fingers and the empty hand floating like a butterfly and Ken joined in. With his spare hand he took hold of hers and together they twirled around to imaginary music, laughing joyously. Eventually they came together chest to chest and the laughing stopped and they looked into each other's eyes and then kissed. It was as if it had been scripted. But nobody called 'cut'.

They walked hand in hand back to the hangar which was a blaze of bright lights after their time under the outside evening sky. The orchestra was in full tune and the milling throngs were talking and drinking and eating from the trays of finger food that were on offer. The ambassador had made the party and was talking with a delegation from the Ministry of Fisheries. Captain Kyoto was talking with a group of people that included Professor Barry Roper and Ken suggested she come and meet a couple of the on board scientists and he led her over to two Japanese ladies who were standing together. Ken introduced Maree to Mai and Ren. They were both first trip scientists and this was also their first cocktail party so they were a bit shy. Their English was good and conversation flowed readily. It was a refreshing discussion on matters that concerned them all. Boring to outsiders maybe, but it was their field and there were no strange ears to cater to. Maree was so relaxed she invited them all to dinner at Maximes the following evening. Her invitation was accepted with much polite but agreeable approval.

Ken said, "Bumper boats – keep moving," and they said bye bye to Mai and Ren and walked toward the dance floor. There was no one dancing and Ken said, "It's string quartet stuff. When the ambassador goes we change music and all hell breaks loose." They were both on their third glass of champagne and were relaxed and happy. Ken said, "I must talk to the Tongan ambassador if I can find him."

Maree looked surprised. "Is he here?" she asked.

"Well yes, he has to be, he is invited and we are going up to Tongan waters when we leave here to carry on more research. We must thank him for allowing us to research in his domain. Your backyard, if you like. You should be able to pick a Tongan plenipotentiary out in a crowd, surely."

Maree looked startled.

"Can't be too hard, he will be portly and middle aged. Obviously will have Tongan good looks just like you!" Ken teased.

Maree said, "I didn't even know that we had a Tongan Embassy here in Wellington – some Tongan, huh?"

"It is the capital city, so this is the place. Well, anything promising on the horizon?" Ken asked.

"No," Maree replied. "Hard to pick out individuals in the crowd."

At that moment the PA system burst into life, requesting Mr Nakamoto to report to the captain's suite.

"Here we go again," Ken said to Maree. "I guess they want us to meet another dignitary!"

The second visit was not so stressful for Maree as she now felt in familiar territory. They arrived sans champagne flutes this visit and knocked on the imposing door and entered into the now familiar stateroom. The captain was entertaining a youngish Polynesian woman, elegantly dressed and seated in one of the cabins leather loungers.

The captain bowed and Ken bowed and Maree bowed.

"Arrow me to present, her excerrency the Tongan ambassador, Mrs Ruisa Tongirava," he said expansively.

Mrs Luisa Tongilava stood up and they shook hands and then they all sat down.

First, she addressed Ken and said how pleased the Tongan Government was to have their research vessel visit Tongan waters to carry out good scientific works. Tongans were the only Polynesian people to hunt whales, she said. She then spoke briefly to Maree in Tongan but continued in English.

"So, Maree, you are one of us but we have never seen you at any of our local functions for Tongan nationals. Are you avoiding us?"

Maree gave the only reply that she knew, which was, "Never knew you existed."

The ambassador seemed a little taken aback by the candour of Maree's reply.

"We don't exactly advertise our presence," the ambassador replied "but I feel sure that if you do need us we will be there for you. Tell me," she said, "now that you have qualified as a marine biologist what are your plans for the future? Will Tonga be the recipient of your life's work?"

Maree was a little startled by the forthrightness of the question.

"I have only just graduated, Ambassador," she replied. "I have no idea what I will be doing tomorrow, let alone further downstream."

"I'm sure whatever you do, Tonga will be proud of you."

"My family are," Maree said. "And I haven't seen them in a while. A visit back to my home is a priority as is finding work in my field. I would like to work in this area if possible."

"Whales?"

"Yes," Maree replied. "Large aquatic mammals, I include seals and also dolphins."

"Admirable, admirable," the ambassador said, standing up and signalling that the interview was over.

They all shook hands and Ken and Maree left the suite and walked back to the hangar and to another flute of champagne.

They both took a plate of finger food and sat together to discuss the meeting.

Ken said, "I know what she was angling at."

Maree looked at him. "I thought that she was damn rude, actually."

"Well," Ken said, "she doesn't have to be nice to us, it's the captain that she has to impress. He's the boss!"

"I don't follow?" Maree formed her reply like a question.

"Well, I am not saying anything that I shouldn't, I guess, but the word is we are looking for extra personnel for the Tongan part of the voyage as some of the existing staff are flying home from here. My guess is that she will suggest – not ask, but very diplomatically suggest, that a certain young Tongan science graduate that is sitting here next to me, gets invited to join the ship."

Maree, who was about to sip some champagne, spilt a few drops down her chin. A few more drops stuck at the back of her throat and caused a coughing fit.

"It's only a guess, Maree, but I would imagine that if the Rady Ambassador has got the ear of our fearress reader Captain Kyoto. You can expect a call to visit the suite again before the night is over."

Ken mocked the captain's accent by replacing the letters 'L' with the letter 'R' and Maree chided him for doing so.

"Anyway," Maree said, "what makes you so special? You know so much about policy. I get the feeling that there is something you have not told me." She fell silent as one does before a eureka moment. "Nakamoto Scientific, same name as your surname – is that a coincidence, Mr Nakomoto?" she emphasized his surname.

Ken was a humorous guy. He placed his champagne flute on the table and crossed his legs dramatically before ceremoniously shaking his head as if he were clearing a large mane from his eyes, and said in an affected speech pattern. "Well, actually, Mummy and Daddy..." he let his voice trail off, blinking his eyes furiously while staring at the ceiling of the hangar.

His actions had Maree in stitches.

"Okay, wise guy," she said, "come clean, I can take it!"

"Nakomoto Scientific is a family owned business. My parents are the major shareholders and I am a son and heir along with five other siblings. Here, I am simply another worker, but I guess by association the captain likes to keep me in the loop, maybe he has been asked to, I don't know. I get no special treatment. I have no input. I work and I get paid same rates and conditions as any other worker on this ship. That's it.

"I would guess if they are looking for young graduates to join the ship they have invited the right people to the party. Your professor is no doubt of some use to them. We have seen him in conversation with Captain Kyoto and the Japanese ambassador. Do you see any other of your classmates here?"

"No I haven't," Maree said. "But then I was the only specialist whale major of my year!"

"Okay, so maybe they want one new recruit and you are it! You are the chosen one. Either way I am innocent of any coercion. Honest."

Maree looked at Ken. "I believe you." She lifted her glass. "Cheers," she said.

"Cheers," Ken said. "It would be great if we were to become shipmates."

True to her word, Maree invited Mai and Ren to the hotel for dinner with Ken and herself. It was to be a double celebration, as Maree had that very day received confirmation from the Japanese Embassy, that she was accepted for the Tongan leg of the voyage on the *Toko Maru No 2*. They would sail in four days. The ship would spend four weeks on their research around the Tongan Archipelago before returning to the ship's home port which was in the Pacific Coast port of Hachinohe in Northern Honshu. Flora sent the table a bottle of champagne from her own collection. She had earlier excused herself from dining with them. These days, Flora ate a hot lunch in the dining room but made herself a light snack in her penthouse apartment, where she liked to watch the evening news on TV.

The four young scientists were able to engage in their favourite topic. They were marine biologists on a whale research vessel. Maree did more listening than talking, being the new recruit, but she was happy to soak up the discussion and ask appropriate questions. Soon she would be talking shop like the rest of them; a working scientist making a contribution to the planet. Their research may be controversial, but needed to be done to ensure the survival of the species. She was upbeat, bright eyed and raring to go!

"We'll be doing a lot of swimming," Ken said.

"Why is that?" Maree replied.

"We will be counting stock – operating from inflatables and tagging where possible, migratory routes of humpback whales is what we are interested in. Oddly enough, we seem to have gaps in our knowledge about the humpback

271

when it leaves the southern oceans. In other words, we are not sure where they all go to."

"Tonga, for sure," Maree said.

"Not all of them. Let's assume that a thousand whales migrate north and we only count, say, five hundred in Tonga – where have the other five hundred gone to?"

"And then there is the question of food," Mai said. "We cannot determine how much food is taken by a whale by observing it feeding. We can, however, get an indication of the frequency of feeding and the amount from our minke whale take in the Antarctic. From that, we can measure stomach capacity to calculate how much may be eaten at each meal. This is further complicated by the fact that whales like ruminants have three chambers. So you have to evaluate food availability and calculate energy requirements as well as digestion rates."

"Yeah, I read somewhere that the smaller whale, like the minke, with a smaller mouth, needs to take more gulps per feed in order to satisfy that equation than, say, a much larger blue whale," Ren added.

"And furthermore," Ken continued, "when the whales move north to their breeding ground they do not give up feeding entirely but at a much reduced rate. Energy demands are less in the warmer waters than the Antarctic and they tend live on their stored fat and the lactating females require greater sustenance. Our observations show that the females are the first to arrive at the feeding grounds and the last to leave.

"More wine?" Ken offered.

The conversation ebbed and flowed as the eager young scientists shared their knowledge with their peers.

Sailing day came quickly and Kaetrin, Linus and Flora were on the quay to wave goodbye as the vessel slipped its moorings. Maree was on the boat deck waving and blowing kisses. Tears of joy and high emotion dripped onto the wooden polished handrail that she was holding onto tightly with her hands when not waving. They sailed at three o'clock in the afternoon. The ship had spent the morning taking on fresh stores and provisions from a local ship's providing company. Within five minutes the vessel had turned and was steaming away from the wharf making any further attempts at goodbyes futile. The dockside farewell party walked quietly back to Maximes.

Maree went to her cabin sat down on the daybed, wiping her eyes and wondering if she had made the right decision. Drained from the emotional departure, she fell asleep.

Ken knocked on the door of Maree's cabin at five o'clock to announce that dinner was being served in the dining saloon.

Maree awoke from her slumber and called, "Come in."

Ken entered and said, "Thought I had better wake you for dinner."

Maree sat up mumbling thanks and holding her face in her hands, then stretched her arms in the manner of the freshly woken. "I think I needed that," she said, "the emotion of leaving drained me."

"You wanna freshen up? I'll come back in five and we'll go down for dinner together – okay?"

"Great, thanks. See you soon."

Ken returned in five minutes and they headed down a narrow corridor that moved slightly. Maree had walked aboard a still structure berthed against a jetty and woken when the ship was at sea. She found her first experience strange if not a bit disconcerting and now understood why there were handrails on the walls. One's foot didn't land where one expected it to and so a bit of compensation had to be allowed for mid gait. Ken noticed her awkwardness and said, "You'll get the hang of it. A couple of days and you will be an old hand."

The mess was well patronised in contrast to her visit when they were in port.

"If you don't eat now," Ken said, "you go hungry. Next feed is breakfast at 0700 hours." He used the twenty four hour clock system. Dinner was buffet style similar to what she had experienced in port. Ken explained the food and they ate the same selection of Japanese dishes which Maree said were delectable. They finished the meal and sat in a lounge watching television; they were still receiving New Zealand television transmission.

"We will probably get satellite signals tomorrow. We never know what's coming up. It seems that the techs tune in to the best picture reception." Maree commented on the lack of people in the lounge and Ken explained that a lot of crew are watch-keeping staff who work the ship and as they work, twenty four seven, a lot will be in their cabins, sleeping or reading before they go on watch. "Day workers like us scientists can be the only night owls, but even then as you will find out, there is plenty to catch up with at sea such as doing your laundry, sleeping, reading etc. When we are on station and we are working, the days can be long so we take the breaks when they come." At 1900 hours Maree yawned and stretched.

"That's me, I'm off to bed!"

"Can you find your cabin?" Ken enquired, standing up.

Maree said, "If I can't I will come back, otherwise, see you at breakfast. Good night," and she left.

The marine biologists held a meeting the following morning in one of the ship's lounges where the head man, a Dr Yasuko, explained the program that he expected the team to undertake during their four week tour of Tongan waters. It seemed that they would be traversing the length of the archipelago, which excited Maree even more as they would be very close to her home island. Apart from team leader Mr Yasuko, there were just four others, Mai, Ren, Ken and Maree.

Also aboard were a team studying atmospheric sciences. Apart from some social activity, their paths would not cross in a working day. The afternoons' activities found them checking out the gear that they would be working with and trying on wetsuits and examining the inflatable boats under the watchful eye of the seamen in charge. Also, there were cameras that had to be mastered for the underwater shots, of which they were told there would be many. There was tagging gear and radio controlled devices that had to be attached when and if possible. Then it was off to the movies to watch whales and marine biologists carrying out the work that they were about to perform. It was daunting stuff, but exciting.

On the fourth morning they were in Tongan waters and were kitted up in their wet suits ready for a launch, and waiting for the first whales to be sighted. The inflatables were ready on the main deck and for a bit of excitement the rubber boats were going to be launched down the slipway that was used to winch the minke whales aboard when in Antarctic waters. The seaman called this method of launching, 'Kamikaze style'. They had done this often when the water was calm and everybody enjoyed the adrenalin rush as the inflatable hurtled down the steep slipway and crashed into the ocean, sending columns of water into the air. Two seaman and two scientists were assigned to each boat and Ken and Maree were paired which left Mai and Ren in the other boat. One seaman would drive the outboard engine and the other would assist the scientists with their gear and also getting them back on board.

Excitement abounded as the parties lounged around on the main deck waiting for the signal to launch. The seamen were tuning in their mobile phones to the ship's network so they would have contact with the mothership at all times. Ken and Maree checked their gear for the umpteenth time. Gear failures were costly and Dr Yasuko was a hard taskmaster. Mai and Ren were doing the same. Catering staff offered the boat teams drinks, which they declined.

"There is no time to pee on this job. Save your thirst for later," Ken had said from past experience. Both inflatables had fitted wheels at either side of the transom which had been designed for this type of launch. Recovery would be the reverse. They would be hauled aboard by the whale retrieval wire rope system. All of a sudden: "Go – launch boats," was relayed over the intercom. They launched in single file to avoid entanglement on the slipway. Suddenly the boats were in the blue Pacific Ocean and speeding away from the mothership in the direction that was relayed over their radio phones. Ahead, wispy white water spouts could be seen as the whales exhaled the warm air from their blow holes into the atmosphere. And then there was the rank smell that accompanies the animals. "It comes from their breath," Ken explained to Maree. "When an animal lives off its own body fat, it converts the fat into ketones which, when expelled in breath or urine, well, there is a smell." The pod seemed to be lying motionless on the surface. "Okay, in we go for a camera shoot – see what we have here." Ken fell over backwards into the water with snorkel and mask in place and camera in one hand. He held his mask firmly sealed to his face with the palm of his spare hand. Maree followed and so did Mai and Ren from the other boat. The boatmen sat and waited for the swimmers' signals to collect them. Maree was no novice to marine dives but was surprised at the warmness of the tropical waters. Certainly nothing like the coolness of Cook Strait where she had done her diving apprenticeship. The clarity she defined as like looking through a bottle of gin. Light beams shafted the surface and expanded in their width as they penetrated the blue abyss and in this wonderful mixture floated some of the world's largest mammals. The humpback is a stout bodied mammal with long flippers that may be a third of its body length. They are black in colour but there are usually patches of white on the belly and undersides of their flippers. Knobbly excrescences adorn the snout, chin and sides of the lower jaw. The fins are scalloped on the trailing edge adding to the whales overall general bumpy appearance. The body length is about twenty meters and they could weigh up to 48 tonnes. Colour patterns were sufficiently characteristic to enable recognition of individuals and whale scientists had been able to build up photographic records which could be used to follow the seasonal migrations of these great whales. Dr Yakuso was aware of this trait and was keen to keep his own records as up to date as possible. Maybe they would be able to recognise individual whales from previous seasons' studies. Maree knew this as she clicked away, cognisant of the creatures' habit of exposing the underside of their flukes before diving. This was a bit like fingerprint territory and was used for individual identification. The creatures swam ponderously and slowly. They were all females, it seemed, having recently arrived from their cold southern waters to breed in the warm Tongan Archipelago. As coastal huggers, the species had been prime targets for aboriginal and commercial whalers because their patterns of migration were predictable. This was the whale that the Tongans hunted until it was banned by the king in 1979. Maree was just 8 years old at the time. It was strange that the memories of her island home should come flooding back while she was busy taking photographs of the whales. She could remember the excitement when a dead whale was brought ashore by the boat crew. The great beast was cut up and distributed equally among the population. Nobody went without a share and for the next few nights the smell of cooking whale meat emanated from the umus. The skin could be made to crust like crackling on a porker and the whole island celebrated their good fortune at God's bounty from the sea that supplied so much sustenance and protein, a valuable commodity. There would be no waste as, excess was used as barter for commodities from island neighbours, who were not so fortunate to have whale hunting skills. Commercial killing ceased around the world in 1964, following decades of hunting that almost annihilated them and they had been a protected species ever since. The scientists were called back to their boats and Maree was surprised to find that they had been in the water for two hours. Their photographic efforts were developed and examined during the afternoon and evening and Maree made for her cabin, had a welcome shower and then bed at twenty hundred hours. It had been a long day. The days did not get any shorter and any glamour that may have existed about a sea voyage in the tropical south seas was soon dispelled as Dr Yokato worked his charges to the limit of the articles that established working conditions for those on the ship. Every day was a working day, but Saturday night was still party night when the bar opened and those not on duty could attend and buy drinks or put them on a tab that would see them deducted from wages. There was comfortable seating around a small dance floor and a jukebox that could be played by inserting washers purchased from the bar. The bar closed at midnight and the ship returned to routine.

Ken asked casually after dinner the following night.

"Which island in the Tongan Archipelago do you call home?"

"I was about to ask you where we were, I would hate to miss my island, we simply must stop and visit, I just couldn't not visit!

"The captain has asked me to confirm with you, I think he has some information from your papers but wants to confirm."

"The island is called Vavai, it is in the Ha'apai group."

Ken looked at his watch, "We can go up to the bridge now, if you like, the chief officer is on watch and he is a helpful sort of a guy, he can show us on the chart exactly where we are. Would you like to do that?"

"Definitely," Maree emphasized, "too right I would!"

"Follow me," Ken said. And off they went.

Maree was surprised when she entered the bridge with Ken. She had been there before when she was introduced to the captain back in Wellington. Then it was day time and the bridge was a large, light, airy place with lots of windows. Now it was dark. There was background lighting coming from instruments and she could see the shadowy figures of three people. One was looking through a pair of binoculars, one was looking at a radar screen and the third came over to greet them. Ken introduced Maree to take, the chief officer, who obviously had been previously briefed by Ken about the visit. He motioned them to a room at the rear with a curtained doorway. The curtain was swaying gently to the movement of the ship. With the curtain pulled back across the doorway opening, Take flicked a switch and a low wattage lamp illuminated a flat table that had charts on it. He pointed at the chart with a pencil and said, "This is our position," he then drew a straight line on the chart using a parallel ruler, made a dot and drew an 'X' on the dot, "and here is your island," he said.

"It doesn't look far away," Maree offered.

"No it isn't," Take replied "but at the rate of knots we go during the day, sometimes we don't move at all, it could take us several days to get there. Also we just cannot go in a straight line as there are shipping hazards such as reefs in the way. But do not worry, I have checked it out and there is safe anchorage outside the reef when we get there. It seems that there is a good navigable passage through the reef where we can shuttle the ship's motorised lifeboats and run our people from ship to shore and back."

"We are going to stop there?" Maree said, surprised.

"But of course! The captain said we can stay for one day and a night."

Maree looked at Ken. "You will be able to meet my family! You'll just love them."

Ken smiled, "That's the idea, we don't want them to get the impression that their precious daughter is working on just any old ship. This should allay their fears." He looked at Take. "What do you say, chief?"

Take grinned, happy to be included in the routine.

"The best ship in the fleet for sure," he said.

An excited Maree spoke to her parents by radio telephone from the ship as they arranged the ship's estimated time of arrival. She had to emphasise 'estimated' because the ship may be held up depending on scientific work which was their prime reason for being in Tongan waters. Both visitors and hosts were in a highly emotional condition.

Maree's father, Robert MacLeod was Kaetrin's younger brother who had come out to New Zealand on the *Rangitata* as a CORB sponsored immigrant in 1940. Flora MacLeod had raised both of her brother's children from her home at Maximes in Lower Cuba Street, Wellington. Robert completed his schooling and started an engineering apprenticeship with William Cables at Kaiwharawhara. He subsequently went to sea as a marine engineering officer on the Union Company's island trader *Matua* and in one of the ship's many calls at Nukua-Lofa, met his future wife, Maree's mother, Tia, when she was doing her nurse training in the local hospital. Robert eventually settled in Nukua-Lofa and married Tia. He started a marine ship repair yard and became a successful local businessman. Robert subsequently sold fifty percent to a working partner and moved with his wife to Vavai, where Maree was born.

Island life was different than Robert had imagined. The first rule he learned was that food was important, but time was not. On Sunday one could relax, go to church and eat and sleep. The island had a limited agricultural industry with the growing of root crops and squash being their primary source of income. Kava ground and unground and also vanilla were new sources of agriculture that could bring in an income when sold to the main island. They had always grown their own kava roots but Robert wanted to expand this and export the excess. Vanilla required new skills that they had to learn. Fresh water came from the sky when it rained, so growing and irrigating crops could be a risky business. Fishing was a good source of protein but never as good as whale meat when they were able to hunt the humpbacks. Their island had two working whale boats before the king's moratorium stopped all whaling in Tonga. They were able to catch surplus to their own needs and so the excess was bartered for goods and services from other islands. Pigs and poultry provided another source of protein.

Robert enjoyed an income from his business interests and without any government assistance and his generosity they had drilled a bore into an underground aquifer for fresh water. They purchased diesel generators to supply electrical power which meant that they had refrigeration. This extended the life of foods stocks considerably. He had also got them started on a vanilla bean plantation which was the El Dorado of island thinking at the time and would at some future stage bring them a healthy income. Tongans think of the whole village as themselves and so what was done by one was done for everyone. Their dwellings, called fales, had either thatched or corrugated iron roofs. Some had wooden walls and some thatched walls. With an abundance of coconut trees, Robert bought a portable sawmill so they could mill their own timber for houses, from the coconut trees. After a severe tropical storm there was a lot of windblown trees available for milling, that otherwise would have been wasted. Any excess timber that was milled could be sold or stored for future use.

Pearl farming, an experiment, was underway in the lagoon. The farms were propagated by Japanese specialists and maintained by locals. The pearls would provide another source of income and there was a question mark after that. Japanese pearl farmers supplied the spat and the expertise. The Tongans supplied the warm and sheltered lagoon and some labour. That was how the partnership operated. The returns were nothing at this end of the operation and could remain nothing for some time until the pearl harvesting came in and then they could assess the quality of the product. In any event it cost them nothing but some hours' labour, of which the island had plenty to give. In this instance, the Tongans were the landlords and the Japanese the share croppers.

The island spokesperson was called the Talking Chief and he happened to be Tia's father. It was Tongan tradition that children addressed their parents by their first names and never mum or dad, mother or father. Tia called her father as Ata, which means 'hurricane' and her mother was Aba, 'born on Thursday'. Aba and Ata had no other children. This was due to a medical condition preventing Aba from becoming pregnant again.

The islanders had constructed a runway, compacted from crushed coral and shells. This was okay for small planes but to realise their dream of opening their paradise up to tourism they would need to be able to land large planes and build tourist fales. Hard cash and plenty of it would be needed and it seemed an impossible dream.

The first landing party from the whale research vessel comprised of Maree, Ken, Captain Kyota, two atmospheric scientists and the ship's purser. They were met on the main lagoon jetty by a welcoming committee and Maree was whisked off to her parents' fale for a private welcome.

After eight years, it was never going to be a quiet affair and Maree broke into a low wailing sob at the sight of her parents. "Aba-Aba," she said and then, "Ata, my father," embracing both in turn and then all together in a huddle with tears streaming down all of their cheeks. When they had gotten over their initial sentimental weep they burst into an incessant chatter attempting to bridge the years apart in a barrage of endless vocalizing. This continued for some time until a figure appeared in the doorway, requesting the presence of the Talking Chief at the official welcoming ceremony.

Holding hands, Ata, Maree and Aba walked to the throng of villagers gathered by the jetty to welcome their visitors. As Talking Chief, it was Ata's job to be the spokesperson for the island at such ceremonies and he walked up to Captain Kyota and shook his hand.

"Welcome, Captain," he said, "you and your crew have the freedom of our island home for the duration of your stay. We have prepared some of our finest pigs for a feast this evening which will be in your honour. I realise that not everybody from your ship is able to attend but we hope to entertain as many as you are able to release from duty, for this momentous occasion. Our first official function is the traditional kava ceremony, in your honour, please allow me to escort you to the ceremony." Ata led the captain to what was their equivalent of the village square where they were seated on tapa mats. Kava is a mild narcotic and can numb the mouth. Captain Kyota, who had a problem with the letter 'L' soon found that he was no longer in charge of 'R' and that some odd muscular backsliding seemed to have afflicted his tongue and lips and there was a whole array of facial contortions that were becoming beyond his ability to control. He had to think very carefully before he chose a word which gave the appearance, to his new friends anyway, that the ship's captain was either deaf or retarded. The hosts were generous and keen to ensure that their guest was included in each pass of the cup. There was no respite for the good captain. And then he had the honour to respond to Ata's wonderful speech of welcome. He beamed at the audience for a long time, working out in his head carefully chosen words to say. That is to say, he thought that he was beaming but subsequent photographs indicated, one side of his mouth had drooped and he looked like he had Bell's Palsy.

"My dea fwends," he began. And frowned. "We so peased to wisit you on your irand home. Since Mawee join ship in Wewington she has given us inwitation to wisit you."

He paused, frowning and searching for the right words.

"Ata and Aba thank you for dewiwerwing to our scientific," and he smiled knowing that he couldn't be tripped up on scientific, "expedition", and another smile, "such a young and dedicated werka. We hope she want to come with us next year when we weturn to the Antarctic for more whale weaserch." He gave another of his beaming Bell's Palsy grins and continued. "I have wots to say but I can't say it wewy well now, me talk water, thank you dear fwends."

The purser spoke next. "Maree told us about your whale hunting prowess and we have brought ashore for you, frozen chunks of minke whale meat, sufficient for the whole island to enjoy after we have left. It has been blast frozen so it will be fresh when you thaw it out." Polite clapping from the hosts indicated that this was a welcome gift and would be enjoyed by the islanders.

A mixture of local singing and dancing followed and then the remnants of the island's whale boat crews were presented to the distinguished guests. There were ten in total and they all carried the tools of their trade. The harpoon irons were freshly sharpened for the occasion and the metal gleamed in the bright sunshine; wooden handles highly polished from use in the sure hands of the throwers and recently oiled to preserve the wood and increase the lustre. The lances were tapered to a needle finish and all of the instruments were fettered to their owners by an intricate woven rope created more for the ceremonial occasion than the plain but functional hunting rope. The owners gave displays of weapon holding and balancing as if standing in a prancing boat advancing on their prey, presenting their tools as they would when hunting the whale. Suddenly, a host of children ran out onto the grass, each holding a coconut and placing them twenty yards away on the ground. The children retreated and the hunters went into a type of ceremonial crouch, contemplating their targets.

279

They went forward onto the front foot and then back, shifting their weight and balancing the weapon in hand, feeling the transfer of weight and the centre of gravity of the weapon while making slight adjustments. A ceremonial chant was started and then on a signal, all of the whalemen shouted a mantra and launched their projectiles in a carefully calculated parabola, reaching the vertex almost simultaneously and dropping toward the intended targets. Without fail, all spears found their mark and cleaved the coconuts in two before becoming embedded in the soft ground.

The harpoon throwers pulled on the slack and appeared to hold tight onto the rope, demonstrating that the harpoon was to tether the whale to the boat and the boat followed the whale until the beast tired. The lance throwers retrieved their weapons that had been ceremoniously discharged and stood with their lances at the ready for when the whale was subdued and close enough to use the lance to pierce the whale's exterior and penetrate its lungs and heart to bring about the kill. It was not a job for the faint of heart, but in the well-documented annals of the hunt, both the hunter and the hunted entered the contest on an equal footing. Neither would be aware of the eventual outcome. Whale boat crews had been beaten to death by the giant flukes of an angry whale feeling the prick of the dart and flailing about with its giant tail flukes, thrashing the water in a blind rage at its tormentors and many a whale had lived a life with harpoon irons rusting in their flesh. Signs of battles past remained, where they had been pursued but won the contest leaving the dead, dying and wounded crews from the commercial factory ships who eventually became so well equipped that the scales of a fair competition became tilted. They were using loaded dice and hunted the whale to near extinction. Aboriginal whalers hunted for the table. Their hunt was the same as a plains Indians hunting for buffalo or a Zulu warrior taking a lion. For the adolescent men it would be their rite of passage into the adult world. Kill or be killed; hunt or starve. It was the call of the wild.

Reluctantly, Maree and the crew of the *Koto Maru No 2* said their farewells. Everybody had a good time and everybody was enriched from the interchange of culture and customs that had prevailed upon both hosts and guests for the past twenty four hours. When the sun came up, the vessel had weighed anchor and sailed for Japan. It was the end of another long whaling season for the crew who were now keen to get back to their homeland and their loved ones and to recharge their batteries for the next season that would come upon them all too soon.

Maree was inundated by requests from crew members for recipes of the delightful food that they had been offered on the island. Tongans ate a lot of seafood, as did the Japanese, but they both prepared it differently and with different ingredients and so it was good to find new ways of preparing and eating the same produce. All of the ship's complement that she had talked with following the visit to Vavai wanted the same recipe. It was for a dish that was made with raw fish and it had coconut milk in it. After much discussion, Maree figured that they were talking about the Tongan national dish which was called ota pusi.

"Okay," Maree said, "I can make this for you, or I can give the recipe to the ship's cooks who can make it for our farewell night on board. 'Ota ika'," she explained, "is raw fish that we marinate in a citrus juice like lime or lemon then, when the outside of the fish is opaque, we add coconut milk and some diced vegetables, we can use cucumber, tomato, onion and some spicy peppers."

Maree went onto explain.

"The word ota means raw and ika is fish. If we use eel for the fish, we call it oka pusi."

The night before the ship made landfall on the northern Japanese island of Honshu, the ship held a farewell party in the main lounge. Everybody got into the spirit of the occasion and Captain Kyoto gave a speech in Japanese that Ken translated for her. He made particular reference to Maree and her family and the wonderful welcome that the island of Vavai had bestowed upon the ship's company and he vowed to return for another visit following their research work in the same area next year, Nakamoto Scientific agreeing, of course. Ken and Maree danced to the jukebox and mixed with their shipmates, saying farewell and wishing each other the best until they met again, hopefully next season when the ship would again head south into Antarctic waters for the minke whale kill and then back up to the Tongan Archipelago to continue their research work with the humpbacks.

Ken asked a question that had been dogging him since their island visit.

"I keep hearing references to the king, the commoner and the whale's teeth," he said. "It seems to be folklore around Vavai. Do you have any idea as to the origins of this anecdote?" he asked.

"It concerns a beached and dead sperm whale and the teeth from that whale." Maree replied

"Tell me," Ken invited, "I need to know."

"A tale of lése majesté no less – here goes." Maree launched into the story.

"King Finau Ulukalala is your man," Maree said, "and as you know, sperm whales' teeth are highly prized in Tongan society. This was before Tongans became whale hunters and the only way they came by these prized gems was when a dead sperm whale was washed up on an atoll. Word got around that such an event had occurred on a small isle occupied by a man and his wife. King Finau had gone there to claim the teeth, as was his right, but when he arrived the teeth had been extracted from the whale's jaw. The male occupant of the isle was questioned about this and he immediately went to his fale and extracted a basket from within the thatch of his dwelling. The basket, however, contained only two teeth. The man suspected that his wife had taken the remaining teeth and hidden them, but she denied this when questioned about it. In his defence, the commoner said that he would not have taken them because as a commoner he had no right to them and if he did have them someone would eventually find out and they would be confiscated by the first chief who came

281

across them. They were not negotiable in the hands of anyone other than the king. Eventually, the king decided that he would jog the wife's memory when he ordered her husband's brains to be bashed out of his skull, in front of his wife who remained stoic and it was not until the club was raised against his head that she led the king to another hiding place where she produced one more tooth. This was an outrage, a violation against the dignity of a reigning sovereign. King Finau was so offended by this lesé majesté that he ordered her to be clubbed to death immediately. Some years later the teeth were discovered by a Tohunga who divined the spot where they had been buried."

"Rather drastic measures," Ken said, grimacing at the thought of bashed in skulls.

"Maybe," Maree said, "but you have to remember that King Finau was acting upon the laws of a society in which he lived and so his actions were legal and natural. Whales' teeth were the exclusive property of the aristocracy and for a commoner to keep them was theft and theft was punishable by death. So now you know!" Maree concluded. "Our monarch is held in high esteem."

Ken and Maree had decided that they would take leave when the vessel docked in Japan. Ken said that Maree could live at his house where his parents lived. It was a big house by Japanese standards and naturally, she had her own bedroom.

"I will show you some of Japan, it is very beautiful," he said. "You will like it. I want to go to Tokyo too. The big city where you can buy anything you like. If it is not available in Tokyo," Ken said, "then it is not available in the world!"

"Really?"

"Yes really!"

"I cannot imagine what I would want," Maree said. "I have everything now. All of my prayers are answered, surely. Maybe I could buy something exotic for my Aunty Kaetrin and Great Aunt Flora. They have been really good to me these past few years when I stayed with them to do my studies."

"Well you have a while to come up with something, we have three months' leave before we are back on the ship and heading down to the Antarctic again. Gosh, you will like that. It really is indescribable. The Southern Ocean. Playing hide and seek with Greenpeace. The planet do-gooders."

"Will we stop at Wellington on the way down or on the way back?" Maree asked.

"Normally on the way back, why?"

"No reason, just a question."

The night was moving on, as was the ship, sliding easily through the northern Pacific Ocean swell and toward their landfall and home port in Hachinohe on Northern Honshu. Their ETA was 0700 hours and Ken said that they would be alongside and tied up by 0800 hours then customs and immigration would board the ship and when all of the paperwork was stamped and declared in order they would be allowed to go ashore.

"I have stood on your home soil, now it is your turn to stand on mine!"

"When you put it like that, it sounds exciting!" Maree replied.

Chapter 18

Genetics and DNA

By the mid-eighties the scientific world had determined a fool-proof system of testing for paternal or sibling DNA to ascertain the correct biological connection between people. Previously, there had been a system of doing this, but it was not fool-proof. Kaetrin was determined that they not get involved in a procedure that might bring them initial joy but subsequent grief and so they delayed their testing until the scientific world was able to deliver absolute proof. This was determined by Richard Van Oldenbarneveldt, who was acting for scientific institutions with a pecuniary interest in patent rights for the procedures involved,

"If they are going for a patent," Richard said, "and they are, you can be sure that they have nailed it!"

As was anticipated, albeit with a little apprehension, the results would confirm what their hearts had already decided some time ago and great joy was celebrated among the MacLeod clan starting with Muriel, Flora and James Peroux, Linus and Kaetrin Levin, Robert and Tia MacLeod, and close family friends such as Marjory Beresford-Amble and Leslie, Bravo and Georgia Thornton.

Flora requested a formal gathering be held at Maximes with the guest of honour attending, having been flown in by Bravo and Georgia in a flight that would coincide with Art 1 Trust business in the immediate or close area. Linus was always able to throw urgent conferences as and when required. This occasion was no exception.

Mahmoud had become a favourite of Muriel's during his sojourn at the hospital. They had stabilised him and he went home to his Mayfair apartment to recuperate as best he could given the circumstances and the uncertainties associated with the new disease. She would have liked him to make the trip with her to New Zealand and he was keen to come but he was really in a fragile condition and prone to the ravishes of infections. He had not been able to travel home to Egypt on a commercial flight but with the Lear Jet dropping an Art 1 Trust executive off at Cairo for talks with the Kaiser and von Hapsberg gallery it was just possible he could be transported there en route to New Zealand with Muriel. They could collect him on the return trip as the plane had to come back for the Art 1 Trust executive.

Mahmoud's condition was not disclosed to his family. It was too complicated and would cause no end of discussion and innuendo. His father was on his last legs and Mahmoud didn't want to be the reason that Abdul finally shuffled off to the family vault.

Muriel had no idea of the wealth her newfound sister had at her disposal, so when Kaetrin had informed her that she would be travelling by private company jet and via Cairo as well, Muriel wondered what she had fallen into.

Bravo collected Muriel from her flat in Paddington on the way to the airport and with Georgia they went to Heathrow where they collected Mahmoud, Lalita his pretty Indian hijra and one of his eunuchs. It was the one that they called Oman, Yousef was left in London to help Gregory at Mahmoud's Mayfair apartment. The party took off for Amsterdam to collect their Art 1 Trust executive and then settled in for the long haul to Cairo.

Mahmoud was carrying his cocktail cabinet of drugs prescribed for his condition by the doctors at Saint Marys Hospital. On the flight, Muriel went over the drug list with Mahmoud and ensured that he was conversant with his dosages and timings, which he was, as he had been on the drugs in one form or another for some time now. The drug ritual was important for their absorption, metabolism and subsequent effectiveness and although Lalita was still struggling with her English, she had become proficient in the administration of the medicine and helped oversee Mahmoud's daily dosage, as prescribed.

The plane was on the ground for two hours at Cairo while they refuelled and the passengers who were alighting there went through customs and then the flight was on its way to Wellington.

Flora had arranged a grand welcome for her second and youngest niece. She had been shown photographs that Kaetrin had taken and also from Muriel's photo album. Doppelganger was a new word to Flora and she had looked it up in her dictionary so was prepared for her first encounter with the newest and youngest member of her late brother's children. Franz-Josef had telexed Kaetrin from Cairo to say that they had pinched another German word, "It literally means 'double-walker'," he said.

Robert and Tia MacLeod had flown in from Tonga which was a bonus for Maree as her parents rarely visited because their time was consumed with island affairs.

Marjory Beresford-Amble was on the organising committee and the official family welcome home party would be held at Marjorees on the first floor at Maximes Hotel. So as not to disappoint patrons, they had selected a Sunday for the event, as that was a day which attracted less casual activity than any other. Those that had already booked for tea at Marjorees were advised that the establishment was booked for a private function and they were offered another booking free of charge on the establishment.

The stage was set for a family gathering that had no parallel in the history of anybody who would be attending the celebration. A family reunion is one thing, but in a manner of speaking it was a union and not a reunion. They were gathering to welcome a long lost member, a person that did exist but whom nobody had ever had any inkling had ever existed. It was a most unusual situation, but it was a celebration, and Flora was determined to ensure that everybody present would cherish the experience for life.

Bravo had a part to play too. His instructions were to deliver Muriel, Georgia and himself on the ground at Wellington Airport at noon. Not jet lagged and requiring sleep, but fresh and ready to attend a party, to celebrate the arrival of a new member among them. Bravo had it planned and that included a twenty four hour stopover in Singapore. Bravo and Georgia would take turns in one of the flat beds in the cabin and Muriel had the double berther at all times.

On the day, Flora went over the proceedings with Marjory to ensure that it would run 'as smooth as a well-oiled Gatling gun.'

"Horace's saying," Marjory said wistfully with the hint of a tear in her eye. Horace had been gone a year and her feelings were still very tender for her late, dear husband.

Almost on the stroke of the clock and as arranged, Muriel alighted from the taxi outside Maximes Hotel in Lower Cuba Street. Bravo and Georgia were with her as concierges came out to collect their luggage from the boot of the cab.

Bravo led the way to the elevator car and they rode up to the first floor where the door opened onto the reception area for Marjorees, and redhead met redhead. It was a defining moment in the dynasty as eldest greeted youngest, each with an outstretched hand and then a hug and then they were enmeshed in an embrace of emotional proportions that expressed over forty years of lost love and happiness that came out in an immense welling of endearment, fuelled by a desire to have and to be held. For Muriel, it was the passion to have her own flesh and blood hold her and for Flora it was the final act of her love for a brother that she would never see again. Her long dead brother was her last relation to cherish this person, whom she was now embracing. Gathered family and friends felt the amplified emotions well up in their breasts and when they thought they would simply burst with the intense joy of the moment, the haunting melody of 'Amazing Grace' burst upon them as a piper, resplendent in full ceremonial highland dress, played that lovely air. He walked past Flora and Muriel and entered the tea rooms, with them following on. Other guests fell in behind and the piper played the entourage into Marjorees where named seating had been arranged in an intimate manner and at the conclusion of the piping an MC invited all to find their allocated place and be seated.

It is not necessary to chronicle the exact details of the following hours in Marjorees as, dear readers, you will by now be aware that Flora orchestrated the most superb soiree. Suffice it to say that the guests lingered longer than anticipated and Muriel proved that she could match Flora in her consumption of scotch whiskey.

Having a brother was a novel concept and one that Muriel was enjoying. Her and Robert got along very well indeed and she was invited to stay in Tonga at some future occasion.

James Peroux said to Flora when they were alone in their apartment, "Muriel reminds me of you in 1942. Doppelganger is a fair assessment. It's the same result every time. One looks in the mirror and sees their reflection and says, I know you but the same view in a three dimensional projection is not so easy to define. You really have to be out of your skin to recognise the other person in it!"

"The fact of the matter," Linus said, "is that Muriel looked the same as Flora did at that age but not now. Muriel now knows what she will look like at seventy four and Flora knows how she looked at forty two which is Muriel's age. I cannot say who has the better perspective!"

All too soon, it was time to return. Muriel was still a working girl and had gotten leave from the hospital for this special occasion but now she had to return. As a parting gift, Kaetrin gave Muriel a brooch that their mother had pinned onto Kaetrin's coat at Euston Station back in 1940, when her and Robert left as CORB children for their new life in the colonies.

Bravo had planned a twenty four hour stopover at Cairo as it would be a bit of a task to load Mahmoud and entourage on a runway layover. He also wanted the plane refuelled and a hydraulic light checked that had been annoying him. Nothing major, just annoying. Georgia, his co-pilot, agreed.

Muriel hurried to Mahmoud's residence and was aghast at the condition of her former patient. He had deteriorated considerably in the two weeks since they had been dropped off at Cairo.

"Why did you not contact me?" she said, scolding him. "You had all of my contact details!"

Mahmoud gave her his best Bedouin's sand storm grin, gritted teeth and lips slightly apart.

"We both know I'm not here for the long haul," he replied. "Lalita has done her best, as has my eunuch Oman. No amount of medical staff could do any more and you know that."

He was right and Muriel thought that he was wanting to die in Cairo rather than return to London. Mahmoud was, after all, an Egyptian national. As much as he had adopted western habits, he was at heart a Bedouin and it seemed to her that he would die a Bedouin and be buried as a Bedouin. The least they could do was to respect his final wishes. Despite this, Muriel rang Saint Marys Hospital in London and talked with the medical staff who confirmed her prognosis.

"Make him comfortable and let him go!" they said. "You have all of the medication to do this at your disposal."

And she did. Muriel asked Bravo to delay the flight or maybe return and collect Linus and Kaetrin. "They will want to attend Mahmoud's funeral," she said. "The hospital have given me leave to stay and see out his last days. Death is imminent. He is very weak. We think he has several cancers. His liver is shot for sure. The end is nigh!"

Mahmoud was quite lucid during his last few days; he was not falling in or out of comas, but did sleep for periods in between his wakefulness. Visitors came and went, including his immediate family. When the pain came, Muriel administered morphine and this induced coma-like trances. Lalita would sponge him and Oman was the bed-panner, although the demand for those services fell away as his appetite for food diminished until Mahmoud was taking minimal sips of fluid and then only by Lalita insisting he wet his lips. When the end came, he was sleeping in a morphine induced coma as the pain had worsened and the dosage increased. In accordance with his wishes, Mahmoud was embalmed. This work was carried out at his home. The embalmers drained his body fluids and injected embalming fluids to preserve the body from decay. They washed, dried and oiled his skin and he was swathed in linen bandages in the manner of the pharaohs of Egypt and placed in a sarcophagus for the final journey.

The final journey was revealed to the von Hapsbergs and Anna and Brigette Kaiser some two weeks before his death so that plans could be made for the transportation of the sarcophagus to his chosen resting place. Bedouin graves were often crude affairs, a shallow grave covered by a cairn of rocks and centuries of sand were often the norm but Mahmoud wanted something a little different. He had prepared a burial chamber for himself at Wadi Gin, one of his favourite Bedouin boltholes in the desert. To get there they would need fast transport and today this would be an aeroplane. The von Hapsbergs and Kaisers owned a fleet of Douglas DC3 planes that they used to seed the desert. They could be converted from a bulk carrier by inserting a passenger pod within the fuselage and Mahmoud had asked Alfred to make a couple available to transport guests and his sarcophagus to Wadi Gin. Refuelling would be necessary at Kufra. Wadi Sheri was nearby, which both the LRDG and the Kaisers and von Hapsbergs knew well from their desert trek back in 1943.

"The desert is my home," Mahmoud had said to his successors. "My spirit will be contained within the western boundary by the Atlantic Ocean, to the east by the Red Sea. To the north by the Atlas Mountains and the Mediterranean Sea and to the south by the Sudan and the valley of the Niger River. These are my boundaries and I shall roam the Sahara as a Bedouin for eternity. But if you want to talk with me you will have to come to Wadi Gin where I shall lie in the coolness of the chamber that I have built for my confinement. Do not grieve for me, for I am a Bedouin, I am a true son of the desert. My name shall be on the wind. My breath will warm you as the sun warms the rocks. And my tears will rain upon you when water is needed!"

Bravo and Georgia had collected Kaetrin and Linus and Neil and Alison Walker from New Zealand and they all had made it to Cairo in time to say their goodbyes to an old friend. Muriel was administering the drugs and said, "The end is nigh, I doubt if he will last the night." And she was right, come morning Mahmoud's spirit was wafting with the desert sands, a free spirit adrift on the sands of time.

True to Bedouin tradition, which included few words but lots of haste, Mahmoud's sarcophagus was loaded and the plane with its passengers and cargo were off to Wadi Gin. With his usual skills Mahmoud had arranged for tented accommodation at Wadi Gin and all guests were treated to the best that Mahmoud's considerable resources were capable of providing. Refreshed by sleep following a sumptuous repast the previous night, the mourners were led into the labyrinths of the cavern at Wadi Gin. They went down past the bathing sluices. It seemed that the underground passages were many and eventually came to a hand hewn cavern that contained Mahmoud's favourite yellow Jaguar and a plinth for his sarcophagus. There was a case each of scotch, gin, vodka and sherry, plus a golden salver with glasses. It seemed that he would want for nothing if indeed he ever needed anything. Mahmoud was ready for any eventuality. Some say he wrote the boy scout motto, 'be prepared', but then historians said, "No – he was not old enough!" There was not enough room in the chamber for many people other than the pallbearers and Lalita and Oman. Once they had completed their duties, other mourners could file past one by one and return to the main cavern. When everyone had filed past workmen started to seal up the chamber with bricks and mortar.

"How did the car get down there?" was the question on everyone's mind.

"It was dismantled and reassembled," came the response supplied by the local headman, whose team had carried out the instructions as given to him by Mahmoud's lawyers. They were handsomely rewarded for their efforts.

The von Hapsbergs and Kaisers dallied at the sluice gates where many years previously they had taken cool welcoming baths following their long camel ride in from the road. Such memories are not easily erased. Otto was not here to exchange experiences with Alfred but all the ladies were here and they had a grand old time memorialising a most pleasant event.

The job being completed, there was now nothing left other than to depart for Kufra which was to be a refuelling stop and an overnight stay. Again all victualling and accommodation would be from the generous hand of the late Mahmoud. This time, assembled guests would be able to linger over toasts and eulogies that could take them through the night, thus replicating one of his Mayfair soirees.

Anna Kaiser was heard to comment, "You know," she said to Neil Walker, "back in 1943 as we finished our trek on camel, I think it was at Mut el-Kharab oasis, my comment was, the next time I cross a desert it will be in an aeroplane!"

"Well Anna," Neil said, "I have to say I do recall you saying that, most emphatically, it was after all one helluva journey. We have a lot to thank Mahmoud for on that occasion."

288

"I agree!" Alfred said, "He was our guiding light and knew all of the ancient Bedouin tracks. May he rest in peace."

Chapter 19

The Foxtrot Boat

"Foxtrot class Russian submarines were made for domestic and export consumption. There were a lot of them made. They are easy boats to run, similar to the German U-boats, of WWII era. The Russians based the design of their post-WWII diesel subs from captured U-boats which they cut up and examined in great detail and replicated with improvements. Foxtrots are now available on the open market at a reasonable price and for us I think it is the best choice."

Linus looked at the brown Tongan faces and the stand-out pale face of Kaetrin's brother.

"This is how we would operate the system," he went on. "We operate the whale catcher from the sub. The whale catcher will be an inflatable type boat like a Zodiac with a powerful outboard motor mounted on the transom. Both items can be stored in the sub, the boat can be tied down on the deck and we can take the outboard into the sub via the forward hatch which is large enough to load torpedoes so we will have no problems getting it through the hatch. We can store this plus any other equipment needed in the forward torpedo room.

"When we catch and kill a whale we can float it onto the deck at the rear of the conning tower and tie it down onto the deck, remember the deck is the outer hull and not the pressure hull, so we have the ability to weld holding down lugs to the deck and we can use standard transport system tie downs to secure the catch. With the whale secured we can dive the boat and proceed to our rendezvous with the mothership, surface the sub and release the whale to the factory ships on board hoisting mechanism."

"Sounds too easy."

Linus looked at the speaker, it was Kaetrin's brother, Robert.

"It's the way of it," Linus said, "most good plans are simple, executing them maybe something else but I feel we can train crew for that. Crew from

290

here, from this island. We will need to retain some of the sub's trained personnel however."

"Russians?"

"Yes Robert, Russians. I would think that we need to retain the captain, engineer, a planesman and at least one trained warrant officer for each of the watertight compartments. There are certain protocols when diving and surfacing the boat so we would need to retain a full complement of the men needed to carry out these procedures and they can train our guys. After the first season we can dispense with them, but we would still need to retain the skipper and engineer. They are essential.

"We need to recruit suitable men from this island who are comfortable with the idea of working on a submarine. If you are at all susceptible to even mild claustrophobia, please do not apply. Once submerged we cannot resurface because someone has developed an attack. If you are keen, please talk to me after this meeting. As an ex-submariner during WWII, I can explain these marvellous machines to you and the features that are probably misunderstood. They are as safe as any other waterborne craft and maybe safer than most because of the additional features that have been built into them, over the years. I will be looking for about twenty applicants.

"Now, carrying on – our deck and whale catcher crew will wear wet suits at all times to protect them from the elements. As you can imagine, in order to float the whale onto the deck of the sub we will have to partially submerge the sub to carry out this procedure. I propose that we have deck crew in wet suits and the whale chaser crew carry out this procedure which we have yet to develop. Once on the deck and suitably lashed down, we raise the sub to normal surface flotation level and open the forward hatch and store gear as discussed. All whale transfer operations will be carried out at night to avoid detection. The last thing we need is to attract attention to our covert operation – it has to remain secretive for obvious reasons.

"Our main prey is the humpback. Japan want about 18 units from us each season. And then maybe a couple of sperm whales at the end of the humpback catch. There is an estimated population of fifteen thousand humpback whales worldwide and, although an endangered species, they are increasing in numbers. The females are slightly larger in size than the males. We will take only males, as the females will be suckling calves. You can expect the average male to be about 15 meters long and weigh between 30 to 40 tons. Nominal swim speed is 3–9 MPH, but they can sustain 16 MPH for short bursts. When spouting, you will see two vertical wispy sprays about 3–4 meters above the surface of the water. Spout intervals are 30–60 seconds following a deep dive. But more about this later. Our seasoned whalers from years gone by will be able to describe whale seascapes to you in infinite detail.

"Now, if we can agree that the proposal is a viable option I can get my guys in London to work on a deal to buy a Foxtrot, which my trust will finance and repayments can be made from the whales that you are able to kill and sell to Nakomoto Scientific."

Those assembled all nodded in agreement and Robert, who was the Talking Chief and therefore their spokesman said, "We are keen to get this project underway as soon as possible, the next season is still six months away so we do not have a lot of time, but enough to get there – just."

"Is the sperm whale larger than the humpback?"

Linus looked up from his paper work at the questioner, a young Tongan man from the island named Sione.

"Good question, Sione. Sorry I forgot to mention Moby Dick." Linus used the name of the most famous sperm whale of them all.

"Now let me see..." he sorted through the papers on the desk in front of him, picking up a paper with the required details.

"Okay, the sperm whale is sixty feet in length will weigh up to fifty tons and can sustain a surface speed for short bursts of 23 MPH. Stories abound from old whalers about being taken on a Nantucket sleigh ride by a harpooned sperm whale. They say that the old flimsy wooden boats used by the whalers back then would break apart from the rigours of such a journey, leaving the hapless whalers floundering among the wreckage in some cases many miles away from their mothership. The mortality rate was high among whalemen back then."

"Big sperm whales are dangerous"

Linus looked at the author of this statement, an older Tongan man with a toothy smile revealing gaps in his dental arrangement and part of one leg missing.

It was Homeguard, one of the old whalers who had been a harpooner back in the day when Tongans killed whales for meat and oil.

"Did you catch sperm whales?" Linus asked.

Homeguard shook his head. "Not many, maybe two or three smaller ones a year, mainly for teeth and bone. The meat is too black – no good to eat. The big sperm whales are too dangerous. We catch the humpback whale, much easier."

Homeguard continued. "Whale meat was very popular because meat was scarce in the Tongan diet. We caught about twenty humpback whales a year, sometimes more, sometimes less, but you were always glad to have whale meat cooking in your umu and the oil makes a good light when burning in your lamps." He smiled as his sensory memory returned the smells from the cooking meat and the burning lamps.

"The skin was deep fried as crackling, like the pig," he recalled with his wrinkled brown skinned face wreathed in a display of memorised pleasure, ghosting back from his past.

Linus let him finish and continued with his outline for the plan to buy a suitable boat.

"We will need a minimum of twelve men to learn to run the boat and they will be in on the delivery voyage, which I assume will be from Vladivostok to here – a short hop across the pacific. There will be two engineer understudies, an electrician, a cook, at least seven seamen and a navigator, this will comprise the delivery voyage crew. While that is being done, we need the whale catcher crew to undergo some form of training here under the guidance of some of the old hands who operated the catchers when Tonga was carrying out legal whaling. This is where you come in, Homeguard; I want you to assemble a boat crew and start training them in the finer points of catching whales. We will not be using hand thrown harpoons, but bomb lances fired from special handheld devices like a firearm. It is important to remember to recruit only men from this island and to maintain strict secrecy. I have ordered two Zodiacs with outboards. They should be here within the week, next supply boat from Nukualofa. Once the boat crews are finalised we can order wet suits to fit the men selected.

"Okay, well then, that concludes the meeting – I'll let you know as soon as I get word from my contacts in London that they have closed a deal on a suitable boat."

He checked himself and continued, "There is just one other thing."

"Is there any place that we can moor the boat undercover, like away from prying eyes, or will it have to stay at sea continually during its time here, which may only be six weeks or however long it takes to catch our quota?"

He got blank stares.

"And another," Linus remembered, "refuelling, we may have to refuel."

Robert said, "Maybe we take on bunkers from the factory ship if at all needed. I read from the blurb that you have given us on the Foxtrot boats that they have enough fuel to do twenty thousand nautical miles, surfaced at eight knots. When submerged we run on batteries, of course, so the diesel fuel is conserved. So let's say we travel five thousand nautical miles to get here and return to Vladivostok at the end of the season and that leaves ten thousand miles to travel during the season here, so at a guess we have heaps of fuel and should not need to take on any bunkers."

"Okay, I'll leave that one with you – it's an option but not a necessity."

"Homeguard," Linus called the old whaleman's name out.

"Yes, boss," Homeguard responded.

"Do you understand what is required from you about training potential whalers? Do you think you can do that?"

Homeguard despatched a toothy grin. "Yes boss, I still have some lances too, as you know but so do most of our old whaling crews. We all keep our lances and harpoons."

"Yeah, maybe, but we will be using bomb lances and other modern devices. It would certainly be beneficial to learn about hand thrown lances, especially the etiquette needed to operate a small boat in close proximity to the prey. I imagine that it could be extremely foolhardy to place your boat in a compromising position, especially if you are having to deal with a mortally wounded beast."

"Yes, boss, for sure." Homeguard pointed at the stump of his leg. "I learned the hard way."

"Yes, you sure did, but I hear that you can still throw a harpoon as good as the next man. You can be the Talking Chief for the whalemen. They respect you and your knowledge."

"Yes boss, you leave that to me, I will give you trained men to be proud of."

Linus called the meeting to a close and said, "We will have a big meeting when the gear arrives, I must impress on you all that the success of the entire operation depends on secrecy. You are sworn to say nothing about this discussion to anyone. Do I make myself clear?"

Everybody nodded solemnly and left the fale.

Chapter 20

Diving

Linus handed out the printed and laminated cards that he had made for each of the Tongan crew members.

"Read and memorise these procedures," he instructed. "This is how the boat will be submerged and surfaced."

The cards were written up as follows in large black print:

The following commands are issued by the duty officer to submerge the boat.

"Prepare to dive."

*discharge sewage

*dump all refuse

*stop diesel engines

*close snorkel [air intake for diesels]

*close diesel exhaust valve

At this stage the duty sailor in each compartment must report to the duty officer that they are ready to dive.

*sound dive alarm.

"Dive."

*The captain comes down from the fin and seals the outside hatch

"Dive to 40 meters, 5 degree trim on bow, course 90 degrees, up periscope."

*this order is a precursor to the next several commands and indicates the final position of the boat when dived. The periscope is raised so the captain can monitor surface traffic as the boat dives.

"Port and starboard motors slow ahead."

*The port and starboard electric motors are engaged at slow ahead speed. At this stage the boat is still on the surface.

"Open Kingston valves bow and stern group ballast tanks."

*The Foxtrot has ten ballast tanks divided into three groups. The bow and stern groups comprises tank numbers 1–4 and 7–10. The Kingston valve is located at the bottom of the tank and allows seawater to enter which causes the boat to submerge.

"Open ventilation valve bow and stern group ballast tanks."

*Ballast tanks are filled with air when the boat is surfaced and this air must be allowed to escape through the ventilation valves before any water will enter through the Kingston valve. With the bow and the stern group of ballast tanks flooded the submarine is partially submerged with only the fin visible above the water.

"Open Kingston valve middle group ballast tanks."

*as above for the middle group tanks 5 & 6.

"Open ventilation valve middle group ballast tanks."

*with all ballast tanks flooded the boat is now fully submerged.

"Extend forward diving planes."

*the retractable diving planes located in the bow are extended.

"Depth ten meters."

*The duty officer is now advising the crew that the boat has submerged to ten meters. Crew members must now check their respective compartments to ensure that the boat is secure for diving. i.e. no water leaks, etc. The duty sailor in each compartment must report back.

"Down periscope."

"Down all masts."

*all other masts on the fin are retracted – antennae, aerials, radar, ESM etc.

"Submarine dive to forty meters."

*the boat will continue to descend to forty meters.

"Depth forty meters, course ninety degrees, trim one degree to bow, pitch zero degrees."

*the submarine has reached the desired depth. The duty officer informs the crew of the condition and depth of the boat.

"Close ventilation valves all ballast tanks."

*the ventilation valves are closed in all ballast tanks. In order for the boat to surface, compressed air is forced into the ballast tanks to flush out the water making the boat more buoyant. The valves must be closed or the compressed air will escape as fast as it is fed in.

*The submarine will alter its depth underwater by using the bow and stern diving planes. The ballast tanks are only used to obtain positive buoyancy to bring the boat to the surface and negative buoyancy to sink the boat.

Surfacing the Submarine

"Submarine surface, ten meters, trim five degree stern."

"Port and starboard motors half ahead."

"Acoustic report on surface traffic."

"Bubble high pressure air through middle group ballast tanks."

*In peacetime, air bubbles to the surface at a depth of 30 meters, 20 meters and 10 meters. This safety measure alerts any surface traffic that the boat is about to surface.

"Prepare quick dive Kingston valve."

*The quick dive Kingston valve is operated by a large lever in the control centre. When engaged, it quickly dives the boat, in case there were danger on the surface.

"Up periscope." [a depth of 10 meters]

*At this point the captain will climb up into the conning tower where the scopes are situated on a mezzanine decked area, and survey the surface visually for any traffic in the area: if clear he will relay the order to the duty officer to surface the boat.

"Blow middle group ballast tanks."

*Compressed air is used to blow all water out of ballast tanks five and six. At this stage the fin of the sub projects above the water.

"Prepare starboard side diesel engine to blow bow and stern group ballast tanks."

*Once the fin of the submarine is above the surface, the diesel engines can be started and the exhaust gasses from these used instead of compressed air, to blow the water from the remaining ballast tanks. Compressed air is one of the most precious commodities on board the submarine. Because the pressure required to blow the ballast tanks when the vessel is close to the surface is considerably less than when the boat is at depth, the exhaust gasses are sufficient for the task.

"Retract forward diving planes."

"Start starboard side diesel engine."

"Blow bow and stern group ballast tanks with exhaust gases."

*Exhaust from the diesel engine is now used to blow the water from these ballast tanks. At this point the submarine has positive buoyancy and is fully surfaced.

"Close ventilation valves all ballast tanks."

"Open Kingston valves all ballast tanks."

*When closed, the Kingston valves keep the seawater from entering the ballast tanks. When the boat needs to dive these are opened. With the ventilation valves closed and the Kingston valves open, the boat can be quickly submerged by opening the ventilation valves.

"Duty officer on the bridge."

*Once the boat has surfaced the duty officer will always be on the bridge. One of his first duties will be to observe that air bubbles have been sighted coming from the Kingston valves indicating that the ballast tanks are empty. The duty officer and duty sailor will keep an eye out for any surface or air traffic.

"Prepare starboard side diesel engine to power the main propulsion motor."

*This command indicates that the starboard diesel engine will be used to power both the port and starboard propellers.

297

"Course 130 degrees, boat speed half ahead."

Linus read through the card with them and said, "You are to memorise these instructions and also the following Russian words that the captain may use in his crew instructions:

"Dive: Pogruganye.

"Surface: Vspletye.

"Up periscope: Podnyat periscope.

"Down periscope: Opustit periscope.

"Quick dive: Srochnoiya pogruganye.

"Full speed ahead: Polney vperyod.

"By the time you board the submarine these will be etched in your memory forever. Understood?"

Everybody nodded solemnly, in agreement.

"Any news from your London agents on a suitable boat?"

Linus looked up from his card and at the questioner, Sione.

"Nothing confirmed, Sione," he said, "nothing confirmed, but I understand that they have been looking at a boat that is based at the Pacific Fleet's port of Vladivostok. I guess all will be revealed at the appropriate time, so we must be ready to move when requested. We have a few weeks to prepare the boat for the coming season and I would suggest that we will need all of that time. If it is Vladivostok that we need to go to then I have arranged for a chartered plane to take us on a direct flight rather than mess about with commercial airlines and their timetables whereby we would be in transit for days – who knows how many days – far too many, anyway.

"There will be a bit of dockside work to be done so that we can tie the cargo onto the outer skin of the boat, not the pressure hull, the outer skin – that's the bits that you walk on. Also we will do some shake down cruises before we depart for Tonga. We will need to get some of the wrinkles ironed out of our technique before we tackle the blue water stuff."

Robert had selected a crew of fifteen islanders including himself. The whale chaser boatmen would not join the submarine until it arrived in Tongan waters. They would be mere passengers in the sub. Their role was to catch whale and deliver them to the sub and subsequently the mothership. They had other skills to hone up on and Homeguard had them drilling on the water daily with the inflatables. He was teaching them how to come up onto the whale, and how to avoid the thrashing whale flukes which could be fatal if they were on the receiving end of an angry thrashing wounded beast.

Chapter 21

Season 1

The Barnevelts London office, on behalf of the Art 1 Trust, had negotiated a deal to purchase a Foxtrot class submarine from the Russian authorities. This had not been easy due to the Russians' traditional distrust of the west. But hard foreign cash was also needed to keep the Russian economy afloat and the Kremlin had recognised since Perestroika and Glasnost that while still adhering to socialism, capitalist principals must sometimes be invoked. And so, the selling off of selected redundant military hardware was proving to be an economic winner. Firstly, the military equipment sold to the west had to be rendered benign. And any subsequent deal scrutinized and agreed upon after serious and rigorous examination of the principals of the purchasers. In the case of the Art 1 Trust, the purchase was intended for marine research. And nobody questioned that!

Independently and privately, former Russian naval personnel were recruited for training and delivery services and there were many agencies operating from Russia, to supply such personnel, under the new cloak of private enterprise.

Linus had talked with the recruitment agency and it had been decided following consultation with the Russian captain appointed for the task, that a minimum of eleven crew members would be needed assisted by a similar number of personnel supplied by the buyer for the delivery voyage and ongoing training for the first six months, which was sufficient time to cover the first season of whaling in Tongan waters. Following the completion of the first season, the submarine was to return to Vladivostok for dry docking and any repairs needed before starting out on the following season. It was a costly business but the sums had been done and the ledgers finely tuned to show a handsome profit after two seasons whaling in Tongan waters.

The Russians wore name tags on their tee-shirts and a description of their job and location of the station that they were to occupy during any ascent or descent of the submarine. There were seven compartments and it was a requirement that each was to be manned by a duty sailor who would report to the control room, that their compartment was secure for diving, that is to say, no water leaks, or any other defects that would present a hazard to a submerged boat and that the watertight door to the compartment was shut and secure.

The Russian sailors in charge in the seven stations were:

Feofan, compartment number one, forward torpedo room. Able seaman.

Andrey, compartment number two, accommodation, battery spaces one and two. Electrical tech-crew.

Vadim, compartment number three, control room, periscopes and access to the conning tower hatch. Boatswain.

Milan, compartment number four, accommodation and battery spaces three and four. He was also the cook, the galley was in compartment four and the Russians wanted someone to prepare Russian food. Russian submariners ate the best food in the Russian Navy and they wanted the standard to continue. Their menu included caviar, borsch and piroschki. Goulash was also a favourite.

Bogdan, compartment number five, engine room machinery space. He was also a motorman or engine room assistant.

Vladislav, compartment number six, main electric motor controllers and motor room. He was an electrician and a former petty officer.

Kliment, pronounced Klee-ment, compartment number seven, after torpedo room and auxiliary electric motor room. The escape hatch is in this compartment. Able seaman.

There were also the specialist sailors:

Sevastyani, who was the specialist planesman. Control room compartment number three.

Lev, the sonar, radar and radio operator, who had been a petty officer. Sonar room compartment number two.

Then there were the two officers, they were the engineer, Nikita and the captain, Franko Melor. The name Melor was an acronym from Marx, Engles, Lenin, October and Revolution. His name had been created by communist parents eager to reject traditional Russian names. But contrary to the sentiments of his parents, Melor was a traditional Russian sailor. Melor enjoyed his social life as much as his professional life as a naval officer. If salt water ran through his veins then vodka displaced the water content of his body mass, which was considerable. His station was in the control room and the periscope mezzanine space, in the base of the conning tower. To access the periscopes, one had to scale a ladder from the control room and onto the mezzanine area.

Nikita the engineering officer had no particular station but was free to roam. His intimate knowledge of the boat's workings meant that he was an invaluable addition to whichever space he occupied. The engineering department was the largest department on any submarine and so with minimum staff he was doubly busy. Nikita had sailed with Melor in the Russian Navy when his status was captain third rank which was as high as an engineering officer could go. Melor, as the commanding officer and captain of a Foxtrot class diesel submarine, was a captain second rank. To become the captain of a nuclear powered or missile submarine he would need to attain captain first rank, but he was not interested in achieving any status higher than he currently held. That he said was for younger smart alecs.

Foxtrots were less glamorous than the large nuclear powered boats, but they were at least a seaman's boat and Melor was a seaman. Messing about with nuclear reactors and ballistic missiles was not his idea of having fun. Having fun was firing a torpedo and looking through the attack periscope, down range to watch his torpedo hit the target. There was nothing like the smell of a diesel boat, too. Hot engine and diesel oil smells, they seemed to penetrate every nook and cranny. Crowded quarters and smelly bodies competed with cooking aromas from the galley. Hot bunking among the crew meant that there were two crew members allocated to each bunk so while one was on duty the other slept. All up, when submerged seventy eight men shared three toilets and two showers. Personal hygiene aboard an operational boat was a challenge.

When surfaced, there was a toilet and a cold seawater shower in the fin and these were used exclusively. The crew could have as many showers as they wanted as there were no water restrictions from the large expanse of water that the boat floated upon.

Life aboard a fully operational Foxtrot boat was a challenge and a busy and smelly existence, but smells were as important as sight and sound, they indicated, as a barometer would, the atmosphere of the boat. A submariner in his environment had the honed instincts of a beast in the wild. Every sound, smell and optical observation required an equal and an opposite reaction. One lived and died on one's responses. It was the survival of the fittest. Being fit was not restricted to a muscular condition alone. The cook played a huge role in food selection in order to contain methane gas production within the body's alimentary canal, the doctor would consult with the cook on the best food combinations to keep the methane levels within the gut as low as possible. Gastric science was an art form, perhaps even a black art. But the lessons learned over the years were practiced with due diligence. Beans were banned and had been for many years.

Melor liked his men to be as fit as was practical given the cramped confines of their diesel electric boats.

Diesel boats surfaced after three days submerged at the most and then fresh air washed through the interior like air conditioning through a high rise building. Smokers could indulge their passion in the fin or on the deck casing and swimming in the ocean was allowed, given certain mitigating circumstances.

Melor contemplated these past memories as he sat in his cabin examining the crew list that had been handed to him by the recruitment company. He had the command of his own boat again and the freedom to carry out that command without any meddling from the political officer. He shuddered as he recalled the men that the ministry of defence had sent to his boat in the capacity of political officer. In the old Soviet hierarchy, the political department was similar to a Ministry of Defence official. The M.O.D. communicated the government's policies to the military and the communications started at the highest possible level with the fleet commander who was the admiral of the fleet of the Soviet Union and the commander of the political department, working together to formulate policy. Every submarine carried a political officer who could attain the office of captain third rank. He would accompany the commander of the boat when they went ashore to receive orders for the coming mission. Also he would jointly sign with the captain for all incoming and outgoing radio transmissions. Melor shuddered at the recollections. The political officer would ensure that orders were obeyed to the political structure dictated and kept the communist doctrine alive among all members of the boats compliment. In the earlier years, a political officer was second in command of the boat but for practical reasons he was subsequently relegated below the first officer due to the folly of having a novice in command of a submarine, should something happen to the boat's commander.

Melor shuddered as he remembered his last trip before his submarine was to be decommissioned. He was given a new political officer, a tyro. A newly commissioned officer, fresh from graduation as a lieutenant.

Promotions were based on merit and loyalty to the communist party and Luka demonstrated that from the moment he stepped aboard; he intended a meteoric rise through the ranks as the best communist to have ever graduated from the academy due to his enthusiasm, zeal and energy and blind devotion to the Communist Party.

The political officer was keen and ready to go to work so he insisted on coming to the boat, in the dockyard, to present himself to the captain. Melor tried to put him off as he would just get in the way of the dock workers, but Luka was eager to show his mettle. Under the captain's instructions, Luka was directed to be brought to the captain's cabin in compartment two. It was the forward-most compartment in the boat, apart from the forward torpedo room and just forward of the four berth officer's cabin where the new man would be allocated a berth.

The armourers were loading torpedoes through the forward hatch and Melor had the new political officer, directed by the shore guards, enter the boat through the after-hatch and walk the length of the submarine's interior spaces. Normally this would not be a problem if the boat were at sea, but being in the dockyard, the interior spaces were cluttered with dockyard workers carrying out repairs which meant that negotiating the various compartments was like walking through a minefield, only the mines were above ground and some of them were very dirty.

At least the kind sentries on the dockside had asked Luka to leave his seabag with them and they would have it delivered safely aboard afterwards.

No one openly admired communist party hierarchy and dock workers were no exception. Their contempt for communist party puppets, especially those with no jurisdiction in their working environment, was legendary and the tales of the unfortunate recipients of dock workers' shenanigans were manifold. The mere fact that the greenhorn had presented himself to his boat whilst undergoing dockside repairs indicated that he was indeed new at the game, as no experienced political officer would dare venture near his boat until clean linen was on his bunk and the boat was in preparedness for sea. But then, Melor had experience on his side and perhaps he was about to have some sport with the new appointee. The boat crews were not able to enjoy such luxury and by their acquiescence due to the duration of confinement, living with a bilge rat was part of the job.

Luka had his first encounter with dockside residual grime when his hands slid down the rails of the escape hatch ladder as he entered the submarine in compartment seven. This was the after torpedo room and while there were no workmen as such in the compartment there were a lot of ropes, lines and hoses snaking down through the hatch and over the deck in the compartment, carrying shore generated compressed air and electricity among other things to the various tools and lighting, employed by the repair crews, working in the machinery spaces.

Indoctrinated as he was in the communist credo, Luka had never dirtied his hands or any other part of his anatomy by undertaking menial peasant and worker activities. While all Russians were equal, Luka had devised a private communist maxim that some were more equal than others. And none were as equal as Luka.

Luka had a privileged upbringing. An only child, his parents were scientists and held down responsible jobs that attracted good incomes. They lived in a roomy and comfortable apartment, where there was always an ample supply of good food and treats and they had a dacha by the sea which was a great summer getaway. As was common with well-off Russian society, communism was embraced as it was conceived to be the reason for their success. At an early age, Luka was indoctrinated into the communist ideology and was fed a diet of privilege. The communist party rewarded the faithful and the faithful were those that had the most to lose. It was the faithful that ensured the oppressed were not equal. And must be kept as unequal as possible.

Luka looked around for something to wipe his hands on, the grime was annoying him. He saw a bundle of rags over by a ladder leading down to a machinery space under the deck he was standing on. He walked across and picked up a rag and managed to remove most of the dirt but some was ingrained into the wrinkles of his palms. It was annoying but better than before. He threw the rag onto the pile and walked toward the hatch separating compartment seven from compartment six and was accosted by an irate, "Hey you!" Luka turned. A workman had appeared standing on a ladder from the machinery space below, with a pneumatic tool that he placed on the deck beside the rags. He lifted up the piece of material that Luka had used and shook it, saying, "This is my tee-shirt mate not a fucking rag – clean it!" and he hurled the crumpled shirt at Luka.

Luka looked at it and said, "Looks like a rag to me!" and threw it back.

The dock worker recognised the insignia on Luka's uniform and smiled. "Jump snake, then comrade." He then turned toward the hatch separating the two compartments and cried out loudly, "welding fumes secure hatch." He then uncoupled the airline hose that was powering his tool and let it loose on the compartment deck. Without restriction, compressed air emerged from the hose end in a powerful jet stream causing the hose to fly about uncontrollably. It made a dull metal to metal sound as the steel end of the hose fitting made contact with the steel deck. It would cause a nasty wound if it were allowed to make contact with soft human flesh.

Luka shook his head in disbelief and said, "Crazy man," as he turned to escape through the hatch into compartment six. The hatch was about to close and Luka called to wait while he exited through it.

The dock worker closing the hatch recognised the insignia on Luka's uniform and said, "Too late, comrade." The round hatch door clanged as metal contacted metal and the heavy securing mechanisms were engaged. Luka was stuck in the compartment with a rampant snake hissing and flailing about like a stock whip, but more lethal by far. The only way out was through the escape hatch and that was close-by, however the unpredictable nature of the tortuous writhing and headless serpent had him pinned to the compartment bulkhead. His eyes widened with terror, thinking he may be struck by the malevolent reptile. When it seemed that his nemesis had retreated to the after part of the compartment, Luka made a dash for the ladder. He had halved the distance between the bulkhead and the ladder when the air hose made an unpredictable turn and came at him, hissing and thrashing. Standing erect like a cobra about to strike, the hose hissed passed his chest. Luka looked down as the hose passed by his feet and in a moment of what he considered at the time to be sheer brilliance he stood on it to restrict the movement. The head of the hose reared up and convulsed at this attempt to restrict free movement and like a mad thing with renewed energy it turned and came back. Luka was no snail and had reached the ladder and started to climb when the steel fitting at the hose end made contact with his buttocks. He was pumped too full of adrenalin to feel pain and climbed up and onto the casing of the boat, panting in short gasps with his oxygen starved lungs feeding the blood coursing through them.

He walked across the gangway connecting the boat with the dock and it was not until he was on the dock that he regained a normal breathing pattern and felt pain. There was a draught around his buttocks too and the backs of his legs felt warm. He placed his hands at the back of his pants and made contact with wet sticky skin. His fingers were covered in blood and he realised that the hose had made contact with his backside and he had sustained an injury. Luka walked over to where the sentries stood and asked them about his bag.

"It's aboard, sir."

"I thought that the forward hatch was unavailable to access the boat because the armourers were loading torpedoes?"

"True, comrade, true, but I asked them if they could place it in the first compartment at least. The hatch is closed between it and the second

304

compartment where the accommodation is and it will stay closed until the armourers open it at the completion of their duties." He continued. "May I suggest, comrade, that you take yourself over to the first aid post on the dockside?" The sentry patted his backside and pointed at Luka's midsection. "You appear to have sustained some damage and it should be taken care of immediately; dockside regulations, you understand."

By now the pain was starting to register and Luka winced as he turned.

The sentry could now see the extensive lacerations, the torn clothing revealing his entire buttock region. It was a bloody ugly mess.

"Here, comrade, cover yourself," and he gave his overcoat to Luka to protect his dignity if nothing else.

And Luka limped away toward the first aid post.

Melor had read the report that had been submitted by Luka and the sentry and he told Luka to stay away from the boat until called upon to report for duty, as was the custom when the boats were in port and under repair. Crew stayed in hostels and went on leave to special sanatoriums for submariners.

"The next time I want to see you," he told Luka, "is when we go to receive our orders from command HQ. Until then, lie low and keep your nose clean."

Melor smiled in reminiscence of the incident. He never did have any trouble from his new political officer, who had been dealt a lesson that Melor would dearly have liked to have given to previous incumbents. He wondered why he had never thought of it before. There was streak of the tyrant running through the old sea dog and he wondered if it were an age thing, perhaps even jealousy – cunning versus zeal? He couldn't say.

Melor had been retired now for five years and apart from the odd delivery voyage, he had spent his days in his dacha. Since Perestroika, dachas that were formerly a holiday home only, restricted by size from modification, were now allowed to be modified for permanent living. As an older bachelor, Melor undertook this work and enjoyed it. Almost as much as he enjoyed his vodka.

Former shipmates would come to visit and Melor was a generous host. His goulash was to die for and the samovar was bottomless, but filled with vodka, not tea. He was looking forward to the adventure ahead and wondered what sort of a motley crew the new owners would present him with.

He didn't have long to wait, because a chartered jet was already en route to Vladivostok, carrying the selected crew from the Tongan island who were to be trained to become submariners during the first voyage from Vladivostok to the Tongan Archipelago.

Melor had assembled his Russian crew and explained to them the task ahead. They would be paid good money; more than a year's salary in the navy and they would earn it for less than five months of work. Their contract was for two seasons and they were free to follow other pursuits during the off season. The main word was secrecy. "No leaks," he said. "What we do is for our eyes and ears only. You may not even realise what it is that we are doing, but I can tell you that it is not dangerous work. Your duties will be confined to within the interior of the boat. The Tongans will do all of the outside stuff, whatever that

305

may be! As in the Russian Navy, when the boat ties up you will be paid off and dock workers will take care of any repairs needed before the next season begins."

The Tongans arrived on the dockside at 0900 hours and Linus was with them. They also had the services of an interpreter. Melor and Nikita spoke passable English and it was also a prerequisite for other hands to have a reasonable command of the English language, but for the next few days when sea trials were underway they wanted to cover all contingencies.

The crew total on the operational Foxtrot Submarine was seventy eight men. The total on *Moby Dick*, as Linus had named the boat, was a mere twenty six. Everybody had a permanent bed. Hot bunking, as they called it on operational boats, was not necessary. Here aboard *Moby Dick*, the conditions could be considered luxurious. Sevastyani the planesman and Lev the sonar and radar operator were to occupy the midshipman's cabin with Vadim the Bosun and Vladislav the electrician.

"We have more room in here than a Kremlin toilet!" Lev said as he placed his seabag on his bunk of choice, "Mine, all mine – no sharing!" he continued, as a reference to hot bunking.

The Russian seamen who were on board first had selected all of the forward bunks and not without reason. There were eight single bunk cabins normally reserved for officers. The captain had his, as did the engineer. That left six, and Melor reserved one each for Linus and Robert. They were the furthest away from the diesel engines and therefore were considered quieter. There was a four berth officer's cabin in compartment number two and the top seamen took that over with the balance opting to sleep in compartment number one, which was the forward torpedo room.

The Tongan seamen had to settle for the after bunk spaces, which were above the propeller shaft and nearer to the engine room. It was considered that they were more prone to noise and vibration. But a tired, well-fed seaman could sleep anywhere. Some wag on an earlier deployment and obviously a resident in the after bunking accommodation area had written a framed citation that hung in the after bunk compartment for all residents to read. It was in Russian, but the new residents had it translated and laughed at the outcome.

"To all resident after bunkers. All complaints should be addressed to the chief engineer who is in charge of noise and vibration, sweet dreams comrades."

Once the crew was aboard and settled in, the loose ends came together extremely well, a phenomenon that had always surprised Linus. It was as if the boat cast off the mess of dock yard life when the ropes were freed from the bollards and slipped into the tide to be stowed neatly in the departing vessel. Suddenly, the boat became shipshape. Prejudices and biases were slipped with the mooring lines and energy was expended in developing an esprit de corps.

The boat had been provisioned and was fully fuelled. Creating a common menu was a problem that could be solved by having a Russian cook and a Tongan cook; rice and meat are in both diets so it was merely the manner of cooking and serving the ingredients that differed. They were breaking new ground in more ways than one and, as with most experiments, the results would be documented and improved upon.

The first experiment was to dive the boat and Linus had put his crew through a rigorous training regime so that they would at least understand the rudiments in time learn to carry out procedures alongside their Russian shipmates. Every crew member had their name and job description and compartment when diving prominently displayed on a tee-shirt especially printed for the expedition.

Melor held an exemption from compulsory pilotage and so he was able to take the boat out of the harbour under his own pilotage. A tug was required, however, to nudge them away from their berth. Melor was on the bridge in the fin with two lookouts and Linus, who was enjoying the moment after forty odd years.

And as they passed the Takanevsky Beacon, Melor sent one lookout below. It was Sevastyani the planesman getting to his station in preparation for diving. The water suddenly would go from sixty fathoms to about a thousand fathoms very quickly and Melor was keen to get the first dive under his belt with the new recruits. He announced, "Prepare to dive," to the boat crew who immediately went into action. The sound dive alarm was activated as he prepared to leave the bridge in the fin.

He called down to the control room and told Vadlim the bosun that he was leaving the fin and to steer the current course and speed in preparation for diving. He then asked Linus to go below, followed by the lookout and then Melor who ensured that the hatch was secured and then he went to the periscope flat and ordered, "Up periscope," so he could monitor any surface traffic as the boat prepared to dive.

It all seemed very well managed and amid strange calls and actions to the Tongans on their first dive they were told that the boat was submerged by their counterparts. The periscope had been retracted and the boat was at forty metres depth. It was strangely silent with the diesels shut down. The boat's propulsion and all other energy requirements were being supplied by battery power. Once the boat's integrity was confirmed the order was given to reopen the inter-compartmental watertight doors and normal life, for a submariner anyway, was restored.

Melor didn't seem at all concerned about the dive and commented to Linus that he must have put his charges through their paces in a well-managed exercise regime. "Naturally we will hone things as the voyage progresses, but for now let's get settled into the voyage. Come over to the chart table, I'm sure you'll find some interesting and familiar items there." Laid on the table was a chart onto which Melor had pencilled his course.

"Here we are now, in Peter the Great Bay, we will sail north and cross from the Sea of Japan into the Pacific Ocean via La Perouse Strait. At the top of Japan, here!" He pulled another chart off the rack and laid it on top of the existing one. "And here," he said, "is our course through the Pacific to Tonga.

I'm sure you will remember how to use a sextant. Well you can take the noon sightings to verify our position against all this modern GPS stuff we now use. I still like to back up my position with the old navigator's reckoning. We are not hiding from a real or imagined enemy so I plan to do plenty of day time runs on the surface, especially through the doldrums, the lads love to swim from the side of the boat in those conditions, unless of course you as the owner say differently!" he looked at Linus for a reply.

Linus nodded, "Yes, I don't have a problem with that so long as we meet our delivery schedule. GPS was not around in my day but I would like to see how it works. I feel like an apprentice again."

"Next stop, my cabin, I have a meeting with Nikita the engineer who will give me his usual run down once we are underway."

Melor opened a bottle of vodka and poured a generous slug for the three men who had assembled in his cabin. "To a successful voyage, gentlemen," he offered.

"Cheers," said Linus.

"Vashe zrodovye," said Nikita.

"Just as we have two sets of diving planes, one forward and one aft, we need two shots to maintain equilibrium, just like the boat," Melor said lustily as he recharged their glasses. Again they toasted and swallowed.

"My dear Linus," Melor said as they were leaving the cabin, "are you interested in taking a watch if required?"

Linus looked surprised. "Yes, I think that would be good for me after all these years."

"You know the drill!" Melor replied. "No heroics. Any problems, you call the captain."

"Yes, captain, I know the drill – you never forget it!"

"The Royal Navy trained their submariners well, yes?"

It was the first reference that Melor had made about Linus and his military background during WWII.

"Well yes, they did. We got the best training available at the time."

"So you saw active service! Did you ever get depth-charged? That must be the worst experience!" Melor said.

"Yes it is, we had a couple of close calls but we had a superb skipper – managed to get us out of a few jams. Lost a propeller once. Lucky we didn't lose the shaft as well, otherwise we would have been… well, you can imagine. I wouldn't be here now. I lost a lot of good mates. There is something about the service. It creates camaraderie beyond any other branch of all the services combined. No doubt the other services feel the same about their particular field of conflict. Near death situations create strong emotional ties."

"Cuba was the nearest thing I ever got to war!" Melor said. "I remember it well as it was my first command, a brand new boat same class as this one, we called them Project 641, NATO called them Foxtrots. It was 1962. We were raring to go had all of our pieces in place, just like a chessboard. Kruschev had a few moves up his sleeve and we had a few torpedoes with Kennedy's name on them too. A lot of sabre rattling, of course, but still serious stuff, you understand. There were five Foxtrots in the area and we all had to surface at one stage to be identified. I remember that much. The upshot was that at the end of the day, Kennedy and Kruschev installed a hotline between the Kremlin and the Whitehouse. It came too close for comfort and they say a nuclear war was avoided… just."

"I remember," Linus nodded. "I'm sure the whole world, or those old enough to understand, will remember the crisis. It lasted for thirteen days."

As Linus left the cabin he heard the cap on the vodka bottle being unscrewed and a clink of glass on glass.

Linus walked through the control room where Vadim the boatswain was on watch. He was also the assistant navigator and was qualified to take charge of a watch at sea. The planesman, Sevasyani, was instructing a Tongan seaman, Maana, in the finer points of keeping the boat on an even keel. He kept walking aft and in compartment four. Lev was in the radio and sonar room where he also slept. He had no understudy but would waken if a default setting on an alarm was activated. It seemed all was in order. Apart from a battery space beneath the main deck, compartment four also contained the midshipmen's cabin, a dry food storage room, and the most important part of the entire boat – the galley. Smells were emanating from the galley, as they always would. Men needed to be fed and the galley was always fixing something. If it wasn't cooking it was preparing. He went through to compartment five, which contained the diesel engines that were silent as the boat was submerged and running on battery power. The engine compartment was empty of personnel and he continued aft into compartment six which, among other things, contained the main electric propulsion motor controllers where he saw Robert, Nikita the chief engineer and Vladislav the electrician, a former officer in the engineering department who would have been in charge of the technical electrical crew. They were discussing the battery's propulsion life and instructing Robert in the finer points of electrical propulsion by batteries. Linus nodded his head in greeting and left them to their technical discussion as he walked past the toilet facilities and stepped through the watertight bulkhead opening and into compartment number seven. The main crew bunking arrangements were in this after compartment and various Tongan crewmen who were not engaged in boat duties were sleeping or resting on their beds. Linus nodded and continued until he reached the four after torpedo tubes that were part of the compartment and felt familiarity with these weapons of destruction. The torpedo tubes had been incapacitated by removing the firing mechanisms, before the Russian Government could agree to the sale of the boat. Standing in the compartment and looking at the four round torpedo tube doors, mounted symmetrically side by side and under and over, reminded Linus of the deadly capabilities of these silent killers and the havoc that one torpedo could wreck when the high explosive warhead was fired at and made contact with the intended target. World War Two may have ended forty five years ago, but age never eroded the sharply etched image of a doomed German freighter off the Greek coast exploding in a bright orange flash as a torpedo ripped through the inch thick steel hull plates of the hapless vessel. It was his first kill and Linus was the submarine's first lieutenant. His skipper had invited him to try his hand. When that happened you knew that they were lining you up for your first command. The flash went off in his mind, as vivid today as it was that dark night in the Mediterranean Sea many years ago. He had scanned the seascape for three hundred and sixty degrees and all was clear. He ordered down scope and then took the boat to 130 feet where they waited in total silence for ten minutes then up for another look. The freighter was on fire from stem to stern but had not sunk. There were a couple of life boats in the water so the crew would have abandoned ship and that was when the skipper said to finish her off. It was a good opportunity to complete the job. And he did. Linus wondered what on earth he was doing now at age seventy two. He was back on a submarine but on a peaceful mission; with regards to mankind, anyway. He wondered how many people his age were as silly as he was. He then altered that thought to how many would have this opportunity. Then, how many never made it this far? "I'm turning a what if into a how many," he said aloud, startled some men resting on their bunks nearby.

The intervening years had been memorable and he was glad that he had survived the wartime hostilities. Surviving life threatening incidents had put a coating over his vulnerability. It did not make him any less vulnerable, rather it transferred the emotion to inevitability. He called it sugar coating the pill of uncertainty. Linus was no hero, but he had learned how to handle adversity.

He recalled arriving at Maximes Hotel in 1946 and his first encounter with the then twenty one year old Kaetrin. Cocky, was the word that came to mind, she was cocky. Now armed with a larger vocabulary he would say 'self confident'. Linus became a permanent resident at the hotel having negotiated a favourable rate with the landlady, Flora MacLeod. Linus subsequently sold his parents' art collection and became an instant millionaire and was already a trustee and the sole beneficiary of the Art 1 Trust. In 1950 Linus and Kaetrin visited London on their honeymoon. Rudi Levin was, it had been rumoured, still alive, but Van Oldenbarnevelts position was clear about the sale and that was that Rudi Levin was deceased. He had perished in unknown circumstances while at Auschwitz, as had thousands of Jews; the Dutch Government said so. The Dutch firm of lawyers were adamant. Rudi was deceased and that was the end of the matter. The Art 1 Trust that owned the collection of artworks that Rudi had shipped out of Holland before the Germans invaded had become a valuable asset that earned the trust a handsome income. It too had investments, originally in iron, coal and shipbuilding, valuable commodities in strong demand following the immense loss to shipping during the war years. They expanded their business interests around the world. Coal mines in Australia, iron foundries in America and ship building yards in Italy, France, Britain and Spain, to name a few. When shipping started to decline they moved into aviation. Today they owned several private Lear business jets to fly their executives around the world in pursuit of their global business interests. It had become an empire that exceeded Linus' business abilities and he was embarrassed by the financial success of the operations. He became a philanthropist doing good works where he could and leaving the hard nose business decisions to highly paid executives. With his financial clout, Linus and Kaetrin, with the approval of Flora and James had the old hotel demolished and rebuilt a new tower on the valuable site. They formed a new company to manage and run the affairs of the new Maximes Hotel, which was now one of the more prominent buildings in the capital city of Wellington. It stood fourteen stories high and was constructed to the highest earthquake building standards of the day. During the three years of the demolition and construction process, Linus and Kaetrin undertook a world trip. They spent four months in Cairo with the Kaisers and two months in Vavai with Kaetrin's brother Robert and his family. Try as much as they did, there was no way that the Tongans would accept any philanthropic approaches from the Art 1 Trust. They would countenance a loan, but the loan must be repaid. If there was no way to repay, there was no loan. It was the Tongan way. Robert spent the money he received from the sale of a parcel of his shares in Maximes on the island. They upgraded the jetty, bought some new generators, renewed and expanded their refrigeration plant, added two rooms to the school house, purchased a new launch that would get them interisland transport and built a two bed hospital with a defibrillator and medical supplies for an emergency. What they really needed to open the way for tourism was a runway with lights capable of taking planes up to the larger Boeing 737 passenger jets and a hotel comprised of tourist style fales or villas. Last but by no means least, they needed a hospital where minor operations could be performed. Linus was mulling over these events that led to Maree's visit which rekindled the locals' desire to hunt the whale for commercial gain. It was one thing for the king to declare a moratorium on whale hunting as the royal family had the money to buy food where the commoners did not. What stuck in the craw was that the royal family were spending aid money, or so it had been insinuated, which had been given for agricultural aid. If the island was to prosper and break into the twentieth century, then they had to do it off their own bat and not rely on empty promises from politicians who, if not members of the royal family, were influenced by members of the royal family. The tale about the king, the commoner and the whale's teeth was ever near the surface. When Maree and Ken had sailed away following the visit to the island by the whale research ship, the islanders held some serious discussions about their future and it seemed to them that Japan was paying good money for whale meat. It certainly was not rocket science, but it became obvious that if they could sell whale meat to Japan, they could solve their economic problems and move ahead. Once established, they would cease whale hunting and consolidate their knowledge on the new tourist industry which was whale watching and swimming with dolphins.

Both Maree and Ken had returned to the island for a visit the following season where these matters were discussed and they formulated the following plan: a whale hunting industry was to be set up whereby the Tongans would kill and sell whales to the Japanese whale catchers. The mechanics of the operation were solved one night when Linus and Kaetrin were visiting and they entered into a discussion on this very matter. It was obvious that the activity would need to be covert. Linus had thought about his training with submarines and in a short time he had come up with the perfect solution.

"This is how I see it!" he had said rather excitedly, "it's an easy solution, as most are when you have the answer. First we need to get hold of a submarine!" They all looked at him as if he were mad. "We use inflatable boats as whale chasers and modern bomb lances that are humane killing devices. Once the whale is dead, we load it onto the deck of the sub and strap it down. The sub submerges and that night it rendezvouses with the whale research ship and the transfer is made under the cover of darkness. The whale meat is processed, that is to say it is cut up and sectioned, packaged and frozen and stored for later sale on the Japanese market. We repeat the process each night until the quota is reached and that's it until the next season!"

Heads nodded in agreement. "What does a sub cost?" Robert asked.

"Not sure," Linus said, "but I know that the Soviets are keen to export to get some foreign cash into their economy. I do have a loose figure of a million in my head. This would be for one of their standard design diesel boats. I would suggest say a Project 641 unit. Or Foxtrot, as NATO call them."

"Where the hell would we get a million!" Robert sounded frustrated.

"Easy," Linus replied, "I lend it to you and you pay it back when you sell your catch. By my early reckoning I say that you will pay for the sub in the first year and pay for your island improvements in the second. You would not need a third. Then you have a sub to sell as well so you are well on top!"

"I'll put it to the council," Robert said. "The plan has merit."

And so it did and here was Linus on the sub that he had purchased and was heading for Tonga. The deal was done and now they had to make it work. *Funny how staring at a set of torpedo tubes stimulates the mind,* Linus thought as he came back to reality.

Travelling through the doldrums, Melor did some daylight surface runs where he would stop the boat and those not on watch could swim in the warm Pacific Ocean. There was a shower in the fin where the crew could have endless sluices when the boat was on the surface and they would wash the interior of the boat by moving at ten knots with the hatches open, allowing fresh air to reach every nook and cranny of the submarine's internals. What a difference a sweet smelling boat makes. Then at night, they would remain surfaced and some crew even slept on deck which was highly irregular and discouraged, but the lookouts in the fin kept an eye on them. By the time the boat reached Tongan waters they had a well-trained and happy crew prepared to go to work. Linus got off and flew back to Wellington. From here on in, the business was between Robert and Ken Nakamoto.

The inflatables were strapped to the deck of the sub and the motors were taken inboard through the forward hatch into compartment number one. The drill was that when a pod was sighted through the periscope the sub would surface and the inflatable launched. With a kill completed, the sub would resurface with just the fin visible so that the inflatable crew would float their catch onto the foredeck of the sub. When in position, the boat would blow the remaining ballast and become fully surfaced. Then the inflatable crew, who wore wetsuits, would tie the catch onto the deck and then tie the inflatable to the after deck and stow away the gear in the forward compartment. The submarine would silently slide beneath the surface with its deck cargo firmly tied in place. As soon as it was dark the sub would surface and rendezvous with the mothership where the transfer was made. The system worked very well and by the time they had caught their quota it was working like clockwork. In the days allocated they had exceeded their quota and both parties were pleased with the results.

Ken Nakamoto radioed Robert and said, "Head office are very pleased with the results, but they have one last request."

"And just what might that be?" Robert asked.

"They want a sperm whale, not a large one, just any single unit will do. So the next time you see Cachelot puffing around the ocean – we want him. They have decided that this would be too good an opportunity to pass up on some serious scientific research."

There was a long silence.

"They are prepared to pay double the rate," Ken added, as if he felt a carrot needed to be offered.

"I don't know…" Robert hesitated. "I need to discuss this with Homeguard. Let you know tomorrow, okay?"

"Okay, tomorrow then," Ken said. "Talk again tomorrow. Bye."

Robert took a Zodiac ride ashore to have a discussion with Homeguard. The Zodiac returned to the submarine and Robert went to look for Homeguard who was in charge of the whalers. He wasn't hard to find, as he was always in one of two places. Homeguard was seated in the shade of a tree outside his fale. He was wistfully honing a harpoon. His old whaling irons were propped up against the wall of his fale and he regularly sat in the shade and oiled the wood and honed the steel. This to Homeguard was like playing a favourite and sentimental tune on a phonograph. He could place his mind in neutral and let the reminiscing walk him through his nostalgia.

Robert said, "They have asked us for a sperm whale!"

Homeguard stopped rubbing the oiled rag along the wooden handle. He squinted as he looked up at Robert standing just beyond the shadow of the tree.

Robert noticed his hesitancy and continued. "They said not a full blown bull; a juvenile would do."

Homeguard's prosthetic leg was standing by the door. Around the house he used a crutch; it was easier. He used the wooden leg as one might use an automobile for longer outings.

"I need to talk with them," Homeguard said. "You need to get a whale crew to me from the sub so we can go over some detail. Get volunteers, it is dangerous to take sperm whales."

313

"Okay," Robert said, "I'll have a Zodiac with crew here within the hour. Be down at the jetty in one hour." He left.

The Zodiac with the volunteer crew arrived within the hour and Homeguard could be seen dancing around on the coral sand where he had drawn the outline of a whale on the beach. He had accentuated the large lower jaw of the creature and the flukes also were larger than life. On each side of his sketch he had placed eyes and from the eyes he had detailed by radiating lines the angles of the line of site for the whale. There were clearly two blind spots, both fore and aft of the whale. It was clear that the whale had to move his entire body to change his angle of vision, it was not just a simple matter of moving the head. The head and body were one unit. In fact, the sperm whale seemed to be all head.

He was pointing out the approaches to a sperm whale. "They have blind spots to the front and to the rear," he said, "where they are unable to spot an assailant. Both ends are dangerous. The front jaw can be three or four meters long with lots of sharp teeth. The rear approach is the best for a clean shot but it is also the most dangerous, as when those huge tail flukes start thrashing you are a dead man if they contact you with a clean blow!" He was dancing about, showing them the moves that one might make in avoiding the tail flukes. "Back in the day with just the harpoon and lance the front approach was probably the best approach but today with your modern gear, you will be best to make the rear approach, but your boatman has to be very quick to control the direction of the boat to avoid the thrashing flukes." And to prove a point, Homeguard leapt out of the way of an imagined fatal fluke blow, which was no mean feat for a man with a wooden leg. Soon they were all practising on dry land what they may have to put into practice on the water and when Homeguard thought that they had the routine mastered, he let them go. "Good luck, fellas," he said as they climbed back into the Zodiac and sped out from the lagoon for a rendezvous with the submerged craft.

Homeguard went to Robert's house. Robert was spending time ashore while the sub was whale hunting in Tongan waters. "All good boss," he said to Robert, "they have learnt a lot in this season alone. Having a couple of the older whalemen in the team helps, but then so does enthusiasm. Myself will be very surprised if the job not done properly!"

"Thanks, Homeguard," Robert sounded thankful for his input. "We both know it's a dangerous job. The best we can do is lessen the odds. I'm certain you have done that."

Homeguard waved and limped away. He had done too much on his stump in a very short time and would be glad when he reached his fale and could park his wooden leg up and get round on his crutches.

The following day, the whale catchers killed a juvenile male sperm bull whale and delivered it to the factory ship that evening. The factory ship left immediately for Japan, having declared the season over and successful. Not only did they have valuable whale meat on board for the Japanese market but they also had compiled an enviable record of scientific data that could be valuable information when sold on the black market.

Having transferred the catch, Melor prepared his boat for departure the next day to Vladivostok. As soon as there was daylight, he surfaced and the two Zodiacs, with all of their crew and gear, were launched and headed off to Vavai, their work done for the year.

Melor nosed the sub out to deeper water before sounding the prepare to dive alarm. He was in the fin with Milan the lookout.

"What's that, Skipper?" Milan asked, pointing at an object several hundred yards away.

Melor scanned the seascape with his naked eye and saw a large blunt object, "Could be a shipping container," he said. "They are a bloody hazard!"

"Looks like it's moving."

"Binoculars," Melor said, "hand me the glasses."

He sighted in the glasses and Milan heard an audible, "Shit."

"What is it, Skipper?"

"It's a bloody whale, a huge bloody whale and he's heading this way!"

All seaman were aware of the story about Moby Dick and other leviathans who had sunk wooden whale boats; smashed them into splinters with their massive locomotive style blunt foreheads.

I think he intends to ram us, Melor said and sounded the 'prepare to dive' alarm. Milan crashed down the ladder and Melor followed suit after closing the hatch. "This is an emergency," he yelled to the control room crew. And in Russian he shouted, "'Srochnoiya pogruganye.' Dive. Dive, dive. We need to go down. Blow all ballast tanks. Twenty degrees on those planes. Sevastyani and full ahead all propellers." The boat deck tilted as the sharp descent began.

The submarine rocked wildly when the whale rammed it. They were still descending to ten meters and obviously so was the whale in hot pursuit. The impact was felt by all on board who had to hold onto fixed objects to stop from falling over on an already reclining deck. Melor levelled the boat at ten meters and asked the sonar operator if he could detect any signals. Obviously the whale had accelerated to attain contact speed and to come back at them again at a similar speed it would need to back off and then charge to attain damaging collision speed, accelerating as it did so. Melor asked for reports of damage from all compartments. They all reported negative damage. "No water leaks!"

He had heard the usual stories from the whalemen about sperm whales that could attain speeds of up to twenty knots for short bursts. With harpoons fixed to the whale, the boat crew would hang on for dear life as they and their flimsy clinker planked craft was towed at great speed by an enraged sperm whale. Nantucket sleigh ride, it was called. Often the small wooden craft would disintegrate under the strain of the hydraulics being applied to the flimsy planked wooden boats, used by whalers in the heydays of the industry, sending many a hapless whaler to a watery grave.

"My submarine," Melor reasoned, "is able to withstand some amazing shocks. It has a twenty two millimetre thick pressure hull and ten millimetre

315

thick outer casing." It was not so much the main hull structure that concerned Melor. Appendages were his concern. The things that stuck out from the hull, but were important for the operation of the craft as a whole. Rudder, propellers, hydroplanes... These items could easily be damaged by a rampaging bull sperm whale. He was reminded about the tales that the whalemen told during their recent sojourn on his boat. At the time they seemed harmless folklore, every industry has folklore, but now he was reminded about the aggressive whales in the whalemens' yarns. There was Timor Jack and New Zealand Tom who, or so it was said, in 1804 had destroyed nine boats before breakfast. Melville's Moby Dick became the whale that sank a ship! And then the most famous tale of them all, the sinking of the *Essex*. Now there was a gruesome tale as ever he had heard. 'But enough of that for now,' Melor said to himself, 'what do we do about this rampaging monster?'

His boat was capable of sustaining a speed of fifteen knots submerged and sixteen knots surfaced. If surfaced, he could see the whale and reasoned that by sailing away from the animal he would most likely out-run it once it had expended all of its energy in producing twenty knots for a short burst. If the whale did manage to hit him when the boat was travelling at sixteen knots and the whale at twenty knots the impact would be reduced considerably due to their relative speeds. It didn't take Melor long. "Prepare to surface," he said, 'up periscope.' He ordered as he climbed into the conning tower flat where the periscope was positioned. He wanted to survey the surface to ensure that they were in a relatively benign position with regards to the charging bull. He spun the lens through three hundred and ninety degrees and saw nothing on the surface and then there was an almighty collision that sent the boat over on its beam ends by some thirty degrees. It was severe and took a lot of the crew off guard. "Periscope down, blow all tanks," he yelled, "start port and starboard diesel engines, full ahead on all shafts!" He was on the ladder leading up to the conning tower hatch when the boat righted. As he opened the hatch, seawater poured over him but he didn't have time to wait for the scuppers to clear the water off the fin. He was standing in the fin surveying the seascape as the diesel engine exhaust fumes were scavenging the last of the water from the ballast tanks. *Just like battle conditions,* he thought to himself. *Fast and bloody furious!*

It was then that he saw the periscope, partly retracted and very bent. The whale must have hit the fin and carried on over the top when the scope was retracting. He still had his navigation periscope so the damage wasn't critical, but they would need to make some temporary repairs. He called Nikita, the chief engineer, onto the bridge to inspect the damage. Melor had posted two lookouts, Bogdan and Feofan were looking for any sightings of the rampaging bull, hell bent on destruction. Or was it revenge?

The boat had built up speed and was now doing thirteen knots and increasing. *Could be a bit of a tide running,* Melor thought, *slowing us down a bit. But, hey, if it's slowing us down it's slowing old Trumpo down.* He couldn't imagine how he came to refer to the whale as 'Trumpo'. *Must have heard it from one of the whalemens' stories,* he mused.

"Whale ahoy," Feofan shouted. "Abeam of us directly off the starboard side amidships." Melor ordered forty five degrees port helm to place the whale directly behind them. They were steaming at full speed now so it was simply a matter of seeing what the whale had in mind.

"He's a big bastard," Vadim said, "seems to have whitish streaks across the forehead. Not unlike the bow of a Foxtrot. Imagine what they were able to do to a wooden boat? Those stories that whalemen regaled us with must have been some truth to them all right. At the time I was thinking yeah right, bullshit! Not anymore!"

"We're gaining, looks like he's slowing down. Hell, he's disappeared, he's gone!"

"Sounded has he? I hear that they are very good at the disappearing trick. We will keep this course and speed up for two hours," Melor said. "Just to be sure. I've no wish to engage that monster again!"

"Vadim," Melor said to his boatswain, "you have the con. I'll be in my cabin if you need me."

Melor retired to his cabin and helped himself to a large vodka. "Mission accomplished," he toasted. "That's one for the forward planes," he said, "now to balance the boat." He poured another for the after planes. "Even keel," he said and swallowed it in one gulp.

Nikita the engineering officer made a temporary repair to the periscope but it was not operational and so they used the navigational periscope only for the return journey to Vladivostok. When the boat finally docked they could see a dent in the outer casing where the whale had rammed it. Melor took a bit of ribbing from dockyard staff about the dent. As with a dent in a car, the driver always gets the blame.

"We were rammed by a rogue bull sperm whale," he told them. "See what he did to our periscope!"

"Yeah, yeah, Skipper," they replied. "And you had a meeting with King Neptune as well." And they made a chug-a-lug sign with their cupped hands, as if drinking a glass of vodka.

Chapter 22

Season 2

Melor had received his instructions to ready the boat for the second season of the whale hunt. Linus had transmitted the funds to Melor's bank account in Russia to pay for fuel bunkers and provisioning of supplies, fresh water and victualling. Freshly laundered linen was delivered aboard and the periscope had been repaired following the encounter with an enraged sperm whale at the end of last season. Melor had made some covert adjustments of his own and had purchased a couple of items and had them loaded away from prying eyes. Nikita the chief engineer had given Melor a list of repairs that he required to be completed to make the boat fully seaworthy for their second voyage to the south seas. All those present on the first voyage had signed on for another tour of duty and they were ready to go, waiting for the Tongan crew members to arrive. The Tongan whalers would join them when the submarine reached Tongan waters. For now, the Tongan crew contingent was comprised of one man for every Russian. They were led by Robert, a marine engineer in his own right.

Melor ran his eye over the Russian crew list.

Able seamen: Feofan, compartment number 1.
Kliment, compartment number seven.
Boatswain: Vadim, compartment number three.
Cook: Milan, compartment number four.
Motorman: Bogdan, compartment number five.
Electrical crew: Andrey, compartment number two.
Electrician: Vladislav, compartment number six.
Planesman: Sevastyani, compartment number three.
Sonar and Radio: Lev, compartment number two.
Engineer: Nikita, no fixed compartment.

Then there was the captain, Franko Melor. His space when diving and surfacing was the control room which was situated in compartment number three. Other than that Melor could be found all about the boat. Probably a little odd for a submarine skipper who usually would rely on departmental specialists to report to him and become his eyes and ears, but this was not the Soviet Navy, but a commercial peacetime mission where economics dictated the logarithmic multiplier as less time and energy was applied to the input, but the downside was more errors, so one had to juggle the equation and Melor was good at juggling. Melor waited alone in the boat for his crew to arrive. He had gotten the dockside electrician to run a shore power cable so he could have heat and power to his essential electrical circuits. In an emergency, he could run on the submarine's battery power but this was not an emergency, so shore power and the amount that he would consume was a minimal cost. An empty ship is a cold, soulless steel tomb, but he had heating in his cabin, a comfortable bed with warm covers and he ran an endless samovar from which he dispensed his vodka. If he got hungry, he could cook himself a meal in the galley and for company there was always the watchman who would play a game of chess with him in the mess. Following an encounter with the large white sperm whale, last season Melor had taken to researching the subject of whaling and was currently reading *Moby Dick* by Herman Melville. Since Perestroika western books were hard to come by, although the laws had been relaxed. In the old Soviet days, Samizdat provided illegal printing of banned material and that was always available if one knew where to go. Melor settled for a copy that he had found in a used bookstore on a recent visit to Finland. It was in English and although he was reasonably proficient in the language, he found that the style and fashion of the writing was hard to fathom in some passages and he kept reading the same pages over and over to fully understand the import of the words. Russians had hunted whales for years and there was plenty of literature on the subject of Russian commercial whaling which he found rather boring. It was facts and figures. Melor was more concerned with the romancing of the whale stories from the industry's heydays and the most prolific writers seemed to be from American whaling ships that roamed the waters of the world's oceans, plying their trade and creating the legends that were as large and often as mythical as the whales themselves. But *Moby Dick*, it seemed, was immortal.

"No one has ever gotten the better of this mammalian monster." Melor paraphrased in vodka vapour breath. "No one has ever had the better of Melor Franko, Captain Second Rank."

Melor was agnostic, as were most Russians indoctrinated into the communist ideology. Older persons held the faith because that was their religion before the Marxist doctrines attempted to obliterate Christian and any other form of religious thinking. Melor had also been studying the whaling practitioners. The Americans were, it seemed, mostly Quakers. This was back in the day when commercial whaling was a profitable industry providing oils, waxes, bones and ambergris to a world that had not yet discovered petroleum products. He had further learned that a large white whale called Mocha Dick, or the White Whale of the Pacific had been sighted in 1810 near Mocha Island which lay off the coast of Chile somewhere near the 38th parallel south. Then on July 5, 1840, according to the *Detroit Free Press*, Mocha Dick destroyed two boats from the English whaler *Desmond*. They were west of Valparaiso, Mocha Dick's stomping ground. Eight weeks later, two boats from the Russian whaler *Sarepta* killed a whale and were towing the carcass back to their ship when they were attacked by Mocha Dick. The rogue whale demolished one of the whale boats and killed two men while the other boat snuck back to the mothership minus their kill. The Russian mothership stayed in the area for a few hours in the hope that it could retrieve their kill which was being guarded by Mocha Dick, but to no avail. The *Sarepta* was forced to abandon her catch, which was found floating alone a couple of days later by a Nantucket whale ship and, according to whaling custom, was able to claim the catch as their own and profit from the prize – a not uncommon practice. The next sighting of Mocha Dick was recorded off the Falklands when a huge sperm whale breached near to the English whaler *John Day*. It launched three boats to attack the whale that subsequently smashed two of the boats, killing four men. The *John Day* withdrew from the fray. The final recorded account with the large whale, if the reports were to be believed, was off the coast of Japan as the large white whale was battering a merchant vessel carrying a load of timber. The attack seemed to be from sheer malice on the whale's part when it charged the merchantman knocking off her stern. The stricken vessel had settled in the water, her scuppers awash. This was observed by three whalers standing by, they were the English *Dudley*, the American *Yankee* and the Scottish *Crieff*. The three whalers' captains were determined to put an end to the rampaging escapades from this dangerous leviathan and hatched a plan to bring about its demise. Somebody, it seemed, had forgotten to tell the whale. Each whaler lowered two boats apiece; the first boat was to be the attack boat and the second would act as a rescue craft. The *Yankee* attack boat drew the short straw and started its attack. The mate of the *Yankee* boat connected with his first harpoon throw that so enraged the white whale that it swam at a furious pace, knocking over a Scottish boat, then it took an English boat in its jaws and crunched it into wood splinters, killing two of the occupants. Those who managed to survive the crunching swam like hell to get away from the mighty flailing tail flukes, but a further two were killed when they got whacked, thus bringing the carnage to an end and leaving four whalers dead. Mocha Dick then attacked the merchantman while still attached to the *Yankee* whaleboat by the line from the harpoon. He rammed the boat so hard that it keeled over. The *Yankee* whalers had seen enough and cut the line that fastened them to the whale and started to row back to their mothership. Mocha Dick, however, had not finished and had a go at the Scottish mothership carrying away the bowsprit and jib boom. He then raced back toward the *Yankee* boat. The crew, who saw this coming had the foresight to leap from the boat and take their chances in the ocean, from where they watched on in horror as the whale took hold of their twenty eight foot boat between his massive jaws and chewed on it as easily as a cow munching grass. In August 1859 a Swedish whaler gave a report on the demise of Mocha Dick when it took a huge white sperm whale off the coast of Brazil. Although this was not the Pacific Ocean, it was assumed that the whale had transited the straits of Magellan. "Certainly not the Panama Canal," Melor had quipped as he read the story. The whale was old and exhausted and put up little resistance. It measured a hundred feet in length and the jaw was a massive twenty six feet. Further examination revealed a huge scar across the head and that it was blind in one eye. When the blubber was rendered down it revealed twenty harpoons that were contained in his flesh, medallions of battles past, carried within his super frame like war medals on a veteran's chest. Lost harpoons became like tagging is today, whereby the harpoon lodged and lost in a whale would tell whalemen, who subsequently hunted and killed the same animal, about its migratory routes as the harpoon would wear the ship's name and the private mark of its owner. Melor was sure that the whale that attacked his submarine was such a beast as Mocha Dick and he was going to come prepared for the encounter should it occur. He was fast becoming an expert on whaling folklore and was as superstitious as the whalers of old who used religion as a shield for protection in the hunt. He had noticed how the Tongan whalers always recited the paternoster before they launched the Zodiac to commence the hunt. Supplications were also offered upon their return. Melor grappled with this display of religious fervour and conceded that it had not done them any harm. Perhaps he should research this as well. Whaling was a complex business, he concluded. He came across names of other large whales who had secured their place in whale lore. There was one they called Timor Jack who supposedly destroyed every boat sent out against him. Then there was the fighting whale of New Zealand, aptly named New Zealand Tom who, it was said back in 1804, destroyed nine whaleboats before breakfast. He was, they said, distinguished by a white hump. Insanely, the whalemen risked life and limb in pursuit of these outrageously dangerous beasts, but for what purpose remained obscure, especially to Melor. A life at sea was risk enough without throwing in the thrill of the hunt, just for one's jollies!

Melor was deep into these deliberations when he heard the sound of leather on steel rungs and then voices announcing the first of his crew arriving for the second voyage to the South Seas. There came a tap on his cabin door.

"Enter," Melor said and the door opened and Nikita and Vladislav came in. They all greeted each other with lusty embraces, handshakes and shoulder slaps and Melor filled two glasses from his samovar and handed one each to his men and they toasted, "vashee zdarovye," which is the popular Russian toast: "your health!"

"That was for the forward planes," Melor said, "to keep the boat on an even keel we need to toast the after planes." He refilled the glasses and they toasted "Your health," again.

"Sit," Melor indicated the daybed, he was seated in a chair at his desk against the bulkhead. The two men sat down and Nikita asked Melor about the repairs that he had listed for the dock workers to rectify.

321

"All done," Melor handed Nikita a clipboard with the list attached. Nikita read down the list nodding at each one that had been ticked off. He handed the clipboard back. "All good, Captain, thanks, we can go to sea. I will check the boat out tomorrow and as soon as Bogdan and Robert get here we will do dockside engine trials."

"Okay," Melor replied. "We sail in five days. I have word that the Tongans are flying in here not tomorrow, but the next day; as soon as they are settled we can get underway. What did you get up to over summer?"

"Got a couple of delivery jobs, one to Cuba and the other to Indonesia, both diesel boats. The diesel fleet is selling like hot cakes at an Eskimo picnic. Went to Rasputin's on the way here. You remember Rasputin's? It was a favourite watering hole with the submarine boys around here. Well bugger me it was half empty and those that were there were all nuclear boys, not a diesel submariner in sight, except Vladislav and myself. That's where I ran into him, eh, Vlad?"

Vladislav agreed, "Yes a sight for sore eyes, a real submariner! Those atomnaya boys are up themselves, they wouldn't know what hot bunking was, living in those radioactive palaces."

Melor smiled at the rivalry which was never far below the surface between the two factions. On a diesel sub you came up for air at least every three days, not like the huge nuclear beast that left port and never surfaced for the duration of its tour of duty, sometimes months at a time. Diesel boats were cramped but the camaraderie was evident in the manner among the sailors whenever they had a run ashore together. Diesel boats were noisy, smelly and cramped. On the surface when the diesels were running there was noise and vibration but when they slipped beneath the waves and ran on battery power they were as quiet as a mouse. You got used to the hot engine oil smells and even missed them when away from the boat for a long period.

Nuclear boats were large steamships with the steam to drive their turbine machinery, which turned the propellers, being generated by heat from a nuclear reactor. There were no noxious exhaust fumes to worry about. No smells. The turbines ran all of the time with the spent steam being condensed back into water before it was reheated and vaporised into steam to do its work again. It was simply clean and efficient and so the boat was able to remain submerged at all times. They were larger, faster and roomier and every seaman had his own permanent bunk. But they stayed continually submerged, generally for the duration of their patrol, that being several months.

"So how's Cuba?" Melor asked, "my last run ashore there was twenty years ago, maybe more."

"Nothing has changed, literally, same as you remember, maybe some paint missing on a few buildings and fresh dents in those huge Detroit barges they drive, but the rum is as good as ever and the cigars are large and cheap. Bought you a box, Skipper," Nikita offered. "You'll have to go topside to smoke the things, up in the fin. I remember doing that, whenever we left Cuba the boat would be full of cigars and the men would line the decks puffing away at the things. We must have looked like a... well I don't know what, but we must

322

have looked like one anyway. I mean the boat is cigar shaped. Can you imagine. A floating, smoking rum palace."

They all smiled, nodding at the recollection. Seaman are great historians. Maritime tales are as safe as salted beef in a barrel of brine, but they last longer. With plenty of lubrication, a seaman's tongue wags freely and the stories run abound. Melor poured another round from the samovar and the men settled in their seats.

"No doubt about it," Vladimar said, "a Habana hand rolled by a top torcedor is as near to the best taste experience that one can expect from a tobacco product. In a way it seems a pity that it is so bad for you."

"Bad is good; I like bad. Vodka is bad, I like vodka!" Nikita added.

"Vodka is good, vodka is bad, reminds me of a parody about drinking alcohol, now let's see, how does it go?" Melor looked pensive as he scanned his memory banks and then his eyes lit up and he started on his poem.

"The horse and mule live thirty years
And nothing know of wine and beers.
The goat and sheep at twenty die
And never taste of scotch and rye.
The cow drinks water by the ton
And at eighteen is mostly done.
The dog at fifteen cashes in
Without the aid of rum and gin.
The cat in milk and water soaks
And then in twelve short years it croaks.
The modest sober bone dry hen
Lays eggs for nogs, then dies at ten.
All animals are strictly dry,
They sinless live and swiftly die.
But sinful, ginful rum-soaked men
Survive for three score years and ten.
And some of them, a very few
Stay pickled till they're ninety two!"

"Very good, Skipper," Nikita said, "on the strength of that we had better have a nightcap."

"I'll drink to that," Vladislav raised his glass, "good one, Captain Boris, you are a poet too, that's commendable!"

Melor looked pleased with his oratory effort and poured himself and his guests another vodka.

The three men sat in silence, then Nikita swallowed the contents of his glass and said, "I'm going to hit the sack, good night, gentlemen." He left and walked aft to his cabin.

Two days later, the boat was fully crewed. Fresh provisions were stowed away in the dry goods store which was in compartment four just abaft the galley. Bananas were a staple of the Tongans and there were plenty of those. They would use the same system as the first voyage when two cooks would prepare two menus. There would be one for the Russians and another for the Tongans. Some dishes were enjoyed by both nationalities which gave one of the cooks a rest from time to time.

Leaving port was easy, as Melor had exemption from compulsory local pilotage. He was in the fin and took the con as the boat left Vladivostok and when he got to Takanevsky Beacon he prepared the boat for their first dive of the voyage. This meant that they had to stop the diesel engines and revert to batteries for propulsive power, close the snorkel, which was the air intake for the diesels and close the diesel exhaust valve. The duty sailor in each compartment made their report that their compartment was prepared to dive and then Vadim the boatswain in compartment number three, which housed the control room, sounded the dive alarm.

Melor came down from the fin sealing the outside watertight hatch and descended to the periscope level on the mezzanine.

"Dive to ten meters," he called, "five degress trim on bow, course ninety degrees, up periscope," and it all happened. Melor smiled.

"Port and starboard motors slow ahead."

"Open Kingston valve bow and stern group ballast tanks."

"Open ventilation valve bow and stern group ballast tanks."

"Open Kingston valve middle group ballast tanks."

"Open ventilation valve middle group ballast tanks."

"Extend forward diving planes."

Melor heard Vadim call out, "Ten meters"

"Down periscope."

"Down all masts."

"Submarine dive to forty meters."

Vadim called out, "Depth forty meters, course ninety degrees, trim one degree to bow, pitch zero degrees."

"Close ventilation valves all ballast tanks."

The interdepartmental watertight doors were opened and Nikita did his check of all the compartments, chatting with the crew as he moved about the boat. Melor sat in the control room for a while then found an excuse to leave and go and check out the samovar in his cabin.

The course was set and the boat was on its way for season number two.

Routine aboard ship is quickly established and they settled down for a voyage of about twenty days. Submerged, the Foxtrot boat was capable of fifteen knots but the fuel registers were pulled back to allow a speed of twelve knots. Nikita had worked out for Melor that they could conserve several tons of fuel per day by travelling at the reduced speed. They were given a fuel allowance but in true capitalist fashion it had not taken Melor long to realise that any savings could be a bonus which at the end of the voyage he would share with Nikita. They made considerable savings on the first voyage and they were keen to do so again.

At precisely the interceding points of the International Date Line with the equator, Melor ensured that they would be at this point at noon and surfaced.

He ordered everyone on board to abandon ship by jumping into the warm tropical sea with their life jackets on. Melor was the only occupant to stay on the boat. All systems were shut down and he relayed his instructions to them through a bull horn. Following a ten minute frolic in the Pacific Ocean he called back aboard those who wanted to come aboard and said that the others could reboard as they wanted. Vadim the boatswain questioned this tactic but he had sailed with Melor for a long time and was aware of some of his erratic and irregular behaviour and did not question it other than thinking he would never have gotten away with such a stunt with a Soviet political officer aboard. The PO would have reported the incident on their return to Russia and Melor would have been relieved of his command and ordered to attend some form of reconditioning.

The crew, however, enjoyed the diversion. To the Tongans it was how things should be. The Russians considered it to be unusual and concluded that it would never be countenanced in the old Soviet Navy. They agreed that their skipper would have been despatched to Siberia for some serious soul searching sans vodka and other delights of a senior naval officer on shore leave.

A much invigorated crew continued on the journey to Tonga, now only a few days away from their destination. It was important that they stay submerged by day, surfacing only during the hours of darkness, to avoid any visual contact from local fishing boats and aircraft flying between the many islands in the Tongan archipelago. The Japanese whale research vessel was on station and had been for some time carrying out their legitimate research work. Homeguard had prepared the whale catchers and their crew and they were waiting for the signal to rendezvous with the submarine. It was a dark night when the whale catchers were launched from Vavai and motored out to the sub waiting on the surface a mile offshore from the island. With practised ease they uncoupled the hardware from the rubber boats and passed them through the hatch into the interior of the boat. The Zodiacs were strapped down onto the deck of the mothership and their crew disappeared through the open hatch and into the dimly lit yellow interior. A muffled metal to metal sound indicated that the hatch was in place and being secured from the interior. The noise of air bubbles popped on the surface water as the ballast tanks filled with seawater and the boat settled as it became negatively buoyant. It could be seen moving slowly forward and a periscope extended when the fin disappeared and then two minutes later the scope vanished leaving disturbed surface water. Beneath the glow of diffused moonlight shining through a cloud infested sky, the bioluminescence of disturbed marine organisms left a lively dance of plankton. It could have been a pretty sight if it did not seem so altogether sinister.

***

Maree took the opportunity to stay with her mother while the research vessel acted as factory ship to the submarine. It was a year since she had last visited and she had been to Japan and then south to the Antarctic where they were

325

researching minke whales and dodging Greenpeace activists. She described them to her mother as, "Crazy people with a myopic attitude toward science. They have no understanding of the principles of scientific research whatsoever. I think that they have mixed political ideology with their version of scientific principles. It seems that they have an agenda fostered by ignorance and perpetuated by their collective ability to raise money to enable a few of the favoured, to achieve a lifestyle beyond the dreams of most young people seeking adventure!" Maree, her mother Tia observed, had developed a scientist's mindset which determined that the end justified the means. But she also tempered that with her belief that the destination is reached by following the signposts marked prudence and fortitude. They were the cardinal virtues and combining these with her Christian teachings she could not see that her daughter could err. These principles were inculcated in her from the beginning, but then she did live in New Zealand while attending high school and university. Maybe some liberal thinking from a freer society was diluting her island teachings. Tia, Maree's mother, contemplated these abstracts as they prepared for church on Sunday.

Tia's parents Ata and Aba accompanied Maree and Tia to the island's Free Wesleyan Church which was well patronised as everybody on the island of Vavai attended. Singing a cappella, that is, without instrumental accompaniment, the harmonised joyous sounds of the congregation filled the wooden structure and passed through the thatched roof. The melodies travelled to kingdom come, where it was intended, by the singers, that their disembodied voices should ascend to.

The pastor surveyed his congregation, noticing the vacancies created by the whalers who were away from the island on a mission. All Tongans attended church on Sunday, no exceptions, no excuses, but Pastor Fatualofa, who was aware of the reason for their absence, knew that wherever they were, they would be observing the Sabbath in true island tradition. He had decided to conduct his sermon this Sunday on the morals and precepts of the story that is in the book of Jonah. He looked over his flock and in a clear but soft voice announced.

"The Lord is merciful and forgave his transgressors."

There was a shuffling of feet on the wooden floor as the congregation considered their recent transgressions, if any, that had caught the attention of their well-loved minister.

"Jonah ran away from the Lord," he announced dramatically.

This time, bottoms shuffled and settled on the hard wooden pews seeking a comfortable position for sitting through what sounded like a lengthy discourse. Everyone in the church, save a few younger people, had heard the story about Jonah and the whale and while many Christian denominations declared it to be no more than didactic fiction, it had a powerful message concerning mercy and forgiveness to those who would repent and believe. Jesus believed the story had happened in eighth century BC and if it were good enough for Jesus to believe, then it was good enough for the good Christians of Vavai to believe. The story was also honoured by Islam and Judaism, so the concept is not peculiar to Christianity alone.

"Repent and believe," said the pastor, "and you shall receive the Lord's mercy and forgiveness.

"The Lord asked Jonah to go to the wicked city of Ninevah and bring them God's message, but Jonah never did that, instead he booked passage on a ship going the other way. He spurned the Lord and ran away, yes, he ran away from the task that he had been asked to do by the Lord. Would you run away?"

The air in the church was still and many hand held fans were at work moving static air that was stifling the silent seated parishioners. Maree wished she could be on a ship at this moment too. 'A cold blast of Antarctic air would be heaven sent,' she fantasised.

"The Lord was angry and sent a storm to frighten the sailors on the ship who concluded after conferring among themselves that Jonah was the cause of the maelstrom. And Jonah said, 'If you throw me overboard the storm will cease!' So they threw him overboard and the waters calmed."

Tia moved the hand held fan wafting air over her neck and face, it had a cooling effect if only momentary. *Calm water is fine,* she mused, *but a bit of breeze would be nice.*

"Instead of drowning, Jonah was swallowed by a large whale which God had provided. From the stomach of that whale, Jonah repented and cried out to God in prayer. He praised God, saying, 'Salvation comes from the Lord'."

Ata was thinking about his days in the whaleboats, a dangerous occupation if ever there was one and how many a time the whale boat crew would cry out for mercy from the Lord when they were in a tricky spot. *Life is precarious enough,* he thought and he didn't fancy his chances in a whale's stomach. God knew, he had cut open enough of them to see the contents spill out. *Not a pretty sight,* Ata contemplated and eased his butt on the pew, where it was getting numb.

"And Jonah was in the whale's stomach for three days and three nights and eventually the whale vomited the reluctant prophet onto dry land. Safely delivered, Jonah obeyed God's instructions and went to Ninevah, proclaiming that the city would be destroyed in forty days unless they changed their ways."

Aba thought, *If I don't change the way I'm seated my left leg will go to sleep* and she wiggled her backside on the hard wooden bench.

"Scholars tell us that the Ninivites paid heed to Jonah's message because of his appearance. Following three days and nights in the whale's stomach the gastric acids had given him a bizarre, ghostly white appearance, his bleached skin, hair and clothing terrifying them. A truly Godly figure as you can imagine." The pastor examined his congregation for the effects from this particular piece of gruesome evidence.

Maree thought about this. She was now an old hand at examining the contents of whales' stomachs. This was, after all, one of the most factual ways of determining how the beast got its sustenance. It told them not only about the whale itself, but about the creatures that it shared its home with. Biological mapping, she called it.

"Because the Ninevites believed Jonah and repented, God showed them compassion and did not destroy them."

Take your eye off the whale for one minute, Ata mused, *and you will be destroyed by one of the mightiest sea creatures that God has provided us with upon this earth. It must be here for a reason and not just to teach Jonah a lesson.* Then he admonished himself for straying beyond the guidelines of the sermon. *Must be the heat,* he thought, *it is a sultry day.*

"In conclusion," the minister was winding up his discourse, "In conclusion," he repeated, "Jonah thought that he knew better than God, but in the end learned a valuable lesson about the Lord's mercy and forgiveness which is extended to all of God's people who repent and believe. It's about being open and honest with your maker and fellow man."

Tia was reminded of the story about the king and the commoner who hid the whale's teeth and had his brains bashed out by his monarch for his troubles. 'No mercy shown there' she concluded. But then, he was only a king, a mere mortal.

The pastor went to the back of his pulpit and bent down. He straightened up and turned around, brandishing a harpoon iron. He raised the weapon above his head and addressed the congregation. "As this is a token of death and destruction, may it also become a token of peace and prosperity to those of you who repent and like the Ninevites of old, restoring their city and lives to working with the will of God. I ask you to stand and join me in prayer."

The assembly recited the paternoster and while still standing, the pastor raised the harpoon into the throwing position. He had, as a young man, been a harpooner on one of the island's whale boats. The congregation gasped as it appeared that he was about to jettison the weapon directly among his assembled parishioners.

"Repent, sayeth the Lord and I shall forgive you."

The pastor looked at his congregation through large bloodshot eyes, the result of his affection for and consumption of kava. His arm holding the harpoon was scribing an arc, the arc of a throw of the javelin that an athlete makes before releasing the missile to flight.

With that he turned at ninety degress and with his powerful arm action, for he still was a very fit man, threw the harpoon toward the side wall of the building where it struck and became firmly embedded in a wooden structural upright. The tail end of the slender shaft vibrated as the polished iron tine buried itself in the soft coconut wood and the abrupt cessation of flight caused the instrument to quiver.

"Please be seated," he told the congregation.

Pastor Fatualofa walked from his pulpit and went over to where the harpoon had lodged in the wood, pulling it easily free with his powerful arms. He held it aloft and said to his congregation, "Just as this weapon represents the bounty the good Lord has to offer, may it also be a prick on your conscience should you ever choose to disobey the will of the Lord. Be true to yourself and to your God and you shall be truly blessed. He placed the harpoon at the back of the pulpit and said, we will now sing, 'Eternal Father Strong to Save'."

The congregation stood. Pastor Fatualofa knew his flock loved this hymn. They were an island people surrounded by sea and the sea gave them sustenance. They launched into the words with strong voices and great harmony. He knew the second verse would reach a crescendo and it did; the small church was filled with a beautiful consonance.

"O Christ whose voice the waters heard
And hushed their raging at thy word
Who walkest on the foaming deep
And how amidst the storm did sleep
O hear us when we cry to thee
For those in peril on the sea."

That evening, Maree asked her parents if Ken Nakamoto could stay with them for a few days. There was after all a spare fale that he could sleep in. They managed to contact the whale research vessel from the island's radio and arranged a suitable time for the island's boat to meet the ship at sea. Ken explained on arrival that the whale hunt was progressing well and in a couple more weeks they should achieve their quota for the season. Ken had brought with him diving gear for both himself and Maree. Two marine biologists on a tropical island were no different than any two kids would be in a candy store. They had a whole island to themselves with a lagoon on one side, falling away to deep water on the other. There was so much to do and see that they were barely around during the day to socialise with the islanders. But then they had all night to do that. Ken had bought some frozen whale meat from the ship and this could be smelled cooking in the umus, a smell reminiscent of the island's whaling background and much favoured by the inhabitants who hankered for the good old days.

There was a small uninhabited atoll about ten nautical miles away from Vavai and Ken and Maree decided that they would take one of the island's boats and carry out some exploratory dives around it. The atoll boasted lovely coral shallows and deep drop offs that were so favoured by the migrating mammals. They needed a boatman and so young Vito volunteered. It was to be their last night on Vavai, as the research vessel had sent a message the previous day saying that the quota was now nearly filled and they were preparing to depart the Tongan Archipelago and head home to Japan. They would be off Vavai to collect their two scientists. "We will send a ship's boat to collect you," the message concluded, "as Captain Kyota wants to renew his acquaintance with the wonderful people he met last year."

Maree said to her grandfather, "No kava, Ata, you know what kava does to Captain Kyota, it totally hijacks his facial muscles, especially his tongue."

Ata smiled, "We will offer him a cup of tea, how's that? He won't be here long enough for any ceremonial stuff anyway – a fleeting visit. His dignity shall remain intact."

"Okay, that sounds just fine. Ken and I are going to Matu for a dive we are taking one of the inter-island boats and Vito will be our boatman as Ken and I will be diving. See you tonight, we should be back by five o'clock." Maree kissed Ata and left.

It took forty minutes for the dive boat to reach Matu and Vito anchored in twenty meters of water. Ken and Maree were togged and tanked up and ready to go. "See you at the anchor!" they said to each other and slid backwards over the side of the boat and into the water. Vito did some line fishing and kept watch over the surrounding water for any signs of a surfaced diver, especially one in trouble. That, after all, is the boatman's job; to assist divers in the water, if they signal that they are in distress and require assistance. It doesn't happen very often but it does happen. He expected them to be gone for the duration of their tank life, which was about an hour. They would all eat lunch when they returned and maybe do some free diving in the afternoon. Without any medical back up, if things should go wrong, Ken did not like to use more than one tank of air in a day. Matu was a small pretty island sitting like a gem in an emerald sea setting. It may have been inhabited at some stage but access was difficult as there was no beach landing or lagoon; it sort of rose up from the water like a molar tooth with steep rocky sides and was festooned on its flat top with coconut palms. You could scale the cliffs in a couple of places and those that had bothered said that it was worth it, as the top was fertile and verdant. Maree's father Robert had wanted to build a cable car to scale the sides. "It would be a great honeymoon destination," he said. "When we get our tourist fales and an airport developed that would be my next challenge!"

Vito unhooked a fish and rebaited his line. He was casting the baited hook when a bright flash on the horizon caught his eye and it was followed by another. Seconds later the boat rocked and then he heard a loud noise like a clap of thunder and then another in rapid succession. The surface water was not disturbed, but the boat rocked again. Vito was uncertain about the events that he was witnessing but he was not taking any chances he started the outboard engine and then went forward to raise the anchor. He wanted to be prepared for any eventuality. The boat was at least one hundred meters from the shore and as the anchor warp came aboard he kept an eye out for his divers. He felt sure that they would have felt underwater sensations and surfaced immediately and he wasn't wrong. Vito picked up their signal and motored the boat over to them. With the two divers alongside the boat, he helped them clamber up the ladder by reaching for an up-stretched hand and hauling them over and through the cut-away transom.

Both divers seemed mildly distressed as they dropped their weight belts and worked themselves out of the harness holding the scuba tanks, dropping them onto the deck of the boat. They then set about clearing their Eustachian tubes by holding onto their noses and applying pressure to the ears, using the Toynbee manoeuvre. There was a lot of eye rolling and then swallowing and yawning. Vito pointed the bow of his boat away from the land and left the wheel to see if he could help his passengers. They seemed to have relaxed a

330

little but he could see that they had experienced some underwater trauma. He poured them both a hot sweet tea from the thermos and Ken and Maree accepted the cups and sat on a thwart and sipped. Ken spoke first.

"I think we have received some sort of shock wave from a detonation. Maybe two detonations, one following the first in close proximity. My ears are still ringing, how about you Maree? How are you?"

Maree looked up, moving her jaw from side to side as if still trying to equalise the pressure in her middle ear. "Something has caused a shockwave," she said. "I remember doing some experiments with underwater transmitted shockwaves and their effects on aquatic creatures. Can be lethal, you know."

Vito said, "I saw a bright light on the horizon and then the water moved and then I heard a noise like a large bang, a loud and scary noise, I can tell you. Maybe there were two bangs one after the other?"

Ken nodded. "Yes," he said, "I am sure we had two underwater shockwaves, the first hit and almost immediately after that the second one of a similar frequency followed. It was as if two identical devices were detonated one after the other. So if you saw a flash on or over the horizon from sea level and your height on the boat, the horizon would be, say, five kilometres away. I recall from my experiments with marine mammals and percussion we found that a 1200lb explosive device could be lethal at say up to 300 meters away. We would have been 5000 plus so we were well outside of the danger zone, but hell, it still registered on our ears!"

"No more water sports for me today," a shaken Maree said, "let's head back to Vavai and a nice safe afternoon pastime like a game of Scrabble!"

Ken agreed. "Sure, my ears need some quiet after that pressure wave. Maybe we'll find out what the hell caused it."

***

With the Zodiacs fastened to the deck and the hardware safely aboard, Melor dived the submarine and headed for the agreed hunting ground and rendezvous with the Japanese whaling factory ship that would take their catch of humpback whales and winch them aboard for processing and blast freezing, to be sold later in the Japanese market.

The submarine crew were jovial as the routine of a long voyage was over and they entered into a new system of watch-keeping. A change was as good as a holiday. Everyone enjoyed a change. The whale boat crew were always a bit gung-ho and chatted endlessly about technique and the kill. Once the first whale had been killed and delivered to the factory ship the season seemed to pass quickly and it seemed over all too soon when the Japanese signalled the quota of humpbacks was filled. They now wanted two sperm whales. Juvenile bulls were okay, but no mothers with calves. Homeguard lectured his team about the dangers of the sperm whale and they even did a couple of sorties where they went hunting as an exercise to examine their own techniques before he would let them loose for a kill on a sperm whale.

Melor had not participated so much in the whaling procedures, preferring to leave the mechanics of the boat's operations to a well drilled crew. They were very slick indeed and could surface and dive the boat as well as any Russian naval outfit that he had ever had working for him in his career as skipper. He spent a lot of time in his cabin reading from his large book collection and tending to his samovar. It was a well-used container indeed and if he left his cabin door open, snoring noises could be heard emanating from within. Chief Engineer Nikita was invited to share a vodka on most evenings, but apart from that Melor drank alone. It seemed that he also ate alone. He was never seen in the mess at chow times.

The whalemen took a fine specimen of a young adult male sperm whale on the second day of their sperm whale hunt and transferred it that night to the factory ship under the cover of darkness which was standard procedure for their covert operation. The Japanese mothership's whale boss said, "Same again, one more, please and we can all head for home!"

The following day when the submarine returned to the hunting ground, Vadim was surveying the sea through his periscope before surfacing to ensure that there was no surface traffic. This was a covert operation and to be seen by an observer outside of the cabal was not a desirable option and may jeopardise their entire operation. Melor had left most of the day to day activity to his trusty boatswain a position holding officer status in the Russian Navy. The seascape proving clear, Vadim surfaced the boat and the whaleboats were launched and away from the submarine when the watch on the fin shouted that well known cry of the whalemen of old. "Thar she blows. Whale ahoy!" Binoculars were trained along the line of the accusing outstretched arm of the author of the cry. It can take some time for an untrained eye to distinguish the change to the seascape that a whale can make as it leisurely puffs its way along the sea tops. One thing is certain and that is that a sperm whale is the most identifiable species when surfaced, with its large blunt head profile and the low and bushy spout ejected forward from a single blowhole that is at a forty five degree angle from the left side of the tip of the snout. It one of the most easily recognised profiles, even at a considerable distance and is unique in whales. Vadim was savvy enough to take a cross bearing, he knew that if a sperm whale sounded it would resurface at the same spot. Whales could stay submerged for long periods so he was taking no chances. With the whale boats well away, he submerged the boat to thirty meters and cut propulsion. They had a floating antennae and would receive a signal from a whale boat when it was time to surface and rendezvous with the returning whalers. "Just like the whale," Vadim said, "I can submerge and I can resurface and I will be in the same spot."

Everybody relaxed, enjoying the moment, no rush, no propulsion, just floating weightlessly in the ocean like a large aquatic mammal at rest. Those on watch tried their best to look busy but there was nothing to look busy about. Occasionally, a hand wielding a rag would polish a gauge glass. Coffee was available on request. Off duty crew slept on their bunks or just lay and read a book or a magazine. A card game in number seven compartment occupied several crewmen. The sound of vodka snores emanated from the skipper's cabin in compartment two. Lev the radio and sonar officer was also in compartment two, but in the sonar room

"We have company," he said aloud but there was no one else to hear him as he was alone in the room. He got up and found Vadim.

"We have company," he said. "I have a signal on the sonar, a rather large object. Too small for another sub unless it's one of those mini jobs, highly unlikely way out here in the boondocks." Radio people pick up foreign vernacular easily.

"Boondocks?" Vadim enquired.

"Siberia – open spaces!" Lev said.

"Oh I see. Boondocks, strange word! Anyway, what is this object that you are picking up on?"

"Can't say exactly, very quiet, no obvious sounds of propulsion, moving silently and it is close to us. Closing even, come, have a listen. I believe that it is some form of aquatic creature rather than an inanimate object. I have heard porpoises many times, they tend to bark and whistle. This does not sound like bark and whistle – clicks maybe."

Vadim put on the headphones, "Skipper's good at analysing sonar signals, I'll get him." Vadim left the sonar and radio room and went to the next door cabin where Melor had recently woken from his slumber and was sitting at his desk reading a book and enjoying a drink form his samovar.

"Lev has a strange contact on the sonar, thought you may like to have a listen, Skipper!"

Melor looked up and seemed a little annoyed about being disturbed. He was grappling with his English edition of *Moby Dick* and had done so all of the voyage, thus far, as each page he had read several times to get the import of the words. It was not English as he knew it.

He was reading a particular piece that Melville had penned and he was enjoying it following the third reading.

"One often hears of writers that rise and swell with their subject, though it may seem but an ordinary one. How, then, with me, writing of this Leviathan? Unconsciously my chirography expands into placard capitals. Give me a condor's quill! Give me Vesuvius' crater for an inkstand! Friends, hold my arms! For in the mere act of penning my thoughts of this Leviathan, they weary me, and make me faint with their out-reaching comprehensiveness of sweep, as if to include the whole circle of the sciences, and all the generations of whales, and men, and mastodons, past, present, and to come, with all the revolving panoramas of empire on earth, and throughout the whole universe, not excluding its suburbs. Such, and so magnifying, is the virtue of a large and liberal theme! We expand to its bulk. To produce a mighty book, you must choose a mighty theme. No great and enduring volume can ever be written on the flea, though many there be who have tried it."

Melor was busy pondering this passage when Vadim interrupted his reverie of thought, where he was embracing the idea of his book, that he would write about whales when this voyage was completed. He had become fascinated by the subject.

"Skipper," Vadim repeated, "Lev asks that you go to the sonar room."

Melor responded with a groan. "Okay, Bosun, coming," he said. "Tell Lev I'm on the way!"

Melor entered the radio and sonar room, Lev was seated in front of the set twiddling with dials. He removed his headphones when he saw Melor enter.

"Thanks, Skipper," he said, "I usually have some idea of what I am listening to, but not this time, I can make a guess – what do you think?" He handed Melor the headset. Melor listened for a while and then smiled as he removed the phones from his ears.

"I say we have a love sick whale who thinks that he is talking to a female whale. Flirting behaviour, I would say. Male to female, one-way traffic, his affections are not being returned. He cannot stay submerged indefinitely so will have to go up for air. When he does, we get out of here." He looked at Vadim. "Full speed ahead, both outer shafts should see us out of range in ten minutes. Carry on!" Melor exited the room and went back to his cabin.

"How long can they stay submerged for?" Lev asked Vadim.

"I heard Homeguard say, according to the whaleman's' rule of thumb, that for every foot of its length a surfacing sperm whale will spout once and at the next sounding will remain submerged for a minute per foot. So a forty foot whale will spout forty times and then stay submerged for forty minutes."

"Well, this sucker had been mooning us for at least twenty minutes, so we could be here for a while yet!"

"Nowhere better to go," Vadim said as he exited the sonar room, "let me know as soon as he surfaces and we will depart the scene, so to speak." Vadim went from compartment two to compartment three which was where the control room was situated. He rang stand-by on the propulsion telegraphs to let the engineers know that they would soon be receiving instructions to get underway and called for a cup of coffee from the galley. In five minutes they were underway, Lev advising of the love sick whale's departure for the surface. "Even lovers have to come up for air," he said.

The whalemen returned empty handed after their day on the water looking for a suitable prospect. Tev, who was the motor operator on Zodiac 1, said, "We saw plenty of females with calves but no juvenile males. Some say they hang out with a different bunch of guys!" Tevita said.

"The mature bulls don't like them hanging around their harems!" Lesindi offered. He was called 'Les' for short and operated one of the harpoon guns.

They would repeat their routine tomorrow, until then it was rest and recreation and when night fell, Vadim surfaced the boat and those who wanted to were allowed to sleep on the top casing. There was no breeze but it was far cooler than the torpid conditions below decks where the air seemed thick with body odour and cooking smells. Nikita the engineer started one of the three diesels to charge the main batteries. He opened the main air inlet valve on the diesel so that it drew its combustion air in from the submarine's interior, thus allowing an inrush of exterior tropical night air to flow in through the open hatches, instead of coming through the exterior snorkel and interior ducting, thus allowing fresh cooling air to flow through the boats interior, continually changing the air and rejuvenating even the farthest reaches of the stale inner pressure hull. It was pleasant but dangerous as it left them vulnerable if they had to dive in an emergency, but Vadim couldn't think of any emergency that might threaten them. Melor was sleeping off his day's ingestion of vodka and Vadim was reluctant to wake him. He did open his cabin door, however, so that the stale air within might be sucked into the passageway as the gyre of fresh air swirled like its ocean cousin, creating a suction from the Venturi effect as the velocity of the air flow increased when it passed through the departmental bulkhead doors. It was a good solution and welcomed by all members of the crew. The air flow was continual and rejuvenated the boat until eventually all crew members who were on the upper hull casing went below to sleep as the diesel engine thumped away like a large air transfer pump, ingesting its combustion air from inside the boat and exhausting it into the outside ambient. When the watches changed at 0400 hours, Vadim ordered the diesel stopped and the boat dived to thirty meters to prepare for the coming dawn.

The submarine rose with the sun and the Zodiacs and their crews were away in the clean morning atmosphere disappearing quickly from the submarine's horizon on a flat sea. Within minutes, the submarine was submerged and would stay down until the whale catchers signalled a kill or returned empty handed at the end of their day. They didn't need to wait until the end of the day, as the catchers returned with a kill early. With practised ease, the whale was strapped onto the top casing of the boat as deck cargo, the Zodiacs were tied in place and the hardware stowed inboard. The submarine submerged and made its way to the mothership to transfer their cargo that night, under the cover of darkness.

As the mothership was heading directly back to Vavai to collect their two scientists Ken and Maree, it was agreed that they would load the Zodiacs and the whalemen and their gear aboard and deliver them directly to their island home. Melor thought that was a good idea. Under floodlights and after much back slapping, the transfers were completed and the two ships parted company. The submarine spent the night on the surface, their diesel engines recharging the propulsion batteries and also flushing the boat's interior with fresh air. Melor retired for the night and said to Vadim, "Tomorrow we will set a course for Vladivostok. Tonight I give you some vodka for the crew to celebrate the end of the season. Wake me at 0500 hours!"

The Russian crew devoured the vodka that Melor had very graciously supplied, but the Tongan crew would need to wait a while before they would fly back from Vladivostok to Tonga before they could enjoy a kava ceremony in honour of their season. It was therefore by a unanimous vote that the Tongans drew the short straw for the overnight watches, thus allowing their

335

contemporaries to celebrate and get some sleep before the morning watch was called and the boat readied for her voyage to Russia.

Pita and Sioeli, two Tongan seamen, were on the fin keeping an eye on the Pacific Ocean as the boat drifted in the currents off one of the deep Tongan trenches. They were in safe water and the GPS repeater told them where they were at all times relative to any islands in the archipelago. A straw light in the eastern sky indicated that dawn was imminent. They had shaken Melor as requested and also members of the crew who would take the early morning watch that had been set as a precedent to their journey to Vladivostok. Coffee smells were wafting up to the fin from the galley below which was in the next compartment to the control room. All hatches were closed except the hatch in the fin and the diesel engines were thumping away, charging batteries. Milan the cook bought two hot coffees to the lookouts on the fin. It was his time in the fresh air, as, when underway, his duties kept him in a very strict rotation between his bunk and the galley. This would be his last look at the world above the water before the boat went down for the start of the journey home. Once he started his labours he was on a conveyor belt of cooking and sleeping and there was more cooking than sleeping. Milan would have one last cigarette before he retreated down into the low yellow light that was the dimly lit interior. It was fast fading too, as the day dawned and the light from either source reached equal potential.

Pita trained his binoculars on a disturbance on the seascape and announced to his watch keeping mate "Whale on the port bow, stationary and spouting!" He had seen the unmistakeable spout of the sperm whale which was sort of off from the horizontal, a bushy column of warm breath and moisture. The large blunt profile was obvious and caused Pita to say to his watch keeping mate, "Better get Vadim or the skipper up here quickly. This fella looks as if he has us under observation." Pita looked again and saw a large blunt object like the front of a diesel locomotive heading directly for them. It must have altered course since he first sighted it; there was no doubt who the intended target was going to be. Forty plus tonnes of angry whale moving at twenty knots sunk many a whale ship back in the day, but they were constructed of timber; flimsy boats by comparison. A modern steel structure must surely be a different proposition, Pita thought as he waited for authority to arrive in the fin. A mere lookout is simply that. He had seen the whale and raised the alarm and as far as he was concerned, he could do no more. It was nerve-racking watching the water gap decrease as the projectile approached. It was now nearer and clearer and was pushing up a sizeable bow wave just like a ship does as it pushes the water aside.

"Captain on the bridge," Vadim shouted as Melor came up the fin ladder and through the watertight door. Melor immediately sighted his glasses and let out an expletive in Russian that Pita could only guess would not be used in mixed company. The skipper sized up the situation and said, "Srochnoiya pogruganye," which Pita knew as "quick dive." He left the bridge, sliding down the ladder like a fireman sliding down a pole: quickly. The dive klaxon sounded as crew ran to their dive stations and carried out their much practised and allotted tasks. Melor had the attack periscope raised for observation as the boat reached ten meters and locked on the leviathan closing in on them quickly. "Down periscope," he called and then, "thirty meters planesman. Full ahead all screws."

Melor said, "This looks like the same whale that rammed us last time!" he said it as if he was welcoming a rematch. "I have been reading up on these creatures. They have been known to wreak havoc among unsuspecting aggressors. Their head is used as a ram to drive off opponents. The old whalemen in their flimsy wooden boats did not stand a chance but we have come a long way since those days. If this fella gives me any grief, believe me, he will be history, of that I can assure you!" Captain Melor was upbeat. He went to the sonar room and said, "Lev, get a fix on that whale and keep me posted. I need to know his every move!" Melor then went to his cabin and had a good helping from the samovar then proceeded back to the control room.

"Whale's diving," Lev transmitted over the intercom from the sonar room. "Hell, he's going down! I have him logged at over twenty knots. He is about three hundred meters off our port beam. You know he could have rammed us, but he's diving and the descent speed is faster now at twenty four knots. That's faster than his surface speed! Holy hell, what a beast!" The control room staff were silent after that report. They were all busy with their thoughts about a whale that could damage their boat. Last time they got away relatively unscathed. Would they be so lucky on this occasion? It got so quiet in the control room that the sonar echoes could be heard coming from the sonar room in the next compartment.

"Close all bulkhead watertight doors," Melor ordered. "Battle station conditions. Red alert. Everybody on their feet." Melor was taking no chances. He grabbed the intercom microphone and talked into it.

"We seem to have attracted the attention of a large sperm whale, this is definitely not the one that was smooching us the other day. This one may even be the big fella that dealt with us last year, who knows? However, back then, he was downright angry and ornery. This one seems to be playing games with us and I can't say what his intentions are. I have been studying up on these creatures since our run in with that brute last year and have learned quite a bit about their behaviour. Back in the day they were perfectly capable of sinking whaling ships, but I hardly need to remind you that those flimsy craft were made from wood and a forty ton projectile could inflict terminal damage with one good charge. I have had Nikita, our engineer, work out that the beast could impact on collision a force equivalent to one hundred and fifty thousand tons, even higher depending on his speed at the time of impact. This wouldn't compromise our pressure hull but would seriously damage the outer casing. What concerns me most is the damage that it could do to our appendages and I refer to our diving planes and rudders and propellers. With these out of action we become a lame duck. Still afloat, but that's about all. Everybody on their toes. Those responsible for life support and abandon ship devices ensure all is ready if we need to make a hasty exit. That is all."

Melor asked Vadim to take the con and went forward to the sonar room to talk with Lev the sonar operator.

"What is he up to?" Melor asked.

Lev had earphones on but the sonar echo was audible to Melor's hearing.

"He's dived and levelled out, stationary at the moment, at a depth of five hundred meters, the dive trajectory was at an angle of forty two degrees and the average rate of descent twenty four point six knots. Now that really is quick. I thought that you had previously told me that they dived and surfaced at close to the same spot?"

"True, true," Melor replied, "but that is when they dive for food, I believe that they hang motionless in the water and their dive and ascent is near vertical. It's a food thing I have read! But this is different, he's up to something, I fear. What's our speed?"

"Ten knots."

Melor rang Nikita on the phone in the sonar room to ask about the boat speed.

"Sorry, Skipper," Nikita replied, when asked, "that's all we can get from the batteries at the moment. They are not fully charged."

Melor asked Lev about the possibility of the whale ascending at a similar angle as it used in its descent. "You know," he said, "they have a sonar device in their head too! I wonder if he has calculated a collision course by doing things this way? He can't catch us in a straight line so, is using his superior diving speed, technique and angle to make contact?"

Lev punched some numbers and a display came up on his computer screen. It showed the position of the boat relative to the whale and by some simple adjustments he was able to plot a collision course which altered depending on the whale's ascent speed and angle, but it did prove one thing and that was that a collision was imminent.

Melor phoned Nikita the engineer. "Can I have more speed for a short burst?" he asked.

"Sure, Skipper, I can turn it on for maybe two minutes then we are reduced to slow ahead speed only for maybe thirty minutes and then we have to start the diesels."

Melor rang through to Vadim in the control room asking him to standby for further instructions and to put the submarine onto collision station alert. "Bit like a depth charge attack, but then we haven't had them for ages, have we? Well, use your imagination," he said, "let's say a big bang!" He then ducked into his cabin which was next to the sonar room and drank a cup from the samovar.

Vadim thought, *The skipper's drunk. Been nibbling away at the samovar and the sun's not even over the yard arm!*

Vadim talked with the seaman in charge of each compartment and made sure that they knew what the skipper was thinking. Keep us all on our toes.

Complacency was not a word allowed on submarines where 'be prepared' was the mantra. Be prepared for anything!

Lev said, "The whale is moving four knots ascending and seems to be positioning, at 20 knots he is about four minutes from contact."

"But he's not doing twenty knots," Melor sounded exasperated.

Lev was busy plotting the various options on his screen and Melor looked at the intersecting lines. "At that speed," Melor said, "if I ask Nikita for two minutes at full ahead we could beat that old bull to the draw, he would miss us."

"Yes, but he may speed up."

Lev had hardly gotten the words out than the whale took off in a huge burst of acceleration.

"Fifteen knots," Lev called then, "twenty knots – shit, he's moving."

Melor rang Nikita and ordered "Maximum speed – avoid collision power!"

Immediately, a vibration was felt inside the boat as the screws reacted to the applied torque from the electric motors. "Hope that's enough," Nikita said to Robert. "It's all we have!"

"You've got less than a minute before collision," Lev called out.

"Okay," Melor replied, "at thirty seconds before impact I will get the helm put hard over to port. That means the whale will have to alter course too and I don't know how good he is at doing that, his tail flukes go up and down and not left or right so once committed he may not be able to alter direction quickly enough, I guess we are going to find out!"

"Thirty five seconds," Lev shouted.

"Rudder hard to port!" Melor relayed his order and the boat immediately responded.

Lev called out, "He'll miss us on current course... that last manoeuvre did it, Skipper. Hang on, the bugger's sped up and veered off his course, I don't know – it will be a close run thing!"

"Hang on," Melor yelled out through the intercom.

The boat was checked and the crockery, nestled safely in in their special galley compartments, rattled, but there were no breakages. In compartment three, the planesman's hand was thrown off the forward diving plane control lever which moved violently. The boat rocked a bit, probably from the wash of the fast moving leviathan and then it settled on an even keel.

Melor got a sailor to open the watertight bulkhead door and moved back into compartment three where the control centre was. He ordered, "Periscope depth," as he passed through the compartment and climbed the short ladder up to the mezzanine that housed the two periscopes. He then ordered, "Up scope," and was squinting through the glass as it broke water at ten meters. Melor swivelled like a well-oiled trunnion pivot, turning quickly through three hundred and sixty degrees, an instinct developed to check surface traffic conditions. His action had been honed following years of practice and a Bolshoi ballerina could not have made it seem more natural and composed. Trumpo it seemed had surfaced and was several hundred metres away, spouting

339

and looking the other way. It seemed he may have been temporarily disoriented from his collision and definitely exhausted from the excess speed work that he had displayed.

Melor ordered the boat to surface and the planesman, Sevastyani, said that he was having trouble controlling the forward planes. "The whale must have hit one of them and they are jammed," he relayed.

"We go straight up!" Melor said, "Blow all ballast tanks!" And up they went, it wasn't a controlled ascent and the boat bobbed about on the surface before settling down. "Send a man to check the forward planes," he said and went to his cabin for a drink from the samovar. Melor thought, *This is the moment, the moment is mine I can do it!* What Melor said next was received with absolute incredulousness by all of his crew. He told them to prepare to abandon ship. "Use two of our inflatable boats." They carried four, enough for a full complement of seventy eight men and had radios and flares aboard, life jackets were to be "donned on deck as you cannot get out of the hatch with them on!"

"Hurry," he called "I don't have a lot of time!" Melor went into the control room and threw a breaker on the main switchboard before climbing up into the fin to observe the whale and also the crew, abandoning ship. He carried a bottle of vodka stuffed into his jacket pocket. When all of the men had climbed into the two rafts, Melor said to Vadim, "Stand off one thousand meters and wait for further instructions from me."

Melor knew that the whale would need to stay on the surface for one minute for each foot of his length, and spout about three times per minute, following the recent dive and physical exertion. He further calculated that he had time available to ready his plan, which if successful, would rid Melor of his nemesis forever.

Melor partially submerged the boat with only the fin visible above the water. He had power on the port and starboard propeller shafts to help steerage of the boat and bought the stern to bear in the direction of the whale. He used his attack periscope to record and transfer cross bearings which he fed into the fire controller together with the distance of the boat from the target. He was happy with how his preconceived plan was working out and took a long drink from his bottle that was sitting in his jacket pocket. He felt euphoric. Melor Franko, Captain Second Rank had never felt such frenzied madness since the Cuban Missile Crisis. 'Christ!' he said to himself, 'that must be thirty years ago, my first command!' How ecstatic did a young submarine commander feel in those anxious times. He thrived on it. A true Russian, his name was an acronym of Marx, Engles, Lenin, October, Revolution. The Kremlin's man ready to tackle the imperialist bastards. His gold braid was the shiniest on the boat. It was also the newest, but would tarnish with time in the salt air. His boat was ready for action, the torpedoes were primed and prepared for destruction. Kruschev and Kennedy were at loggerheads. The two great nations were on a war alert footing. There had never been a moment like it in Melor's career, this was what he was born to do! And then the leaders backed down. Well, Melor was not backing down this time. It was to be his war, his showdown and he would show them. This was not going to be another Cuban stand off!

The whale was on the surface and had turned side on and had one eye trained on the fin protruding from the water some twelve hundred meters away. He was puffing away leisurely, now having recovered his strength from the previous dive. His muscles, having restored their myoglobin, were fully charged with oxygen and ready for another dive.

Melor waited until all coordinates were in the sweet spot and he pushed the button. A torpedo exited one of the after torpedo tubes and hissed through the near surface water toward Trumpo with its payload of eight hundred pounds of high explosive. Melor took a swig from his bottle and squinted through the periscope lens to watch the bubble wake fizz across the flat surface of the ocean. He could elevate the periscope lens for a clearer view, as the missile raced toward the target with its lethal warhead.

"Stupid whale," he said aloud. "Mess with me at your peril." And he laughed a vodka induced cackle.

He looked at the second hand on his watch. The journey would take just under a minute and there were twenty seconds left. Melor peered through the eye piece and gasped as a strange thing happened. The whale, which was on the surface, did a sudden and magical disappearing act. He had heard about their ability to suddenly sink, it was a now you see me, now you don't, sort of a trick. The next thing that Melor saw was a huge fluke from the whale's tail in the air and then it crashed down on the surface of the water. What happened next was beyond belief, as the torpedo was flicked into the air where it scribed an arc of one hundred and eighty degrees before falling back into the water. The whale had flipped the weapon with his fluke and reset the device, sending it back in the direction from whence it had come. It took Melor at least ten seconds to realise that the torpedo was on a new trajectory; his brain had slowed down from vodka infusion. He knew what he must do and he had just thirty seconds to do it. He started flooding the middle section ballast tank group to give the boat negative buoyancy to sink. And then he had to climb into the fin and shut the watertight hatch. The projectile hit the submarine at about the same time as Melor's feet hit the deck plates in the control room. There were two explosions. The first was when the live torpedo struck the submarine and the second when the spare torpedo sitting in the rear torpedo tube exploded.

It subsequently became obvious that Melor had purchased two torpedoes on the black market and had some modifications carried out in the docks at Vladivostok that would enable him to remotely fire the devices, without the need of additional manpower to assist him.

It didn't take Vadim, or any other member of the crew watching from the rafts, long to realise that they would not be returning to Russia by submarine. The explosion was horrific. At a distance of one thousand meters, the percussion left their eardrums ringing profusely. The submarine leapt into the air with the first impact and the after section was totally severed with the second detonation. Debris from the detonations rained down on their little convoy and someone said that they saw a hand floating past clutching a bottle. There was no attempt made to retrieve it.

The water surface was littered with flotsam and jetsam and oil stains. Paddling through the rubble they salvaged some items of personal effects that were recognisable and Vadim asked his radio operator to raise the mothership and organise a rescue.

There was no sign of a whale on the surface.

The Tongan crew members were returned to Vavai and the Russians were taken to the Japanese ship's home port of Hakodate from where Linus organised an airlift for them to Vladivostok.

Chapter 23

Tonga

Robert had overseen the entire project for the island's transition into a tourist destination. The contract was let in Wellington to a firm of civil engineers experienced in runway construction. Sub trades were selected by them for the building of the fales and the hospital. A convoy of ships delivered the plant and equipment for the works in hand, from New Zealand to the island, and special accommodation was constructed to house the construction workers who came for the duration of the project. The contract stated that all uncontracted labour would be made available from the island's population. The men provided the muscle and the ladies the victualling. There was to be no work undertaken on Sunday – it was stipulated in the contract. All financials were taken care of by the Art 1 Trust who held the money from the whaling project in a special account. This meant that no money went through the kingdom's banking and financial systems that were wholly owned by the royal family. An option was for runway lights. It was an extra and would require a special backup generator required by the aviation authorities but it guaranteed a safe landing day or night and that increased the incoming air traffic bringing in the tourists.

Following completion, Ata, who was the island's chief, received a visit from a government official who flew in one day unannounced. It seemed that the royal family were interested to find out how, without any financial assistance from the government and without special funds from foreign aid they were able to finance such an undertaking and how they intended to pay to the government taxes that would be due from the profits generated by the new enterprise.

Ata sent for his son-in-law Robert who explained that he had contributed money from his private means. He was a fifty percent partner in an engineering business in Nukualofa and in addition his aunty in Wellington who owned a prominent hotel had gifted the majority of that business enterprise to himself and his sister, who ran the place.

Furthermore, the island had been given to the occupiers by a benevolent Queen Salote Tupou III during her reign and since that time they had never received any financial assistance whatsoever from the government or royal family. Their choices back then were to make a go of it or leave the island and return to the mainland. The islanders made a go of it, mainly because back then whaling was a profitable venture for them and they were able to use their whale catching skills and use any excess whale meat to barter for other goods and services from neighbouring islands.

When King Tupou IV magnanimously banned whaling in the kingdom of Tonga, the residents of Vavai never gave up and through sheer determination and some financial input from Robert, were able to sustain a modest existence. Tourism now would ensure prosperity for them and as far as the island was concerned, the government, who had spurned their requests for financial assistance all of these years, could take a hike!

There was a hitch, the government official pointed out. That was the financial system in the kingdom, whereby all monies earned had to be banked and all transactions made through the bank of Tonga which of course was owned by the royal family. They would, of course, need to deduct the usual levies from those deposits. He didn't need to say what those levies were, but Ata and Robert knew that they would be creative and there really was no alternative other than secede from the kingdom. The story of the king and the commoner who hid the whale's teeth was never far from the surface.

The crown prince of Tonga, resplendent in bowler hat and with an eye monocle clamped in place, visited an Art 1 Trust display in Hong Kong where he resided when not in London. Or, as sometimes was his wont, in the palace at Nukualofa, when he visited his family.

None of the valuable works of art on display were for sale. The brochure, purchased by patrons entering the exhibition, explained that these were some of the pieces that had been saved by the late great art dealer and raconteur, Rudi Levin, who had been mysteriously killed in Amsterdam. The collection was spirited away from Holland prior to the Nazi invasion during WWII. They were owned by the Art 1 Trust, who were involved in good works. They had become a charity who lent money to developing nations and worthy Jewish causes. The brochure explained that the late founder's son, Linus Levin, was a philanthropist and gave large wads of money to needy causes. The crown prince was impressed. He got his staff to obtain contact details and was delighted to learn that Mr Levin was in Hong Kong for the opening of this current exhibition. They were in fact both staying at the same hotel where the Tongan prince occupied a permanent suite.

Prince Tupou V decided that it was time to hold a party and the Art 1 Trust received an invitation.

Kaetrin had opened the mail when it was delivered.

"We have been invited to a party that the crown prince of Tonga is giving in his suite," she had said to Linus. "All we have to do is take the elevator to penthouse level, I'm sure you would want to go. I believe that he is an art patron."

"Yes," Linus replied, "the staff at the exhibition say that he attended our current exhibition and is impressed with the work on display."

"Do you want to go?"

"Yes, I do, he sounds like an interesting fellow."

And so Linus and Kaetrin appropriately dressed for the soiree, had returned the RSVP card and attended.

It was a fine affair in a fine apartment that was decorated with fine paintings. The crown prince was indeed an appreciator of paintings. Linus was taken by surprise at some of the works that he knew about but had no idea where they were. They were artworks that disappear only to be seen by their owner. He was pleased they had made the effort and mentioned it to Kaetrin. He added, "I have seen a Chagall and a Picasso, a Renoir and a Monet. These have been out of circulation for a very long time indeed. We talk about them but that is all. I will forward their location to the Jewish Mediation Committee to make sure that they are not stolen holocaust art."

Kaetrin looked aghast. "Hardly," she said, "I simply cannot imagine a prominent figure owning stolen artworks!"

"They may not know that they are stolen. By stolen, I mean Nazi loot as taken from German Jews during WWII. There are some unscrupulous art dealers who get hold of these things and flick them on. They are never auctioned, it's tap the side of the nose and say no more, I can get them for you before they come to market. You would pay a lot more on the open market, if you understand my meaning?"

Kaetrin nodded. "I know what you are saying," she said and she did. She had been around art now for some time and was beginning to understand the nuances of black market art trading. It was rife and very active. Scruples were for mere mortals in the art business. Forbidden fruit was the tastiest morsel of them all.

Linus made some notes in a notebook and they mixed with the Hong Kong 'in-crowd' at the party. They chatted with the crown prince who was a very nice man. He had been trained at the Royal Military College, Sandhurst and was delighted to learn that Linus served in submarines in WWII. "I was not born until 1948," he said. "You people had all the fun."

Linus must have received this comment with his father's Auschwitz Camp survivor's look.

"Well, you know what I mean!" the Prince said

"Yes I do," Linus replied. "It was a strange time for everyone."

"How opportune to meet you," the royal continued. "Perhaps you will lunch with me, I have some business that I would like to discuss with you."

"Sure, you have any date in mind?"

"Next Wednesday at the Pink Pelican, they do delightful lunches, make sure that Kaetrin is with you. My sister will join us too. She is visiting from Tonga. You must excuse me, I have a weak disposition and need to have a break. These affairs tire me quickly." They shook hands and the prince left the room, waving and nodding to guests as he went.

"What do you suppose all this will be about?" Kaetrin asked Linus.

"Sounds like a proposition regarding money, I would say. Let's hear what they have to bring to the table. They are a stable country with a struggling economy."

"The royal residence here does not seem to show any signs of struggle!" Kaetrin said.

"Right, but I suppose you can't have the first family running around as paupers. They need to mix and entertain and then ask favours."

"I suppose," Kaetrin said. "What about the paintings?"

"I'll ask Miss Lightfoot to get some of her spooks to take photographs. I'm sure that she has contacts in the Hong Kong bureau. They can access the royal apartment with all their trickery." Photos would be better than my description. No doubt Rudi would know them off by heart. I'm not Rudi."

Barbara Lightfoot had worked as the head of overseas displays for the Art 1 Trust for many years. She also was an MI5 operative and her position with the trust gave her a good operating cover as she moved around the world with the exhibitions. She was also a handy courier. While the Levins lunched with the royals it was proposed that the apartment could be entered by bogus hotel servicemen who would photograph the paintings that Linus had targeted as possible Nazi war booty. It was then a matter of sending the prints off to HQ in London who would send copies on to the various mediating factions in Europe that were constantly on the lookout for looted artefacts and when found, mediated with the German Government for their return to their rightful Jewish owners, should they still exist. Many had been exterminated in the Nazi death camps during WWII. It was a touchy subject as the persons who currently owned the artworks, would have purchased them in good faith from a dealer. The German Government would pay compensation, but that was not the market rate.

The Pink Pelican restaurant was a good choice for a business luncheon. Linus may have been the richest person in the restaurant, but that didn't outrank royalty. The crown prince was obviously a popular patron and so they received the best of service and the food was great. Prince George Tupou V's sister was the Crown Princess Tuita who had a very engaging personality. Rumours said that she was the richest woman in the South Pacific. The Art 1 Trust research team had done their homework.

"The thing is," the crown prince said during the main course, "the thing is, we have a shortfall of capital to expand our business plans and bring prosperity to our people."

"Most small nations do," Linus said. He had, after all, heard the same opening statement from many a ruler. And most of them had access to the

346

family cash accumulated over many years at the top of the realm. But that cash was the ruler's cash; it was not the peoples' cash. The people had to earn their own cash and a good and conscientious ruler would help his people to achieve this. Which was what this luncheon was all about.

"We need to expand our agricultural and horticultural base," the prince said.

"And what are they?" Kaetrin enquired. She knew what her brother was doing on Vavai.

"Vanilla, fresh and chilled fish, ground and unground kava, root crops and squash," Crown Princess Tuita replied. "We need to teach our farmers sustainable farming practices. We also need vanilla curing facilities and education in vanilla curing. There are a wide range of subjects to address. Unfortunately, this requires a large capital input before we start getting a return. In other words, we are seeking foreign aid to develop these industries. And what about the royal family's money, I hear you say? Why don't they invest in their own economy? The answer is, we do – we have – we are the biggest employers in the kingdom. We restrict our interests to banking and finance. Which is exactly what we are discussing now!"

Kaetrin and Linus were impressed with the dialogue delivered by the princess. She would prove a capable negotiator.

"This is the Art 1 Trust's business, for sure. If you can get me some figures I'll give them to our London office to have a look at. Our people will probably need to visit Tonga at some stage in the not too distant future. They would need to hold talks with the appropriate government departmental heads and come up with solutions. I assume this can be arranged?" Linus asked.

The royal siblings looked at each other, then nodded simultaneously in tacit agreement.

"Yes, we can arrange that," the prince said. "And now for dessert. This place has the most amazing dessert trolley!"

On leaving the restaurant, the crown prince gave Linus his business card. "Feel free to contact me anytime." And he meant it. As a departing shot of feel-good camaraderie, he said, "my close friends call me George!"

Kaetrin and Linus flew in the company's jet to Amsterdam to visit Werner who was now seventy seven. Werner's parents had passed away some years back and he was living in the old Levin residence on his own. A housekeeper attended to the everyday household chores and cooked meals for him. The microwave oven was an invention that complimented Werner's lifestyle as he could drink with his circle of friends and come home to a delicious meal. Three minutes was all it took in the microwave and he was eating. Art is something that older men can do which requires little physical input and although Werner was no shirker he had degenerative muscle loss which was par for the course at his age.

"We are mere guardians of these masterpieces," he would say, referring to the paintings that were now his life's work. "We are in transit, but the painting stays!"

The heavier paintings in the gallery were moved by his younger staff of which there were two permanent ladies. Linus wanted to show Werner pictures of the paintings that were taken in the Hong Kong apartment of the Tongan prince.

"They will be sent through the normal channels for identification but I would like you to dredge your usual spawning grounds to see what comes up. Be advantageous if we knew who sold them to the prince, if they do happen to have been stolen by the Nazis!"

Werner looked at them. "Yes, I see what you mean, well known but missing from circulation for years. Disappeared into that big black hole! Good spotting, Linus. Rudi would be very proud of you. As the subject has come up, how about we go to the cemetery tomorrow to pay our respects?"

"Yes of course, we had it down on our list of things to do."

Their next stop was London, where Linus was keen to get the Tongan Government's request for foreign aid underway. The process could take some months as the Art 1 Trust auditors would need to visit Tonga to examine the industries requiring the cash injections. Plans would need to be put in place to ensure that the projected outputs would be achieved and of course the return on their investment managed according to their actuarial calculations, as used by modern economists in their financial reasonings. The Art 1 Trust used modern financial logic and were now leaders in their field. The Art 1 Trust's economists had identified obstacles; the biggest hurdle being supply. Pacific Island countries faced barriers that limited potential exports. There were bureaucratic wrangles concerned with onerous country of origin rules and quarantine standards to comply with, which was the modus operandi of every customs service in the world. Other vulnerabilities identified were small and dispersed populations, small domestic markets, sparse resource bases, distance from international markets although better air services were kicking in. They were vulnerable to natural disasters. Tropical storms could flood an atoll and carry away entire villages and destroy all crops and other forms of cultivation. There were few good deep water harbours. It was indeed hard for Pacific Island exporters to compete internationally. This made investors nervous. The Art 1 Trust was not nervous. Their methods were well researched and managed. They were their own insurers. It was called captive insurance and many large conglomerates found that managing their own risks was far more economical than buying insurance from a commercial insurance provider who, at the end of the day was out to make a profit from their activities. In a captive insurance a calculated amount of money is set aside but retained rather than paid out to a commercial insurer. The savings were great and the monies were kept in a special account to be used against one's own internal claims if and when they were made. The Art 1 Trust's insurance reserves were immense and had been accumulated over many years of trading. They were also used to underwrite loans to economies, where assets were not able to be claimed when payments became defaulted on by the debtor. It was a good system and Linus was pleased that he had insisted they adopt it although he did receive some opposition from his suggestion when he first mentioned it at a board meeting. Mr Van Oldenbarnevelt Senior was against the idea. It was the first time that the two had disagreed on any matter at board level. Linus discovered that his fellow director was also a director of a large insurance company who wanted the trusts business. A conflict of interest, Linus declared to Mr Van Oldenbarnevelt, who, when confronted, withdrew any opposition to the suggestion. That had been many years ago now and Mr Geradus Van Oldenbarnevelt had retired and his place on the board had been taken by his son Richard Van Oldenbarnevelt. The Van Oldenbarnevelts were an old Dutch legal firm that Rudi used and nothing had changed. Richard was born and schooled in England and spoke passable Dutch. Linus would often start conversations with Richard in Dutch to keep his fluency in the language, but invariably they would revert to English which was preferred for technical discussions. English was the lingua franca of the global business world. Richard ran the London office for the old Rotterdam legal firm. All European business was still conducted through the Rotterdam office.

It was Richard who reported to Linus about the paintings that were owned by the Tongan crown prince. They were enjoying a drink after work in a pub in Knightsbridge when Richard drew a piece of paper from his coat jacket pocket.

"This arrived today in our bag from Rotterdam," he said unfolding the type written page and placing it on the table between them.

"Now let's see – the Chagall first. Painting owned by the Popitz family from Frankfurt, according to our sources. The family, survivors from the Holocaust, can establish legal ownership so I guess that one has to go back to Germany." And he then added, "Perhaps."

"Picasso, another straightforward ownership declaration. The Tuttleman family descendants, again survivors from the Holocaust, have declared and can prove legal ownership so that one goes back." Again Richard suffixed his comments with, "Perhaps," reinforced with a "Maybe!"

"No traces for the Renoir, although at some stage it was owned by the Mingelsheim family from Berlin. There are no surviving members from that prominent Berlin family, having perished in the Nazis' extermination campaign, obviously. Our records go back to 1923 when it was purchased by them at auction. Legally it may still be a German treasure but it may also have been sold before the war, outside of Europe. More work needed here, maybe?

"And the Monet. The Gumberich family from Cologne owned this fine work of art and the survivors are keen to have it back. We have a counter claim from another family who say that they purchased it from the Gumberichs in 1936. A very disturbed year indeed in Germany. The Nazis did keep excellent records but it does not surface on any of the searches to date as having been sold by the owners and purchased by the Yiedels who claim that they can supply a bill of sale. So we have a dispute there. Nonetheless, it seems that we have three confirmed stolen and one in dispute. What do you do now? How do you explain to the crown prince that he owns stolen artworks? It's a delicate matter. And he wants a loan too!"

349

Linus took a swig at his beer. "He gets compensation. The German Government has to pay him; they do not just take them. Also it's a conscience thing. Some owners have refused to part with their stolen artworks. Many museums worldwide are just coming to grips with Holocaust Art! Fifty years after the end of the war!"

Richard gave his lawyer's nod. "There are ethical points that apply and are most prevalent in cases between 1899 to 1954. There is no international mechanism in law to enforce this. The arguments therefore are left to national laws. I mean how strange is that? Imagine if you will, Germany trying to recover artefacts from Russia and Russia had plenty looted from her by the occupying Germans – Rudi could have told you about that! The Germans would need to go through a Russian court where their chance of recovery would be nil. Especially in light of the fact that when, during the Germans' short occupation of western Russia in WWII, they looted and destroyed 2000 churches, 43,000 libraries and two million works of art. They wouldn't stand a snowball's chance in hell of winning anything back from Russia!"

"When you put it like that, no!"

They finished their drinks and Linus went to the bar and replenished them.

"Consider the Swedes," Richard said. "The thirty years war against the Holy Roman Empire was all about plunder." Richard paused for a drink. "Greed and plunder," he repeated, "and the Swedish Queen Christine wanted it all. Talk about bloody excesses! Prague Castle contained a fabulous collection of artefacts collected by the Holy Roman Emperor Rudolph II. His paintings alone took up seven walls in the sprawling Prague Castle. There were valuables beyond belief, the best known being the Silver Bible or *Codex Argenteus* as it was called back then, the book in which the four gospels of St Mark were transcribed in gold and silver ink. Can you imagine?"

"Not really," Linus said, "but carry on, it sounds interesting."

"It had been created in the sixth century – the book that is," Richard said. "And for the next thousand or so years its movements were lost to history as it no doubt passed from owner to owner who enjoyed the documents contained within its jewel encrusted covers. And the whole item as a work of beauty and great value too! At one point, or so the story goes, one of its vellum leaves were torn out and hidden with the relics of a saint. The remaining 187 leaves came into the hands of Benedictine monks. By the time it had reached Prague it was so old that the language in which it had been written was forgotten. Today, in fact, its pages represent half of all surviving examples of the Gothic language. I mean, how amazing is that?"

"It's a good story so far," Linus opined, as he sipped his beer.

"Well, the Swedish queen wanted that above all else and boy did they plunder that Prague Castle and send ship loads of loot back to Sweden. Now, nearly four hundred years on, the book is still in Sweden. It is the most valuable book in all of Sweden and the Czechs want it back. They had a go after they rid themselves of their communist shackles in the late 1980s, I think that was, but were not successful. Also, consider that Prague was

350

Czechoslovakia when Rudolph lived in the castle, so how come the Czechs think it belongs to them now that Prague is conveniently in Czech Republic? Surely, with countries' borders being shifted… it's a bugger's muddle!"

"The plunder stays with the plunderer," Linus said. "That's the way it has always been, despite universal condemnation from today's liberals. Some plunder has been in the hand of the plunderers now, longer than it was ever in the hand of the plundered and who knows how they ever came by it in the first place? Probably plundered!"

"From memory, I think that Rudolph II's collection contained some weird artefacts that they had obtained over the years. Richard avoided using plundered. There were two nails purported to be from Noah's Ark, a horn from a unicorn, and a jawbone from one of the sirens who tempted Ulysses!" Richard swallowed a hearty draft following his discourse. He did like to talk on subjects that he was knowledgeable on and prior to law he had completed a history degree.

"So you see," he concluded, "there are obstacles and lots of precedents. It seems that we have always taken whatever we wanted if we had the means to do so. The conquering armies plundered the vanquished as a matter of course. Also consider the pay."

"What?"

"The pay was not the best, you got what you plundered. No victory, no plunder. The soldiers back in the day never went shopping for mementos to take home to their loved ones at home, no sire! It was plunder! Plunder, pillage, rob and rape!"

"That's human nature," Linus said. "We always want what the other guy has. Never happy with our lot and I won't have a lot if I don't get back to our hotel," Linus said looking at his watch. "Kaetrin has us going to a show tonight. She is a stickler for punctuality. And rightly so, I believe. Her father, who perished in WWII, always insisted that she treat time like a close friend."

"I don't get it," Richard said.

"Neither do I," Linus replied, "but that's what she says. You don't have to get it!"

"See you tomorrow then."

"Yes, tomorrow, we have a lot to do."

The Art 1 Trust auditors flew to Tonga and spent several weeks working with Tongan government officials who were very helpful. On the way, they dropped Kaetrin and Linus off at Wellington. Kaetrin phoned her brother in Vavai to tell him what had transpired. She said that the negotiations were going well and whatever happened they would not jeopardise the economy on Vavai that the inhabitants had worked so hard to establish.

"We even lunched with the crown prince in Hong Kong," she said to Robert during the phone call.

"Who, George the fiver?" he replied.

"The very one, a nice man too I must add."

"Yeah, well, we're all nice when we want something, did you tell him about us?"

"He knows nothing about our relationship. Vavai was not even mentioned."

"Good. Anyway, enough of that speculation. We are planning a big opening party. Island festivities that will announce to the world in general, and our Pacific neighbours in particular, that Vavai as a tourist destination and a whale watching experience, is open for business. So, any ideas, sis, let's have them!"

Kaetrin sounded breathless. "That's wonderful news, what can we do to help?"

"Don't know yet, but we have eighty fales now that we can fill with guests. The airport is fully operational and the whale watching is underway. Kava production is at full swing. I guess it's time to party. Maybe you know some people in high places who might like to tackle the island experience and then go home and talk about it.

"See what you mean. Okay then, I'll put my thinking cap on here and get back to you."

"Bye bye."

"See you."

"PS..."

"What?"

"Maree and Ken are engaged."

"Great news – whoopee!"

"It could double as an engagement," Linus had said when Kaetrin broke the news to him after she had finished her call to her brother Robert in Vavai.

"No!" Kaetrin was adamant. "You don't share your engagement with another event. Big or small. We will do the engagement separately, let's do the island opening first. One at a time."

A lead-in time of several months was given for the invitations to the official island opening and Kaetrin was given the job of coordinator. Robert and Tia considered it to be a family affair but as Kaetrin pointed out it was the travel industry who would be selling the place as a holiday location so it was all about the travel industry. Family could be present as there really was not a lot of family outside of Tonga to invite. "We have to invite the travel industry representatives," Kaetrin concluded. "Basically we fill a 737 with travel reps and ship them up to Vavai for a few days of R&R. Feed them and give them some drinks, take them whale watching, reef diving, involve them in some kava ceremonies. Yeah, that's it really!"

"You will have to invite some Tongan government officials for sure," Linus replied. "Minister of tourism at least, plus minister of fishing and agriculture to see the whale watching at work. You know the sort of thing, a general interest observation, can't leave them out!"

"Okay, I'll get started on the list!" Kaetrin threw up her hands as a signal of compliance, which she agreed with anyway.

A week later, Linus got a call to go to Hong Kong and talk with the crown prince. I seemed that some Art 1 Trust official had gotten a bit off side with the monarch over a comment or two about the current loan discussions and the royal had asked to talk with his friend Linus. Linus rang him using the number given to him when the prince handed Linus his business card following their luncheon at the Pink Pelican in Hong Kong.

The prince answered his phone in a relaxed manner; obviously only a few invited persons had the number.

"Hello, George here," he said.

"Hello George, this is Linus."

Linus had been around enough persons of high rank to know that if you were given a private number you responded by echoing the name given when answering. It's the royals' equivalent of the hot line between the Kremlin and Westminster or the White House or the Vatican.

"Hello Linus, how nice of you to call, I seem to have run into a small problem, can you come and have an informal meeting with me here in Hong Kong?"

"I can," he said. "I haven't clarified the time zones yet, but I will be on my way in eight hours. Call you when I land, or at the first suitable business hour."

"Thanks, Linus, I really appreciate that, Goodbye."

"Goodbye sir."

Familiarity kills the intrigue, Linus learned that lesson a long time ago. Intrigue is 110% of any business negotiation. Leave a bit for the mind and a bit for the soul and walk into the room with your reputation whole. Intact was a better synonym, but it didn't rhyme.

The meeting was held at the prince's residential hotel suite seated in comfortable armchairs and serviced by a hovering waiter who bought tea and coffee as requested. The person was obviously a trusted aid to the prince as he came and went and the flow of conversation remained unrestricted. The two men addressed each other as George and Linus. As a Sandringham graduate, George would have been just one of the boys and he enjoyed that and exercised the discretion with people he trusted and of course respected too. It seemed that a zealous employee from the Art 1 Trust had somehow spilled the beans on certain stolen artworks. It had come to the trust's notice that the prince may, unwittingly of course, own such pieces. The founding principles of the Art 1 Trust, was in preserving and returning pieces of art that was looted during WWII. The prince cut to the chase.

"I get the impression that our application for aid is in jeopardy because they say that I own some paintings that may be war booty taken from the Jews by the Nazis. I find that attitude distasteful. I buy paintings as an avid art collector from reputable dealers. I am aware that there are a number of pieces that may have black market connections. I'm in the business, but not stupid. When I buy, I get a full disclosure certificate from the dealer that the piece is free of any questionable history. I.e. war booty and the like. Or, I get my money back. Cannot be a more open disclosure than that! My other question is; are they simply flying a kite and how do they know what I have in my collection? I have private showings only. Who knows what my collection consists of?"

353

Linus considered his own reputation and relationship with the royal who was obviously disgruntled that his personal integrity should be questioned. He was. After all, an honourable man.

"I am the beneficiary trustee of the Art 1 Trust, the other two trustees are professional trustees. Executive decisions are a matter for the board, which consists of us three trustees. Individual employees have no executive rights whatsoever. They merely report their findings to the board for a decision. If they have spoken about matters other than the application they are processing, then they are out of order and shall be dealt with. In fact, all contact in this matter was to be through me only.

"As you are aware the trust was originally formed following the end of WWII when the paintings and other artefacts that my late father Rudi Levin exported from Holland prior to the Nazi occupation, were found to have no surviving claimants other than myself; all other owners had been exterminated or died from other causes during the war. As sole survivor, I inherited the lot. Subsequently, it was discovered that my late father was in Russia where he had been sent following the Russians' liberation of Auschwitz. During his years in Auschwitz, he and two others had catalogued over 4000 works of art that were confiscated from the incoming prisoners, Jews, who would be exterminated."

"Unbeknownst to them and at the same time, a German industrialist was shipping his and another family's art collections to Egypt, hidden as part of an armoured car and spare parts delivery for the Africa Corps Campaign. These two factions actually had pre-war connections although they never realised it at the time. Subsequently, between all parties and intermediaries we have established an organisation to seek out and reclaim the stolen artworks for the affected families. Not unlike that Jewish organisation that hunts down Nazi war criminals and brings them to justice! It's quite a network and contains an enviable array of knowledgeable art dealers who can just about verify the entire European art collection pre-war and subsequently between them they have catalogued thousands of missing paintings and their last known legal owners. Quite a feat, but it has taken nearly fifty years to compile this information."

"Commendable," the royal said, "most commendable."

Linus nodded, tacitly agreeing with the sentiment.

"I noticed, when I visited your apartment," he continued, "that you had on display several paintings and I was intrigued to find that a couple at least may be on that missing paintings list. I made a mental note and asked our organisation to check it out. Professional interest only, you must understand. It seems that the Chagnall and Picasso are posted as missing, believed stolen. There is a Monet which has a disputed ownership between two German families, also on the missing list and the Renoir is inconclusive. We have had a lot of experience in this area and I can tell you that it is a morally challenging business. Furthermore, there is no legal international system in place to enforce anything, other than voluntarily offering up the disputed works. You would receive remuneration, of course, from the German Government, who must pass it back to the original owners from whom it had been expropriated. In no way will any of this or the outcome have any influence on our decision for your request for aid. I personally guarantee you that! Also the entire matter remains in-house and is subject to non-disclosure clauses with penalties, same as our aid agreements."

The crown prince received this information with the greatest of respect. He knew that he had been addressed by a world authority on the subject and as an educated man he respected knowledge above all else.

"Thank you for clarifying that for me," he said. "As a future ruler of my people it is important that I am able to distinguish right from wrong and do the right thing. Make the right decision. God knows I shall have enough of those to have to make in due course, so a bit of practice now will hold me in good stead for the heady days of office. I appreciate your candidness and congratulate you on your demeanour. When I am ruler, those are the qualities that I would seek in my minister of foreign affairs. I could not offer you the job because you have to be Tongan. I think that you can gauge my sentiments from that statement. Maybe you could become some sort of ambassador at large!" He smiled.

Before leaving, Linus said that the aid programme was approved and required rubber stamping by the board and then they could present their proposals to the Tongan Government.

"Our team will be in Tonga to do this next month. Now let me tell you about Vavai, then I must go and catch a plane."

***

Kaetrin was well advanced with her planning for the coming Vavai Island opening as a tourist destination. She had organised the lease of a Boeing 737 which would fly 190 travel agents to the island where they would be accommodated in the new fales. There would be sufficient fales left for family accommodation. It was up to the island fale management and staff to arrange for victualling to sustain their guests for four days and nights when they would be loaded back onto their plane and delivered back to the various New Zealand destinations from where they would spread the gospel about holidaying on a tropical island and whale watching and diving on coral reefs and kava ceremonies.

Kaetrin and Leslie were now retired and the hotel was run by a professional team of managers reporting to the board of directors consisting of Kaetrin, Linus, Robert and Flora. Flora never divulged her age, it was a Flora thing and you asked if you dared. No one dared, but a popular guess was 'eighty mumble'. Kaetrin and Robert were her two successors and she had some twenty years earlier gifted to them shares in the hotel. Robert had since sold a parcel back to Linus to help fund the Vavai island project. Since the discovery of Muriel, Flora had gifted shares to her newest and long lost niece. Vavai's future was further enhanced when Nakamoto Scientific announced that it wanted to fund a scientific institution on the island, specifically for the study of large aquatic mammals. Ken and Maree were to head the project which would mean that there would be a steady stream of scientists from Japan as well as other nations, collectively gathering and sharing information about one of the world's greatest marine resources. Nakamoto Scientific had agreed to totally fund the project and in so doing, would construct a building to house the laboratories, lecture rooms and display areas that were required from such an undertaking. Homeguard had agreed to be the permanent janitor, a trusted position with a modest honorarium. He would be given a battery operated mobility cart to make the commute from his fale to the new laboratory, a distance of 1200 metres.

Those travel agents who were in transit from other parts of the country assembled in Wellington and all flew out directly to Vavai where they were greeted with a typical Tongan welcoming ceremony and allocated fales for their stay on the island.

The *Koto Maru No 2* lay off the island just beyond the lagoon where the ship's lifeboat ran a shuttle service for the crew, ferrying them to and from their floating accommodation. Ken and Maree would use the ship as their base while the island's accommodation was full to capacity with visitors. Mr and Mrs Nakamoto Senior were on board and would be given an official welcoming ceremony in front of all assembled guests, when they would announce the Nakamoto Research Foundation's intention to establish a laboratory on Vavai. Captain Kyoto, who was now an old friend, was told that his visit would be free from any official duties so he was free to take an active part in the kava ceremonies. This news was received with much enthusiasm by the genial captain. His Japanese gene pool had endowed him with his ancestors' dedication to official ceremonial decorum, requiring his total application and attention to cultural detail. The release from this obligation was therefore immense. To drink kava and then give a speech undermined his ability to maintain concentration on his deportment and elocution. The soporific effect that drinking kava had on his facial muscles, including his tongue, which acted like an uncontrolled writhing serpent, placed him in a most embarrassing situation. Pronouncing English words was difficult for him and he had to practise linguistic gymnastics to allow for vowel and consonant clarities, in his speech pattern. However, following a sip or two of kava it became impossible to control the malevolent tongue twisters devised by the demon architects of said language. Captain Kyoto couldn't stop smiling; he was upbeat now that he was unencumbered from officiating in any way. His ever smiling countenance earned him the islanders' appellation of 'Toyota Tooth.' A reference to that popular Japanese vehicle with a shiny chrome grill similar to a gleaming and toothy smile.

Linus had managed to get Bravo to pilot a company Lear Jet to Vavai. He was fresh from flying some Art 1 Trust personnel to Nukualofa for on-going business. The deal with the government had been signed some weeks back but as with any aid programme the beneficiary could be expected to be visited regularly by their benefactors who kept a close eye on how their money was being spent. His former co-pilot, Georgia, was now Mrs Bravo Thornton and she and Bravo lived at their London home with their offspring. It was her first pregnancy and Georgia gave birth to twin girls, much to Leslie's delight. These days, Linus found that he couldn't leave home without Leslie hitching a ride with him to visit Bravo, if he were home, and her daughter in-law, Georgia and her two granddaughters, Roma and Paris. Georgia and the twins had been staying with Leslie at Maximes, waiting for Bravo to return from Nukualofa to collect them all.

In Wellington, they added Flora and James, and Kaetrin and Linus, and also Muriel, Kaetrin's long lost sister who had now integrated into her new family. She had flown out from London with Georgia and the twins. It was the first time ever that they had all been together at one time. It was a joyous band of travellers that landed at Vavai to a rapturous welcoming committee consisting of Tia and Robert, Ata and Aba and Ken and Maree. There were smiles and shrieks of delight and tears of joy as the full gamut of family emotions were demonstrated by a proud dynastic display of joyous unity. This caused Flora to take stock of her life and reflect on a journey that saw herself and her late husband Murdo, leave Scotland in 1933 to start a new life half way around the world in New Zealand. Kaetrin and Robert had really cemented her social acceptance as a de facto parent. Although they were her brother's kids, he was killed in WWII, as was his wife and so they were enriched by the accident of being a family seeking refuge from the ravages of war-torn Europe. This family was founded on the concept of sharing the good times as well as the bad times but overcoming adversity and regaling in their triumphs. Flora had schooled them all in the act of perseverance and the tough lessons were taken on board and they were all enriched from the experiences. Ata and Aba had added the Tongan attributes with Tia and Tia and Robert were passing on their combined inheritances to Maree who it was soon to be announced would be engaged to Ken Nakamoto of Japan. Leslie and Doug had given the world Bravo and he and Georgia responded with Roma and Paris. Flora felt sad that Kaetrin and Linus never found the time to have children, but on reflection, Flora never seeded progeny either. And hey, contributions come in other forms. It needn't be solely a mercantile approach either, Flora had reasoned. There was a myriad of ways that social and moral issues may be advanced and it seemed that they had concocted a pretty potent recipe for advancement, enjoyment and enrichment of the human condition. All in all, Flora conceded, "We did a good job!"

Flora and James were given the best double bed unit in the fale compound. It was separated from the others by a solid fence, fashioned from concrete blocks and plantings that would absorb noise which was expected to come from the travel agents as they partied after dark. The fales held a liquor licence and the tap was turned off at 10pm.

The kava welcoming ceremonies took care of most of the first evening. There were various kava circles and everybody took part and felt welcomed. Whale watching was to be a full-on, all day activity for the travel agents and the boats were scheduled to work all of the daylight hours in order to get through their heavy schedule.

Bravo was first to bed, even beating Georgia and the twins. "I have some flying duties to perform tomorrow," he said.

"Where are you going?" Georgia asked.

"Never you mind, good night, my love."

"Good night, Bravo."

Bravo was away before the island had woken to another sun soaked day in paradise. They didn't have a long flight but it was to be a round trip and he was not sure of the length of time that they would be on the ground at either end of their journey. He had instructed his co-pilot to be prepared for a long day and therefore said to him, "get an early night, I think we are going to need it." Bravo never tired over flying above the archipelago and looking down on the seascape dotted with atolls, islands, reefs and whales casting shadows like cigars, then broaching and making white water frills like lace doilies as they splashed back onto the blue sheet of flat ocean. They flew low and so the view was much more intense and vivid than a scene from a high altitude.

At Nukualofa airport they had barely taxied to a standstill when a black limousine flying a pennant drew up and three men and one women boarded the plane. Bravo welcomed the party and showed them where to sit for take off and they were away.

Linus had arranged for a special airport welcome for the return of Bravo's flight when it landed at Vavai Airport. He had to do this without the knowledge of Robert and his immediate family but he had arranged with the faithful Homeguard to have villagers set up a dais with four seats and a lectern with a microphone and seats in front of the dais. Runners were then sent around the island requesting that all of the island's inhabitants that were able to do so, be present at the airport reception area at 11 o'clock in the morning. It was one of those requests that sounded so far out of the ordinary that one would want to attend out of sheer curiosity if nothing else.

On the dot of eleven, Robert and Tia, Ata and Aba were driven to the airport in the airport shuttle, an open air, extended body golf cart, festooned, island style with aromatic local tropical blooms, as was the dais. It all seemed rather grand and nobody on the ground other than Linus knew what was about to unfold. Those officials attending were told to wear their best ceremonial clothes and that included the ta'ovala, the traditional Tongan woven mat-like outer covering. It could be said that it was similar to a westerner wearing a suit as a sign of respect for a special occasion.

When all official guests were seated, a jet plane appeared in the sky and approached the airport from the sea. It flew leisurely above the runway, circled and came in to land. The plane taxied as directed by ground staff to within fifty meters of the dais where it came to a stop. The whine of the jet engines decreased as Bravo shut them down and then the door in the fuselage opened and the steps were extended hydraulically from the plane and a government aid walked down the steps and stood on the runway.

The crown prince appeared, followed by his sister, then a personal aid and all four made their way to the dais. The assembled crowd gasped in disbelief and then burst into a loud cheer of approval. The prince approached the dais and held up his hand and silence fell over the assembly.

A beaming royal announced to the assembly that he had heard through the grapevine that a transformation had taken place on the island of Vavai and he was compelled to come and have a look for himself to ascertain the facts and congratulate those responsible for such a phenomenon. He was a man of action rather than words and before too long Ata and Aba were invested by the prince with the Royal Order of Tonga. He pinned a lovely jewel to their chests and then called on Tia and Robert to come forward and invested them with the King's Service Medal. It was in turn a shock, an honour and a privilege.

The prince congratulated the recipients for their achievements and what they had been able to accomplish for their fellow Tongans and asked to be taken on a tour of the island's hospital before saying farewell and boarding the plane for the return flight to Nukualofa. The royal party were on the ground for two hours. It was the first time since Queen Salote had gifted the island to the inhabitants seventy years ago that any member of the royal family had set foot on the place. This was indeed a grand moment and set the scene for a continual celebration that took place for the remainder of the week until the travel agents departed, having witnessed the best moments of their travel experiences, ever!

It didn't take Robert long to put two and two together and in a quiet moment he singled Linus out to have a talk with him alone.

"That was some stunt," he said.

"The prince doesn't do stunts, Robert!" Linus replied, "He is for real."

"And you know?" Robert looked accusingly at Linus.

"Actually I do, I have had some very close and personal discussions with him lately and I think that we have developed a mutual respect for each other. He is genuinely impressed with what you have done here on Vavai and has expressed that gratification, in the only way that he can. And that that is in the form of an investiture."

"What did you tell him?" Robert sounded accusing. His hand brushed the jewel that the prince pinned on his shirt.

"Only what you can see – you have built an airport and a hospital, got agriculture and fishing underway as a commercial venture. The island is self-sufficient and will no doubt be making some serious profits when the tourism bug kicks in!"

"That's the problem," Robert said, "I had a visit from some government officials who want a share of the action, after all of these years of avoiding us, avoiding any form of financial aid and at the first whiff of a profit they are here to get their claws into our hard earned cash."

"That will not happen," Linus said.

"What?"

"I said that will not happen, your profit is yours to reinvest in your economy."

359

Robert started to respond when the new mobile phone that Linus had invested in rang. It was the first call he had received in Tonga.

"Hello? Yes, George, loud and clear... Yes, I am just talking with Robert now... Okay, I will do that... Next week is fine, see you then... Bye bye, sir."

Robert's eyes were as dilated as Linus had ever seen them, he looked at Linus. "Was that who I think it was?"

"Who do you think it was?" Linus teased.

"Him. You know, the prince."

"Yes, it was he."

"You called him George!" Robert's tone of voice rose several octaves.

"I did," Linus replied, "we are on first name terms, he calls me Linus and I call him sir!"

"But you called him George, I heard you."

"Not a word to anyone, Robert, not a word. Okay?"

Robert smiled. "Sure, you can rely on me. The recipient of a King's Service Medal at your service!"

Robert was not to be denied his question. "Now as I was about to say this tax thing what's going on here?"

"Let's say by mutual agreement, and you do know that the Art 1 Trust has been negotiating an aid agreement with the Tongan Government. George – I mean, the prince, feels that as a part of our extended aid agreement, you should be allowed to reinvest the fruits of your endeavours back into your economy for the next five years. I guess it is a bit like a tax holiday."

"But to be renegotiated then," Robert said.

"Yes," Linus said, "at the same time as our aid programme, so I would expect the status quo to continue."

"You're a wily old fox," Robert said.

"As James Peroux would say, you have just landed in a mink lined fox-hole!"

Robert mused over that for a while. "Tell me," he said, "your insurers paid out on the submarine, was that another sleight of hand?"

Linus looked bemused. "Certainly not, all above board, I can assure you. You paid the insurance it was all included in the contract."

"You have a very understanding insurer, then." Robert replied. "Typically the wriggle room is so great in that industry that they train with Hula Hoops – one wrong move and you've lost it!"

"We carry our own insurance," Linus replied. "Only way to go."

Robert rolled his eyes and then looked at his watch. "Better get back to my place," he said, "the family has gathered for an after party following the investiture. The family jewels are on display."

Night had not yet fallen and the smell of pork roasting over open pits was redolent throughout the island. Robert and Tia's fale could not house everybody indoors, so apart from Aba and Ata sitting in the interior shade and visited regularly by admirers who were lining up to congratulate them, the main body of family and guests were sitting outside. Cold beer and wine were on offer as was the Tongan favourite, kava, it was a mild narcotic and had a calming effect. No one went home until the kava bowl was dry. A new favourite iced tea was making inroads now that refrigeration was available in most homes. Bravo had returned from delivering the royal party back to Nukualofa, and together with Georgia and their twins Roma and Paris, had gone to the lagoon for a swim. When Tongans swam they did so with their clothes on, so it was a constant amusement to them to watch the palangis change into a swimming costume to undertake the ritual of bathing in the ocean.

Kens parents and Captain Kyoto had paid their respects and had returned to the ship. The heat was oppressive and aboard ship they could turn on air conditioning. Flora and James were sipping iced tea and mingling and Kaetrin had just caught up with Linus who had been on the organising committee for most of the day and now they were both seated in the shade of a large Casuarina pine and enjoying a cold beer.

"That was really some coup," Kaetrin said.

Linus looked at her squinting in the glare. "If you mean a stroke of genius, I agree."

"I mean nice work, a good idea. Robert has delivered the stroke of genius ad you made it possible I suppose, in a very subtle way. You do subtle very well."

"You know Robert, if he had an inkling this could happen he would have towed the island and all of its inhabitants to another location."

"Absolutely," Kaetrin said.

"The prince will one day be king," Linus continued. "He is keen to bring the whole monarchy system into the modern world. One thing will never change and that is an investiture. It's something only he can do. At a fair you win a kewpie doll. Here, you win the real thing. It's a reward for good hard honest slog for the betterment of your fellow citizens. We talked about it at length, George and I that is, and I can tell you that he was genuinely surprised and very pleased that progress was being made off the produce of one's own spade. You are only what you can produce. Produce nothing and you have nothing. And so, Vavai has gone out and grabbed its piece of pie. The feedback that I am getting from the travel agents is stuff you cannot buy. This island is going places. Health and prosperity. Not a bad lump of coal to retire to my dear, what do you say?"

Kaetrin saw a large grin on her husband's face but never called his bluff.

Homeguard arrived to pay his respects to Ata and Aba, Tia and Robert. He came on his electric scooter; Robert had fashioned a special holder for Homeguard's crutch. He alighted and went into the fale and paid his respects to Ata and Aba, emerging some time later to find James Peroux admiring his scooter.

"You want to take it for a ride?" Homeguard suggested.

"I would," James said, "maybe I could get one of these."

"You just sit on it and I will tell you what to do," Homeguard said, he was delighted to be able to give instruction to James.

361

James sat on the scooter and Homeguard said, "Okay, now hang onto the handlebar and pull that lever. The harder you pull it the faster you go, that's all you do, let go of the lever and you stop. Easy, eh?"

James took off and did a circuit of the exterior compound that housed the two fales that Robert and Tia and Ata and Aba occupied. He was riding on a crushed coral and sandy track and moving nicely. He arrived back with a big grin on his face, like a kid in his first pedal car.

"I like it, Homeguard," James said, "I'm gonna buy one when I get back home. The terror of Cuba Street. How about that, Flora?"

Flora laughed, "You're a big kid, but I guess they don't call them mobility scooters for nothing. Yeah, why not. Maybe we can get one each!"

"Nice one, Homeguard," James said, "thanks for the ride – I like it!"

James Peroux was the first double amputee that Homeguard had ever seen. In fact, apart from himself, James was the only amputee that Homeguard was aware of. Considering the regional confines of Homeguard's domain, it was conceivable that the only way a person may lose a limb would be in circumstances similar to his own misfortune. Homeguard considered his options and eventually with curiosity overcoming any inhibitions and also with a hint of awe compounding the circumstances, he went up to James and said.

"That must be one very angry fish that damaged your legs. My fish was angry but he only got one leg!"

Realising the significance, for James had been acquainted with Homeguard's accident at the hands of a rather lively and large sperm whale, James replied, "not one fish but two, I guess that must have been Ahab's legacy!"

"Yes," Homeguard replied, "Big fish, big trouble, small fish no trouble."

The End